Jane
and the
Jackal

or

All Her Turkeys

Jim Pinnells and Isabel Otto

from a manuscript by
Charles Hawkins

Copyright © 2024 2024 Jim Pinnells and Isabel Otto

The moral right of the author has been asserted.

Apart from any fair dealing for the purposes of research or private study, or criticism or review, as permitted under the Copyright, Designs and Patents Act 1988, this publication may only be reproduced, stored or transmitted, in any form or by any means, with the prior permission in writing of the publishers, or in the case of reprographic reproduction in accordance with the terms of licences issued by the Copyright Licensing Agency. Enquiries concerning reproduction outside those terms should be sent to the publishers

This is a work of fiction. Names, characters, businesses, places, events and incidents are either the products of the author's imagination or used in a fictitious manner. Any resemblance to actual persons, living or dead, or actual events is purely coincidental..

Matador
Unit E2 Airfield Business Park,
Harrison Road, Market Harborough,
Leicestershire. LE16 7UL
Tel: 0116 279 2299
Email: books@troubador.co.uk
Web: www.troubador.co.uk/matador
Twitter: @matadorbooks

ISBN 978 1 80514 362 8

British Library Cataloguing in Publication Data.
A catalogue record for this book is available from the British Library.

Printed and bound in the UK by TJ Books Limited, Padstow, Cornwall
Typeset in 11pt Garamond Pro by Troubador Publishing Ltd, Leicester, UK

Matador is an imprint of Troubador Publishing Ltd

Jane and the Jackal

or

All Her Turkeys

This book is dedicated to the author of the words:

"Mrs Weston's poultry-house was robbed one night of all her turkeys - evidently by the ingenuity of man. The result of the accident was…"

CONTENTS

Author's Preface   ix

1	The Fortress	1
2	The Gathering	29
3	Betrothal	65
4	Psyche	88
5	Eight Winds	119
6	The Mosque	133
7	Release	152
8	The Assault	181
9	An Alliance	202
10	Flight	216
11	A Mistake	231
12	The Shot	245
13	Convergence	260
14	Fever	282
15	The Ring	303

Postscript	317
Editing Jane and the Jackal: A Note	323
Resources	325
Explanatory Notes	327

AUTHOR'S PREFACE

Some nine years ago, in the summer of 1845, I was staying in the newly opened Queen's Hotel in Cheltenham Spa. Whenever I stay in a hotel, I pay particular attention to the guest list. As a not-unfashionable doctor, I scan the list for the names of ex-patients, preferring to spend as little time as possible in their company. The names of two guests were distantly familiar: Mrs George Knightley and Miss Fanny Price, *Emma* and *Fanny*, as we shall come to know them. They had taken a suite together, the *Akropolis Suite*, and the Greek word stirred a distant memory: these two ladies had been in Athens with my uncle, Edward Trelawny, at the height of the Greek uprising against the Turks some twenty years earlier.[1]

You may have heard of my Uncle Trelawny. You may even have read a book he wrote some years ago, *Adventures of a Younger Son*. In his youth he had been a sailor, a privateer and, almost certainly, a pirate. He counted famous poets among his friends, Byron and Shelley in particular. He proposed marriage to a half-sister of Mary Shelley and burned the drowned body of Shelley on a beach in Italy. Though some of Uncle Trelawny's stories are, to put it politely, unverifiable, most are, despite exaggeration, simplification and romantic embellishment, true, at least in their own way. Some of his tales were repolished with every repetition during his long life: many were not.[2]

As a young man, of course, I believed every word of his after-dinner yarns which turned so often on battles at sea, on curious love affairs, and particularly on the war between the murderous Greek rebels and their unspeakable Turkish overlords. He had been in Athens during that war and become entangled with what he called a *gaggle* of women trapped there by rapine, murder and the threat of general mayhem. I was young, remember, and Uncle Trelawny's tender attachment to one of these women, Fanny Price, fired my youthful imagination. And there, in Cheltenham, undergoing treatment for an unmentionable complaint in an unmentionable part of my anatomy, I had the chance to meet the heroine of my uncle's tales and of my own youthful dreams. Fanny Price, the exquisite Fanny! Not that I expected to see my uncle's peerless angel. Twenty years had passed, and time leaves none of its daughters unscathed: what is charm itself in a lass of two-and-twenty can become in a woman of four-and-forty, at least according to my uncle, as pitiful as a buttered bun.[3]

At breakfast, I asked the waiter to point out Miss Price and her companion, which he did. Later, I found them sitting together in a sunny corner of the orangery. I introduced myself, as casually as I could, as the nephew of a man they had both encountered in Athens years before, Edward Trelawny.

For most of us, and for women in particular, life is not packed with adventure. I was certain that these two ladies, bored to excruciation in a brash, unfashionable spa, would jump at the chance to revisit the most exciting months of their lives. And if the revisiting took place in the company of a presentable young doctor (luckily, they were unaware of my complaint), then so much the better. My first meeting with the two of them lasted a good hour. We talked again on many occasions in Cheltenham and later in London. Their frank gossip, coupled with memories of Uncle Trelawny's yarns, made me eager for more. I started to make notes, and, finally, I came to contemplate the narrative which I have here pieced together.

Unfortunately, I have never written anything longer than a medical report, and my reading, though extensive, has been haphazard. My only literary acquaintance is a woman I sometimes meet at gatherings of the British and Foreign Anti-Slavery Society, Miss Charlotte Yonge. She had just enjoyed extraordinary success with her novel, *The Heir of Redclyffe* (of which I confess to reading only the first chapter). I decided to ask her opinion of my idea for a narrative. She was interested, perhaps even enthusiastic. She suggested that I present the whole plan to a Mr Gregson at Tauchnitz and offered to recommend me.[4] Mr Gregson received me with the distant politeness of a man much in demand. Unlike Miss Yonge, he expressed no particular interest, but informed me that my proposal, properly written up, might be marketable: it might perhaps appeal to a historically curious reader unable to cope with a Gibbon or a Plutarch, who had some tiresome hours to while away. Painfully aware that I was imposing on his time, I explained to him my principal difficulty: I am a doctor and for a while I'd been surgeon's mate on a third-rater. Worse, my Uncle Trelawny's yarns, which supported some portion of my story, were largely unprintable. Accordingly, my literary style might display, to put it mildly, some rough edges: fastidious readers might find it insufficiently polished, others might find some aspects of the subject itself offensive. With at least a show of understanding, he advised me to set down my text exactly as I saw fit, to ask some person of literary discernment, perhaps Miss Yonge herself, for help with the most blatant infelicities. I could to leave the final polishing, if there was to be one, to Tauchnitz. And that is how I have proceeded, although another hand than that of Miss Yonge has been my trusty guide.

And so, dear Reader, as I begin this work, I imagine you in a few years' time sitting in the corner of a first-class compartment perusing my book, and dreading, perhaps, days of travel ahead until you reach Brussels, Berlin, Bologna, or whatever your destination might be. And I promise myself that the book[5] you are holding will have been subject to an expurgation ruthless enough to spare the blushes of the most unenlightened maiden and to a revision of its syntax and orthography thorough enough to satisfy the most unyielding governess.

Charles Hawkins,[6] London, 1854

Chapter 1

THE FORTRESS[7]

Another perfect day. The sea glittered, the breeze blew fresh and salty, and the cloudless sky stretched blue for ever. Despite the smiling heavens, Fitzwilliam Darcy and his wife were silent and gloomy, huddled in the bow of their yacht. In the shining haze ahead, they glimpsed the towers and ramparts of their destination, the ancient fortress of Medoni, at once stronghold, refuge and prison.

'Another hour, my dear,' Mr Darcy said, holding his wife affectionately close. 'Two at the most.'

'And then?' she asked. 'What then, Fitzwilliam?'

'Excuse me, ma'am. Excuse me, sir.' It was Tilney. She had padded, silent and barefoot, toward them along the deck. 'Hawkeye would like a word with Mr Darcy.'

'I'll be damned if I'm at his beck and call. On my own ship. Infernal corsair and his Arab impudence!'

'Go,' his wife told him. 'You're his prisoner. This used to be your ship, but now it's his. He can sink it, set fire to it, or sell it to the Turks. Just as he sees fit.'

'Confound him.' Mr Darcy stood up wearily, clinging to the forestay to keep his balance. He hadn't slept since the *infernal corsair* and his rabble had boarded the *Pemberley*, despatched the servants to the slave-market in Tunis, and butchered the crew, all but one. To sail a ship like the *Pemberley* with its unfamiliar, modern rig, the corsair needed a helmsman, and he'd chosen Darcy's man, the irreplaceable bo'sun.

'How is Jane?' Mrs Darcy asked Tilney, who was her daughter's governess. 'Is she still crying?'

'Still crying,' the governess confirmed with a sigh. 'But after what she's been through…'

'Do what you can for her,' Mrs Darcy said with an impatient shrug. 'I've tried, but whenever I talk to her, she just looks the other way and pretends to be deaf.' Mrs Darcy must have heard the petulance in her own voice: she grimaced and slipped into the irony which so often protected her feelings. 'To be honest, she takes as much notice of me as I took of my own Mamma[8] when I was twelve.'

Mr Darcy felt uncomfortable. 'Perhaps if I talk to Jane…?' he offered tentatively.

His wife nodded. 'But Hawkeye first,' she said, though so quietly the wind carried her words away. Fitzwilliam was fond of Jane. At home in Derbyshire, they rode around the estate together, questioning the bailiff about the crops, and the gamekeeper about the pheasants. At one time, they'd made up stories about the rabbits who lived in the sunny banks of Pemberley, though Jane was too old for that now. Sometimes he sat through the piano lessons that his sister, Georgiana, gave her niece twice a week. In general, it was one of his pleasures to treat Jane as a little lady, and one of hers to play along. Bringing her on the cruise had been his idea: he enjoyed her company, and he wanted her to see a little of the world – not, of course, the world in all its diversity, but at least such part of it as might be seen from the security and luxury of the family's new yacht. Elizabeth Darcy[9] had also hoped to see more of young Jane, and perhaps get closer to her. But neither for Jane's mother nor her father was anything going to plan.

Elizabeth Darcy was one of a family of five sisters. Her own upbringing had been desultory at the hands of an ignorant mother and a laconic father. Elizabeth and her older sister, Jane, had scraped together a handful of social graces, and these, together with their brilliant good looks, had secured them the love of young gentlemen rich enough to marry girls without a dowry. Elizabeth's younger sisters, Lydia in particular, had been less successful. In fact, spoilt, light-hearted young Lydia had humiliated the entire family by flinging her virginity at the first man, or more accurately at *one* of the first men, who had fondled her backside. After this disgrace, one of Elizabeth's chief concerns had been, understandably, that little Jane should not be similarly 'spoilt.' Jane had two younger brothers, little Fitzwilliam and young Charles, and, inevitably, their mother kept them on a looser rein: after all, boys will be boys. Perhaps if Miss Elizabeth Bennet had had brothers, Mrs Elizabeth Darcy would have thought differently. When Catherine Tilney had agreed to take over the business of governessing young Jane, the chief requirement had been clarified at least a dozen times: the child was not to be *spoilt*. Tilney was, however, some ten years older than Mrs Darcy, her mistress. In her own youth, she'd been something of a tomboy and nothing of a scholar. She remembered those times with pleasure and did her best to lighten Jane's burden, rather than to break her spirit with unbending injunctions as to what was, and what was not, allowed to a gentlewoman in the making.

'If Jane is still crying...,' Mr Darcy pursued.

'Let her have her cry out,' his wife replied, 'before we reach this dreadful Greek place.' Incautiously, Tilney raised an eyebrow. For two nights, the child had hardly slept for nightmares. Jane had been on deck when the Arabs had cut the throats of the crew and tossed their bodies into the sea. The crew: Jane knew their names and their nicknames. She called the carpenter *Chips*, and the cook *Slushy*. Her merry *Aye, aye, Bo'sun* rang out whenever Robb, the bo'sun, gave an order. The men liked her. She was nearly thirteen, full of laughter, and 'pretty as a pitcher,' as Robb more than once remarked. The men took turns teaching her to row the little boat that her father had bought in Genoa for just that purpose. When the Arabs had ordered all hands on deck, Jane had not anticipated what must inevitably follow. Then, as the butchery had unfolded, she'd screamed and struggled and vomited over the taffrail. It had been all Tilney could do to stop the child from flinging herself at the murderous, laughing Arabs.

Mr Darcy shook his head. 'Poor Jane,' he said, remembering the scene with a shudder.

'Fitzwilliam, my dear,' his wife prompted. 'Hawkeye is waiting.'

'I'll need you to translate,' he muttered. 'You come too. Please.'

Hawkeye, as they called him, was the leader of the little troop of corsairs who now occupied their ship. His outlandish dress, part Berber, part Ottoman, but mostly Arab, together with his black and grey beard, his hawkish eyes set too close together, and his beltful of weapons, made him a nightmarish figure. His crew aped his style. Hawkeye, like Elizabeth Darcy, spoke a little French with a smattering of Italian. It was enough for the two of them to hold a conversation. Darcy himself remembered only a handful of French words from his schooldays, and no whisper of French syntax.

At this point, the Reader may wonder by what mishap of geography an English family, complete with governess, had fallen into the hands of North African pirates, and was now ploughing the Ionian Sea in time of war? The answer requires us to step back a little in time.

After 1812, it became fashionable among the English aristocracy to build yachts. The Darcy family, great landowners in the county of Derbyshire, were early followers of the fashion. Not long after Waterloo, Fitzwilliam Darcy became a member of the Royal Yacht Squadron on the Solent. At first, the owners simply raced their yachts in their home waters, but then cruising became fashionable, probably because it allowed ladies to accompany their husbands, to accompany them and, remembering the 8,000 prostitutes reputed to have lived, moved and had their being in Portsmouth, to keep an eye on them. A crew? With so many discharged navy-men looking for work at that time, it was easy to pick up seasoned sailors. At first the cruises were unambitious explorations of the English Channel. Then, as the western Mediterranean settled down to peace and prosperity, its warmer seas and milder winds attracted the yachtsmen. As you may recall, Percy Shelley was sailing in a yacht, the *Don Juan*, when he drowned off the coast of Italy in 1822. If the Reader does indeed recall that drowning, it may be of interest to note that it was my uncle, Edward Trelawny, who designed the *Don Juan* for Shelley, and who was widely blamed for its falling apart in little more than a mild breeze.[10]

In the spring of 1823, Fitzwilliam Darcy hired a cook, a captain, a first mate and a bo'sun as well as half-a-dozen English sailors. They were to sail his yacht, the *Pemberley*, to Genoa, though as yet he would not be aboard. The *Pemberley* was all that English taste and Essex craftsmanship could make her: fast, nimble, and comfortable. The name had been the subject of a prolonged debate between Mr Darcy and his wife: he wanted the *Elizabeth* while she preferred the *Pemberley*. To settle the matter, Mr Darcy had put it to his children, certain that they would prefer the name of their mother to the name of their ancestral lands. But he was wrong. Though young Fitzwilliam, the heir, rejoiced in the word *Pemberley*, his brother wanted to call the ship *Lizzy*, since that was his mother's real name. Their older sister, Jane, was attracted by the romance of her father naming a ship after his wife, but, when it was Jane's turn to vote, she voted with her older brother. And so, the *Pemberley* it was. Not, the boys said, that the name mattered much: they preferred riding to sailing, and usually spent the summer with their favourite aunt, Jane Bingley, in Hertfordshire.

In planning their excursion, the Darcys decided to devote a week to Paris, to cross the Alps in a hired diligence, and then to join their yacht in Genoa for the summer. With Mr Darcy and his wife, would travel their daughter Jane, and their daughter's governess, Catherine Tilney, as well as a handful of maids and a valet. The cruise began auspiciously. The first goal was to visit Naples and the excavations at Pompeii, now newly re-opened. After that, in September, the *Pemberley* would seek out the legendary haunts of Scylla and Charybdis in the Straits of Messina. It was the particular wish of Mrs Darcy to see this place: in her father's study in Longbourn, he had spun for her the tale of Odysseus, and she'd never forgotten it. Elizabeth's sister, Jane, had shared this shred of enlightenment, but the younger sisters had heard nothing: their father saw them as brainless romps and escaped their company whenever he could.

In the Straits of Messina, as the Reader already knows, the *Pemberley* encountered neither the monster Scylla nor the whirlpool Charybdis, but she did chance upon two ships manned by Barbary corsairs, old-fashioned galleys with a single bank of oars and two lateen sails. The galleys were among the last of their breed. Just a few years earlier, the French had blockaded the coast of North Africa, seized Algiers, and begun to eliminate piracy. Mr Darcy's captain and his first mate, backed by the bo'sun, requested permission to go about and make a run for Naples or Palermo: even in a light wind, the *Pemberley* could outpace a couple of galleys. Mr Darcy, however, was too proud to turn tail and run. In any case, he apprehended no great danger to a yacht flying the white ensign of the Royal Yacht Club and sailing in waters belonging to a British ally, the Kingdom of the Two Sicilies. So, the *Pemberley* sailed calmly toward the pirates. When, at a range of 200 yards, the pirates rolled out a cannon and fired a shot across the *Pemberley*'s bow, the Captain hove to and the pirates boarded. The carnage that followed has already been described.

And what did Hawkeye plan for the ship and its owners? The day before, partly in words and partly in ferocious dumb-shows, he had explained to the Darcys his view of things. One of his galleys had already sailed southward for Africa bearing the four English maids: whatever they fetched in the slave-market would be distributed as a small reward among his hard-working sailors. The *Pemberley* was his booty, but there was a problem: how could he turn such a ship into cash on the west coast of the Morea? Impossible. The only marketplace was in far-away Constantinople where the Sultan's fleet was desperate for fast ships. What to do? The plan was this: the *Pemberley* and Hawkeye's one remaining galley would sail to the nearest Turkish fort, Medoni. There Hawkeye would sell the yacht to the local governor, the *Sanjakbey*.[11] The *Sanjakbey* would pay in cash and himself despatch the yacht to Constantinople. That dealt with one problem. But how to dispose of the Darcys themselves? As Hawkeye explained, that was not so easy. Times had changed since Nelson thrashed Napoleon at Aboukir. These days, the slave markets simply sold slaves: in Algiers, the days of fat ransoms paid by fond relatives were long over. Proper accommodation for hostages had vanished, and ransoms were uncollectable. In 1823 in North Africa, you simply couldn't trust anybody. So? Darcys are fish-food? Hawkeye asked rhetorically. Probably not. As Hawkeye explained, butchering English lords and ladies was dangerous since it invited retribution by the all-appalling British navy. The old ways, or so Hawkeye believed, had been more civilised, better for both sides. In these decadent times, he had no choice but to leave the Darcys and the *dama di compagnia* in the hands of the Turkish *Sanjakbey* along with the yacht. Would they be safe? They might be lucky. Or they might not. A simple corsair, they must understand, was powerless to protect them. It was regrettable, but his hands were tied. Finally, in accordance with tradition, he would confiscate everything of value he found on the yacht.

The Darcys quickly reconciled themselves to the loss of the *Pemberley*: the ship was insured, and with luck the insurance company would pay. As to finding themselves in Turkish hands, all was not lost: London and Constantinople had diplomatic relations.

But that had been yesterday's conversation. Now? This minute? What did Hawkeye want *now*? Perhaps the Reader will sympathise with Mr Darcy's ungentlemanly choler as he strode down the deck toward the corsair, who sat sprawled in an elegant chair next to the mahogany and brass wheel and the bo'sun who manned it. Mrs Darcy and the governess stayed out of sight, though they had quickly veiled their hair in Moslem style: Hawkeye had explained his wishes on the subject of head-coverings. 'And you, Tilney,' Darcy ordered churlishly over his shoulder. 'Put some shoes on.'

Hawkeye ignored the prisoner's approach. He was watching how the bo'sun handled the boat: one eye on the binnacle and one eye on the wind spilling from the mainsail: it seemed that the bo'sun would be sold along with the *Pemberley* and would sail her to Constantinople. Mr Darcy stopped a few paces from the corsair. '*Eh bien*,' he grunted. Hawkeye wore a heavy white *keffiyeh* tight round his head, almost as though he had toothache. It made him hard of hearing, as Darcy already knew, and it made the expression on his vulture face hard to read.

'*Je veux parlare con vous*,' Hawkeye said with what might have been a smile, if a vulture can be imagined smiling.

Darcy gave a shrug. '*Si vous vouloir*,' he said.

'Begging pardon, sir…' It was the voice of the bo'sun, a gruff whisper on the wind. Darcy nodded quickly: Hawkeye had heard nothing.

'…they've found a box in your cabin, sir. With money. And they're packing up your clothes in bundles. So Mrs Tilney told me.'

'Miss Tilney,' Darcy corrected him.

Sensing rather than hearing the conversation, Hawkeye raised a hand for silence.

'Begging your pardon, sir,' the bo'sun continued quietly, 'but I believe she's a married woman.'

'*Dov'è votre Madame?*' Hawkeye asked. '*Où vostra zawja?*'

At that moment, Elizabeth appeared with Catherine Tilney, still barefoot, immediately behind her.

'I thought I told you to put your shoes on, Tilney,' Darcy began immediately. 'I won't have you walking round my ship half-naked.'

Tilney said nothing, but lowered her eyes to avoid the need for excuses.

'They took Mrs Tilney's shoes, milord.' The bo'sun again, but louder now. 'There ain't much the buggers ain't taken, if the ladies'll pardon *my* French.'

'*Miss* Tilney,' Darcy corrected him forcefully. His ship had been commandeered, his crew and his servants had been murdered or sold into slavery: for a moment, it seemed to him that the word *Miss* somehow stood between him and the apocalypse.

'Fitzwilliam, for heaven's sake,' Mrs Darcy whispered urgently. 'We only call her *Miss* because she's Jane's governess. One can hardly call a governess *Mrs*. But I told you already: she's the daughter-in-law of General Tilney. For pity's sake, make an effort.'

Her husband made an effort: 'You're beginning to sound like my Aunt de Bourgh,' he said, and then shook his head.

Hawkeye stood up. '*Basta*,' he snarled, gesturing Darcy and his wife to the carved mahogany taffrail. There he directed a flood of words at the husband, not pausing for the wife to translate. When he'd finished, he raised his chin in enquiry. The Darcys glanced at each other and Elizabeth nodded. Interpreting the nod as acceptance, the corsair stalked off in the direction of the saloon.

'What was all that about?' Darcy asked.

'He says in an hour we arrive in Medoni. When we get there, he'll hand us over to the *Sanjakbey*.'

'The governor? He told us that already.'

'Yes, but there's more. He's been thinking things over, and he's not altogether happy, our corsair.'

'I'm sorry to hear that a guest on my ship is unhappy.'

Elizabeth detected a change in her husband's tone: the testiness was draining away, his urbanity was returning. If only he could recover that Darcy sangfroid! That had been one of the things she'd cherished most in the man she had led so unexpectedly to the altar.

'Hawkeye is afraid the *Sanjakbey* may think badly of him,' she said with provoking ingenuousness.

'May think he's a stinking bloodthirsty cockroach perhaps?'

'Not my words, but...'

'I apologise, Madame, for any unseemliness,' Mr Darcy bowed ironically. 'But what does King Cockroach want us to do?'

'Hawkeye wants us to say that we've been well-treated. Honourably treated.'

'Honourably? After he sold Browne? And Brinkley? Made slaves of them. And butchered my Captain?'

'He wants your word of honour, as a gentleman, that you will report kindly to...' She shrugged. 'If he's going to sell the ship, maybe he wants to seem respectable.'

'Report kindly, or?'

'Or. Yes, there is an *or*. Or Jane will not...'

'...will not land with us?'

'Yes,' Elizabeth whispered, forced to think the unthinkable.

'God help us!' her husband said, with a sudden and deadly seriousness.

'It's a small price to pay,' Elizabeth said, knowing that her husband would sacrifice anything, even his honour, to save Jane.

'We have no choice then,' he said gravely.

'None,' she agreed.

'And that's all we have to do? Tell a few lies to this infernal Turk?'

'There's more, but it's not bad.'

'Hawkeye wants a *lettre de marque* signed by the Admiralty in London?'

'No. Much easier. Hawkeye says if the *Sanjakbey* sees us dressed as matelots he'll think...'

'...he'll think Hawkeye stole our clothes.'

'Exactly. So, he says I can take two of my dresses with me,' Mrs Darcy continued. 'One on my back, one in my trunk. Likewise for Jane and Tilney.'

'He allows you to wear your own clothes. The perfect gentleman. And me?'

'You can take one suit. *Your* clothes, a gentleman's clothes, fetch a better price in the market.'

Darcy sighed. 'I see his point. He is obviously a fair-minded, decent man, and that is what I shall tell the Turk. Word of honour. You can inform Hawkeye that we accept the bargain.'

'I've already accepted. I nodded.'

'But you nodded at me.'

'That's not how Hawkeye saw it.'

'Confound his insolence. And our money? Bo'sun says he's found that too.'

'Perhaps you should caution him against theft, Fitzwilliam. Tell him you're a magistrate. Tell him he'll finish up in Australia.'[12]

Mr Darcy shook his head and smiled: they could wring their hands and howl in misery at their impotence, or they could banter about it. Faced with such a choice, no Darcy would hesitate. 'I'll tell him if I get the chance. Remind me: what is the French word for *transportation*?'

'And one last thing,' Elizabeth said slyly, keeping the best till last.

'Only one?'

'Wait till you hear it. Hawkeye has been thinking. The *Sanjakbey*, he thinks, will want to be rid of us as soon as he can. If we ask nicely, he might put us on a boat to Ionia. Tomorrow.'

'More cockroach…,' Mr Darcy began, but then reconsidered: 'Is there a chance he's right…' But Elizabeth was already on her way to the saloon to choose her dresses, her shoes, and perhaps even a couple of bonnets. Fitzwilliam shrugged and went with Mrs Tilney to find little Jane.

Jane and her governess shared a tiny cabin that had already been ransacked. Jane was lying on her bunk with her face to the wall. Dry sobs still heaved her slight frame. Her long, fair hair was unkempt and spread wildly across her pillow.

'Jane, my precious,' her father said gently.

Jane smothered her breath and clenched her fists, trying to control herself. The sobs stopped abruptly. Mr Darcy bent forward and rested a comforting hand on her shoulder. He looked back at Mrs Tilney. She returned his look, unsure and herself close to tears.

'We'll soon be arriving in Medoni,' Mr Darcy told his daughter softly. 'We'll be taken off the ship. You'll never see these frightful men again.'

'Never,' the girl said in a tight, dry voice. 'I hate them.'

'If you could get up now, wash your face, tidy your hair. Try to look proud. Show you despise them.'

'I'll try,' the girl whispered. 'Catherine will help me.'

'Catherine? Who…?' her father asked. A quick movement behind him answered his question. So, Tilney was not only a *Mrs*, but her first name was *Catherine*. That was two scraps of information about her he hadn't known the day before. Even with their arrival in Medoni imminent, he found a moment to reproach himself for his ignorance of the people around him, people he paid to look after him, people he had betrayed into slavery and death. Sharing a smile of understanding with Jane, he went back on deck to join his wife.

From the sea, the fortress of Medoni looks impregnable. Once, when I was surgeon's mate aboard the *Fortunate*, we put in there. While the ship took on water, the crew, or some of them, took on the Neapolitan bone-ache, the Famagusta flux or the Portuguese pox according to which of the local whores they chanced to lie with. The town is girdled by crenelated walls, high towers and massive gun emplacements. To enter the harbour, a ship must pass beneath the watchful eyes of fifty batteries of cannon ready to blast it out to the water at the first false move. A strong sea wall jutting away from the Bourdzi Tower,[13] encircles and protects the dozens of boats moored in the harbour: fishing boats, traders, and the light galleys of the harbour guard.

The *Pemberley* hove to outside the harbour and dropped anchor. To the east of the harbour, a long, sandy beach circled the bay. Palm trees and a tangle of oleander, hibiscus and tamarisk lined the beach. Behind this fringe, shacks, sheds and simple cottages straggled up a slow hill; a few were built of stone, but most were of wood, mud and reed-thatch.

The Darcys were ordered below, a guard was set on them, and the curtains were closed. Even so, footfalls on deck, and the clatter of a light galley coming alongside amid shrill whistles and bellowed orders, hinted at what was happening outside.

'It seems…,' Mr Darcy began, but the guard silenced him with a gesture of slitting his throat.

They heard the galley pull smartly away and then, while the pirates continued to ransack the *Pemberley* and bundle up their booty, the Darcys made ready for the trip ashore.

It was already twilight when the galley returned with its crew of six: a Turkish officer, and Hawkeye were installed on a padded thwart. Mr Darcy and his womenfolk were standing for the last time at the taffrail of the *Pemberley*, dressed as if this were Naples and they were to spend the night at the royal palace. Little Jane stood beside her governess, a look of unnegotiable pride on her no longer entirely childish features. A single cabin trunk stood beside them, all that the Berbers had allowed them to remove from the ship.

The galley drew alongside the *Pemberley*. The Turkish officer handed Hawkeye aboard then spoke to *Monseigneur Darcy* in French: he would now escort *Monseigneur* and his women to the quayside. For now, *les corsaires* were to remain on board the *Pemberley* with their plunder.

The captives boarded the galley with their trunk, and the Turkish officer gave the order to toss oars, to let them fall, and then to give way together. There was no breeze. The oily water was flat. For weeks they had been cruising in the bright air of the Mediterranean. As they neared the fortress, its pestilential stink struck their English noses hard. Jane heaved.

'Keep it in,' her mother whispered. 'What happens to us next depends on how we behave.'

'Yes, Mamma,' Jane said. 'I'm trying.'

'Did you hear?' Mr Darcy asked his wife. 'The Turk called me *Monseigneur*.'

'You've the bo'sun to thank for that,' Mrs Tilney ventured. 'He always called you *milord* when Hawkeye was around, and Madam was always *milady*. He thought it might help.'

'Well, Jane?' her father prompted. 'That makes you a *milady* too.'

'I don't feel like a *milady*,' Jane replied. 'What should I do different?'

'Just carry on exactly as you are. You're doing perfectly,' he told her. 'What do you think, Lizzy?'

'Yes,' his wife agreed. 'Much better than I feared.'

'Must I meet the Governor?' the girl asked, holding the hand of her governess possessively.

'The *Sanjakbey*? Yes, I should think so,' her father replied.

At the Turkish word, the officer took a sudden interest in their conversation. '*Sanjakbey?*' he repeated, and then erupted into Turkish. Darcy ignored the man and his incomprehensible jabber. No more was said until the galley bumped against the quayside. The officer gestured his four prisoners to climb the stone steps. With exaggerated politeness, Darcy handed his wife onto the worn marble wharf.

'Thank you, *milord*,' she said, dropping him a curtsey. It was a game, and perhaps a silly one, but Darcy welcomed it: Lizzy had faced the ire of Lady Catherine de Bourgh, Darcy's formidable kinswoman, without blanching: it seemed she was confronting the terrors of an Ottoman fortress with equal address.

An escort of four heavily armed janissaries[14] awaited them on the quayside. Wardens? Gaolers? With luck, neither: everything might turn out as Hawkeye had predicted. In just a few hours *Lord and Lady* Darcy together with young *Lady* Jane and the daughter-in-law of a British General might well be on their way to Ionia and the protection of Sir Thomas Maitland, the Lord High Commissioner. Mr Darcy pictured the map: the Ionian Islands weren't far off. Zakynthos, the nearest, was only seventy miles to the north. For centuries, the islands had been part of the Republic of Venice. Then, no doubt as the result of some dastardly manoeuvre, they'd fallen into the clutches of the French. Finally, in 1815, they'd been properly ceded to the victorious British.

It is hard for anyone who knows only the stench of English cities to imagine the ingrained, festering loathsomeness of a Levantine fortress in late summer. No rain has fallen since spring. The narrow streets are hard with trampled excrement, animal and human. The gutters are choked with rags, ashes, rotting food, and unidentifiable scraps of dead creatures that even the rats won't eat. The walls are smeared with a foul-smelling, dried paste of heaven knows what origin. Yet the streets are busy, especially in the evening hours. Tradesmen, hawkers, citizens on their way to the baths, the shops or the brothel, elbow each other gracelessly. There are no beggars: none is allowed inside a fortress. Donkeys staggering under unwieldy trunks or huge bundles scrape the walls, forcing passers-by into foetid, menacing alleyways. Through this chaos, the janissaries, two ahead and two behind, herded the Darcys and Mrs Tilney. With Jane trying out the postures of a *milady* and the two older women standing resolutely on their dignity, the passers-by must have found them a curious sight.

The lower town was secluded from the upper town by a curtain wall.[15] The only portal in this massive construction was heavily guarded. The square in front of the portal, with its fountains, wells and mosques, was swept by cannon ranged along the parapet. Mr Darcy was no expert on fortifications, but he had once visited the Tower of London: Medoni, he saw, was far better defended. The escort halted at the gate and their prisoners with them. Words of challenge and response were bellowed in a strange language, and the gate swung open.

The upper town smelled no better than the lower, but the streets were wider, and they had been swept. A magnificent bastion dominated the upper city, the Bembo Tower as the Darcys soon learned. The tower was the residence of the *Sanjakbey*, and it was their immediate destination. They passed two more gates and climbed flights of stone stairs with guards at every landing. Finally, they entered a large and richly furnished audience chamber. The windows stood open, and a pleasant breeze stirred the many-coloured muslin curtains. The stench was gone, purged, or perhaps masked, by attar of roses. Signs of civilisation abounded: bronze candelabra, gilt-framed mirrors, and an inlaid mother-of-pearl table with a crystal bowl of fruit. Embroidered cushions softened ornate chairs and sofas. The first janissary ushered his prisoners into the room but did not accompany them. The tall, double-leaf door clicked closed behind them. There were several similar doors in the room, all of them guarded by impassive Turkish soldiers armed with pistols, daggers and curved scimitars in scabbards chased with brass and silver.

Darcy and his wife advanced into the room; Tilney and Jane hung back. 'Shall we sit? Or stand?' Darcy asked, looking round the room.

'Stand, I suppose,' his wife replied uncertainly.

'Treat him as our honoured host, that sort of thing? What happens if he's like Hawkeye?'

'Fitz,' she confessed in a whisper. 'I'm as lost as you are.'

'I doubt it,' he said quietly, taking her hand. He felt her fingers close round his in companionship and trust. 'Keep our wits about us,' he said. 'Specially you.'

They stood anxiously for ten minutes listening to the sounds that penetrated the room from the courtyards below: orders, marching feet and hooves on flagstones. Then one of the doors opened and a figure entered dressed in Ottoman regalia and carrying a staff of office. 'It's not him,' Darcy whispered, sensitive to the protocol of courts though he'd never been a courtier. 'Just a steward.'

The *Sanjakbey*, when he entered, was dressed in a gold-embroidered caftan. He wore a turban and long, pointed slippers. His beard was white and neatly trimmed. He carried neither sword nor firearm, and he was smiling. He made a slight bow of welcome to each of his guests, perhaps a shade lower to *Lord* Darcy than to the women.

'*Parlez-vous turc?*' the *Sanjakbey* asked, gesturing them to sit down on one of the heavy gilt sofas. The women sat: Darcy remained standing.

'No, sir,' he replied. 'We speak only English.'

'*Nous besoin traducteur,*' the *Sanjakbey* said. He fired some brisk, incomprehensible words at his steward. As the man left the room, he ushered in two barefoot, veiled and colourfully draped serving women. The women were carrying a low table on which stood a golden jug and half-a-dozen crystal goblets. They set the table down in front of the sofa. The *Sanjakbey* gestured at the jug. '*Sher-bet?*' he offered his guests. He went to the table himself and picked up the jug. 'Milady?' With the slightest shake of his beard, he dismissed the two servants, who retreated from the room without taking their eyes from their master.

'Thank you, Lord Governor,' Mrs Darcy replied with an open smile. If she was to be *milady*, then she would treat the Turk with equal politeness. 'You are most obliging.'

Before all three women had a glass of sherbet in their hands, the steward returned with a girl dressed in chiffon trowsers and an embroidered halter. A fine muslin headdress covered her head and her mouth. Something in the attitude of the *Sanjakbey* hinted that the newcomer belonged to a different order of beings from the serving women who had just left.

The Turk gave orders in his own language, and the girl replied, her voice subdued and deferential. One more command from the Turk, and the girl let slip her veil: her eyes were blue, though her hair was dark. 'Aslan Bey says welcome,' she translated, bending slightly to put her veil on one of the tables.

'And who is our charming interpreter?' Mrs Darcy asked with a warm interest which, though feigned, sounded real enough.

'Cora,' the girl replied. 'Cora Shrubb, milady.' The harshness of London streets grated in her voice.

The *Sanjakbey* sat down, and Cora, as she called herself, poured him a goblet of the sweet, lemony sherbet. As she neared his chair, she sank to her knees, bowed her head, and, with a sort of meek pride, offered him the drink. He took it, and she remained kneeling while he explained something to her in Turkish. She replied in the same language. They talked earnestly back and forth until he gestured her to stand.

Darcy watched the girl carefully. She was beautiful, but not in the way that Elizabeth had been beautiful, was beautiful still, with her brilliant eyes and fresh complexion. Cora conformed to a harsher model: tough, submissive and satiated. She was a slave, that was clear, and she must have been a slave for some years to speak Turkish with such fluency. Even so, she seemed hardly more than seventeen. Her figure was slender, and enough of it was exposed to give an unnerving sense of the rest.

''E wants to know 'ow it comes you're 'ere,' Cora said, her accent blossoming. ''E's already spoke wiv the Berber what you come wiv. You gotta tell me ev'ryfing firss, so I can tell 'im.'

In Turkish, Cora's voice had sounded languid and mellifluent: in English it had the aggressive rattle of the costermonger. They began to tell their story, but Cora broke in on them time after time, demanding more detail, more explanation. They asked her questions too. Why did she speak English? She *was* English, she told them. How long had she been among the Turks?

'Me muvver was in service wiv Lady 'Amilton, you know, Lord Nelson's buntling.[16] Not a lady's maid or nuffink, just a mopsqueezer.[17] Anyway, when Milady went to Naples, me and me muvver got dragged along after. It was all right in Naples, for a while any'ow. Then Milady sailed orff wiv Nelson and the Queen, and some'ow we got leff be'ind. No work in Naples, nuffink, so we tried our luck in Malfi. 'Uge plague 'orspital there. English sailors, sick wiv God knows what, 'undreds of 'em. Me muvver got work as a scrub-girl. 'Orspitals is always lookin' out for scrub-girls.' Cora looked at them enquiringly. 'But you prob'ly know that already. Don't ikspeck there's much I can tell *you*.' She didn't say *swells*[18] *like you*, but it was in her voice.

'What happened then?' It was Catherine Tilney who asked the question. Cora interested her. If the girl had picked up English from her scrub-girl mother and the sailors in a lazaret, it explained her accent and her earthy vocabulary, but it didn't explain her evident self-esteem or her coherence: Cora was clearly no fool.

'Me? I was juss a kid, so I couldn't work, only 'elp out and, well, you know… Then them A-rabs from Tunis raided Malfi. I got took. Got sold to some Bulgar. Soldier. 'E sold me to a Turk. Then I got give to Aslan Bey. Sort a bribe, I fink. Been wiv 'im a few years now. F---in' paradise after them uvver two.'

When enough had been said to satisfy both sides, Cora went and stood behind the chair of the *Sanjakbey*, the man who owned her, body and soul. She whispered for a long time in his ear. He nodded, glancing occasionally at the Darcys, and particularly at young Jane who stared back with an expression of defiance that showed she had no idea what might be afoot.

'Don't look at him like that,' Mrs Darcy whispered. 'Look at Cora.'

'Is Cora his wife?' Jane whispered, transferring her stare as she'd been told. 'Why hasn't she got any clothes on?'

'She *has* got clothes on,' her mother assured her.

'But I can see her…'

'Shush now,' her mother ordered. 'She's standing behind the chair so there's nothing to see. And even if there were, you wouldn't be allowed to look.' Jane grimaced. Not allowed to look? She never knew when her mother was joking: it was one of the many things that had begun to annoy her.

The *Sanjakbey* now embarked on a long explanation. Cora

listened to him carefully. The words *Zakynthos*, *Ionia* and *Ahmed Azmi Pasha* were among the few the Darcys could guess at. When the explanation was over, Cora returned to Milord and Milady. She explained to them in her brassy, half-forgotten English what exactly the *Sanjakbey* had in mind. It came to this: in one way they were his guests, but in another they were his prisoners. He could not allow them to leave Medoni until he'd talked to the *Kadi*. *Who was the Kadi?* The judge: they might meet him in the morning. But even the *Kadi* could decide nothing till he knew what Ahmed Azmi Pasha was going to say. *Who was Ahmed Azmi Pasha?* A general that the Sultan had sent to run the Morea[19] during the war. *And where was the Pasha?* Perhaps in Tripolis,[20] over a hundred miles away, though no one knew for sure. Milord and Milady, as Cora put it, was stuck in Medoni, maybe for *mumffs*.

Mr Darcy protested. What about Zakynthos? What about the Lord High Commissioner in Ionia? He insisted on writing a letter immediately to Sir Thomas Maitland, and on the letter being sent that night. The *Sanjakbey*'s behaviour was outrageous. Great Britain and the Ottoman Empire had diplomatic relations: no subject of His Majesty, George IV, could be exposed to such indignity.

It took a while, but finally the *Sanjakbey*, with the help of Cora and a small map, clarified the Turkish view of local diplomatic relations. It was true that Sir Thomas Maitland was Lord High Commissioner of the Ionian Islands: the islands were independent, and they had been British for eight years now, ever since the French had surrendered them. The capital was in Korfu. Mainland Greece, however, including the fortress of Medoni, was part of the Ottoman Empire. The British ambassador to the Ottomans was in Constantinople. The British had consulates in Athens, Smyrna, and a handful of other places, but none of these was the direct concern of Sir Thomas Maitland in Korfu. If letters were to be sent, they would be sent to Constantinople, and they would be sent by the *Sanjakbey*.

Mr Darcy began to argue: the Ionian Islands were less than a hundred miles away. Constantinople was more like a thousand. Neither Cora nor the *Sanjakbey* appeared to hear.

'So my husband may not write to Sir Thomas?' Mrs Darcy asked finally. Cora translated.

One word, *hay-r*, came from the *Sanjakbey*. Cora nodded. 'That means *no*,' she translated. 'Or, as me muvver mighta said, milady, *less 'ope than a dog's fart in 'ell.*'

Mrs Darcy drew in her breath sharply, controlled her features, and then said with a frigid smile: 'That's clear enough anyway.'

If escape to Ionia was impossible, how were the Darcys to be accommodated in the immediate, and perhaps in the indefinite, future? Stumbling and often lost for words, Cora began to explain to them the arrangements within the fortress. The lower town they'd come through was built on arches. Below the arches was a huge magazine, badly lit and so filthy your feet stuck to the flagstones. Gunpowder, cannon balls and all manner of things were kept there. Prisoners too. Down there it was always dark and cold. The prisoners, mostly Greeks and a few Albanians, didn't stay long. Every day, corpses were thrown over the sea wall for the crabs and the gulls. If Milord and his people were sent to the magazine, they'd be kept in one cell. Milady and her maid were women. Lady Jane was a girl. In the magazine there was no way to hold back the janissaries, the guards, or anyone who slipped the guards a *kurush* or two. A muff[21] is a muff, but you don't find English muff every day. If it turned out to be popular, so much the worse for them.

After every few words, Cora glanced back at the *Sanjakbey*. Evidently, he'd told her to frighten the English strangers: was she doing it right? Or was she going to be punished? He smiled at her, obviously pleased. He said a few more words to her, and her explanation took a new turn.

The *Sanjakbey*, she said, was sorry for them. He might, perhaps, invite them to stay in the fortress as his guests. There were pleasant rooms, and he'd enjoy their company in the evenings after work. All Lord Darcy had to do was give his word of honour that neither he, his wife, nor any of them, would try to escape, nor would they write letters or send word to anyone. In the fortress, in the Bembo Tower, she herself, Cora, would help look after them.

'You really are his slave,' Mrs Darcy said in reply. 'His…' She struggled for a word: *lick-spittle* was too insulting, and *creature* did not convey her meaning.

'So what if I am?' Cora agreed. 'You know what 'appens, if I crawss 'im. 'E'll make me sorry I was born.'

'You'll be whipped?' Mrs Darcy asked.

'That, and a lot else. Some come back in one piece, some don't.'

Mr Darcy gave his parole.

Cora led them to two airy rooms, not uncomfortably furnished: the beds were soft, and the coverings were clean. A handful of books in Italian and in what looked like Arabic decorated a small bookshelf. Tall doors opened onto the ramparts where there was a cool kiosk and a garden with plants in pots. Half-a-dozen officious house slaves, with Cora in command, were soon attending to the Darcys' needs, real or imagined. A copper tub was carried into each of their rooms, and hot water was brought in copper jugs. There were fragrant soaps, soft towels and bathrobes. Dinner would be served later, when it was cool, on the *Sanjakbey's* terrace.

To head off a charge of robbery, Hawkeye had left a few gold coins in Mrs Darcy's trunk. Even so, Darcy realised, he'd need money, and soon. Next morning, on the orders of the *Sanjakbey*, a moneylender was found outside the fortress who was ready to negotiate a draft on Lord Darcy's bank in London. For a note worth 100 English sovereigns, Darcy received in Ottoman silver 1,500 *piastres*, perhaps half the going rate.[22] The *piastres* wouldn't last long, but they saved the Darcys from looking cheap in the eyes of the *Sanjakbey's* servants, and especially in the eyes of Cora Shrubb on whom their comfort, and perhaps their survival, might depend.

Days of waiting followed, days of walking on the ramparts of the upper city, days of boredom and frustration. They gazed from the fortress, across the dry moat, into the squalor outside the walls: Arabs, Albanians and Greek riff-raff lived there, anyone the Turks distrusted. In a sense, the outsiders lived in freedom: in another, they were the most abject of captives. Occasionally, the Darcys discussed this paradox, but in general they spoke only of their immediate concerns: the intentions of the *Sanjakbey* and the insolence of Cora Shrubb.

From the beginning, Cora was demanding. When she'd 'become a woman' at fourteen, the *Sanjakbey* had given her a title of respect, *Melek Han-m*. Cora insisted that the English guests use it. Cleverly, and unscrupulously, she used the little information at her disposal to assert her power over them. For example, when they asked her what was in their food, Cora refused to tell them: they should eat first. Then, after a bite or two and a swallow, she inflicted a thousand horrors on them: millipedes, dogs' eyes, offal of every kind. Cora had in full measure the despotism of the slave and the malice of the victim. She had seen inhuman cruelties, cruelties had been inflicted on her, and now she had her own subjects to practise on. She passed on the *Sanjakbey*'s orders with the curses and blasphemies she remembered from her childhood. She quickly realised that singling out Elizabeth as her special butt and being open and friendly with the others, especially with Jane, was especially humiliating for Milady. Cora commandeered Elizabeth's clothes, flaunting herself as an English lady, and *Why not for once in me f---ing life?* she asked. She demanded that Elizabeth try on the dresses of the harem: the *Sanjakbey* would be amused. But here Cora failed. Mixing obstinate silence with outbursts of fury, Elizabeth refused. Cora laughed: if the *Sanjakbey* was upset by Milady's refusal, God help them all. Subtly, Cora saved her sharpest barbs for when she and Elizabeth were alone together. Frequently she reported, exaggerated even, the charms of girls she'd seen on sale in the lower town: why didn't Milord buy himself a couple? No man was content with just one woman, and certainly not with a woman such as Milady who had lost her youth, her figure, and her complection. Elizabeth was thirty-three, she had preserved her appearance with remarkable tenacity, but nevertheless Cora's thrusts went home. Slave girls, Cora pursued, were cheap, and Milord could sell them again when he left Medoni. Pitilessly, taking another tack, Cora appraised what young Jane might fetch in the marketplace, wondering whether she was worth more now with a little girl's notch,[23] or if she'd be worth more later, wondering if a Turk, a Greek or an African would be most likely to buy her, wondering how many times you could sell a girl's virginity. In Malfi, her mother had sold hers so often she'd lost count. 'Same fing might 'appen to Jane. You never know 'ow life's gunner work out.' One crowning piece of villainy, however, Cora failed to bring off. Her plan was to get close to Jane and to persuade her that it would be great fun if the two of them appeared one evening dressed as girls from the seraglio, girls like Cora herself. She and Jane discussed the matter in all its aspects. How a little discreet padding might make Jane seem a year or two older. How astonishing it would be if Jane learned one of the harem dances, and they performed it together. Jane knew, of course, how annoyed her mother would be if the plan were carried out, but perhaps that was part of its charm. Luckily, in her excitement, Jane betrayed the plan to Catherine Tilney, Catherine warned her mistress, and Jane was forbidden to appear in any clothes but her own on pain of being locked in her room for the rest of her time in Medoni. The failure of her little scheme did nothing to improve Cora's behaviour.

    Elizabeth Darcy had despised many people in her life. She'd felt nothing but disgust for her sister Lydia and Lydia's husband, George Wickham. But she came to hate Melek Han-m with a dangerous virulence. She hated the slave's spiteful, bullying manners, she hated the uncouth sound of her voice, and her unending stream of filthy words. She hated the sleek body immodestly concealed beneath the silks and chiffons of the harem. She hated the slave's cringing subservience when the *Sanjakbey* was looking at her, and her smirking arrogance when he was not. Elizabeth put her hatred into glances of contempt, vicious curlings of her lip, and savage, clever sarcasms which passed over the slave's head.

Catherine Tilney saw the hatred and guessed where it might lead. Without seeming to put herself forward, she headed off much of Cora's mischief, coarsening her own voice, trading occasionally a curse for a curse, and letting herself be amused by the slave's indecencies. She flattered Cora's vanity with praise of her good looks, and made her little presents, paid for, it goes without saying, by Milord. Milord was by nature insensitive to the intrigues of the seraglio, yet he could hardly fail to see that Elizabeth's hatred of Cora might endanger them all. He began to observe, and then to admire, Mrs Tilney's resourcefulness. They started talking to each other. They were much of an age, and Mrs Tilney, to his surprise, had read many of the books he had read himself. He had no literary tastes in common with Elizabeth, who sunk herself in epics of drawing-room conspiracy that left her husband cold. On the other hand, Catherine, as he began to call her, was happy to share with him the dread and distress she so relished in *Vathek*,[24] *Udolpho*, or even *The Monk*. She told him her own story too, how she'd married General Tilney's son, Henry, when she was still a slip of a girl. Her husband had been ordained, but, coming from a military family, he'd still joined Wellington's army in the Peninsula, not as a soldier but as a chaplain. He'd died in *Wellington's Lines* in front of Lisbon in 1810, a victim of bad provisioning and the typhus. He'd left his wife with two children and a tiny pension. Although the General and his daughter-in-law had long-standing reasons to dislike each other, he'd invited her and her children to live with him at Northanger Abbey, and they'd settled down uncomfortably together. Her children, two boys, had both been taken by the sour throat[25] in 1818. Then in 1819 the General had lost most of his fortune in an American cotton speculation. The abbey had been rented out to a war profiteer, and Catherine had lost the roof over her head. Her first idea had been to go to the Queen's Lying-In Hospital in London to train as a midwife even though the course took seven years and the wages during training were negligible. After six months of training, she had taken up governessing to keep body and soul together. Her first position had ended in acrimony when the family found fault with her music. Her second position... Well, Mr Darcy knew all about that: it had landed her in a Turkish fortress with no apparent prospect of release, though, she had to say, with a sweet girl like Jane, governessing itself was no hardship.

Each evening round the *sofra*,[26] the *Sanjakbey* watched Cora play her game of cat and mouse with Lady Elizabeth. It amused him, though he understood none of the details. Occasionally, with Lord Fitzwilliam, he broached the subject of the war or of European politics, but Cora's powers of translation were too feeble to sustain a serious conversation. When the *Kadi* ate with them, the two Turks discussed, interminably, issues of which the English guests had no inkling whatever.

The Darcys had already endured two weeks of servitude when, late in September, unwelcome news arrived from the Pasha in Tripolis. No decision, he wrote, could be made locally: they must wait for a reply to a letter that had been sent to the Sublime Porte in Constantinople. At the earliest, this reply might arrive in late October.

In November, when the decision of the Porte finally arrived, it was a surprise to everyone including the *Sanjakbey*. The Darcys were to be taken overland to Athens and there handed over to the British Consul. A *firman*[27] was enclosed with the orders, giving Lord Darcy and his party the protection of the Sultan in all Ottoman domains.

In the meantime, by daily exposure to the *Sanjakbey*, Cora had improved her position to that of favourite slave. She hung affectionately over her master as she helped him explain to the

Darcys the difficulties of their journey. Perhaps she exaggerated a little, but the bare facts, honestly translated, would have been disquieting enough.

War had been raging now for two years. Before the war, the land between Medoni and Athens, the Morea, had been in the hands of the Turks. Now the Greek rebels controlled the Morean countryside, while the Turks held the fortresses and little else. A year before, the entire army of Mahmud Dramali Pasha, 17,000 Turkish soldiers, had been ambushed and butchered by the *khlepts*[28] in the Dervenakia Pass. And that was just one of the many passes on the Darcys' route. If the Greeks decided to attack their convoy, no escort could defend them. Of course, one of the *Sanjakbey's* best men would command the escort, the man would swear to die in the defence of his charges, and his eldest son would be kept hostage for his father's good behaviour. Even so, the escort would abandon them if the Greek attack looked dangerous. But would the Greeks attack? In winter, the *khlept*s and the other bandits, *dirty dogs, all of 'em, 'id their 'eds in their 'oles, and burrers*. In practice, the late rains were as threatening as the *khlepts*. There were two Turkish strongholds on the route where they might find shelter, but most nights they would have to camp in a ruined village, or in the open under their cart. They had 200 miles of hard terrain to cross. As Cora put it: 'No plice for a dandy prat.'[29] By ship, it would be no easier. Since the summer, the Greeks had blockaded much of the Aegean: only warships got through. According to a rumour the *Sanjakbey* had heard, even the *Pemberley* had gone missing. The land route was tougher but, all in all, it was safer.

As a parting gift, the *Sanjakbey* gave each of the three women a silk carpet made in the Grand Seraglio in Constantinople and bearing the imperial seal. To Lord Darcy he gave a pair of flintlock pistols inlaid with gold. He trusted that the Darcys would give a good report of him when they arrived in Athens or returned home to England: he had always held the English in the highest esteem.

As soon as the journey began in mid-November, it was clear

that the *Sanjakbey* had told no less than the truth. A month of cold, wet and exhaustion followed. It wasn't until 15th December that the three Darcys and Mrs Tilney straggled the last few miles toward Athens. The Porte had informed the British Consul, George Knightley, that Lord Darcy and his party would reach Athens at some time during December. Mr Knightley had posted a lookout five leagues outside the city on the track that the Darcys must inevitably follow. Alerted by his scout, the Consul himself rode out to meet his guests when they were still a mile from the city. Meanwhile, in the comfortable consulate, his wife, Emma, built up a good fire and prepared to welcome the famished newcomers.

Chapter 2

THE GATHERING

Lord and Lady Darcy? Emma Knightley had scoured the fourteenth edition of Debrett's *The Peerage* on the subject of the Darcys and found neither Lord nor Lady. And why was there no copy of *The Baronetage* in the consulate? How could a lady treat her guests correctly if she was ignorant of their rank? In her uncertainty, she consulted Fanny Bertram, wife of the consular Chaplain: would it not, she asked Fanny, be a grievous *faux pas* to treat commoners as though they were nobility? Even more grievous perhaps than treating nobility as commoners? But Emma found no succour in the Chaplain's wife. As Fanny understood it, the Darcys had been captured by Berber pirates and spent months in a Turkish fortress. Now they were trying to cross the Morea in winter. Their daughter was with them, a girl of only twelve. What difference did it make if the girl was Lady Jane, Miss Jane, or just plain Jane with no frills? The family should be welcomed, looked after, and helped in any way possible.

Mrs Knightley found the attitude of the Chaplain's wife painfully unethical: respect for rank, she maintained, was a Christian duty. The Chaplain himself happened to pass by at that moment, and, in search of an ally, Mrs Knightley referred the question to him: Was respect for rank a religious duty? Or was it not? As always, Chaplain Bertram avoided answering until he had confirmed the lie of the land. Had the Consul expressed an opinion on the matter? Or Mrs Knightley herself? The Consul's wife was immediately eloquent in support of her view: rank must be upheld at all costs. Now on safe ground, the Chaplain declared that, among the Christian virtues, respect for rank fell little short of faith,[30] hope and charity.

Sadly, the scene had an unpleasant epilogue. Half an hour later, Mrs Knightley overheard the Chaplain upbraiding Fanny for her foolhardiness in contradicting the Consul's wife. She heard Fanny make a spirited response, and then the sound of a hard slap followed by a little cry of pain, quickly suppressed. In revulsion, Emma decided, and not for the first time, to refer no more questions to her termagant Chaplain.

Later Emma asked the Consul for *his* view: how much importance should she attach to the rank of the visitors? He resolved the issue with quiet diplomacy: the Darcys should be accorded the honours of lordly rank. If they turned out to be imposters, these honours could be reduced in proportion to the degree of imposture.

When she next saw Fanny Bertram, Emma glanced at her face: one cheek was swollen and inflamed. Emma shuddered. How frightful to be hit like that by one's own husband! Thank God, her George had never laid a finger on her. Emma's better nature urged her to comfort poor Fanny, but the right words did not suggest themselves, and she said nothing.

When unequal couples live in one house, their communal life is likely to be unstable, hovering between wrangle and reconciliation. This was certainly the case with the two couples who lived in the consulate, the Knightleys and the Bertrams. Some things they had in common: language, religion, and the English way of life, at least the English way of life as practised in prosperous country houses. The Knightleys, husband and wife, had arrived in Athens in late 1822. At that time, the Bertrams had already been in the city for almost a year, though they had no love of it. Mr Bertram claimed that pagan temples held no charm for a priest of the Church of England. He conducted the Knightleys on no tours of the sites, he had no conversation to offer them on any subject whatever, and, worst of all, he had an aversion to card games and to all other forms of entertainment. Temperamentally, he was ready to take offence, though not to quarrel: his power of opposition, or so George Knightley discovered, was limited to a sour face and an evasive eye. George Knightley disliked him. Emma, always sociable, had tried to patronise the Chaplain's wife, to 'draw her out' as she put it, but to little effect. Fanny was ready to make herself useful, but she believed herself inferior to the Consul's wife in wealth, in social position and in education, beliefs that Emma fully shared. The barrier was difficult to surmount. Temperamentally the two women had little in common: Emma found Fanny unpredictable, sometimes mocking and flippant, sometimes cheerless and censorious, but seldom good company. When Fanny was in a gloomy mood, she predicted dark days ahead: an end to the villainous *khlept* government in Athens, an end to the futile British occupation of the Adriatic islands, and an end to the social prohibitions that Emma called *respect for rank*. Fanny's interest in politics and history, untutored though it was, struck Emma as pretentious. Emma herself was seldom troubled by the future. A Cassandra[31] such as Fanny Bertram and the cheerful, even-tempered Emma, were, at this stage of their lives, painfully unsuited to each other's company.

    Fanny's relations with Emma's husband, George, were warmer. Every day, after his mid-day meal, the Consul took a walk as an aid to both digestion and reflection. Emma never accompanied him on these walks, preferring to temper her own digestion with a nap. One afternoon, seeing Fanny hemming bed sheets, George asked her if she would like to walk with him. It was a kindly impulse, typical of the man. Fanny accepted, the walk was pleasant, and

Mr Knightley learned more about Fanny's history in an hour than his wife had gleaned in many months. To his surprise, he found Fanny entertaining: her comments on the Greek world around them, in particular on the inner life of the consulate, were related with a subtle, feminine wit that George frankly enjoyed. The walk was repeated and extended. When Emma, with natural curiosity, asked if her husband did not find Mrs Bertram's company tedious, he replied, evasively, that her health was his main concern and that she was finding the fresh air beneficial.

After a few months, these walks had an unexpected consequence. One morning Edmund Bertram confronted his employer, cringing and sour-faced perhaps, but nevertheless with manly intent. As a personal favour, the Chaplain began, might he ask the Consul to discontinue his daily and public excursions with Mrs Bertram through the streets and fields of the city. 'Why so?' the Consul asked. The Chaplain mumbled a reply: 'She is not a person who needs exercise.' The Consul assured his Chaplain that he was talking stuff: did he expect his wife to waste away in the airless confines of the consulate? Whatever air Mrs Bertram might, or might not, be allowed to breathe, her husband retorted, was hardly the Consul's business. Tempers rose. The Chaplain hinted at breaches of Christian duty and threatened to preach a sermon the following Sunday anent the seventh commandment. The Consul expressed his condolences for any woman unequally yoked to an imbecile and a bully, though without naming the imbecile and bully he had in mind. This was hardly diplomatic, but George Knightley was by nature hostile to tyranny. There was perhaps another motive for the Consul's defence of his walking companion's right to fresh air: on the previous afternoon, Fanny had been particularly amusing on the intricacies of female life in the naval dockyard where she had spent her childhood, and Mr Knightley was keenly looking forward to the next episode. 'The day on which you forbid your wife to walk in the afternoons,' he growled at his Chaplain, 'will be your last day in Athens.' With these words and a flick of the wrist, he dismissed further religious counsel.

The Chaplain preached no mutinous sermons, hummed no Marseillaise, and forbade no postprandial perambulations, but, to his dying day, he bore the diplomatic service a grudge. Although he was no consummate husbandman, to use a phrase of my Uncle Trelawny's, he did resent other men waling his potatoes or plucking his rosemary.

Why did George Knightley not dismiss his Chaplain there and then? In fact, the Consul did write a letter to London seeking advice on how best he could rid himself of Edmund Bertram. The Foreign Office replied that the Chaplain could be dismissed at any time if given six months' notice. Unfortunately, the Chaplain chanced upon a copy of the letter in the Consul's office: it did nothing to ease his resentment or to sweeten his sour face.

Apart from these two English couples living in the consulate, the only British citizens in Athens were Marianne Brandon, a middle-aged relic of Lord Elgin's pillaging campaigns, and two deserters from the Mediterranean fleet. These Hampshire lads bunked in the stables and earned an occasional crust running errands for the Consul. Sad to say, such crusts were rare during the spring of 1823. In all these months, Mr Knightley found little call for diplomatic activity beyond the resolution of disputes between the wife of his bosom and the wife of his meddlesome priest. Some men, finding themselves without regular occupation, sink into lethargy, some collect antiquities, breed dogs, compile a dictionary or chase some other hobbyhorse, while still others, and perhaps this is the majority, seek out the company of Silenus, Peitho or the Nepenthes[32] until failing health drives them back to their ancestral estates. But George Knightley took none of these courses. Instead, helped by the other consuls, French, Russian, Austrian and Dutch,[33] all of whom had been in Athens for some years, he began to examine the current political trends in Greece, indeed in the Ottoman Empire at large. After an initial burst of clarity, he found that the more he learned, the less he understood. If there was an overall picture, he surmised, then no one, and certainly no one in Athens, could fathom it. What then did he know with certainty about this city, his city and Emma's, where they must live and perhaps grow old together? At least this: in 1821 and 1822, before their arrival in Athens, the Greek rebels had twice besieged the Akropolis where the Turks were well ensconced. During the first siege, the Turkish garrison had held out. During the second, it had been less fortunate: in July 1822, the Turks had run out of water and surrendered to the Greeks. During the Greek war, such capitulations were normally followed by the rape, pillage and slaughter of those surrendering. Greeks slaughtered surrendering Turks, and Turks slaughtered surrendering Greeks. It had become, as they say in another connection, the custom of the country. However, in 1822, the Turkish garrison in Athens had been more astute. They had agreed to surrender if, and only if, the foreign consuls in Athens supervised the surrender and guaranteed their safety. No British consul had been in Athens at the time, and so the British had played no part in the affair: the Dutch had taken the lead.

George Knightley and Emma had arrived in Athens some months after the surrender. They had arrived not from Constantinople, as might have been expected, but from Korfu, capital of the United States of the Ionian Islands. An eighteen-gun sloop, the *Sparrowhawk*, Captain Stewart commanding, had transported the Knightleys from Korfu to Korinth. A dozen of the *Sparrowhawk's* Royal Marines had then escorted them from Korinth to Athens. Emma was no coward, and she had seen the trip as an adventure. She'd enjoyed her role as *prima donna*, the attentions of the officers, and the good-natured jests of the marines. On the other hand, she immediately took against the 'insufferable gang' of domestics who had remained in the consulate hoping to serve (and betray) the new consul as they had served (and betrayed) his predecessor. She quickly replaced the entire motley crew, apart, that is, from the Bertrams and one old woman, Mother Yeter as they called her, who did no recognisable work, but who could speak Turkish, Greek and English, at least when it suited her.

George Knightley was a country gentleman by breeding and by nature. The curious reader may wonder how such a man with such a wife ended up as His Britannic Majesty's consul in a backwater such as Athens. It may, therefore, help if I devote a line or two to the Knightleys' history.

Donwell Abbey in the county of Surrey was George Knightley's home, and Emma, his wife, was the daughter of his nearest neighbour. George's brother, Henry, had married Emma's sister, Isabella, so the families were unusually close. George had fallen in love with Emma when she was thirteen, still a child in some ways, but already blithe, impertinent and promisingly opulent, altogether, as the expression has it, *as tight as a gooseberry*. Her mother was dead, her father, though he was gentle and considerate, was senile, and her governess, who later married a man by the name of Weston, let Emma have her own way in everything.

Emma Woodhouse had ruled George Knightley with a rod of adolescent iron until, after a futile dalliance with one of the Churchills, she had agreed to marry him, much to his astonishment be it said. At the time of their marriage, Mr Knightley of Donwell Abbey was thirty-eight and Emma some sixteen years younger. Not long after their nuptials, the narrow scope of the Knightleys' rural life was radically enlarged. Fuller's earth,[34] easily accessible and of the highest quality, was found on Donwell land. Within weeks, a consortium of speculators in the City of London made an offer to buy the adjacent estates of Donwell and Hartfield, Emma's ancestral home. Henry Knightley, George's brother, was a lawyer well-connected among the bankers and investors in the City. He advised acceptance. The offer was generous, and it was in ready money. It covered Hartfield complete and that part of the Donwell lands under which the fuller's earth was thought to lie. Donwell Abbey itself would remain with the Knightleys. Negotiations dragged on. Even the mention of mining on the Hartfield estate was enough to put Emma's father, *poor Mr Woodhouse* as everyone called him, in his grave.

If Donwell had acquired an heir, the lands might never have been sold. Unfortunately, however, unlike the marriage of her sister Isabella, Emma's marriage was not blessed with children, and so the contract was signed and the land was lost.

Rich from the sale of their property, grieved by their lack of offspring, and disturbed by noisy mining work on the demesnes of Donwell, the Knightleys decided to travel. They toured Scotland, they visited the Alps, they explored the beauties of Italy, but nothing was satisfactory. Emma detested the shabby inns and insolent couriers. George surfeited quickly on the landscapes, the paintings and the churches he was forced to admire. Both rebelled at the hordes of vulgar and disrespectful tourists, all bound on the same mission of cultivated awe. The Knightleys longed for a more genteel, for a less exhausting, way of seeing the world. As it turned out, the diplomatic service was the answer, and Sir Thomas Maitland was the connection.

Sir Thomas, as my Reader may know from newspaper reports, was a colourful character. A slight digression within a digression will, I hope, be forgiven for the sake of those Readers who have never heard the name of Maitland. In the year 1805, Sir Thomas had been appointed Governor of Ceylon. He had been a soldier of some distinction; even so, his fame, his notoriety perhaps, depends on a tunnel. This tunnel he ordered to be dug from the wine-cellar of the governor's palace in Colombo to a well in the garden of a Singhalese dancing-girl named Lovina.[35] Sir Thomas used the tunnel to pay clandestine visits to the joy of his heart. As it turned out, the visits were not as clandestine as he had imagined. British officialdom condemned his burrowing activities, and Maitland was moved to the Governorship of a far smaller island: Malta. In Malta, as far as is known, he dug no amatory tunnels. Two years later, in 1815, when the United States of the Ionian Islands first became a British possession, he was given an additional post as their Lord High Commissioner.

Maitland, as it happened, was a distant cousin of George Knightley. When Sir Thomas returned to London for a consultation with Lord Castlereagh[36] in the summer of 1819, the Knightleys read about the visit in the *Morning Post*. At Emma's urging, George wrote to his brother Henry, who lived in London. Henry was asked to host a dinner at his house in Brunswick Square so that George and Emma could meet Sir Thomas. At this entertainment, the lustrous Emma played the piano, and sang with touching rusticity half-a-dozen English folk songs. She made no attempt at Singhalese dancing, but, had the success of her project depended upon it, I'm sure she would have darkened her skin and rehearsed the necessary steps. One result of this dinner was a three-year appointment for George Knightley as vice-consul in Marseilles. Then in 1822, on the personal initiative of Sir Thomas, came promotion: full consul in Athens. Sir Thomas, be it noted, had no authority to make the appointment. That authority lay with Lord Strangford,[37] the British ambassador in Constantinople. Sir Thomas was, however, the driving force. Why? Why did Sir Thomas go to so much trouble? Is there perhaps a hint here of a flirtation between the Lord High Commissioner and Emma? For years afterward Emma repeated a phrase of Sir Thomas's that she had clearly taken to heart. *Lovely and well-remembered*: that is what he had called her in his invitation to the Knightleys to sojourn in his half-built palace in Korfu before they travelled on to Athens. It was a visit Emma often mentioned: the magnificent new palace, the idyllic views of Epirus, and the help Sir Thomas had so often solicited from her on details of domestic convenience or park design. Sir Thomas, of course, had the expert counsel of his architect, George Whitmore, and his reason for troubling Emma Knightley for her inexpert advice is unclear, though her being *lovely and well-remembered* may have had something to do with it.

If the scene in Athens has now been set, I must ask my Readers to turn their attention once again to the arrival of the Darcys from Medoni and to the details of their reception.

The two men, George Knightley and Fitzwilliam Darcy, first met, as we have already seen, on a rugged track not far west of Athens. Mr Knightley's little cavalcade reined in. The Darcys' bedraggled convoy slithered to a halt: ten janissaries, a man and a girl on horseback, and two covered carts. Mrs Darcy had left Medoni in a well-sprung carriage not unlike a barouche-landau. Unfortunately, a wheel of this conveyance had collapsed in Pylos, and she and Mrs Tilney had continued their journey in one of the baggage carts.

'Lord Darcy?' the Consul inquired of the rider.

'No, sir,' Mr Darcy replied frankly. 'Plain Mister.'

The men tipped their hats, recognizing immediately that the other was a down-to-earth Englishman with no bigodd nonsense about him.[38] Jane, who was also riding, hung back shyly. The *Sanjakbey* had found no side-saddle for her in the depots beneath his fortress, and so she was sitting astride her horse. Her nascent sense of propriety warned her not to speak to an English gentleman at such a disadvantage, so she slid off her horse, gave the rein to one of the janissaries, and joined her mother in the covered cart. A minute later, peering into the back of the cart, Mr Knightley greeted the three ladies, taking care to speak kindly to Jane: he had seen her embarrassment and understood its cause. If she needed reassurance, she would certainly have found it in his warm and welcoming voice.

As the procession continued, the two men rode together. By the time they reached the consulate, Mr Knightley was familiar with the adventures that had befallen his guests, and he was ready for Emma's raised eyebrow of enquiry as she welcomed them.

'Mrs Darcy,' he began, 'allow me to introduce to you Emma, my wife. Emma, this is Elizabeth Darcy, Fitzwilliam, her husband, their daughter Jane, and their companion, Mrs Tilney. They have been through a distressing time, and our house must now be open to them.'

Emma understood: no milord, no milady, but she was to behave 'as if.' George seldom took to people, but evidently he had taken to Fitzwilliam Darcy. Accordingly, she concealed her disappointment, which was slight, and beamed at her new guests as though they were long-lost cousins.

When Emma Knightley felt the call to be charming, few women were her equal. She indulged her new friends with baths, food and animated conversation. A French dressmaker, an Italian milliner and an Armenian moneylender danced attendance at the consulate, and, in a few days, the Darcys were snugly at home. Mrs Tilney, promoted to the position of *companion* because Elizabeth felt it awkward to include a humble governess in her retinue, was embraced without question. Little Jane quickly became Emma's special protégée.

Much of what now follows will be incomprehensible unless the Reader is introduced to a formidable Greek captain, Odysseus Androutsos. Odysseus was, at this time, Governor of Athens, and, as he often boasted, nothing happened in his city without his knowledge, and little without his approval. The Reader must therefore make ready to spend some time in the company of one of the most unsavoury villains in modern history, and in a climate of treachery and brutality which has no parallel in our own British history since… Well, to be honest, since the massacre at Culloden[39] and its grisly aftermath.

Odysseus was a *khlept* by birth, a free spirit, a warrior of the islands and mountains who owed allegiance to no one but himself, his family, and his men. Physically Odysseus was as tough as an anchor chain, and just about as sentimental. Most accounts of the Greek War of Independence agree on one thing: it was the ferocity, the unscrupulousness, the shameless duplicity of the *khlept* captains that led to the Greek victory. Matched against the tyrannical Ottoman system of appanage, the intricacies of Ottoman taxation, and the sloth of the imperial bureaucracy, the *khlepts* could hardly have lost. In fact, the only serious threat to a *khlept* captain such as Odysseus was the hostility of his fellow captains. And hostility there was in abundance: it is hard to imagine a more foul and pestilent congregation of vipers.

The National Greek Executive in Naflion had allowed Odysseus to assume the Governorship of Athens and of the territories around Athens known as East Romelia. After all, it was Odysseus who had wrested the Akropolis from the Turks. After becoming Governor, he had allowed the foreign consuls to remain in his city. His hope, and the hope of the Executive, was that the European nations would take the Greek side against the Ottomans: as Odysseus saw it, there was no point in expelling the consuls when money and weapons might well be on their way from France, from England, or from the Christians of orthodox Russia.

Odysseus was a despot. He had been a servant, and then chief pipe-bearer, in the notorious pleasure-dome of the Albanian, Ali Pasha.[40] Ali Pasha, the Lion of Ioannina, had been famously butchered and beheaded not long before the Knightleys arrived in Athens. From the Lion, Odysseus had learned the secret of enforcing obedience. The method is both painful and indelicate: accordingly, a lady Reader might wish to avoid offence by passing over the following paragraph.

A person offending the Lion of Ioannina was impaled on a sharpened pole some eight feet long violently inserted into his (or her) fundament. The post was then mounted in the ground, and the sufferer left to scream himself (or herself) to death, which might take a few hours or a few days depending on how many internal organs had been penetrated by the pole. Should the heart be penetrated, death was, mercifully, instantaneous. If every slight offence is punished robustly and publicly, then serious offences are held to be unlikely, much as, in our own enlightened country, the hanging[41] of the few is held to reduce the criminal proclivities of the many. On one occasion, the provisional Greek government, the so-called Executive, sent envoys to East Romelia to censure Odysseus's abuse of power. He received them and impaled them to the last man. No further envoys were sent to Athens on such suicidal missions.

Some two years after war broke out, and not long before our story began, the Greek Executive split. This left Greece with three governments: the still-undefeated Ottoman administration and two rival Greek governments in waiting. Against this background of chaos, war and civil war, the mighty Odysseus seemed indestructible.

Indestructible or not, when Odysseus met the Darcys not long after they arrived from Medoni, something about the family took his fancy: in a rare flush of hospitality, he offered them the use of a carriage from which to see the local sights in comfort. He also mentioned an English woman who, with his permission of course, showed visitors round the town. What was she called? He snapped his fingers, and Mrs Knightley provided the name: Marianne Brandon. So it was that the Darcys, in a coach provided by Odysseus and under the expert guidance of the widow Brandon, visited every stick and stone of note within ten miles of the Akropolis.

Mrs Knightley accompanied her guests on many of their outings. Her husband observed his wife's hospitable efforts with pleasure: Darcy and his womenfolk greatly enlivened the consulate. On the other hand, the political situation was worsening, and the quicker the Darcys were gone, the better. One of the deserters from the consular stables was sent to Korfu with a message to Sir Thomas Maitland: the four English refugees had arrived in Athens. When should they continue their travels? And what financial contribution did London propose to make toward their support in the meantime? It was the lad's first serious employment: more was promised if he proved himself worthy.

While they waited for Sir Thomas's reply, Christmas came, Christmas was celebrated, and Christmas went. On the day after

St Stephen's Day, Odysseus arrived at the door of the consulate arm-in-arm with a dear, albeit a recent,[42] friend, Captain Edward Trelawny. Edward Trelawny, as the Reader may recall, is a relative of mine. Uncle Trelawny, as I have always called him, is my mother's brother.

A visit by Odysseus was no novelty. During the previous autumn, Odysseus had been a frequent visitor, spurred on by rumours that an Englishman, Lord George Byron, was on his way to Ionia from Italy with a shipful of treasure. When would Byron arrive? Where would he land in Greece? And how much money would accompany him? To these and other questions, Odysseus sought urgent answers. George Knightley had received no briefing on the subject and had no ready answers: diplomatically, however, he adopted a knowing look and kept his cards close to his chest.

Odysseus and Trelawny arrived just as the Darcys and their hostess were settling down to a morning of the *Traveller's Tour Through Europe*, a board game published the year before in New York and sent as a Christmas novelty by Emma's sister, Isabella. Emma's quick ear caught the sounds of her husband at the entrance hall welcoming not one visitor but two, and inviting them in for coffee. The game was packed up, hair tidied, and the maid ordered to fetch coffee before the guests had set foot in the drawing room. Introductions were effected, though with conspicuous restraint. The Consul prepared himself to deliver a helping of those sturdy platitudes beyond which British diplomacy seldom strays, at least in public, Odysseus prepared to probe deeper into the mysteries of Lord Byron's whereabouts, while his guest, my Uncle Trelawny, gave no sign of life whatever.

Emma Knightley did not like Odysseus, though it could hardly be said that she *disliked* him, at least not in the way her gorge had once risen against Mr Elton, her parish priest back home in Highbury, or against the duplicitous Frank Churchill. How could she dislike Odysseus? He was a form of male human life wholly beyond her experience.

She scrutinised him now, as he sat stiffly in her drawing-room, a picture of invulnerability and of everything foreign to her world. His right hand was tucked into his wide sash, and a fragile coffee cup was perched uncomfortably in the other. At least, Emma thought, he had left his arsenal behind today: his magnificent sword and the array of pistols stuffed into his sash. Only the gold-hilted dagger that was always ready to his hand had survived. At the end of Odysseus's first visit to the consulate in the autumn, George had objected to the armoury: even a king had no authority to bring weapons into a foreign consulate. Sometimes Odysseus remembered the caution: more often he did not. Today was one of his good days. Although he was her guest, Odysseus made no attempt to engage Emma, or the Darcys, in conversation. He scarcely glanced at the four English ladies except, as Emma fleetingly imagined, to compare their fair skin with that of the swarthy local beauties, or to speculate on what exactly an English lady might be wearing underneath her pretty day-dress. Odysseus addressed the little he had to say to the Consul. Mostly he asked questions to which he received fluent, convoluted and largely meaningless replies. His friend, Kapetan Trelawny, aped the manners and the dress[43] of the Lord Governor, but he went one step further: having once stated his name, he preserved a stony and unmannerly silence.

As we have said, Odysseus appeared stiff and invulnerable, but in fact he was ill at ease. He was an unlettered man, an uncouth man: he could, of course, have had the Knightleys and their guests publicly impaled at a moment's notice, but, in his own eyes, that authority did not make him their superior, or even their equal. Language was one hurdle. English was the language of the Knightleys, French was the language of diplomacy, and Italian was the *lingua franca* of the Adriatic. Odysseus spoke none of them fluently. He sensed that the Knightleys looked askance at the Albanian dress which he had been privileged to wear at the court of Ali Pasha and which he wore still. He knew, too, that his European acquaintances objected to his custom of impaling those he disliked: such behaviour was irreconcilable with the *age of enlightenment* in which they claimed to live. One day, perhaps, he would enlighten them as to the age in which they really lived, but, until then, he held his peace and strove manfully to despise them as heartily as he imagined they despised him.

After some twenty minutes, this unrewarding dialogue was interrupted by a hammering at the front door: a despatch had arrived from Sir Thomas Maitland in Korfu. Mr Knightley had the despatch brought to him in the drawing-room. He opened it and read it to himself while his wife and his guests, even young Jane, sat in respectful silence.

The despatch contained long-awaited news of Lord Byron and of a certain Colonel Stanhope. Like many of Sir Thomas's letters, this one hovered between gouty irascibility and imperial fury. In mid-December, he wrote, Stanhope had arrived in Mesolongi, a swamp-town in western Greece. Immediately after Christmas, Byron was to sail from Argostoli, in Ionia, and join Stanhope in the swamps of Western Romelia. And why? What was their mission? In London, it seemed, a gang of incompetent ninnies and candidates for bedlam had formed themselves into the London Greek Committee. Their task was to establish a *Greek Loan*: a loan for exactly what asinine purpose? Sir Thomas thundered. To make public display of their fashionable respect for liberty? To express their undying hatred of the Mussulman? To find a peace-time occupation for a standing army? 'In my view,' Sir Thomas declaimed, 'if syphilitic imbecility isn't at the root of it, heaven knows what is.' And what a loan it was! 10 million English pounds in gold: half the wealth of the East India Company as declared in 1822 amounted to little more! Of course, such huge funds would take a while to negotiate. In the meantime, Lord Byron and Colonel Stanhope, the Committee's pathetic emissaries, had been despatched to Greece. Byron had with him cash to the tune of 24,000 Spanish dollars, not an enormous sum, but a significant part of his private fortune. Byron's pieces-of-eight, or so the Committee hoped, would finance the Greek cause until the full Loan was negotiated. In addition to the cash, Byron's two ships were loaded with boxes of modern small arms. Stanhope carried no cash, but his willingness to parrot the words *10 million pounds* would, Sir Thomas believed, guarantee him a hero's welcome wherever he roamed in Greece. And the sting in the tail! What final sweetmeat was to drop into the gaping, greedy collective mouth of the worthless *khlepts*? An artillery corps under William Parry had already left England and was due to arrive in Mesolongi in late January.

If the Greek Loan had been the brainchild of Daniel O'Connell[44] and the Whore of Babylon, Sir Thomas could hardly have liked it less. He believed in strict neutrality. The Ottoman government had diplomatic relations with London. The Greek rebels, rival gangs of brigands and tax-farming extortionists, had never so much as nominated a leader to speak for them. Since nobody could guess the outcome of the war, British interests were best served by keeping out of it. Hold the line, preserve the peace, and above all keep Odysseus on a tight leash: those were the Lord High Commissioner's recommendations to the Consul.

Here were the answers to all Odysseus's questions and to others he had not yet dreamed of asking. It was fortunate that they were sitting in a lady's drawing room and that even Odysseus, the bandit chief, felt bound by at least some rules of diplomatic behaviour.

In a post-script, Sir Thomas noted that this would be his last despatch for a while. He was leaving Korfu for Malta. In his absence, business in Ionia would be conducted by his deputy, Sir Frederick Adam.

Seeing the Consul absorbed in his reading, Odysseus watched him intently. Trelawny, who had still said nothing, took his cue from Odysseus.

'Gentlemen,' the Consul said at length. 'I must ask you to excuse me.' He stood up, and perforce his guests stood up too.

'And your now despatch?' Odysseus asked impudently in his fragmented English. 'I can ask...?'

'You may *ask*, Lord Governor...,' the Consul smiled.

'...but you not can tell.' Odysseus completed the sentence with a malicious tug at his moustache.

Mr Knightley smiled again.

'Lordship Byron is in letter? Is possible?' Odysseus pursued blithely. 'What you think, Edgardo?'

For the first time, Captain Trelawny smiled: Odysseus was twisting the tail of the British lion, teasing the appointed instrument of King George IV, and evidently the Captain enjoyed such scenes. When Emma Knightley saw the ugly smile, she winced: Odysseus on his own was an unwelcome visitor, but when Odysseus and Edward Trelawny entered the consulate together (mercifully without their bodyguards), she felt that a magic carpet from hell had landed on her well-polished pine floors.

A Greek brigand and a Cornish buccaneer. What was it, in fact, that attracted them to each other? To answer that question, we must leave the confines of Emma Knightley's drawing-room for a moment.

Uncle Trelawny was a man given to hero-worship. Such men do not always choose their idols wisely. They revere cruelty and ruthlessness more readily than wisdom and discretion. They revel in public show, exotic costume, and elaborate ceremony. They enjoy a bold and ostentatious cult of pain and daring. They gleefully watch their current hero treat his allies with disdain and his enemies with scorn. Women, of course, are ignored or dismissed with contempt, though the hero enjoys (or claims to enjoy) a disproportionate share of their favours. In Athens, Edward Trelawny believed that, after long searching, he had found in Odysseus a man to match his own epic imaginings. For a while he was overwhelmed: he imitated Odysseus's Albanian dress, his uncouth behaviour, and his bragging style of speech and silence. To match Odysseus's bodyguard, Trelawny increased the size of his own gang of Suliot guards,⁴⁵ raised their pay, and boasted everywhere of their dog-like loyalty.

And what attracted Odysseus to his friend Edgardo? The answer is simple: the smell of English money. Edgardo was a friend of Lord Byron, and Lord Byron was, according to rumour, bringing unimaginable wealth to Greece. No more need be said.

Meanwhile, folding his despatch back into its original creases, the Consul began his explanation: 'The subject of my letter is indeed Lord Byron and the Greek Loan,' he stated simply. 'Perhaps, indeed, no letter can be written today that does *not* have the Greek Loan as its subject, at least indirectly.' He smiled unhelpfully. 'But before you go, gentlemen, let me invite you to a small, informal gathering my wife is holding on New Year's Eve. Just a few close friends and our English guests.' He indicated the Darcys who had so far taken no part in the proceedings. *Hold the line, preserve the peace, and keep Odysseus on a tight leash*: a gathering on the last day of 1823 seemed to Mr Knightley an apt way of following Sir Thomas's instructions. Mr Knightley's invitation, politely given, was curtly accepted.

In the event, the party hosted by the Knightleys on 31ˢᵗ December was neither small nor informal. One might say that in four frantic days, Emma and her English helpers put together one of the most glittering affairs Athens had seen since the first days of the war. Everything needed for a party was in short supply: food, wine, musicians, silver, cut-glass, even rosewater. The problem with candles may serve as an example. Normally the Greeks burned either olive oil in clay lamps or tallow formed into candles: beeswax had disappeared from the marketplace. Emma had no choice but to take into her confidence an Englishwoman of whom passing reference has already been made: Marianne Brandon. A few words about Marianne will allow us finally to complete my Uncle Trelawny's 'gaggle' of six women.

I have never met Marianne, so my information about her is second-hand. Marianne Brandon was born Marianne Dashwood.

Until she married at eighteen, she had been no sillier than most girls of her age. Fanny Bertram believes her to have been a lively, pert sort of girl, what Uncle Trelawny might have called *a smart little tit*. Her marriage to a man of sense nearly twice her age, a certain Colonel Brandon, occurred after a young scapegrace did her the favour of first wooing her and then deserting her. Reprehensible as it was, his behaviour did at least teach her the value of bricks and mortar, good farmland, and a deep pocket. A useful lesson, but apparently not learned until Marianne had all but died of a broken heart. As a reasonable woman, Fanny Bertram was unsure about Marianne's broken heart[46]: however, such cardiac catastrophes were the fashion at the time and are not unheard of even in our own more rational age.

Broken-hearted or not, Marianne married the good Colonel, and, though he was a soldier not a sailor, she *l'arned him a rare hornpipe*. Nobody knows better how to spend an ageing husband's money than the cast-off *inamorata* of a heartless young blackguard, and, intending no evil, Marianne bled her piss-proud[47] colonel white. She persuaded him to rent a house in Grosvenor Square, she patronised musicians, encouraged tributes from budding poets, and took drawing lessons with distinguished masters. Mixing, as she did, with the artistic rakes and romps of the time, Marianne chanced to meet a very famous personage, Thomas Bruce, 7th Earl of Elgin, the man of the marbles. In the year 1799, Elgin was much occupied with commissioning a company of artists to work under an Italian named Giovanni Lusieri. Lusieri was to go to Athens, there to sketch and to cast in plaster the sculptures of the Parthenon and other notable monuments. The matter was urgent: the Athenians of the day were energetically smashing sculptures from their settings and selling the fragments to travellers. The rape of Athens was the talk of fashionable London. Marianne was nothing if not fashionable, so she begged her Colonel to invest heavily in a trip to Greece. By 1799, the Colonel was borrowing money to support his wife's extravagances in London, and the cost of an expedition to Greece appeared to him ruinous. Marianne, however, dismissed his parsimony with a single, heart-rending question: Was she to be denied the chance of saving the ancient world? Her artistic talent was too meagre for her to join Lusieri's crew, but when Lord Elgin in person encouraged her to abandon London for Athens, the Colonel caved in.

At this point Fanny's version of *Marianne and the Colonel* diverges somewhat from Emma's. Which of them should I trust? Which of them would you trust, dear Reader? Let me put the case. When I first met them in Cheltenham, Emma was fifty-three. She had gone to seed: her complection was liverish, her hair was grey and without lustre, her breath was touched with brimstone. She seemed to me a battle-hardened gossip, a woman who revelled in scandal.

Fanny was different. Though a year or two older than Emma, she was altogether better preserved. She was in Cheltenham for the treatment of a dislocated elbow, the result of a fall from a horse. I could easily picture Fanny Bertram as she must have been as a young woman, the heroine of my Uncle Trelawny's tales, unblemished, ardent, intelligent and beautiful. But trustworthy? For sure, she was refreshingly down-to-earth: she preferred information to inference, she took a kindly view of her fellow creatures, though when that was impossible, she had colourful ways of calling a spade a spade.

In the orangery at Cheltenham, Emma repeated to me a rumour she'd picked up in consular circles some twenty-five years earlier: Marianne Brandon, the rakish wife of the good Colonel, had been more than just a member of Lord Elgin's circle. She had been his mistress. When I asked Fanny about this gossip, she dismissed it out of hand: in 1799, Lord Elgin was newly married to the elegant, much-admired and wealthy Mary Nisbet. Even if Countess Mary had married his Lordship simply for position and title, a new bride seldom allows her husband to take a mistress quite so casually. I have seen a portrait of Mary Nisbet,[48] and, on the strength of her unblinking eye, I incline to Fanny's view: Marianne may well have flung herself at Lord Elgin, but the idea of packing her off to Athens originated, in all probability, not with Milord, but with his strong-minded new Milady. How, dear Reader, is one to be sure? Was Marianne a mistress or simply a hanger-on? In any case, what does it matter? It all happened many years ago, the Elgin marriage ended in a spectacular divorce, and the impoverished, syphilitic peer died in squalor a few years later.

Imagine, then, the city of Athens, not many years into the present century. Each day, poor Colonel Brandon on his mule gamely follows his wife's mare to the heights of the Akropolis. The heat, Marianne's irrepressible flirtations with Lord Elgin's artists, the monotonous food, and his struggle to fulfil his young wife's ambitious enjoyment of her conjugal rights (as Emma assures me): with all this, the old man's strength must have been sorely tried. Not that he was, chronologically speaking, so very old, but in the sense that a fashionable lady calls a ball gown 'old' after she has worn it but once, the Colonel *was* old, perhaps even palaeolithic. Old or not, there, in Athens, far from the battlefields on which he had so honourably fought for King and Country, Colonel Brandon breathed his last. I can give no proper account of Marianne's financial situation at the time of his demise. According to Emma, Marianne found herself trapped in a hostile world with little more than the shift she stood up in. How she kept body and soul together must, in Emma's words, 'defy the imagination of a respectable woman.' As usual, Fanny's story differs. Marianne, she says, was left a competence by her Colonel, she had a small circle of admirers in Athens, she bought a small house in Piraeus, and she eked out a living in a small way. Marianne attached herself to foreign visitors arriving in the harbour, and she invited them to take supper with her. For a consideration, she would show them the local sites, which she knew well from sketching them, and she would sell them her sketches, antique fragments she had found, and bronze forgeries cast by a Greek of her acquaintance. Luckily, it matters little to my narrative how she survived. By the time my uncle met her in Athens, she was forty-three, her body was opulent from the wine, the bread and the olive oil, her face was raddled by the sun, and her little-girlish manners were still those that had attracted Colonel Brandon in the dying years of the eighteenth century. One point of agreement then: my female informants (and incidentally Uncle Edward) all concur that Marianne's behaviour was often silly and occasionally ridiculous. If anyone in Emma's circle qualifies for the epithet *insufferable*, then poor Marianne must be the leading candidate.

To return to the New Year's celebration, Emma knew that Marianne Brandon, impoverished, struggling Marianne, had wide connections among the tradesmen of Athens and Piraeus. Though Emma normally steered clear of Marianne, what would a party be without beeswax candles? As it turned out, the fake bronzes that Marianne peddled were produced by a sculptor in Piraeus who knew a chandler who happened to own a supply of beeswax. Overnight this was turned into 120 candles and sold to the consulate for half its weight in silver. In fact, without Marianne's intimate knowledge of Athens and its hidden resources, the New Year's festival would have been a tawdry affair. Even the musicians, Italians who still occasionally played together, were old acquaintances of Marianne's, dating back to her Elgin years. After benefitting from her help, of course, Emma had no choice but to invite Marianne to the party. At first Marianne declined: she had no clothes suitable for such a grand occasion. Accordingly, with considerable tact, Emma advanced her the money to deck out her substantial frame. The advance earned a quip from the Consul: a loan to Mrs Brandon, he said, was like a loan to the Greeks: you only made it when all else failed, and you knew it would never be repaid.

Emma was, naturally, the paymistress and the loudest voice inside the consulate, or within a hundred yards of it. She worked on the theory that all servants and tradespeople, especially dressmakers, work better when they are told that they are *insufferable* and are threatened with dismissal at least twenty times a day.

Elizabeth Darcy, on the other hand, quietly concerned herself with choosing the music, with drilling the servants, and with drawing up the menus. Making plans was something she enjoyed, and, from grand occasions at Pemberley, she knew exactly what was needed. But who attended to the thousand critical duties on which the success of any social event depends? Fanny Bertram, of course, and her new friend Catherine Tilney.

Although they were ten years apart in age, Fanny and Catherine quickly discovered that they had much in common: both had married clergymen though neither had gained much joy from the union, both had learned to manage on very little, and neither was afraid of hard work. They could easily have sat on their hands and claimed that the party was none of their business: Fanny owed no great loyalty to the Consul's wife, and Catherine no great loyalty to Jane's often disparaging mother. However, if we accept the view of the ancient Greeks that destiny is character, the characters of these two women destined them to work late into the night, to share between them the tedious responsibilities of the day, and to expect no gratitude for their efforts.

Elizabeth formulated the text of the formal invitations, and Emma, whose handwriting was exquisite, wrote the cards. Diplomats from the foreign consulates, the incumbents of, and the heirs to local fortunes, Greek traders, financiers, Orthodox dignitaries, garrison commanders from the towns and villages around Athens, all were invited, and, despite the short notice, most accepted. Married men were invited with their wives and unmarried daughters, the men anticipating the latest gossip on the Greek Loan, and their womenfolk anticipating gossip on a thousand other subjects, together with the rare pleasure of European dancing.

The guests of honour were, of course, Mr and Mrs Fitzwilliam

Darcy of Pemberley in Derbyshire and their lovely daughter, Jane. As a young girl, Emma had always enjoyed the thrill of being the 'lovely daughter' of the house: her sister Isabella, whom no one had ever called lovely, had conceded the title without dispute. In fact, it would be fair to say that Isabella was Emma's greatest admirer, something unusual in a sister. In Jane that evening, Emma re-lived her early triumphs. At first, Jane's mother was only vaguely aware of what was to be attempted on her daughter's behalf. Then, as the family met on the upper landing before descending to the reception rooms, Elizabeth saw a proud slip of a girl, not quite thirteen, simply but exquisitely turned out, and as poised as a princess.

'So this is what you and Mrs Knightley have been plotting,' Elizabeth said to her daughter. Her words had an edge of irony to them, but pride was in her fingers as she tidied an errant lock of Jane's hair. She saw Jane, but at the same time she pictured herself as she had been at thirteen: at Longbourn, there had been no money, no taste, and no opportunity for such modestly elegant display. And now little Jane had been given her chance through what might be seen as the *interference* of Mrs Knightley. Elizabeth, however, forgave the offence, if there was one. Though Emma was regrettably pampered and painfully self-indulgent, she had meant no harm, and, so far, none had been done.

'Jane looks perfect,' said Mr Darcy, not without a hint of surprise. Since Medoni, he had stopped treating Jane as a youngster, but nothing had prepared him for this self-confident and graceful stranger, definitely a lady and almost a woman. Her long, fair hair was arranged in the chaste style of a Raphael Madonna rather than in the confusion of curls that fashion dictated. Her white dress fell straight and simple from the high waist to the gold key-pattern embroidered round the hem. 'Perfect,' her father repeated. He turned dutifully to his wife: 'And you too, my dear,' he bowed. 'And Mrs Tilney,' he bowed again. 'I find myself overwhelmed and at a loss for words.'

Elizabeth looked at him and burst into sudden laughter. It was a sound he hadn't heard since they'd sailed out of Naples months before. It was a magical sound to his ear, and always would be. 'Dearest, loveliest Elizabeth! What do I not owe you?' he whispered, words that evidently harked back to their courtship.

Elizabeth shook her head mischievously and laughed again. Jane looked at her father in wonder: she'd never heard him say anything half so gallant. He sounded like a character in a book, in fact like a character in the kind of book her mother had forbidden her to read. Darcy caught her expression and smiled. 'Your first night of being grown-up,' he said. 'Thanks to Mrs Knightley.'

'And thanks to Mrs Tilney,' the girl protested. Her hand went to a small cross at her throat on a simple chain. She hesitated and blushed slightly: 'And to Mamma, of course.'

Mrs Tilney cleared her throat: 'Actually the cross was a present from Mrs Bertram,' she said modestly. 'Don't forget to thank her.'

'What a lucky girl you are,' Elizabeth remarked. And then to her husband: 'It's a pity the boys aren't here to enjoy the fun.'

'That is a remark worthy of your dear Mamma,' he replied, though without malice. He had long forgiven Mrs Bennet's silliness: after all, it was in her bedraggled nest that, by some miracle, his beautiful and quick-witted wife had been hatched and fledged.

'The older I get,' Elizabeth sighed, 'the more I understand how difficult life must have been for my poor, benighted mother.'

The Italian musicians now struck their first chord in the big drawing-room downstairs. They followed the chord with a short voluntary, and then swung into the most light-hearted of waltzes.

'Time to go down,' Elizabeth said. 'Time to show Mrs Knightley how much we appreciate her handiwork.'

There was no dancing before supper, the space was not sufficient. As soon as supper was over, however, tables were moved, chairs were arranged along the walls, and dancing could begin. Mr Knightley, little as he enjoyed it, opened the more energetic part of the evening with Elizabeth Darcy, his guest of honour. She had already arranged for three other couples to form with them a set for a fashionable quadrille: Mr Darcy danced with Emma, the Austrian consul, Georg Gropius, the youngest dignitary present, was inveigled into dancing with Miss Jane, while the Dutch consul danced with the wife of his French colleague. Before twelve bars of the music had erupted, two further sets had formed, and Emma's drawing-room became a sea of vigour, colour and merriment. After the success of the quadrille, Elizabeth told her musicians to risk a waltz or two. For a moment, the more respectable of Emma's guests hesitated to join the waltz: it was a dance of which they had heard little good and, an even greater obstacle, which they did not know how to dance. Luckily, however, the young people, led by Jane and her new Austrian conquest, had no such concerns, and the ladies of Athens soon dragged their reluctant partners into the fray.

The Chaplain, of course, would have none of it. He had seated his wife in an inaccessible corner of the room. He stood stiffly beside her chair, more like a guardian eunuch than a husband, his usual sour expression tightened into a disapproving frown. Although Fanny enjoyed dancing, and although she received more than one offer, she declined them all under the chilling authority of her lord and master. Seeing this, Mr Knightley, who had already accomplished his one obligatory quadrille, stepped up to ask Fanny for the pleasure of the next dance, a waltz as it chanced. The Chaplain, sourly remembering old grievances, nodded permission. The waltz, a set of three graceful melodies, lasted barely fifteen minutes, but when the Consul escorted Fanny back to her chair, a faint but cheeky smile struggled with her efforts to repress it. Emma saw the smile and wondered, perhaps with a shade of jealousy, what George had said to amuse the Chaplain's wife. Still wondering, she scrutinised Fanny's dress more closely: certainly, it was a year or two behind the fashion, but it was tastefully clinging, and, Emma had to admit, it flattered Fanny's slender figure. And her hair? The tangle of pretty curls was not at all unbecoming, and, Emma decided, far from accidental: there was more to Fanny Bertram than met the eye. A woman, or so Emma firmly believed, makes the most of herself only if… She glanced again at Fanny's churlish husband: he appeared to disdain his wife altogether. And the other men in the room? All well beyond Fanny's reach, Emma decided firmly. For a second, she felt sorry for the Chaplain's rejected wife. Whatever George had said to amuse poor Fanny during the waltz, he was forgiven.

And the Darcys? What was happening there? Emma watched as Fitzwilliam sneaked up behind Elizabeth and whispered something in her ear, something mildly improper, to judge by his smile. Elizabeth, with her back to her husband, was obviously amused, but, when she turned to face him, she assumed a look of icy rejection. He piteously begged her pardon, though for what offence Emma could not make out: she moved closer. Her immediate reward was the words, *She is tolerable, but not handsome enough to tempt me*, spoken by Mrs Darcy with a haughty sneer. Then, unaccountably, something Emma had never seen before: Mr Darcy and his wife, with their arms around each other, helpless with laughter, that exquisite, liberating laughter that eases the heart and frees the spirit. For a second, Emma smiled at their happiness, but then she glanced again at the Bertrams in their grim corner. Something had to be done for Fanny. But what?

Card tables had been set up as custom dictated, but they were not popular, not even among the elderly and cantankerous. Just for tonight, the dancing was everything: the magic of the music supplanted thoughts of the long war, the iron rule of Odysseus Androutsos, and the uncertainties of the next months.

Mr Knightley circulated politely among his guests, but he danced no more. After supper, he offered to show the French consul an ancient marble head he had recently acquired. The two men retired to the consular study. There, before ten minutes had elapsed, Emma interrupted them with the news that Odysseus and

Edward Trelawny had arrived and were already casting a chill over the merrymaking. The Consul hurried to greet his special guests, but then, catching sight of them, he stood for a second, unsure what they expected of the evening, or what he expected of them. They were standing arm-in-arm, not quite sober, surveying the dancers. They were dressed, as always, in the exotic red, white and gold of the Albanian court, and armed only with ornate, though serviceable, daggers. The Consul watched as garrison commanders tendered nervous bows to the overlord of East Romelia, bows which Odysseus acknowledged with a slight narrowing of his dead eyes. Then something caught Odysseus's attention: he pointed to one of the dancers, a girl going through the steps of an allemande with a young man in the uniform of a Russian diplomat lavish with gold braid. Odysseus whispered something to Trelawny. Trelawny whispered something in return that looked very like, 'No, I don't think so.' The girl was Jane, and Odysseus's observation of her at her first dance began a chain of events which, before long, proved fatal to at least one of Mrs Knightley's guests.

There was a sudden shrill cry from among the dancers. 'Oh, my dear Herr Gropius! I'm old enough to be your mother!' It was Marianne, cheerfully proclaiming to the world that she was still young enough to be the target of an indecent proposal. 'Yes, indeed,' the Austrian consul agreed, adding in an unnecessarily loud voice, 'Even older perhaps.'

Mr Knightley winced and hurried toward Odysseus. 'My Lord Governor!' he said. 'And Mr Trelawny! You are more than welcome to our humble celebration.'

'Two despatch more, Mr Knightley,' Odysseus replied, ignoring the forms of politeness. 'My men tell: two messenger arrive today. From Korfu.'

'Then your men have told you nothing but the truth,' Mr Knightley replied. 'Shall we...?' He indicated a French window which stood ajar to let fresh air into the room. The three men stepped outside. On the terrace it was cold, but ignoring physical discomfort was part of Odysseus's cult of the *khlept*, in the same way that ignoring tasteless outbursts by middle-aged women was part of George Knightley's cult of the gentleman.

'The two despatches contain firm information,' Mr Knightley began. 'And I am authorised to share this information with you. But not with…'

'Trelawny? What you say me, you say Trelawny. He is friend Milordship Byron. Despatches talk Byron? Or no?'

Mr Knightley began his explanation. There had been many rumours, but now he could state the facts: thousands of Spanish dollars, millions of English pounds, a cache of small arms and a complete artillery corps were on their way to Greece. Despite his cold-blooded mien and an expression as stony as that of Ozymandias,[49] king of kings, Odysseus was impressed, or so it seemed to George Knightley.

They talked, Odysseus asked questions, and Edward Trelawny sharpened the questions where the answers were unclear or evasive. The Consul watched the ambitious Governor of Athens slowly grasp the extraordinary extent of his opportunity. Even in the candlelight, he saw Odysseus's heavy brow knit together, plotting and planning. Not that the goal of Odysseus's scheming was in any way obscure: it was simply to ensure that the money went to him, and not to the incompetent, avaricious, insatiable bandits who sat on the national Greek Executive, on the two Executives, or on however many Executives there might be. Odysseus was a man who could think with one part of his mind and talk with another. As his plan took invisible shape, he launched into a declaration of sublime patriotism, somehow identifying passionate Hellenism with the brotherhood of *all* men. George Knightley admired the show despite its infantile mendacity.

'Yes,' the Consul agreed, 'we shall work together for the greater good of the race that gave the world Plato, drama and democracy.' Not to mention olive oil, Byzantine treachery, and backgammon,[50] he added to himself.

Odysseus soon diverged from the glory of Greece to a more familiar theme: his own glory. He had been born on the island of Ithaka, home of that other Odysseus...

'...son of Laertes,[51] seed of Zeus, resourceful Odysseus,' Trelawny added.

Odysseus nodded sagely, and began to explain how for 3,000 years the men of Ithaka had defended their flocks, their homes and their honour, a model for the rest of the world, not that the rest of the world could rival what generations of Ithakans had achieved on their small island. There was more in this vein, much more, before the three men re-joined the company.

The advice that George Knightley had received from Korfu was unequivocal: since those brainless apes on the London Greek Committee were determined to throw away their money, the Consul should buy the loyalty of Odysseus Androutsos with promises of a good share of it. But promises only. Although Odysseus might be useful in the short term, he'd be lucky to survive the next twelve months with every *khlept* captain in Greece thirsting for his blood.

At midnight, Edmund Bertram, in his capacity as chaplain, proposed a toast to Saint Sylvester. He (the Chaplain, not the Saint) cut a laughable figure with his skinny legs, scrawny neck, and long untidy hair. And why Saint Sylvester? Nobody, not even the Chaplain's wife, understood his choice of saint. The Greeks would have toasted Saint Basil. The English, who until 1752 had celebrated New Year's Day on 25th March, had neither saint nor tradition, and might perhaps have toasted the Holy Circumcision, although the word *circumcision* is rarely breathed by English Christians, let alone made the subject of celebratory toasts, and in any case that feast falls a day later, on 1st January. Luckily, the toast to Saint Sylvester was short, and the mood in the consulate was forgiving: Rumour had already established that 1824 would be a prosperous year, at least for the Greeks among Mrs Knightley's guests. Sadly, I must here relate that the Consul himself was disconsolate: his French counterpart had assured him that his prized marble head was a shoddy and recent copy of an ancient original now on display among the glories of the Louvre.

Odysseus took his leave shortly after midnight. He kissed the hand of his hostess, and that of Elizabeth Darcy. He hugged little Jane as though he were a favourite uncle. Emma observed the hug and drew from it a conclusion by no means flattering to Odysseus.

Fanny Bertram once (or perhaps more than once) said to me that, much as she had always loved dear Emma, and much as she loved her still, the poor woman was obsessed with matters venereal. In the consulate in Athens, according to Fanny, Emma's favourite pastime had been the detection of lustful glances: male glances or female glances, Greek, Turkish or English glances, rich glances or poor, glances Moslem, Orthodox or Anglican. No licentious glance escaped her, and many that were far from licentious were so interpreted. We all know such women, their heads bubbling with copulation while their deportment would not disgrace the wife of a Wesleyan grocer.

Odysseus probably knew that his whiskery kisses and bad breath earned him no indulgence, but he was not a man to be influenced by trifles. What did it matter what women liked or what they didn't? If he wanted a woman, he took her, or he bought her. If neither approach seemed practicable, he looked elsewhere.

To Emma's surprise, Edward Trelawny did not leave the consulate with his friend Odysseus. Trelawny, as the saying goes, had other fish to fry.

Toward women, Trelawny often struck a pose of light-hearted Byronic contempt, but in truth he was as susceptible to female charm as any crack-voiced Cherubino. Earlier that evening, when Trelawny and Odysseus had entered the drawing-room, Elizabeth Darcy had been entertaining the Austrian consul with some pretty gossip. It was months since Trelawny had seen an English beauty dressed to kill, and Elizabeth's shaft had struck home instantly. Now, with Odysseus out of the way, he could pay his homage, or so he hoped, delicately and without unnecessary swaggering.

(All this, of course, he explained to me much later, and so it may be invention in part, or even in whole.) An extraordinarily fine woman such as Mrs Darcy, he calculated, would abhor a swaggerer. The moment was propitious. Mrs Darcy was congratulating her hostess on the success of her evening. Another woman, the wife of the dreadful English Chaplain, was standing with them, apparently on a similar mission of felicitation. Trelawny approached the three women with a touchingly shy smile and a modest demeanour.

'And may I be allowed to add my congratulations to those of your guest of honour?' he asked his hostess, lowering his soft, west-country voice as though reluctant to attract their notice. For a moment he regretted his exotic, Odyssean outfit. On the other hand, as he well knew, such detriments can readily be turned to advantage. He simply had to tell himself that every man in the room envied his splendid livery: tell himself, listen to himself, and believe himself.

'Mr Trelawny!' Emma greeted him as though his facile congratulation were the crown and glory of her evening. 'We hardly had time to speak when you visited us the other morning.' Her husband had warned her: this party is for Odysseus, so make him uncommonly welcome. And if he comes with Trelawny, be nice to him too.

'No indeed,' Trelawny concurred. He was hesitating between two styles, the polished and the saturnine. In the end, he chose neither: these two women, three if the Chaplain's wife were included, were subtle and intelligent: they'd see through a pose immediately. 'Though, of course,' he added with a smile, 'I found the visit regrettably short.'

He turned to Elizabeth: 'I caught but a glimpse of you the other morning,' he said. 'But now I have the honour of a fuller acquaintance.' The phrase was trite enough, but he injected a deliberate sincerity into the word *honour*. Emma, with her usual acuity, noted the sincerity and drew her conclusions.

'Mrs Elizabeth Darcy,' Emma broke in. 'May I formally

present Captain Edward Trelawny.' She turned to the Captain: 'Mrs Darcy, as you already know, has been our esteemed and welcome guest since before Christmas.'

'Then I must thank her as the *onlie begetter* of our festivities tonight.'

Emma looked puzzled.

'Just as Mr W.H. was the *onlie begetter* of Shakespeare's sonnets,' the Captain explained, 'Mrs F.D. is the *onlie begetter*...'

Politely the women feigned amusement, and at the same time masked their surprise: this friend of the frightful Odysseus, this strangely dressed man of whom any extravagance might be expected, was familiar with the sonnets of Shakespeare. 'It is whispered,' said Emma, sensing that a discussion of poetry might be in order, 'that you are a friend of Lord Byron.'

'Why should it be whispered?' Trelawny asked, familiar but respectful. 'It is a friendship which neither I nor Byron has reason to conceal.' The west-country accent had all but disappeared. George Gordon Noel, 6th Baron Byron of Rochdale, was indeed a friend of his, though perhaps not such a close friend as Trelawny imagined. More of that later, dear Reader.

'You're an admirer of his poetry, of course,' Emma ventured.

'Some of it. In truth, I'm a far greater admirer of Percy Shelley.'

'It was *you*!' Elizabeth broke in suddenly, her dignity overwhelmed by her excitement. 'I remember now, reading about it in the newspaper! It was *you* who cremated Shelley. Lit his funeral pyre.[52] In Italy. Am I right?'

'On the beach at Via Reggio, ma'am. The unhappiest day of my life.'

Pausing for effect, Trelawny rolled back the gold-embroidered cuff of his Albanian blouse. The skin of his forearm was scarred with burn marks, still unbleached by time. The women studied the burns, unsure but impressed: no gentleman, and certainly no English gentleman, paraded his mutilations in the drawing-room of a lady. But perhaps, on this one occasion...

'I saw that his heart would not burn,' Trelawny said with deliberate nonchalance. 'So I snatched it from the flames. It is buried now. In Rome.'

'*Holy the air, the water, and the fire,*' Elizabeth quoted quietly, her fine eyes masked with sudden reverence.

Trelawny rolled his sleeve down to his wrist again. '*Psyche,*' he said with matching veneration. 'John Keats. Maybe one day we'll have time to read it together.' He sighed. 'But for now, I must be on my way. My men are waiting for me in the street. I dread to think what might happen if they became restive.' He bowed politely to Elizabeth, then to Emma and to Fanny Bertram, turned, and made his way out of the drawing-room.

The women watched him go. 'Superb,' Emma said. 'I doubt the Prince himself could have made a better exit!' By this time, of course, the Prince Regent had been King George IV for nearly four years, and Emma had never seen him make an exit either as prince or king, but she had heard the remark at one of Sir Thomas's receptions in Korfu, and now she had the chance to repeat it.

'And Shelley's heart! What a story!' Elizabeth echoed.

'Perhaps it's true,' Emma said. She turned to Fanny sympathetically, trying to bring her into the conversation: 'What do you think, Mrs Bertram?'

'Yes, what do you think?' Elizabeth repeated the question.

Fanny blushed: seldom was her opinion sought on any subject, great or small. 'Yes, there really was something in one of the newspapers, about eighteen months ago,' Fanny said with a shy smile. 'I saw it too.'

'We keep all the newspapers, don't we?' Emma asked vaguely.

'In the cellar,' Fanny offered. 'Shall I try to find it? Tomorrow?'

'What a good idea,' Elizabeth said. 'Well,' she continued, 'burning heart or not, he certainly knows his poetry. I thought *Psyche* was by Wordsworth.'

'And you quoting it like that!' Emma exclaimed. 'You must know it by heart.'

'Far from it. Somebody wrote two lines in my Visitors' Book, and I happened to remember one of them.' Mrs Darcy caught Fanny's eye, and they both smiled, the small, subversive smile of practised irony.

'Well, that's one more line than your Fitzwilliam knows, I dare say,' Emma risked.

'Or your George, unless I much mistake me,' Elizabeth countered. 'But what do you think of Captain Trelawny's idea? A poetry reading?'

'George will throw Trelawny out of the house if he catches a whisper of *Psyche*, or anything like it. He hates poetry worse than Dr James's Powders.[53] Keats in the consulate! Heaven forbid!'

'Milton in the mission!' Elizabeth pursued, glancing at Fanny, inviting her, or perhaps challenging her, to join their badinage.

'Landor in the legation! Chatterton in the chancellery?' Fanny suggested, and the three women laughed together, suddenly closer and more trusting than before.

'Well, if George throws the Captain out of the house, Fitzwilliam will kick him down the front steps to help him on his way,' Elizabeth promised.

'Gentlemen and justices of the peace,' Emma laughed. 'Models of sensibility!'

'But... Did I understand that we are to plan an at-home?' Elizabeth asked innocently. 'For later in the week?'

Chapter 3

BETROTHAL

The next day a sleepy silence fell on the consulate, broken only by the sounds of Fanny Bertram and Catherine Tilney, with the help of the consular servants, setting the place to rights. The extra cooks and footmen had been paid off the night before and escorted watchfully to the back door. Despite the vigilance of the two women, the usual perquisites had vanished: some gallons of wine, most of the uneaten food, and all the candle ends, enough beeswax to light Evensong in a small country church.

Halfway through the afternoon, not long before the work was finished, Jane appeared in the scullery downstairs wearing her everyday cotton frock. Her hair was festively dressed much as it had been the night before, though without the benefit of Mrs Tilney's expert hand.

'Have you come to work or to gawp, Miss Darcy?' her governess asked.

'Work,' Jane replied.

'After the triumphs of last night?' Fanny asked with a hint of a smile.

'Mrs Bertram,' Jane began. 'I didn't have the chance to thank you properly last night. For the cross.'

'It was a pleasure,' Fanny replied with a quick nod. 'If you have time, you can help me put the silver away – properly.'

The consulate's table silver had spent the night in its special cupboard where it had been locked the night before. Fanny had kept the key. Now the silver was spread chaotically across the draining board and its boxes were stacked on the table. 'We have to wash each piece separately so it won't get scratched,' Fanny explained.

'What about polishing?' Jane asked.

'You do that next time, before you use it again.'

At first, as the three women worked in the scullery washing the silver, drying it, and sorting it into its velvet-lined boxes, Jane wasn't quite sure of her place: she had seldom worked at household tasks. Then, as they settled down, Mrs Tilney excused herself: she had matters to attend to upstairs.

Jane, working carefully, felt more comfortable with her governess out of the room. 'What made you think of the cross, Mrs Bertram?' she asked at last.

Fanny smiled. 'I used to live at a place called Mansfield Park,' she explained, 'with my Uncle Thomas and his family. Two aunts and four cousins. There was a ball. My brother, William, had come to visit me. He was a sailor. He had to re-join his ship, so my uncle decided to give a ball: in William's honour, and in mine, though at the time I could hardly believe it.'

'How kind. How old were you?'

'Eighteen.'

'Did he often do things like that, your uncle?'

'Not for me. I was the *poor cousin*, if you know what that means.'

'I think I can imagine,' Jane replied. 'A bit like the way my brothers get preferred to me.'

Fanny shook her head: evidently her young friend had no idea of poor cousins. 'William gave me a cross,' she explained. 'Made of amber. He'd bought it somewhere on his voyages, in Sicily, I think. I wanted to wear it. And my cousin Edmund…'

'Edmund? You mean the Chaplain? Your husband?'

'Yes. We're cousins.'

A sudden reluctance made Fanny frown, and she fell silent.

'What were you going to say?' Jane asked at length. 'About Mr Bertram?'

'He gave me a chain... For the cross.' The answer was as hesitant as the question.

'And so you...?' Jane pursued, still unsure of her ground.

'And so, when I knew it was *your* first grown-up party, I bought *you* a cross and a chain to go with it.'

'I asked Mrs Knightley if she knew anything about it,' Jane said, relaxing suddenly. 'But she didn't.'

'No. We don't talk about things like that,' Fanny replied.

There were, of course, many aspects of her life that Fanny had never talked over with Emma Knightley. On the other hand, Emma's piecemeal account of Fanny's early years and of her marriage, as I picked it up fragment by fragment, was colourful and reasonably close to the truth. As a coherent narrative, it went roughly like this:

At the age of ten, Fanny had been plucked from the licentious dockyards of Portsmouth, and translated to the chaste and unimpeachable residence of her aunt, Lady Maria, wife of Sir Thomas Bertram, in the county of Northamptonshire. There, for the next few years, she was bullied, put upon, underfed and overlooked. Although her lot was better than that of the slaves on Sir Thomas's plantation in Antigua, it was not entirely dissimilar. Fanny's Aunt Norris, Lady Maria's sister, was the fiercest bully in the pack, a woman scarcely less vicious than the famous slave-captain, Robert Norris, whom William Wilberforce[54] so forthrightly denounced in the House of Commons. Though Fanny's Aunt Norris could not have been a relation of the frightful Captain, they were undoubtedly two of a kind.

As young Fanny entered her teens, she suffered from what Emma Knightley gingerly referred to as 'a common complaint among young females.' Emma was speaking, of course, of the green sickness, the late onset of the menses, caused, as we now know, by anaemia and treated, today, with iron and potassium carbonate. When the problem had first manifested itself in Fanny, the treatment had been savage: bloodletting, frequent and thorough purgatives, violent emetics, and cold baths. Sadly, through all this, Fanny had no friend to take her part. The only inhabitant of Mansfield Park who took the least note of her was her cousin, Edmund. Not that he was genuinely solicitous or offered her constant support. Occasionally, however, he made a kindly gesture in her direction, much as he might have thrown the gristle off his dinner plate to a three-legged dog, and for this he earned her childish loyalty. As the Reader already knows, Fanny and Edmund were later married, so the fact that they grew up as children in the same house, is not without interest. Though they existed at the highest and lowest levels of the family hierarchy, they *were* both members of the family: in a sense they were brother and sister. As the second son, young Edmund was destined for the priesthood, whether he was so inclined or no. Unfortunately, like many designated young reverends, he fell in love with a charming romp, Mary Crawford, who chanced to be staying in the village. Mary, as it happened, had no plans to throw herself away on a beggarly country curate. So Edmund, rejected and in despair, proposed marriage to little Fanny. Though Fanny had once been not much more than a skivvy, she was now a young lady of sorts, the companion of the idle Lady Maria, Edmund's mother. Edmund proposed and Fanny accepted. As the Reader has already seen, the next years were plagued by violence, which is far from rare in English marriages: less common, the marriage was never consummated. This is what Emma told me: Fanny Bertram, helpmeet of the Chaplain to the British consulate in Athens, was a virgin-wife. Was this to be believed? When Emma first spun me the story, I immediately doubted some parts of it: I did not believe, for example, that despair could be any man's motive for marriage. More probably, Edmund sought to revenge himself on his disdainful charmer by a none-too-subtle insult. The fact that Fanny's marriage to Edmund had failed on the wedding night and never recovered, that seemed to me slightly more probable. My Uncle Edward's attitude to Fanny had, in a way, prepared me for it: in his yarns about Athens, his youthful dreams had centred on Fanny Bertram, ethereal, elusive and romantic. Now a scamp like Edward Trelawny would hardly fall for a vicar's wife unless (in addition to her being uncommonly handsome), she had some teazingly unusual quality about her. Married virginity was perhaps fascination enough: the body unblemished, the heart all but disengaged, and the spirit lacerated. To abandon fable and gossip for a more reliable source, let us return to Fanny as she and Jane clean silver in the consular scullery.

'I expect you enjoyed it, your ball at Mansfield Park,' Jane said expectantly.

'In a way yes. But I was very nervous.'

'Not about dancing with William, surely?'

'A little, maybe. Brothers and sisters didn't dance with each other, not in those days.'

'What about your cousin then?'

Fanny was wiping a serving spoon. She turned it so that a distorted reflection of her face stared at her from the bowl. 'My cousin Edmund...' She paused, remembering. 'I danced with him. Two dances, one after the other. But he was in a sulk. And all he said was *Let us have the luxury of silence.*'

Jane was shocked. 'How rude!' she exclaimed, and then looked away, sensing that her words were childish and tactless.

'Yes, it was,' Fanny agreed. 'But you see, Edmund...' She hesitated and swallowed awkwardly: it was an unprecedented step she was taking, revealing her past to a girl of twelve, in fact, revealing it to anyone at all. 'Well, you see...,' she began again, finding sudden comfort in the idea of recruiting Jane as an ally, '... Cousin Edmund had fallen for a girl from the village.'

'A village girl?'

'Certainly not. She was staying at our parsonage. Mary her name was. She lived in London, she was beautiful… And she had £20,000 of her own, so it didn't matter whether she was beautiful or not.'

'But why wouldn't Edmund talk to you?'

'He'd quarrelled with Mary. She'd turned him down. Flat. During the first dance. That same evening.'

'She loved someone else?'

'She loved no one. No one at all.'

'Oh dear.'

'It was worse than *oh dear*. It turned him into the man he is now.'

Jane was puzzled. What was the Chaplain's wife trying to tell her? 'And you were…?'

'I was what?'

Jane shrugged. 'I don't know…'

'Jealous, you mean?'

'Were you?' It wasn't a proper question, as Jane realised, but for a moment her curiosity overcame her sense of propriety: it was more or less her first grown-up conversation.

'Yes,' Fanny confessed. 'When I was little, Edmund was kind to me. Not always, but now and again. In my silly way, I half thought he belonged to me.'

'Do men belong to women? Like we belong to them?'

'Far from it,' Fanny shrugged. 'But I was very young.'

'I don't think being jealous means you're silly. I think Mamma was jealous once, a long time ago.'

'Did she have a rival?'

'My father teases her about it sometimes: *Perhaps I should have married Caroline Bingley*, he says.'

'He doesn't sound very serious.'

'No, he isn't. It's one of their jokes. But you? And Mary? Everything was all right in the end?'

'What do you mean?'

'Well, your cousin married you, didn't he? Not her?'

'Yes,' Fanny reluctantly agreed. 'He married me. *The Lord giveth and the Lord taketh away. Blessed be the name of the Lord.*'

'Not finished those spoons yet?' Mrs Tilney's voice unsettled the calm of the scullery. 'I think everything else is done. Time for a nice cup of tea.'

'I'll tell Cook to boil some water,' Fanny replied and disappeared into the kitchen, her hand brushing the sleeve of Jane's dress as she left.

While she was gone, a clattering of hooves in the yard and a hammering at the back door signalled the arrival of a courier. Fanny let him in and told him to wait in the hall.

'Is Mr Knightley up yet?' Fanny asked, poking her head round the scullery door.

'He's out, taking a walk with Mr Darcy,' Mrs Tilney replied.

'And the ladies are still abed, I assume,' Fanny said flatly. For four weeks now, the Consul had taken his afternoon walk with Mr Darcy, and she missed, grievously, what had become the highlight of her day.

'That's what ladies are for,' Mrs Tilney replied. 'To keep out of the way till the work's done.'

Jane laughed. 'But you're trying to make me into a lady,' she said. 'That's why you're my governess.'

'Actually I'm no one's governess,' Mrs Tilney said gravely. 'While we're in Athens, I'm your Mamma's *companion*.'

'Why does she need a companion when she's got a husband?' Jane asked, with the kind of shrewdness that prefigured perhaps the kind of lady she would become in just a few years.

The two women looked at her with amusement. 'Wait till you're older. You'll find out, all in good time,' Mrs Tilney assured her with mock severity. 'That, and a lot of other things beside.'

'Wait till I'm *married* you mean.' Jane shrugged, for the first time in her life playing an audience along. 'But maybe I won't get married. Maybe I'll become a slave like Cora Shrubb. Whatever she said about getting her head cut off, I think she could twist that old Turk round her finger.'

'Cora Shrubb indeed! That baggage!' Mrs Tilney said putting on a cross voice. 'Don't let your Ma hear you say that, that's all.'

'Mamma? She'd rather I was a slave than *spoilt* like Aunt Lydia.' It was the purest nonsense: the three of them laughed and settled down to the serious business of making tea.

After tea was made and drunk, Mrs Tilney went off to see if her mistress needed any further help with her morning toilet, though, in fact, it was already dusk. As soon as she was gone, Fanny Bertram folded her arms and looked seriously across the table at Jane. 'Tell me about Cora Shrubb,' she said.

Jane looked at her quizzically, grimaced, and then explained what little she knew.

Fanny nodded. 'It sounds as though you were sorry for her,' she said.

'Of course I was.'

'Mrs Tilney called her a *baggage*. You don't agree?'

'That's not what Mrs Tilney really thinks. In a way, they quite liked each other.'

'But you just told me Cora Shrubb could be cruel?'

'She was very cruel to Mamma. Mamma got in such rages about her. I think she really hated Cora.'

'But *you* didn't?'

'She was strange. She went around with hardly any clothes on.'

'That's an odd reason not to hate her.'

'She used to talk about all the terrible things that might happen to me. It scared Mamma, but I think she was trying to warn me. She had a horrible life.'

'Despite what you said about the old Turk and winding him round her finger?'

'That was a joke.'

'I couldn't tell. You didn't laugh when you said it.'

'It was a serious joke, like my mother makes. Even my father doesn't understand her half the time.'

'And your Aunt Lydia? You don't hate her either?'

'Not at all.'

'Because she walks around with hardly any clothes on? Or some other reason?'

'Once she went swimming in our lake with no clothes on at all. Or so Brinkley told me.'

'Your Aunt Lydia can swim?'

'Quite well. She learned when she was at Brighton.'

'Brighton?'

'She was visiting an army camp. I think it was part of her being spoilt.'

'And can you swim?'

'Aunt Lydia tried to show me once. In our lake. Mamma was furious when she found out.'

'Your Mamma can't swim?'

'No. She says it's not ladylike, and there's no point in it anyway.'

'It could save her life one day.'

Fanny's words had a strange ring to them, somehow threatening, and Jane hesitated to reply. 'Mamma doesn't think so,' she said at last.

For a moment the conversation flagged. Then, 'And who is Brinkley?' Fanny asked brightly. 'Your mother's maid?'

'She was. Till the pirates sent her to Tunis. To sell. It's so horrible. Papa was very upset about it. I think he still is.'

Fanny nodded.

'He says he'll try to find her. When we get back home.'

'I hope he does,' Fanny said, her mood brightening.

'I hope so too,' Jane agreed with a gentle mix of gratitude and pride.

'Is your father a magistrate?' Fanny asked, giving the conversation a new turn.

'Yes. Why?'

'Does he send people to prison?'

'We live in Derbyshire. There aren't many criminals there.'

'Why not? Because your father locks them all up?'

Jane laughed. 'No, of course not. There was a murder in Matlock once…, before I was born. Sometimes people steal things because they're poor. Or hungry.'

'What does your father do with them? With the thieves?'

'It depends. I think he's rather soft on them. He gets in terrible trouble with Mamma sometimes. For being too soft.'

'Soft?'

'He let a woman off once, and gave her half a sovereign.'

'And what did your Mamma say to that?'

'She said…,' Jane shied away from the question. There had been a row about it that had lasted for weeks: the memory was still painful.

'…the woman would spend the money on drink?' Fanny suggested quietly.

'How did you know?'

'That's what people always say.'

'But not you, Mrs Bertram.'

Fanny thought carefully for a second, weighing a risk. Then, almost as if it were part of the same subject, she said: 'Have you heard of a woman called Elizabeth Fry?'[55]

'No. Who is she? Does she live here? In Athens?'

'Yes,' Fanny replied lightly. 'She's Mr Knightley's secret slave. He keeps her chained up in the attic.'

'Not him,' Jane laughed. 'He's too much of a gentleman.'

'Yes,' Fanny smiled, and then turned the conversation back to what interested her. 'Elizabeth Fry is a Quaker. In England. I met her when she came to Northampton.'

'Northampton? Why?'

'She was visiting the prison.'

'You weren't…?'

'No,' Fanny laughed. 'Elizabeth Fry visited women's prisons.

The place where the Cora Shrubbs of this world finish up. If they stay in England.'

'Mamma says that's where my Aunt Lydia will finish up if she doesn't change her ways.'

'Poor Aunt Lydia.'

'She'd be better off if she didn't drink so much, that's what Mamma says.' Jane paused, sensing that Fanny had no interest in Aunt Lydia, drunk or sober. 'So, why was this woman visiting prisons?' she asked.

'Because she thinks it's disgraceful, the way we keep prisoners, especially women.' She paused. 'I won't go into it, but she's right. So everywhere she goes in England she asks the people, the rich ones, to help her raise money.'

'To give to the women?'

'Not really. Her idea is to teach them how to read and write. So they can find work when they get out of prison, if they ever do.'

'And you?' There was a touch of wonder in Jane's voice. To her ears, the story was new: a woman like Fanny Bertram, a poor woman but nevertheless a lady of some sort, concerning herself not with clothes and balls and beaux, but with *the Cora Shrubbs of this world.*

'Me?' Fanny pondered the question. 'I did what I could. It wasn't much.'

'But it was something?'

'Are you interested?'

'I've never thought about prisons before.'

'Well, in prison, the women need a lot of help. Most of them can't read and write, so they can't write home. I can do that for them. And I can read them the replies, if any come. Sometimes they need a pennorth of medicine for themselves or their babies. I can fetch it. Simple things.'

'And the others? At Mansfield Park? Did they help? Were you married already when you met this woman…?'

'Elizabeth Fry.'

Jane nodded: she hadn't forgotten the name, but somehow it didn't sit easily on her tongue.

'Yes, I was married,' Fanny told her. 'Not that it made much difference.'

'But your husband,' Jane stammered. 'He's a priest. Surely *he* would be the first…' Jane fell silent, arrested by Fanny's grimace of pain.

'There are husbands and husbands,' Fanny said enigmatically. 'There are priests and priests.'

After a moment or two of awkward silence, Jane tried to begin again: despite her blunder about Edmund, there was much that Fanny still wanted to tell her. 'Can I ask you something else?' she whispered.

Fanny nodded.

'Why was she so important to you? Elizabeth Fry?'

'Well,' Fanny began thoughtfully. 'You see, I thought I'd been badly treated at Mansfield Park, not when I was grown-up of course, but when I was younger. I thought running errands for my Aunt Norris was somehow shameful. And then, when I married my cousin, I knew that deep down he still preferred Mary Crawford. And I knew why: it was obvious to anyone. But it seemed so unfair, cruel even. Then I visited that prison with Mrs Fry. It made me feel ashamed. I actually cried with shame.' She paused. 'My God, Jane, when I saw those women and heard their stories… What were my problems compared with theirs, and…?' Her voice choked. She glanced at Jane to see if she'd understood. 'Can you imagine?'

She saw tears swell in Jane's soft eyes and roll down her cheeks. 'I think so. But my life…,' Jane whispered, '…so different.'

Fanny held out her hand across the table, and she saw Jane's hand move impulsively toward hers. For a moment they sat, hand in hand.

Boots clattered at the front door. 'Sounds like the gentlemen back from their walk,' Fanny said, with a grateful squeeze of Jane's fingers. 'Do you think they'd take us with them next time, if we asked?'

'I expect so,' Jane replied, but there was still the catch of tears in her voice.

Fanny had told the courier from Korfu to wait in the hall for the Consul's return. She had found him a chair and a thin cushion. As the Consul entered his front door, the courier sprang to life, tendering his despatch. The despatch was from Sir Frederick Adam. It informed the Consul that shortly after Christmas Day, Lord Byron had set sail for Mesolongi as planned with two ships, a slow *bombard* and a fast *mistico*. Neither ship had arrived. The *bombard* had been intercepted by the Turks on suspicion of carrying supplies to the Greek rebels. It had ended up in the Turkish harbour at Patras. Byron himself, on the *mistico*, had vanished from the face of the earth and his Spanish dollars with him.

No sooner had the courier been sent to the kitchen to eat, than the knocker of the consulate hammered again. This time it was Odysseus and his friend Trelawny paying a courtesy call to thank Mrs Knightley for the New Year celebration. The Consul accepted their thanks on her behalf. And something else… Perhaps the two of them might spare him a moment in his cabinet? Odysseus raised no objection. As soon as Mr Knightley was alone with his guests, he informed them of the disappearance of both Lord Byron and a great deal of money: did they have any information on the subject?

'Yes,' replied Odysseus. 'I know where is Lordship Byron.'

'And where is that?'

'In Astakos. You have map?'

The Consul produced a map showing the whole of Greece. To the north of the Gulf of Korinth, a vertical red line divided West Romelia from East Romelia. Odysseus was nominally governor of East Romelia, though his real control extended only a few miles outside Athens. Astakos was a small harbour on the coast of West Romelia, almost 200 miles away. Odysseus pointed to it on the map.

'I see, Lord Governor,' the Consul said, 'that Astakos is opposite your home, Ithaka.'

'You are right. I go Astakos many time.'

'And you have heard that Lord Byron is there. Is he safe in Greek hands, may I ask?'

Odysseus nodded evasively. 'Receive information, yes.'

'Through your semaphore?'

'You think Greek has semaphore?' Odysseus frowned. Though his signalling system was the common gossip of Athens, he somehow resented this English milksop's knowing about it.

'Given to you by the French, wasn't it?' The consular smile was as innocent as a bowl of cream. 'A semaphore is an excellent thing,' he continued, in the hope that a little needling might cause Odysseus to say more than he intended. 'We now know that Lord Byron is in Astakos. And that he is safe.'

Odysseus nodded. 'You have messenger from Korfu. He eat now, in your kitchen. Tonight he take your message Korfu: *Odysseus say Lordship Byron safe.*'

'You are well-informed about my messengers,' Mr Knightley said with a flash of feigned resentment, and a frown that was almost a match for Odysseus's own masterly display.

'I know what is happen in this city,' Odysseus retorted. 'Nobody enter, nobody leave Athina with not I inform. No foreigner walk my street with not I know. Today, you walk with Lordship Darcy. You want, I tell you where?'

'No. Tell me what we talked about?'

Manfully squaring his shoulders, Odysseus rose to the challenge. 'Lord Darcy wish go home England with wife and so charming daughter. And you say, not possible.'

The Consul was taken aback: he had indeed discussed the Darcys' return to England. They'd been walking through the marketplace, but he'd not been aware of anyone eavesdropping on their conversation. How could he get back at Odysseus, and quickly? 'Lord Governor,' he said. 'Do not confuse *Lord* Byron, who is an English lord, with *Mr* Darcy who is not.'

Odysseus flashed a smile at Captain Trelawny: the skirmish with the Consul had been brief, but he felt that he had come off the better. Trelawny nodded by way of reply, and Odysseus decided to strike while the iron was hot. 'I have plan,' he said abruptly. 'We,' he turned to the Captain with a slight bow, 'we have plan.'

'I'm sure you do.'

'You know our plan?'

'I also have my sources of information,' the Consul replied evasively. A plan? Almost for certain, their plan involved Lord Byron and the English money. Such a plan would necessarily fail without the support of the British consul. It was time to stop bandying words with the Lord Governor and to start listening. 'But tell me anyway,' he said.

'You know,' Odysseus grunted, 'Greek revolution have many leader.'

'Of whom Odysseus Androutsos is the chief and principal.' This was far from the truth as the Consul was aware. Though he had no network of spies, George Knightley had contacts within Odysseus's own circle. For example, Iannis Gouras, Odysseus's deputy, slipped regularly into the consulate for a few words. Gouras seldom betrayed a secret, but he did confirm the stories that the Consul picked up from other sources. He had confirmed, for example, the rumour that the entire Greek leadership hated Odysseus with the kind of passion that only one *khlept* can feel for another. As commander of the guard, Gouras had more than once unmasked an assassin sneaking into the Akropolis.

'Chief leader?' Odysseus repeated. 'Perhaps true. Perhaps not. But if Greece can live, Greece must kill every Turk. For this Greece is have army. Big army.'

'Paid for by foreign money.'

Odysseus nodded. 'And must have *one* leader, not many. Only one. Is true? Yes or no?'

'That is exactly the thinking of the London Greek Committee, or so I read in the English newspapers.'

'Newspapers,' Odysseus said with contempt. 'How is *your* opinion?'

'Lord Governor, I am a diplomat. I have no opinion.'

'Lordship Byron bring money. He bring gun. Gun and money for one great leader. One. But how? Greek have no leader. No great man.'

'That could be problem, I agree.'

'Must be conference,' Odysseus said. 'All Greek come together. Choose one great leader.'

The Consul looked again at the map, thinking, calculating. He saw the whole plan now: set up a gathering of many leaders to establish Odysseus as their chief. Then Lord Byron and his money-bags would be led to the conference by Odysseus's good friend, Edward Trelawny.

'A congress held in *East* Romelia, I should imagine,' the Consul said.

'A *congress*. Better word. *Conference* not so good word. Thank you.'

The Consul nodded.

'Congress meet East Romelia. Amfissa,' Odysseus pursued, indicating on the map a town near Delphi.

'Aren't you pointing at Salona?'[56] the Consul queried.

'Greek name Amfissa.'

The Consul nodded: it might be so. 'But what will happen if you call a congress? Will the other leaders come?'

'Kapetan Trelawny,' Odysseus clapped his hand roughly on his friend's shoulder, 'is already promise.'

'Promised? What?'

'Promise London Committee say *yes*. And promise his friend Lordship Byron come to Amfissa. If Byron come, everyone come. Yes?'

'I am delighted to hear that Mr Trelawny is in a position to make such promises.' The Consul turned to Trelawny who was taking his ease on a chaise-longue, listening to the sounds coming through the unceiled joists: the ladies upstairs dressing for the evening. 'Mr Trelawny?' the Consul prompted.

'Byron, I imagine, will go along with it,' Trelawny said amicably. 'London too, in all probability. Whatever else, it's a damn huge heap of money: crime to throw it away.'

'I agree with you entirely,' said the Consul, standing up. 'Absolutely and entirely.'

'Agree heap of money? Or agree congress?' Odysseus asked, shaking his heavy head.

'Absolutely and entirely,' the Consul repeated. 'And now, gentlemen, if you will excuse me.' He rang the bell on his desk.

The Consul had expected one of the consular servants to answer his ring, but instead the door was opened by Jane Darcy. 'I'm sorry,' she said, stopping short with her hand still on the door handle. 'I didn't realise…'

Odysseus and Trelawny were both on their feet. Odysseus made a slight bow toward the door and the young girl. 'Lady Darcy,' he said ingratiatingly.

Jane replied with a stiff curtsey, closed the door behind her, and fled.

'Lordship Darcy so charming daughter,' Odysseus said. He felt a restraining touch on his sleeve: Trelawny's hand warning him. The Consul observed the touch. A quick suspicion crossed his mind, but he dismissed it. That Odysseus Androutsos or Edward Trelawny had designs on little Jane was out of the question. I have often observed how decent men, men like Mr Knightley, are slow to suspect villainy in others. In a country squire, such a trait is endearing: in a consul, it is perhaps a blemish.

The visitors left the consulate and joined their bodyguard and their weapons which were waiting in the street outside. On the cold January flagstones, grooms were walking two fine horses, keeping them warm. Odysseus and Trelawny resumed their armoury, mounted their animals, and the party set off toward the Akropolis, the bodyguard jogging to keep pace with their masters.

'He agree congress? Or no?' Odysseus asked Trelawny. 'He is difficult understand man.'

'Knightley's a diplomat. Unless you open one of his despatches, you'll never know what he thinks. And maybe not even then.' The noisy flagstones ended. A few hundred yards of hard-packed, uphill debris lay between them and the first gate of the Akropolis. The gate stood open, though it was well-guarded.

'Knightley is not so important,' Trelawny continued. 'If my friend Byron is on your side, you'll get your congress.'

'You are promise?'

'I know that if Byron meets you, he'll like you. He's already written a dozen poems about you.'

'Not possible.'

'*The Corsair*.[57] If he's anyone in the world, he's you. *The Giaour, Mazeppa* and all the others.'

'And he come, this poetry Lordship? With money? To congress?'

'That's the plan. To Salona.'

'It is your plan, Edgardo. This congress. It is good plan. I like this plan. But for you, perhaps is dangerous. So why you want it? I not understand *why*.' There was more than an edge of doubt in Odysseus's voice. Why was this strange Englishman with his exotic Italian name so helpful? What did he want? What treachery was he planning?

'A congress is the easiest way to get the money,' Trelawny replied.

'Yes,' Odysseus agreed, not quite satisfied with the answer. 'Money.'

'Millions, or so they say.'

'Lordship Byron? He know this plan?'

'Not yet. But I'll write to him. Today. We are old friends: he'll do what I ask.'

The guard at the gate came to an approximation of attention as the two horsemen passed into the citadel. The bodyguard halted at the gate, watching their masters amble toward a cluster of buildings at the edge of the Akropolis. The Venetian Tower, as the place was collectively known, was protected by a system of walls, outbuildings and ramparts. This was where Odysseus lived out his well-guarded life, and where Kapetan Edgardo, his friend, was staying as his guest.

'And little girl?' Odysseus said with a deep sigh.

'Little Jane?'

'She is beautiful,' said Odysseus seriously.

'She's not quite thirteen,' Trelawny reminded him.

'Same age like my sister, Tersitza.'

'Tersitza looks older.'

'Yes, you look her,' Odysseus remarked, deliberately casual. 'I see you look her.'

Trelawny could hardly deny the charge: he'd feasted his eyes often enough on Odysseus's budding half-sister. 'She is such a flame of beauty, no man could fail to look at her,' he said, intending a compliment.

'If man look her... If I not like...,' Odysseus said. 'I cut him. I bullock him.'

'And perhaps Jane's father thinks the same about her.'

'You say this? To me?' There was no obvious threat in the words, but, with Odysseus, violence was never far away.

'We are friends, Odysseus,' Trelawny said quietly. He did not say, *And without me you will not meet Lord Byron, and your fellow captains will cut your throat at the first opportunity,* but he was sure Odysseus took his meaning.

'You are look my sister,' Odysseus said, without obvious rancour. 'Every man in Greece understand this look. Same if I have wife. You look my wife. And you tell she is beautiful. Perhaps in cold-blood England is no problem. In Greece, is problem. Is insult.'

'You'll have me murdered before we reach the Venetian Tower?'

'Possible. But... You not have wife?'

'No, I divorced my wife. Years ago.' Trelawny spat from his horse onto the flagstones.

'Then marry with Tersitza. Marry, and I forget insult.'

'And…?' Trelawny laughed. Odysseus was proposing a deal though the details were still obscure.

'And? What are you mean *and*?'

'I marry Tersitza, and…?'

Odysseus laughed. 'Yes, *and*. *And* is this: I want Lady Jane Darcy under my hand.'

'You wicked old devil.'

'For me, she is so perfect, Edgardo. So young, so yellow hair, so white skin, so beautiful.'

The guard at the Venetian Tower gave an order, and the heavy gates swung open.

'Say *yes*,' Odysseus laughed. 'Or I bullock you now, and crow-food you before supper.'

Trelawny laughed. 'Yes,' he said lightly. 'Definitely yes. But you must tell Tersitza tonight: she's to marry me, before midsummer.'

'Midsummer? What year?'

'This year. That's already a long, long wait.'

Laughing together, the two men entered the tower.

That evening, as Trelawny, the *khlepts* and their womenfolk sat round the big table eating and swilling wine, Odysseus announced that his beloved sister was to marry his great and best friend, Edgardo. A splendid dowry would be found somewhere. Edgardo would be a rich man.

'Αλλά δεν μπορεί να μιλήσει ελληνικά!' Tersitza exclaimed. 'Πώς μπορώ να τον παντρευτεί?'

Her objection[58] was drowned in ribaldry. Trelawny kissed her in front of the company. There was no going back: Tersitza and Edgardo were already as good as man and wife.

A Jane for a Tersitza? Or more correctly: Jane Darcy and Byron's millions in exchange for Odysseus's precocious sister and a share of the millions once they were in Greece? If Edgardo wanted to keep his head on his neck and his backside unimpaled, there was no way now to wriggle out of his bargain.

Note

This note is found on four unnumbered pages lodged after Chapter 3 of the original manuscript. Although it is an afterthought rather than an integral part to the narrative, the editors decided to include it as offering a further insight into the behaviour of Edward Trelawny.

It was indeed a scandalous bargain that Uncle Trelawny made with Odysseus Androutsos. But what drove it? How is it to be understood? At the most superficial level, a twelve-year-old girl was exchanged for another, the one blonde and chaste, the other dark-haired and with more than a hint of youthful lubricity. Was lust, then, the driving force? I think it was not. In offering Tersitza to Trelawny, Odysseus sought to bind Trelawny by a blood-tie. In offering Tersitza *in exchange for Jane Darcy*, Odysseus was seeking to strengthen the tie by a sign of good faith on Trelawny's part. Such an exchange would be an act of friendship, of brotherhood even. If the English millions really did flow, and flow to Odysseus, he was going to need all the brothers he could muster. With treacherous schemers like Iannis Gouras snapping at his heels, a brother-in-law would be someone Odysseus could rely on, though not trust of course: Odysseus trusted no one, and no one trusted him. Seen in this light, Captain Trelawny's arrival in Athens at this crucial time was, for Odysseus, a godsend. Looking a little deeper into the Lord Governor's schemes, he had set up a bolt-hole in the mountains, a cave,[59] obscure and inaccessible, on the rugged north-eastern slopes of Mount Parnassus. Here he had concealed the booty of a lifetime. It was to this cave, and not to Athens, that the hoard of English cash would be taken after it arrived in Salona. For Odysseus, the cave was both a treasury and a fortress of last resort: if he lost control of Athens, he could retreat there with his Ithakans, with his half-sister, Tersitza, and, mayhap, with her buccaneer husband, Edward Trelawny.

And Trelawny? He was an adventurer. At this stage of his life, though not exactly destitute, his entire wealth took the form of gold coins secured in a bandolier he wore under his shirt. For him, a marriage with Tersitza balanced a danger against a hope. The danger lay in Tersitza herself: nothing about her suggested that she was the material of which biddable English wives are made. Already at twelve, she was the bright-eyed toast of her brother's murderous crew of Ithakan bandits. Already Odysseus had half-promised her to Iannis Gouras, not entirely, it seemed, against her inclination. If Tersitza's character was the *danger*, her connection with Odysseus was the *hope*: she offered Trelawny the right to enter Odysseus's cave and to participate in the wealth concealed there, now and in the future. Whatever might eventually transpire, Trelawny was ready that January day to surrender Jane Darcy to Odysseus in exchange for a marriage with Tersitza, for access to the cave, and for a negotiable share of the English money.

And Jane as a bargaining counter? She was, of course, to serve as a sign of Trelawny's good faith, but what else did Odysseus promise himself from the possession of *so yellow hair, so beautiful* Jane? Perhaps nothing else. Obviously, Odysseus had conceived no passion for little Jane: power was his only passion. Looked at in another way, of course, power may offer the clew to his unrelenting pursuit of so young a prey. Jane was a Darcy, of the same tribe as the Knightleys, and this tribe despised Odysseus and his ilk with scarce a fig-leaf to cover their scorn. With Jane in his power, Odysseus could strike back. Traditionally the *khlepts* looked at rape and torture as the way in which one tribe stamps its superiority on the body of another. Simply put, rape and torture were tokens of ascendancy. More chillingly, or so my Uncle Trelawny has assured me, a *khlept* finds a sinister amusement in savaging the flesh of his enemy. At the court of Ali Pasha, the Lion of Ioannina, torture in all its variations was common. Often this happened simply because no other form of entertainment offered itself: it was a natural, everyday proceeding. Odysseus, perhaps, saw no reason why Jane should not provide him and his Ithakans with a pastime they understood and found enjoyable.

Or perhaps, and this possibility also emerged from my Uncle Trelawny's ramblings, Odysseus intended to show off the generosity and nobility of his character by first getting little Jane into his clutches and then by restoring her, unharmed, to the bosom of her family. Such a course of action on the part of a soulless despot might seem unlikely, but it is far from impossible. Odysseus's obsession with disguising his inferiority and with inflating his greatness were to claim many victims during the next few months. Whether Jane was one of them will become clear if the Reader pursues this narrative to its bitter end.

Chapter 4

PSYCHE

The next despatch from Korfu confirmed Odysseus's report: Byron's *bombard* and its cargo of rifles had indeed been taken to Patras. The skipper had destroyed a budget of Byron's letters that he was carrying and had convinced the Turks that the rifles were intended for a hunting expedition in Albania. The Turks, reluctant, perhaps, to offend their British ally, had released the *bombard*, and, in a few hours, it had sailed across the Gulf of Korinth to Mesolongi arriving there on 4th January. Lord Byron in his fast-sailing *mistico* had arrived in Mesolongi on the next day and promptly moved into the house of Leicester Stanhope, his fellow dispenser of English gold. At this portent, the Greek vultures began to circle, with Alexander Mavrokordatos[60] the first to arrive. The initial meeting between Byron and Mavrokordatos went well. Unlikely as it might seem, the Greek politician had read some of Byron's poetry and memorised a few lines: after a well-timed quotation, the two men struck up a friendship. All this news was in the despatch from Sir Frederick Adam.

During one of Odysseus's now daily visits to the consulate, George Knightley offered him British diplomatic confirmation of Byron's arrival in Mesolongi. The advice from Sir Frederick was to keep Odysseus hopeful and his Salona Congress high on the agenda. This was not as easy as it sounded. Odysseus and Mavrokordatos had been at daggers drawn for years: any report that Byron and Mavrokordatos were on good terms might poison Odysseus's always suspicious mind and precipitate mayhem.

Meanwhile on the domestic front, Emma Knightley had decided that a literary at-home would inflict social butchery on poor *Psyche* and on any other poem they might choose to read. An at-home would mean a general invitation: *Mrs George Knightley is pleased to inform you that she will be at home...* No! Quite, quite insufferable. The guests should be people of sensibility, women mostly, who could be trusted to say the right words in the right places. No tag-rag-and-bobtail at-home then, but an exclusive poetry-reading.

Though at first glance Mrs George Knightley had foreseen few obstacles to the planning of a simple, though select, poetry-reading, especially with the knowledgeable Elizabeth Darcy on hand and ready to help, obstacles began to emerge immediately. The first was the character of the male protagonist, Edward Trelawny. On New Year's Eve, an extraordinary change in Trelawny had coincided exactly with Odysseus's exit from the consulate. It was, of course, the civilised version of the man that Emma wanted to parade in her drawing-room: her Trelawny was to be the bosom friend of English poets not the devotee of a *khlept* despot. To achieve that, the despot himself, Odysseus Androutsos, must somehow be excluded.

And Trelawny himself? Who was he really? Emma's impression of him, albeit fleeting, was that he was handsome in a darkly ferocious sort of way, though his costume and his manner must be scored against him. But was he a captain? Was he really a friend of Lord Byron? Had he, in truth, plucked Shelley's heart out of the funeral pyre with his bare hands? Emma realised that she should know the answers to such questions before she sent out her invitations. Fanny had offered to rummage among the consulate's old newspapers in search of answers, and this she was asked to do. After some hours of searching, Fanny produced a mildewed copy of the *Morning Post* for 25th August 1822. A man named Edward Trelawny, Emma read, really was a friend of Lord Byron and an acquaintance of John Keats. According to the paper, Shelley's funeral pyre had indeed been lit by Trelawny on the beach at Via Reggio. For Emma, the *Morning Post* had much the same authority as the Holy Scriptures though without their obscurity. The damp, smudged story relieved Emma's lingering doubts: the Trelawny who had presented himself at the consulate was genuine, and his story was true. The article also revealed that Edward Trelawny was, in all probability, a privateer sailing under a *lettre de marque* issued by the French government; in fact, as Fanny suggested, he was little better than a pirate. At the word *pirate*, Emma's cup was full to overflowing: what could be more romantic?

With the putative career of Edward Trelawny resolved, Emma turned to the management of the husbands, Messrs Darcy, Knightley and Bertram. Sadly, Emma acknowledged, all three men lumped together lacked a single ounce of poetic feeling. Worse, all three saw Trelawny as a ridiculous swaggerer and spoke of him, if at all, with contempt: a less encouraging audience would be hard to imagine. If the husbands were there, her evening would fail, and Emma longed for success. Her inner ear heard her drawing-room throbbing with passionate voices. Her inner eye saw firelight flickering across spellbound and ecstatic faces, and she saw herself, for the rest of her life, subduing every dinner table with the tale of how, during the Greek War, she and a pirate captain had declaimed English poetry while the Turks and the revolutionaries blew each other apart in the streets outside.

Emma talked over the invitation list with Elizabeth Darcy, omitting, of course, the charm of piracy: the Darcy family had a recent and well-founded dislike of pirates. Elizabeth immediately agreed on exclusivity. She also agreed about the social usefulness of the story in later years, and suggested, with her usual irony, that a few timely pistol shots in the street outside would lend authenticity. Emma liked the idea of the shots, but she felt that they could be added to the narrative later: that would preserve the romance while avoiding the risks that always attended the use of firearms. Elizabeth also agreed that Odysseus should be excluded and probably the husbands too. On the other hand, she saw a danger in making Trelawny the centrepiece of a roomful of women. They needed more breeches, but what other men in Athens could they invite? Might Marianne Brandon have an idea? And so, despite her ridiculous sally with the Austrian consul on New Year's Eve and other improprieties too numerous to mention, Marianne was invited to tea at the consulate and quizzed about the men of Athens. Despite the ravages of time, this was a subject on which she could speak with authority.

Marianne, who knew every Athenian worth knowing, mentioned three Greeks who admired, or claimed to admire, Byron's poetry, and who had at least heard of John Keats. They might pass as gentlemen if they were warned in advance and given time to compose their manners. Among the three was Marianne's friend, the sculptor of fake bronzes. She also put in a word for the Austrian consul, the only foreigner in Athens with a modicum of sensibility, as she described him. Even though it meant inviting Marianne to the poetry evening, her advice was accepted.

With the guest list settled, Emma had to fix a date. This was an even greater conundrum. The Consul could hardly be banned from an event in his own consulate: Mr Darcy was just as difficult to exclude. And Odysseus? If he heard about the evening and decided to come, he would come. Ruin threatened in all directions. If only Emma could find a date when the Consul, Mr Darcy and Odysseus would be 'otherwise occupied.' And Mr Bertram? He was, the two women agreed, a different problem altogether. Since he had no duties apart from the Sunday services, he was never 'otherwise occupied.' Might he, perhaps, be tolerated? It was possible that he could understand poetry just from hearing it read aloud: after all he'd been at Oxford. How exactly undergraduates at Oxford occupied their time, Emma had no clear idea, and Elizabeth could not enlighten her, but the idea seemed hopeful. Mr Bertram then? Or no Mr Bertram? In fact, as they quickly realised, the question was superfluous. The Chaplain was a nobody: he kept his sermons short and in line with the prejudices of his tiny congregation, he gabbled the appointed prayers like a notary, and he read the appointed passages of scripture omitting all but the first and last verses. He had no culture, and his address was as stiff as his priestly hat. How on earth his poor wife put up with him, the two women had no idea. Emma's distrust of her spiritual guide had taken deep root. She knew that he slapped his wife occasionally, and she had begun to suspect worse: now that she looked for them, she saw bruises where none should have been, and, now that she listened for them, she heard words that no reasonable man would say to his wife. Even so, for the time being, she was prepared to let sleeping dogs lie. Elizabeth surmised that, even if asked to the reading, the Chaplain would stay in his room and sulk. Emma nodded hopefully.

By the middle of January, Emma and Elizabeth had still found no suitable date for the poetry evening, and none was in prospect. Worse, half-a-dozen times a day, George Knightley insisted that the Darcys must leave Athens as soon as possible. From Elizabeth's point of view, leaving Athens was not a problem. She was tired of the place and the meagre company it offered: to leave the city and never to see Edward Trelawny again would not have cost her a single tear. Emma, on the other hand, was trapped in Athens, perhaps for years. She was thirty-one already – and how few of those years had been in any way noteworthy. She needed Elizabeth to stay: if the mistress of Pemberley went, the poetry evening would fail miserably. Emma remembered how Trelawny had gazed at Elizabeth on New Year's Eve, and the modest sincerity with which he had spoken to her. If Elizabeth disappeared, then Tilney and young Jane would disappear with her. Without them, would Edward Trelawny condescend to read *Psyche* in public? It seemed unlikely.

Then, interesting news: a fresh despatch from Sir Frederick in Korfu. As the family sat round the lunch table eating its daily mutton and greens, the Consul read aloud part of Sir Frederick's letter. 'It seems that our friends the Turks have learned that Lord Byron has landed in Greece.'

'That's not a secret, is it?' Mr Darcy asked.

'No, sir, it isn't. Nor, unfortunately, is the fact that the Committee in London is sending millions of pounds to the rebels.'

'With Byron as their cornucopia,' Mr Darcy added.

'What's a cornu…? Whatever you said, Papa?' Jane asked.

'A horn of plenty,' Mr Knightley broke in. 'You sometimes see a statue with a huge horn on one shoulder, pouring out all manner of fruits and other blessings.'

Jane smiled at him: he always had a kindly word for her. 'So, Lord Byron has arrived with his horn full of money,' she said.

'Exactly,' Mr Knightley agreed.

'Money for the Greeks?' Jane pursued.

Jane's mother emitted a quick *tut*. Elizabeth could suggest many things with one click of her tongue: on this occasion it was that children in general, and young ladies in particular, should be seen and not heard.

Mr Knightley took a different view. 'Yes, Jane, for the Greeks,' he said.

'Why do they need so much money?' Jane asked, looking directly at Mr Knightley and away from her disapproving mother.

Elizabeth rapped the table with the flat of her hand. 'Jane, my dear, that's quite enough,' she insisted.

Now it was Emma's turn: 'I think it's interesting to hear what Jane has to say,' she broke in.

Fanny Bertram nodded agreement, but said nothing.

'I'm sure you'll find,' Mrs Darcy sniffed, 'if you ever have daughters of your own…' Her blood was up, and things were becoming serious.

'With your permission, Mrs Darcy, I'll put the matter in a

nutshell for Jane,' Mr Knightley said mildly. 'The British are officially allies of the Turks,' he explained. 'Me, I'm Consul to the Sublime Porte in Constantinople, resident in Athens. Now, the Greek Committee in London is giving the Greeks money to fight a war *against* the Turks, and the Turks are unhappy about it.'

'Unhappy, yes,' Mr Darcy asked. 'But do they have any plans?'

'Unfortunately they do,' the Consul replied. 'As a result of Lord Byron's antics, the Turks have closed the Gulf of Korinth to British ships.'

'God forbid!' Mr Darcy exclaimed. This was serious news indeed: with a rapid glance, Elizabeth and Emma suspended hostilities.

'How can they close the Gulf?' Mr Darcy asked. 'What will they do exactly?'

'Well,' Mr Knightley explained. 'The Gulf is very narrow at the western end, near Patras. And the Turks have two forts, Rio and Anti-rio. One on either side of the water.'

'Guns?'

'Mr Knightley,' Elizabeth broke in. 'Can we spare Jane the details? I don't want her frightened to death.'

'I don't think Jane is so easily frightened, my dear,' her husband assured her. 'She survived the horrors of Medoni. Right, Jane?'

'Yes, Papa,' Jane said very quietly. 'Right.'

Mr Darcy nodded. 'And my question, Knightley? What sort of guns do they have? In the forts?'

'French twelve pounders. Dozens of them. So I'm told.'

'And a British ship, a warship even, would be caught in the middle?'

'It would if it tried to force a passage. And don't forget Lepanto, stuffed with cannon. Lepanto overlooks the whole thing.'

'So, the Turks control the narrows,' Mr Darcy shrugged. 'And there's nothing we can do about it.'

Despite the rebuke from her husband, Elizabeth was still listening with close concentration. 'But surely our warships…?'

she broke in, the legends of Trafalgar and British hearts of oak burning in her words.

'Not even if we took the *Victory* out of retirement,' the Consul shook his head. 'If the Turks say no, it's no.' He paused letting his words sink in. 'In other words, you have no choice but to stay here until either you can go overland or the Turks lift their blockade. It could be months.'

'That really *is* bad news,' Mr Darcy said. 'Especially after what you told me yesterday.'

The Consul caught sharp looks from both his wife and Elizabeth Darcy. He shook his head again, more emphatically. 'That was between ourselves, Fitzwilliam,' he said. 'And it's only a rumour. Nothing to worry about.' He beamed around the table.

'Nothing to worry about, thanks be to God,' the Chaplain echoed, though he knew no more of the matter than the gecko on the wall.

George Knightley raised his eyes to heaven. God, in his opinion, had a consistent attitude to matters diplomatic and military: He consigned them to the lowest pit and cut them off from His hand. *Selah*.

'So we have to stay here,' Jane interrupted. 'Why is that bad news? I like it here.'

'Jane, my dear,' her mother said holding back her anger and frustration. 'If your father says it's bad news, perhaps you should think twice before contradicting him.'

'But let me say in extenuation, Mrs Darcy,' Mr Knightley broke in, easing the silence that followed this rebuke. 'Emma and I are delighted that Jane is happy here.'

'Yes indeed,' Emma concurred.

Elizabeth smiled her perfect, social smile, cold as a January night in Aberdeen. 'Fitzwilliam,' she said. 'Before you take your afternoon walk with Mr Knightley, might I have a word with you?'

'Naturally, my dear,' he replied. 'I should like it of all things.'

In their room, as soon as lunch was over, Elizabeth tackled

her husband. 'Why do you always take Jane's side against me?' she asked.

'I wasn't aware that I did.'

'You said nothing when Mr Knightley contradicted me. I call that taking Jane's side.'

'To be honest, I don't think Jane has a side. She was just trying to say something nice when we were all being so gloomy.'

'I don't think Emma Knightley was particularly gloomy. I think she's trying to wheedle Jane away from me, and I don't like it.'

'She has no daughter of her own, so I suppose…'

'Suppose what you like, it's not my fault she can't have children.'

'Maybe…,' Fitzwilliam said, making for the protection of the door. 'Maybe…'

'And another thing: what did Knightley say to you yesterday?' Elizabeth watched her husband give up his half-hearted attempt at escape and cross to the window.

'I was going to tell you,' he said, looking out across the yard. 'But it isn't easy.'

Elizabeth made no reply. She had him trapped: he'd hold back nothing now.

'George said this: as long as Odysseus is strong, Athens will stay peaceful. How long that will last, nobody knows. If…' He paused to correct himself. '*When* Odysseus loses the upper hand, we can expect…' Another pause. 'No point beating about the bush: his exact words were *murder*, *rape* and *mayhem*.'

Elizabeth sat down on the bed with an undignified *plump*. Murder. Rape. Mayhem. She felt alarm shade into outright fear. For a second she fought to rein herself in. 'When?' she breathed.

'When? Nobody knows.' Mr Darcy sat down on the bed beside his wife and put his arm round her shoulders. 'We got away from the pirates. We got away from Medoni. And you never lost courage. Not for a second.' He paused, waiting for her to catch up.

He felt her slip her arm round his waist. His Lizzy. 'I'm so proud of you,' he said. 'You've no idea.'

'Proud of Jane too,' Elizabeth added quickly. 'You were right. She wasn't frightened.'

Darcy nodded. 'The way she strode through that fortress. I'll never forget it.'

'But this now, this business with Odysseus? It's serious, isn't it? Life-and-death serious?' Elizabeth pursued.

'We need a plan,' he replied. 'There might be a way out across the Aegean. But more likely some way out across the mountains.'

'The mountains! You remember, back home, the fells in winter,' Elizabeth objected. 'Horrible, uncrossable. And Mount Parnassus is three times higher, or so Knightley told me. Perhaps the couriers might know something.'

'I've already asked them,' Darcy replied. 'They gave me a list: Turks, bandits, floods, and snow. And top of the list: dogs.'

'Same list the *Sanjakbey* gave us in Medoni.'

'Apart from the floods and the snow.'

Elizabeth sighed agreement. 'We should start planning then,' she said.

'When it comes to planning, Lizzy, you're the planner,' Mr Darcy said tenderly.

Elizabeth nodded quickly picking up the pieces. 'I'll talk to the couriers again,' she said, as though the problem were as trivial as the choice of the colour for a riding habit.

'And one other thing George said,' Fitzwilliam added.

'I like George,' Elizabeth said, waiting.

'He said that recently he'd been faced with decisions. Hard decisions. And he needs help.'

'You?'

'If we're forced to stay in Athens, would I become vice-consul? That's what he asked me. Acting vice-consul anyway.'

'You?' Elizabeth repeated, though in a different tone. 'Actually, Fitzwilliam, I can see his point. You know the militia, so you're more of a soldier than he is. You don't panic. You're a magistrate, and a good one: everyone says so. I'm sure you'd be useful here…, if we have to stay.'

Mr Darcy looked at his wife who was sitting resolutely on the bed looking up at him with the simple candour he remembered so well from the first days of their marriage. He nodded gently, accepting her praise as he accepted her chiding, with husbandly composure.

'Take your walk with him now. Make some excuse for my behaviour at lunch,' Elizabeth said.

'That makes a change from *you* finding excuses for *me*,' he said, and they smiled at each other, a warm smile, full of the trust one sometimes finds in a strong marriage.

As it turned out, Mr Darcy said nothing to excuse Elizabeth's show of temper. One subject the two men generally avoided on their walks was the behaviour, whether exemplary or regrettable, of their wives. As country gentlemen, they had many concerns, from poaching to landscape gardening, that were more interesting than conjugal relations and at the same time less threatening. Further, as Englishmen sequestered in an alien and dangerous world, they confronted many troubling issues. One problem in particular had distressed Fitzwilliam Darcy ever since he'd lost the *Pemberley*, and he brought it up halfway through their walk that afternoon: after his people had been kidnapped, what had happened to them? Might someone, he asked, be sent to North Africa to hunt down Brinkley and the others and, if necessary, buy them out of slavery? Mr Knightley doubted it. In the past, the unpaid British consul in Algiers had sometimes ransomed English captives on behalf of their relatives or friends. Today, sadly, Tunis and Algiers[61] were simply slave markets, ruled by the Dey, but with no consular presence. In any case, it was now weeks since Darcy's people had been seized: they could be anywhere in Africa or the Levant. And who could be trusted with the money necessary for such a ransom? Perhaps when Darcy was back in England, he could find someone.

'Or,' Darcy said, 'perhaps I could go myself. What do you think?'

'I should think it *admirable*,' the Consul replied.

Fitzwilliam Darcy, one might say, had his roots in an earlier age, a feudal age, when not only were servants expected to protect their masters, but masters were expected to protect their servants. It is a romantic concept, almost superstitious, alien in every way to what Karl Marx has recently called the *class warfare*[62] of our modern, Victorian world.

Admirable, Mr Knightley had said, though he was not a man much given to enthusiasm. Perhaps it was his admiration that prompted him now to repeat his offer of the previous afternoon. With Elizabeth's words of support still fresh in his ears, Mr Darcy accepted. So it was, that when the two men returned from their walk, Fitzwilliam Darcy was sworn in as His Majesty's Acting Vice-Consul, resident in Athens. A despatch was prepared asking Lord Strangford, the ambassador in Constantinople, to confirm the appointment.

Not long after sunset, another courier arrived from Korfu, and the new vice-consul, together with his senior, read his first despatch. It concerned the arrival of artillery from Scotland. A battery of ten light mountain cannon and three heavy naval guns would arrive in Ionia later in January. The guns would be commanded by William Parry, a navy firemaster who had served under Nelson. With Parry would arrive a workshop for producing ammunition. Sir Frederick Adam, the Deputy High Commissioner, was himself an artillery man and a veteran of Waterloo. He disliked the Turks and broadly favoured the Greeks. He was sending a soldier, Lieutenant Chalfont Beadle, to Athens to discuss with the Consul how field artillery might change the balance of power in favour of the Greeks. If possible, Lieutenant Beadle should stay in the consulate. Sir Frederick was aware that the consulate was at the moment crowded, but he was sure that the resourceful Mrs Knightley etc., etc.

Resourceful? Though Emma preferred epithets such as *lovely* and *well-remembered*, she was, in most ways, an amiable woman who settled for what was on offer. She quickly fitted out a room in the attic for the sprightly young lieutenant she imagined would be her guest. Elizabeth helped her. In other words, the two ladies stood side by side chatting, while the Greek housemaid set up the bed and the simple accoutrements gleaned from other rooms in the consulate.

'Will Lieutenant Beadle meet with George *and* Fitzwilliam?' Elizabeth asked with a hint of conspiracy in her voice.

'Interminably I should think,' Emma replied. 'George says Beadle has to brief them on artillery tactics.'

'And will there be a meeting with Odysseus?' More conspiratorial overtones.

'With Odysseus? How clever you are,' Emma laughed, catching Elizabeth's drift. 'A meeting in the Citadel. Beadle and Odysseus. George and Fitzwilliam too. But Trelawny won't be there. Beadle won't talk artillery with a French privateer. So the Captain will be…'

'…heaven knows where.'

'I'll suggest it to George.' She put on a wifely air: 'If you want to flatter Odysseus, my love, why not introduce him to Beadle? *What a good idea, Emma, my darling.* And if you don't want Trelawny to be there, Elizabeth has thought of such a clever way to keep him busy.' Perhaps it is graceless to use a word such as *giggling* to describe a fine lady, but at this juncture Elizabeth Darcy most certainly giggled, and Emma along with her. The wifely scheme was successful. Yes, the Consul agreed, a meeting with Beadle would keep Odysseus sweet, exactly as Korfu required. Organising a poetry reading for Trelawny on the same evening was a stroke of genius: he was deeply grateful to Elizabeth.

The arrangements for Emma's evening could now be perfected, though the *date* was still unsure: it must depend, of course, on the arrival of Lieutenant Beadle who was now struggling against stormy seas, snow, floods, Greek bandits, wild dogs and Turkish patrols, to reach Athens from Korfu.

Meanwhile a search began for a copy of *Psyche*. As it turned out, the only text in Athens was the property of Marianne Brandon. The poem had been published in 1820 in a book entitled *Lamia, Isabella, The Eve of St Agnes, and Other Poems*. Marianne had obtained the book from an English visitor in exchange for an antique head of Poseidon, freshly cast, and an unrecognisable watercolour of the Lyceum. So that the three principals, Emma, Elizabeth and Edward Trelawny, might prepare their reading, Jane was instructed to make two handwritten copies of *Psyche*. However, when she asked her mother what exactly an *amorous glow-worm* might be, and what it meant *to make delicious moan upon the midnight hours* or to *leave a casement ope at night to let the warm love in*, Elizabeth decided to do the copying herself. She even hinted that Jane might be banned from the poetry evening altogether. At this threatened tyranny, Jane rebelled, and a tempest loomed. When Elizabeth sought the counsel first of Mrs Tilney and then of the Consul's wife, those ladies took Jane's part. Predictably, her mother's failed attempt to exclude her from the poetry reading raised Jane's curiosity to boiling point, and she eagerly scanned the remaining poems in the book. There was a great deal she didn't understand, but that in itself was exciting: she had much to learn. Jane asked no immediate questions. She guessed, however, that any enquiries she wished to make would be better pursued with Emma Knightley, or even with Marianne Brandon, certainly on points of detail. And once they were back in Pemberley? Then she'd best ask Aunt Lydia. Odd, the similarities between Aunt Lydia and poor Marianne: both were the daughters of gentlemen, yet neither could fairly be described as a lady, both could be raucous and unruly but… With the imperatives of adult life beginning to impose themselves, Jane could see that the breach of a rule might sometimes prove more entertaining than its observance.

Lieutenant Beadle arrived on Saturday 17th January with

one of Sir Thomas's couriers as guide. Sadly, Beadle brought no additional sparkle to the consulate, as became sadly obvious during his first tea-drinking in Emma's drawing-room. He was older than his rank suggested: perhaps fifty. He had been with Wellington in the Peninsula and served at Waterloo under Alexander Mercer,[63] commander of G Troop, Royal Horse Artillery. Lieutenant Beadle evidently thought that the name of Captain Mercer would command instant respect within the little circle at the consulate. Emma, who had met, charmed, and promptly forgotten dozens of war heroes during her time in Marseilles, knew the appropriate expressions of surprise and esteem. The other women sat tongue-tied, and the men simply nodded. Even the information that Beadle had always advocated the use of shrapnel shells and that these shells had, possibly, won the battle of Waterloo, was tepidly received. Finding himself, if not rebuffed, then at best unrecognised, Beadle retreated into brandy and hot water in his room together with a pipe of strong tobacco. He excused himself from the Sunday services: he had no time for fingerposts,[64] as he candidly told his hostess. He took lunch in his room, and early in the afternoon joined the Consul and the vice-consul for their first briefing.

After the briefing, George Knightley was delighted. He tried to explain to Emma the true beauty of the shrapnel shell as he now understood it. She gratified him with a sudden interest in artillery, and tactfully pressed her real concern, the meeting with Odysseus. Beadle, her husband told her, had agreed to take supper with the Lord Governor, and Tuesday evening had been fixed for the meeting: to help the whole thing run smoothly, she should go ahead with her poetry-reading if she would be so kind.

Tuesday then. Emma and Elizabeth set to work immediately. Exactly as hoped, Beadle and the consuls, vice and principal, were to sup at the Venetian Tower leaving the consulate free for the delights of poetry. Accordingly, Trelawny was invited for Tuesday evening, and Trelawny accepted. He suggested that the ladies read the *Ode to Psyche*, and that he would read in addition Shelley's *Ode to the West Wind* and some fragments of *The Corsair*. Keats, Shelley, Byron: with or without gunshots, it was going to be an evening to remember.

On the evening of Odysseus's supper party, the duty of guarding the Akropolis fell to Iannis Gouras, the deputy governor. Most guard-commanders are content to drink, play cards, or simply doze in the guardhouse. Gouras was different. He was a prowler, constantly checking that the sentries knew the passwords, that doors were locked and windows fastened. It would be fair to say that Gouras was hated. His system of discipline was modelled on that of Odysseus, and ultimately on that of Odysseus's old master, the infamous Ali Pasha. Several times a year, Gouras ordered the immediate punishment of a sentry whom he caught sleeping (or claimed to have caught sleeping) on duty. So that the entire garrison could witness the proceedings, the men were formed up in platoons on the flagstones in front of the Parthenon. In practice, impalement was the only punishment, and it always followed the same ritual. To enhance the drama, it was performed at night by the light of dozens of torches. During the torture, Gouras himself stood a few paces from the upright, trembling pole, impassive, apart from an occasional injunction to his victim to stop screaming and to 'die like a man.' After an hour, the garrison was dismissed, and the victim was left to expire in his own good time. The *coup de grâce*, though often begged for, was never given.

The night of Lieutenant Beadle's visit to the Venetian Tower was, unsurprisingly, free of such rituals. Gouras, instead of prowling, stayed in one place: the doorway of the columned chamber where Odysseus and his English guests were feasting. Cries for more food, more wine, tobacco pipes, *tsipouro*,[65] and later in the evening for music, meant that the door was seldom closed: it was finally wedged open to allow the dancing girls ease of entry and egress. Although Gouras could hear only half of the conversation at the table, and although his understanding of

English was anaemic, he soon pieced together what Beadle was offering: guns, field guns pulled by horses, something the Turks didn't have and couldn't match. Greek victory out of the barrels of English cannon.

A Reader familiar with *Othello* will remember the hatred Iago feels for his commander, especially after Othello makes Michael Cassio his lieutenant. Iannis Gouras felt much the same about his own commander: Gouras had watched the friendship between Odysseus and Edward Trelawny spring up in a few weeks. Quick as a brushfire, Gouras had become obsessed with hatred for *dear Edgardo*. Edgardo, the promised husband of Odysseus's own sister! Of Tersitza! For more than a year now, Gouras had been given to understand that he was the chosen one, he would marry Tersitza, not now perhaps, but in three years' time when the girl would be sixteen.

Somehow, despite his hatred, Gouras kept a clear head: Edgardo was vital to the Greek cause. He was a friend of Lordship Byron, the English madman, newly arrived in Mesolongi with a shipful of money. To get his hands on the money, Odysseus needed the support of Edgardo, even if it meant the sacrifice of his sister, Tersitza. Odysseus was planning a congress in the spring: Gouras knew all about it. If the congress had the support of the English government, it would put a huge sum of money at the disposal of Odysseus, it would declare him the Great Leader, in effect, King of Greece. Never! Once the money was safely in Athens, nothing would be easier than to blast Odysseus from his imaginary throne and his dear Edgardo with him. For such a blasting, Gouras not only had materials to hand, but he anticipated the task with pleasure.

As a conspirator, Gouras was neither as clever nor as malevolent as Iago, but he had two strengths. For some years, he had kept the Greek Executive in Naflion informed of Odysseus's every movement, much as he had, though on a lesser scale, kept George Knightley informed. In all that time, Gouras had been ruthlessly truthful: as a result, the Executive (Theodoros Kolokotrones, Petros

Mavromichalis and the others) trusted his information, though naturally they distrusted Gouras himself. Having established himself as a source of unassailable truth, a single but credible lie, for example a story that Odysseus was negotiating with the Ottomans for the surrender of Athens, would discredit Odysseus completely. And who would succeed Odysseus? Gouras could imagine no one but himself in that powerful and happy position. And that, of course, was Iannis Gouras's second strength: he admired no one, loved no one, and honoured no one but his own pitiless self.

When George Knightley returned to the consulate not long before cock-crow, Emma roused herself, lit a candle, and asked her husband if his meeting in the Venetian Tower had been a success. 'Yes, not bad,' he replied. 'Quite useful really.' When, in return, he asked about her poetry evening, she deluged him with detail that considerably outlasted the slow January dawn.

Uppermost in Emma's mind was the impression that Captain Trelawny, as she now consistently called him, had made. His powerful voice with its hint of Cornish crags had fettered his audience. He had been play-acting, of course, but with an intensity that was shocking: quite, quite shocking. Naturally, Emma had watched Trelawny's eyes closely. At first, he'd directed his every glance, his every word, at Elizabeth Darcy. Elizabeth, Emma explained to her husband, had been wearing the same low-cut gown she'd worn on New Year's Eve. Such a cheap way of attracting men's glances!

'Really?' he enquired, recalling the gown Emma herself had worn at the last of Sir Thomas Maitland's banquets, a gown that had been considerably more eye-catching than Elizabeth Darcy's. 'I thought in Korfu you said…'

'There's no point in discussing such things with you, George. If you really can't see the difference between a respect for fashion and tasteless flaunting…!'

'I'm not sure I can: it isn't always easy,' he agreed mildly and cocked his ear for further enlightenment. The amount of bosom a lady might display in the name of fashion was a subject he had often pondered. At a ball, it gave him something agreeable to contemplate while the rest of the company was dancing or playing cards.

Quickly, however, Emma reverted to what interested her: namely, Captain Trelawny. Elizabeth's appearance had, once again, impressed the Captain. But then his eyes had flitted to little Jane. The look had changed: it had become assessing, knowing, but not lustful. Some men liked girls of Jane's age: Mr Knightley himself, she reminded him, had fallen for her when she was only a few months older. Admiration, however, had not been the purport of Trelawny's glances, not if Emma knew men. His look had suggested a slave-trader eying a pretty youngster.

'And *Psyche*, or whatever it's called? How did you ladies handle that?' George asked, uncomfortable at the direction Emma's narrative was taking: surely even the dubious Trelawny could have formed no designs against a child such as young Jane.

This time, Emma rose to the bait. 'Well, we divided *Psyche* into five. Five ladies, one piece each. Unfortunately, reading a poem isn't just getting the words in the right order, you need some idea of what they *mean*. Elizabeth has none, none whatever. She reads like the wife of a village carpenter. Catherine Tilney is no better. And Fanny Bertram makes Keats sound like her husband gabbling through the prayers on Sunday morning. Marianne is the only one with a hint of sensibility, but even she has no idea how to read Keats.'

'And you, my dear?'

'Well, I thought I did well, but you'll have to ask the others for a proper opinion.'

'No. I think, after all these years, I know when I can trust you.'

'Well, I hope so, George,' Emma preened. 'But there was one surprise.'

'A surprise?' Evidently George did not find the idea of a surprise particularly exciting, but his wife was used to his stoicism.

'After the reading was over, we had some slight refreshment.'

'No surprise there?'

'Of course not. It was just that Captain Trelawny sat on that little sofa, you know the one I had re-covered in green mohair, and spent almost an hour gossiping with Fanny Bertram.'

'Her husband was not mounting guard over her?'

'He stayed in his room the whole evening. With the headache.'

'How lucky for his wife.'

'But what do you make of it? Fanny Bertram and Captain Trelawny?'

'Fanny Bertram is a thoroughly sensible woman. Witty too, when she likes. I'd rather spend an hour talking to her than five minutes with your Marianne, for all her sensibility.' The Consul's words were not particularly diplomatic, but he sensed an injustice in his wife's mockery, an injustice that required correction.

'Yes indeed,' Emma retorted, rising to his provocation. 'I know all about you and Mrs Bertram. You and your afternoon walks! Every day, come rain or shine.'

'But, you must admit, no longer.'

'No, not since the Darcys arrived.'

'Am I then accused of neglecting my perambulatory duties toward Mrs Bertram?'

'Not at all. You may walk with whom you please. Though what she did to convince you that she's a *thoroughly sensible woman* I can't imagine. No woman with the slightest sense would have married a blockhead like Edmund Bertram. And now you tell me she's witty into the bargain!'

Mr Knightley added no further fuel to the fire: his wife always defended, with daggers drawn, any right of hers, real or imagined, from violation by another woman. Indeed, she had decided to marry her George only when pricked to it by a fit of territorial jealousy. And who had whetted her protective instinct at that crucial time? A certain Miss Smith, an aristocratic bye-blow lodged at a local boarding school, gawky, silly and penniless: in fact, no threat at all.

'But then,' Emma pursued, 'you always were a shocking judge of character.'

It was a familiar charge going back to the aristocratic bye-blow just mentioned. 'What on earth do you mean?' he asked innocently.

'I'm sure you remember my brainless little friend, Harriet Smith?'

'Vaguely,' he lied.

'Vaguely! You wanted to marry her at one time, if I remember rightly.'

'Emma, my dear, you do not remember rightly! Nothing could be further…'

'But she *was* pretty, I have to admit,' Emma pressed, ignoring his protest. 'Sometimes she took a bath in my hot water after I'd finished. Things were desperately cramped, you know, at Mrs Goddard's.'

'I never said Harriet was a gargoyle.'

'You've no idea how delightful she was in what she used to call her *birthday suit*.' Emma paused and eyed him provocatively. 'Such a vulgar expression, so typical of the girls at Mrs Goddard's.'

'Why are we talking about Harriet Smith?'

'You know, George, there's something I've never understood: why men are so easily led by the nose if a woman has a pretty figure. It never ceases to amaze me.'

'Oh, I see.' It was now the Consul's turn to be provoking. 'If you're saying that Mrs Bertram has a pretty figure, I might find it in my heart to agree with you.'

Emma saw her danger immediately. She reined in, backed off, and took a new track. 'I refuse to waste my time discussing Mrs Bertram's figure. I imagined we were talking about Captain Trelawny.'

'We were indeed. About his rudeness in ignoring you and in talking to…somebody else?'

'Ignoring me! Did I say he ignored me? I'd like to see him

try! In fact, we spent some considerable time together, and he complimented me on my reading of Keats. I might have been born with Keats's poetry lisping on my infant tongue. Something like that. Uncommonly flattering.'

'Yes, uncommonly,' her husband agreed, struck by Trelawny's ability to turn a left-handed compliment: so far it was the only sympathetic trait he'd found in the Captain.

'But listen,' Emma pressed. 'While he was gossiping with your *witty* and *thoroughly sensible* Fanny Bertram, he was eying young Jane, in the same way I told you about before.'

'Was he indeed?' For a second, Mr Knightley was inclined to take his wife seriously.

'Yes. And then, later on, the Captain asked Jane why she hadn't taken a turn at reading.'

'What did she say? *Mamma wouldn't let me*, I suppose.'

'No. She said, *Perhaps you'll allow me the pleasure of reading for you on another, less public, occasion.*'

'The minx!'

'But it was a good answer, wasn't it? She reminds me so much of myself at her age.'

'And what did he reply?'

'He asked her if she liked riding.'

'Riding?'

'She said she loved it, after all, she'd ridden all the way from Medoni to Athens. But there was no horse for her at the consulate.'

'Did Trelawny...?'

'Yes. He offered to take her riding.'

'And...?'

'She said she'd have to ask her father.'

'Never. I'll warn Darcy. I'm beginning to wonder about this so-called Captain Trelawny.'

'Do you think riding lessons mean that a man has evil intentions?' Emma asked archly. 'Surely not. I remember, when I was Jane's age you could hardly wait to get me mounted, or so it seemed. Wasn't that what you said: *I was old enough to be properly mounted?*'

Ignoring his wife's pretty chuckle, Mr Knightley became suddenly serious: 'Please don't compare me with a man who's been a privateer for the French government and who's attacked ships flying the flag of the East India Company. The man can't be trusted.'

'Jane Darcy's not a ship. He's not going to seize her cargo and sell her for prize money.'

'But that's exactly what you just said: *a slave-trader eying a pretty youngster.* Your own words. The question about a man is: can you trust him? Yes? Or no?'

'And the question about a woman?'

'Just the *Yes or No* part.'

Emma laughed: it wasn't often she tricked even a mild indecency out of her exemplary husband. 'I'll warn Jane not to fly the Union Jack with the thirteen stripes,' she smiled.

This was the kind of conversation into which George seldom let himself be trapped, full as it was of indelicacies, ugly assumptions, and unlikely, though imaginable, villainies. 'I'll have a word with Darcy,' he said. 'The man won't be asked here again.'

'I think he might,' his wife replied mischievously. 'He also had a few words with Elizabeth.'

'On what subject?'

'She asked him if Odysseus was as solid as he looked. Asked him outright.'

'Did she now?'

'And what chance she had of getting to Korfu across the mountains if there was trouble.'

'Elizabeth is...' He rejected *thoroughly sensible* as likely to cause difficulties and groped for a less offensive expression. 'She's far from being a stupid woman.'

'Far from stupid,' Emma repeated.

'So, what did Trelawny answer?' George continued quickly.

'Be nice to me, George, and I'll tell you.' She put on the coy expression he knew so well and had no way of resisting despite the rigours of his night at the Venetian Tower.

'You're a disgrace, Mrs Knightley,' he said, capitulating without a fight.

'I thought that was why you married me.'

'So, what *did* Trelawny say?' he asked, untying his already loosened stock.

'He said he was at her service. If the situation in Athens got out of hand, she should apply to him, and he'd see that she and little Jane arrived safely in Korfu.'

And with that we shall close the curtain on the proceedings in the British consulate for the rest of that day.

Two days after the poetry evening, a note arrived from Sir Frederick Adam: Lieutenant Beadle was to leave immediately and go to Mesolongi where Firemaster Parry and the artillery were about to arrive. The courier who brought the despatch would show Beadle the road to Mesolongi.

In itself, the news about Beadle's move was of no particular interest to the women at the consulate, but it gave Elizabeth the chance to glean more information on the route westward. She sought out the courier in the servant's quarters. What was it like, she asked him, the track to Mesolongi? *You go Mesolongi?* came the reply. No, she was going to Korfu: how long would it take her to get there? In a courier's simple English, he divided the journey westward into three parts. The first part went across the plains and through a range of low hills to Thebes, then on to Salona, Amfissa as the Greeks called it now. A man on horseback attracted no attention, so it wasn't dangerous. The distance was something over a hundred miles: a hard day's ride.

'But a horse would be exhausted, wouldn't it? After such a distance?'

'Three horse keep in Salona and three in Athina, only for courier.'

'Why Salona?'

'Athina to Salona is flat.' He held up his forearm horizontally to show her the plain. 'This is easy part. Then mountain.' His arm swung up almost upright. 'Very bad. Horse is problem. Better mule.'

'Why go over the mountains then? Isn't there a coast road?'

'Turk have coast road.'

'But we're allies, the Turks and the English,' Elizabeth objected. 'Friends.'

'Perhaps government is frenn,' the guide countered. 'Turk soldier not is frenn. He steal Greek, he steal English. He steal Turk, I think so.'

'So, the way through the mountains? What's that like? With mules?'

'Very bad. Not one way: more is ten way, hundred sheep-way.'

'Easy to lose the track.'

'So many ravine, steep like wall.' The vertical arm again. 'You lose the track. You go one ravine, another ravine, another ravine. Then you loss. Maybe you die. Sometime die in summer. In winter, snow is cover track. Then you know face of mountain better like you know your mother face, or you loss and die.'

'Men too?' Elizabeth asked.

'Man loss. Woman loss. Only courier not loss,' he smiled.

'How long does it take? To cross the mountains?'

'In winter, two, three day.'

'And after the mountains?'

'Road. Very old road. Two day, three day, then you Astakos. From Astakos, boat go Ithaka. Ithaka is English. Good for you. Then ship go Korfu.'

'And if *I* wanted to go?' Elizabeth asked when she'd exhausted her other questions.

'You, milady?' the courier smiled. 'Over mountains? In winter? Impossible. You muss go ship. From Korinth.'

'But the Gulf is closed.'

'Now is close,' the courier agreed.

'And it's impossible for a woman...?'

'Over mountains? For woman is possible...,' he began. His shrug as he glanced at her clothes was eloquent, '...but not for lady.'

Elizabeth thanked the man and gave him a silver coin engraved in Arabic script, the size of an English crown. His eyes glowed with a sudden light that Elizabeth failed at first to understand. 'Thank you, milady,' he said. 'This evening...' His voice trailed off.

Elizabeth took the point. 'Yes, enjoy your evening,' she said, interested to know but unwilling to ask, how much dissipation her silver might buy. He bowed, albeit gracelessly, and scurried off to spend his windfall.

Some days later, despite the warning words of George Knightley, a way was found for Edward Trelawny to go riding with young Jane: Mr Darcy would go with them. Trelawny offered to find mounts for them in Odysseus's stables, as well as the necessary side-saddle for Jane. Jane was kitted out with a warm riding outfit stitched together overnight by Fanny Bertram and two seamstresses from the town.

On the morning of her first riding lesson shortly after eleven o'clock, six horsemen (Trelawny and five of his Suliot guard) together with two saddle-horses clattered to a halt in front of the consulate. The door opened, and Jane appeared with her father. The two deserters sprang into view, one to hold the rein of Jane's horse, and one to offer her his back as a mounting block. Bedroom curtains twitched, and Mrs Darcy waved to her husband as the cavalcade set off. She would never have allowed her daughter to ride alone with Captain Trelawny, or with any other stranger. And riding? She herself had started very late, and she'd never quite overcome her fear of sitting so high on an unwilling animal. But Jane should learn to ride properly: it was a necessary accomplishment for a modern young lady.

To the south of the consulate, the massive plateau of the Akropolis towered above the riders. In every other direction, the fields lay just a few minutes away. The Captain suggested that each day Jane should choose the direction of their ride, and she soon learned to do so with a maidenly flick of her whip.

For the modern visitor, it is not easy to imagine Athens as Jane must have seen it. In 1824, it was still the city it had been for more than a thousand years, the city I saw when I was surgeon's mate on board the *Fortunate*. A handful of ancient structures survived, but most of the temples and palaces had been quarried for stone to build barns, sheep-pens and dry-stone walls. The Akropolis lies two or three miles inland from the harbour of Piraeus. Today Athens sprawls in every direction, as I see from Murray's *Handbook for Travellers*. When Jane took her rides, empty fields and groves lay between the harbour and the town. Nothing had been built there for half an eternity. The town itself was little more than an untidy cluster of buildings huddling in the northern shadow of the Akropolis. When I saw the place in 1828, the British consulate was one of the few two-storey buildings still standing. It was a fine, airy house in the Mediterranean style. The street outside the consulate was untidily flagged with stones ripped from roads laid down when Mark Antony had ruled in the city.

Jane, of course, enjoyed every minute of her rides attended by her father and the exotic Captain, but she was puzzled. Why did Captain Trelawny devote half his morning to showing her and her father around places about which he knew nothing and in which he showed only the most superficial interest? Each morning her mother warned her to avoid familiarity with a man nobody knew anything about, and Mrs Tilney echoed the warnings, which meant they should be taken seriously. That Trelawny was a friend of George Byron made him a welcome guest at supper parties, but it also made him an entirely unsuitable[66] companion for a young girl, even in winter, even on horseback in the open air, and even at eleven o'clock in the morning.

Jane rode between the two men, listening to their conversation. She heard her father let fly an occasional *Well, I'll be damned*, but the pirate captain was almost painfully decorous. Trelawny, in fact, seldom spoke to Jane at all, at least not directly. Despite his promise of lessons, he made little effort to teach her. On the first morning, she mastered the art of trotting without a bounce. After that, she never so much as tried a canter, let alone took a fence.

At first Mr Darcy, warned by the Consul, kept his eyes and his ears open, but he soon lowered his guard and began to enjoy Trelawny's company. The man had a wealth of stories. He was familiar with exotic places: the East Indies, the *Isle de Roi*,[67] India itself. And he knew how to spin his yarns to entertain the father while, at the same time and invisibly, intriguing the daughter.

One evening after they had retired to their room, Jane addressed with her governess a subject she had avoided for many months: the capture of the *Pemberley* by the corsairs. There was much that Jane could not clearly remember and much that she did not understand. Why, for example, had the *Pemberley* not turned tail and made a run for it? If they'd run, the bo'sun had told her more than once, *they'd of been safe as 'ouses.*

'You'd better ask your father,' Tilney had told her. 'He knows more about it than I do.'

Next morning, before their ride, Jane did ask her father. 'Papa. If we were faster than those Arabs, why didn't we run away?'

'Let's not talk about it,' he replied slowly. 'To be honest, it's a question I still ask myself.'

Trelawny arrived, and they set off together much as usual, though Mr Darcy was far from his usual cordial self. Then, thoughtfully: 'Trelawny! I'd like your opinion.'

'On what subject?' the Captain asked.

'Your *professional* opinion.'

Jane was startled: as far as she knew the Captain's profession was piracy. Was her father going to ask him about the *Pemberley*? Surely it was impossible.

'Ask,' the Captain replied, perhaps as puzzled as Jane.

'I think you've heard how we came to lose the *Pemberley*.'

Jane drew in her breath sharply. So it was *not* impossible.

'Mrs Bertram told me a little about it,' Trelawny agreed. 'No details, of course. After all, she wasn't there.'

'The *Pemberley* was a two-master, schooner-rigged. Beautiful boat.'

'Fast, I should think.'

'We raced her on the Solent. Twelve knots in a good breeze.'

'And a couple of corsairs overhauled you? Or how was it?'

'We were making for Messina with a good wind on the beam.'

'Southwards?'

'Out of Naples.'

'What happened?'

'We ran into a couple of corsairs. Galleys.'

'I suppose you turned tail and ran for it.'

'That's what the skipper wanted to do.'

'And you didn't?' An edge of disbelief touched Trelawny's voice.

'I couldn't see the danger. Flying the British flag. In friendly waters.'

'So you sailed on till it was too late?' Disbelief shaded into irritation.

'That's what it comes to.'

'And you want my opinion of that? Speaking professionally? As a pirate?'

'I didn't call you that.'

'I'll give you a pirate's opinion anyway, though you may not like it.' He reined in his horse and the others stopped beside him. 'You had your wife and your daughter on that ship, and other women as well. You failed, you miserably failed to protect them from the worst imaginable danger.' He paused, turning toward Jane. 'I'm sorry, Miss Darcy, but it's true. In fact, sir, you behaved like the incarnation of selfishness, high-handedness and pride. If the corsairs had hanged you from your own yardarm, it would have served you right.' He had become almost breathless with anger.

Jane let out a little cry of disbelief. Appalling insults had been exchanged. In every novel she'd ever read, only one outcome was possible.

'It's all right, Jane,' said her father quietly, his head slightly bowed. 'I asked for his opinion. And, thank God, he told me. It's what I've often thought myself.'

The Captain said nothing. He'd just burned his boats. The morning rides were over. He'd never see the inside of the consulate again. What kind of fool was he, who couldn't keep his feelings locked up and his tongue in his pocket?

'Let's ride on,' Mr Darcy said. 'Let's go down to the harbour.' He touched his horse's flank with his heels. 'Thank you, Trelawny. If I want the truth in future, I'll know where to come.'

The truth? In practice Uncle Trelawny was economic, if not parsimonious, with the truth. For example, during all his time in Greece, he never breathed a word about his marriage to an Arab girl, Zela, a girl of much the same age as young Jane. It was several years after he left Greece that he first publicly broached the episode in *Adventures of a Younger Son*. In the book, Zela's father, dying of terrible wounds, bequeaths his daughter to Trelawny with his last breath. With the ancient gesture of joining their hands, the expiring man makes them, by Arab custom, man and wife. Trelawny accepts his child-bride. She travels with him on his adventures, and he falls deeply in love with her. She is everything European women are not: close to nature, unspoilt, sincere, always affectionate, and devoted to her husband. Was Zela real? Or was she a fantasy? Did she exist on the same planet as the Englishwoman Trelawny had married ten years before and divorced under the most shameful and scandalous conditions: Caroline Addison. Caroline's evil spirit, turned inside out, may be what inspired the portrait of Zela.

Why do I bring this up here? Most of what the world knows of Edward Trelawny is harsh, violent and callous. Yet here I describe him escorting a twelve-year-old *demoiselle* round the plains of

Athens day after day with scarce a word or a gesture out of place. Is that likely? If we study his descriptions of Zela, also twelve years old, and of his manner toward her, it seems that the cases are parallel: both reveal respect, gentleness, consideration, and an unusual sensitivity. Herein lies a paradox, but also perhaps a flat contradiction. Trelawny treated young Jane with the greatest delicacy, yet he planned to enslave her.[68] In fact, he treated her with delicacy *in order to* enslave her. It is a key part of the puzzle that is Uncle Trelawny.

Jane's horseback rides, to conclude this chapter, came to an abrupt end when, during an attempt to ford the River Ilissus, which in early February was in spate, Mr Darcy's horse lost its footing and tumbled its rider into the freezing water. Despite a canter back to the consulate and a hot mustard bath, Mr Darcy took chill and could not leave the house for almost a week. Jane missed her rides, but, at least for a few days, her father's illness removed the threat of her abduction from the plains of Phalerum.

Chapter 5

EIGHT WINDS

Mr Darcy was seldom ill, and the treatment of his current ailment presented a puzzle. Had the Darcys been at home in Pemberley, his wife would have released him into the care of a local nurse with a visit from the doctor each morning. She would have stopped by two or three times a day to secure her husband's recovery by the authority of her presence. But, situated as they were, far from the trusted physicians of home, Elizabeth was undecided. She saw Mrs Tilney's offer to sit with the sick man, and, perhaps, read to him if he was bored, as familiarity bordering on disrespect. In any case, Tilney's inexpert reading was more likely to induce catalepsy than to promote healing. Fanny Bertram took the austere view that a chill without a fever was no sickness at all, and that Mr Darcy would be better chopping wood than taking to his bed. Emma's lavish advice, in Mrs Darcy's view, came close to officiousness. As part of its service to British travellers, the consulate was required to keep a list of dependable local doctors. The list was short: just a Swedish physician resident in Piraeus, Dr Hampus Hult by name. Mrs Darcy did not like the name, and refused to call in 'the Baltic butcher' as she unkindly labelled him. Accordingly, Mr Darcy was left to recover with the aid of his own unspoilt constitution, plentiful supplies of hot water, lemon juice and brandy, and the moral support of young Jane who sat with her father for hours at a time playing draughts or mastering the intricate strategies of tric-trac.[69]

Naturally, Jane and her father did not sit in silence. Timidly at first, but with growing confidence, Jane poured out to him the thousand questions that had puzzled her since the pirates had seized the *Pemberley*, questions about Cora Shrubb and slavery, questions about Fanny Bertram and the women in English prisons, questions about Athens and the appalling Odysseus. Already on New Year's Eve, Mr Darcy had begun to see his daughter in a new light. Until the party, he had assumed that Jane would become a younger version of his wife, perhaps not so devastatingly pretty, but, under the guidance of her Aunt Georgiana, a better pianist, and, under his own tutelage, a little more tolerant of the failings of others. In many ways, though, the emerging Jane took him by surprise. If she was not the summation of what had gone before, was she, perhaps, an intimation of what lay ahead? He brooded over what he had seen in recent months. His men, the crew of the *Pemberley*, had idolised young Jane. He remembered her thanking them for her rowing lessons with the frank familiarity of a princess. For Jane, the sailors were not, as they were for her mother, necessary but bothersome menials. And an image from Medoni flashed often on his inward eye: Jane walking on the ramparts with Cora Shrubb, a lost soul with whom she had nothing in common but youth and gender. Their two heads, one dark as a secret cave, the other all sunshine, had been close together, sharing confidences. Where had Jane acquired the trick of intimacy with her inferiors? Was it the spirit of the time: Tom Paine, the rights of man, *liberté, égalité,* and Jack's as good as his master? Or was it some quality in Jane herself? Of course, Jane's sociability didn't end with slaves and sailors. She and the buxom Mrs Knightley enjoyed a surprising familiarity, and she spent hours gossiping with Fanny Bertram. Even Odysseus Androutsos had smiled at her, though such smiles were not always easy to interpret.

Darcy had expressed his surprise to his wife, but she saw things differently. Jane was, of course, a perfectly charming young lady blessed with advantages that few girls enjoyed. She was, to put the matter in a nutshell, *Pemberley's only daughter*. Perhaps, Elizabeth suggested, indulging Jane was how people like Mrs Knightley and Mrs Bertram showed proper respect for the Darcys and their position in society.

On the third afternoon of her father's detention in the sick-room, Jane finally asked him to explain a scene that had puzzled and confused her. Edward Trelawny (Jane's mouth went dry as she recalled the scene) had called her father selfish, arrogant and high-handed; for losing the *Pemberley*, he should hang from his own yardarm, the Captain had said. And her father had swallowed it!

'Strange fellow, that Trelawny,' her father replied evasively. And then, trying to lighten the tone: 'You think I should have challenged him to a duel?'

'Not at all! You might have lost! But what you said to him: "Thank you, Trelawny. If I want the truth in future, I'll know where to come."' Jane looked away hesitantly. 'Did you mean it?'

'I suppose I did,' her father conceded, making a careless move with one of his draughtsmen. 'It isn't often a man dares to speak an unwelcome truth. It usually means you can trust him.'

Jane pulled a wry face.

'You don't trust him?' her father asked.

'I'm not sure I believe all his stories.' As she spoke, she jumped one of her draughtsmen over three of her father's pieces and landed on his back line.

'I think you're going to win this game,' Mr Darcy said. 'Again.'

'Only because you don't concentrate properly,' his daughter chided. Darcy smiled, detecting the tones of her mother's voice. 'The other day…,' Jane picked up the thread again.

'The other day I asked his opinion, and he told me. I think he was right.'

'Right?'

'Yes. It was all my fault. If I'd listened to the skipper…'

'Is that what Mamma thinks?'

'No.'

'Did you tell her…what Captain Trelawny said?'

'Yes.'

'Did you say all those words?'

'I think so.'

'And she said he was wrong?'

'Of course she did, my treasure. But only to comfort me. Your mother is the sweetest and kindest woman who ever lived.'

Jane fought back the tears that welled in her eyes, stood up and went to the window.

'Jane?' Her father's voice was soft and melancholy. 'I lost the ship. I lost most of my people. I could have lost you and Mamma. It was a rotten day's work. But now… Now I think we'll get home.'

'And Captain Trelawny will help us? You trust him to help us?'

'Yes,' Mr Darcy replied, though without conviction.

Jane heard the reluctance in his voice. 'No, you don't,' she said. 'If you trusted him you'd let me go riding with him on my own.'

Darcy paused, pulled up short by her shrewdness. 'Is that what you'd prefer? To take your rides without me?'

'No Papa,' Jane replied, pained by his lack of understanding. 'I want *you* to ride beside me. Always, always. If you're not there… Don't make me go with him. Please don't. Only with you.' Standing uncomfortably by the window, Jane slowly melted into tears, the first she had shed since they stepped off the *Pemberley*.

'I won't. I promise,' Mr Darcy said very quietly, partly to comfort her and partly because her tearful dependence was a source of comfort to him. And his promise to Jane? To a Darcy, of course, a promise was sacred. If he gave his word, even to pacify a crying child, he could never take it back. Such men are sometimes wretchedly vulnerable in their dealings with the world, but Fitzwilliam Darcy also had a tough streak in him, a certain shrewdness. After all, he'd tracked down his sister-in-law Lydia and forced George Wickham to marry her: it was an achievement beyond the scope of most country gentlemen.

By the middle of February, Athens was ill at ease, awash with bad news and disquieting rumours. With Lord Byron now in Mesolongi, most of the tattle concerned him or the aid he was famously bringing to Greece. According to one story, the promised artillery had proved a miserable disappointment. Firemaster Parry, it seemed, knew exactly what his title suggested: how to direct cannon fire from a warship. He was a sailor. Of artillery in the field he knew little, and of the manufacture of shrapnel shells, nothing at all. He worked badly with Lieutenant Beadle: Parry's view was that the guns had been placed under the command of the senior service, and that the army had no license to intrude. In any case, even if the two men had worked well together, the new weapons would have taken months to prepare for action. A cluster of more scurrilous stories concerned Alexander Mavrokordatos. For weeks he'd been urging on Lord Byron a plan of action in the Gulf of Korinth. The Turks, as the Reader already knows, had closed the narrows near Patras to British shipping. 250 years earlier, those narrows had been the scene of a great victory: at Lepanto (or Navpaktos as the Greeks call it), Don Juan of Austria had famously destroyed the Turkish fleet. The site of the battle was still guarded by the huge Turkish fortress of Lepanto. Byron found the story engrossing. While he zealously refreshed his sixteenth-century history, the castellan of Lepanto was totting up his meagre hoard of *kurush*. Like everyone else, he knew and believed the story of Byron's millions. Matching his needs with his opportunities, the castellan intimated to Mavrokordatos that the Turks would abandon their fortress to the Greeks on two conditions. First, that Mavrokordatos put up a substantial sum in gold. Second, to save the castellan's face, that the Greeks mount a plausible attack on Lepanto. As Mavrokordatos presented the case to Byron, the capture of this legendary fortress, with the support of the new artillery, would be the perfect Act I of the English campaign.

Byron was hooked. The comparison between his own club-footed person and Don Juan of Austria, the flower of knighthood, Byron found particularly appealing. And so, although gold braid was scarce in Western Romelia, Byron ordered a splendid uniform in which to lead the attack. He was already paymaster to a large force of Suliots. He would lead these fearsome warriors into the second battle of Lepanto, and win for himself undying military fame. The Suliots, however, like all mercenaries, were more interested in pay than in fighting. At the first rumour of an attack on Lepanto, they demanded more pay, pay in advance, pay at levels quite beyond Byron's resources. And fighting? Even supported by British artillery, attacking a Turkish fortress simply did not interest them. Their attitude is understandable, though it seems to have shocked Byron, despite his years of posing as a world-weary, clear-eyed cynic. He became vindictively angry on the subject of their cowardice and greed, indeed about the cowardice and greed of almost everyone who approached him. He once wrote to the London Greek Committee:

What they most seem to want or desire is – Money – Money – Money.

More poetically perhaps, my Uncle Trelawny wrote,[70] and often quoted:

The instinct that enables the vulture to detect carrion from far off is surpassed by the marvellous acuteness of the Greeks in scenting money.

That winter, Byron's anger worsened into apoplexy and then into epileptic fits to which he had been subject in the past. Between fits, he paid off the cowardly Suliots on condition that they disappear from his sight for ever. Rumour, scandal and calumny added sacksful of grist to the mills of the rumour-mongers. More realistically, with no soldiers, no artillery, and the commander-in-chief struck down by epilepsy, the attack on Lepanto was perforce abandoned.

There were other stories too, other rumours, and George

Knightley spent a great deal of time, some of it at the bedside of his vice-consul, trying to disentangle the credible from the incredible. Surprisingly, young Jane was often included in their discussions. She listened closely, learning more from the subtle and searching conversation of these two men than she'd ever learned from her painful mastery of the sequence of English monarchs or the conjugation of French verbs.

At about the time Byron dismissed his Suliots, he received two letters: one from Odysseus Androutsos suggesting a congress in Salona and one from Edward Trelawny supporting the idea. Byron needed no persuasion: a congress to unite the quarrelsome, money-grubbing Greeks was exactly what he himself wanted, and here the gloriously named Odysseus offered it to him on a platter. Byron decided that Colonel Stanhope, his co-delegate from the London Committee, should head for Athens immediately. Lieutenant Humphreys, a young Philhellene with little to recommend him beyond a well-stuffed purse and a smart new uniform, would travel with Stanhope. They should be with Odysseus in Athens before the end of February.

The arrival of Colonel Stanhope and his young friend took the consulate by surprise. The two men, accompanied by Odysseus and Captain Trelawny, hammered on the door just as Chaplain Bertram was saying *Amen* at the supper table. Loud voices, at least two of them unfamiliar, offered boisterous apologies: *Terribly sorry, but was Mr Knightley at home? The business was urgent.*

The Consul stood up quickly. 'I'll go and see what it is!' he said. 'No need to interrupt your supper.'

Mr Darcy stood up too, though slowly. He'd left his sickbed the day before but still lacked his normal vigour.

'You stay too, Fitzwilliam,' Mr Knightley said, leaving the room and closing the door behind him.

Mr Darcy sat down, but the door did not stay closed for long. Emma sprang up from the table and opened it a crack, sufficient to hear the conversation at the front door. She exchanged a grave look with Elizabeth Darcy: there was fear in their eyes, and the fear was justified. Two days earlier, George had learned from 'an informant in the town' (Iannis Gouras, of course) that the threatened noose round Odysseus's neck might soon be tightening. The *murder, rape and mayhem* which the Consul had predicted were perhaps closer than they had feared.

Already a state of siege had gripped the consulate. Nobody but servants ventured outside its four walls except to perform vital tasks. Trivial happenings took on new, alarming meanings: a distant pistol shot, running footsteps in the street at night, a rattling of the shutters that might be the breeze but might just as easily be the practitioners of mayhem in search of candidates for mutilation. Not that the consulate was completely without defences. Doors and shutters were firmly bolted. Unfortunately, none of the servants, not even the two navy deserters, could be trusted with firearms. The Consul had, however, polished up an old pair of duelling flint-locks he'd bought in Korinth as a souvenir. Fitzwilliam kept by the bed the gold-inlaid pistols given him by the *Sanjakbey*. At first, Elizabeth had been more afraid of the loaded pistols within her bedroom than of the shadowy felons without, but one day she had resolutely taken heart and asked her husband to show her how the guns worked. The other women, all but Mrs Tilney, had wanted pistol lessons too. Reluctantly, Mr Darcy had taken them to the stable yard and taught them how to load, how to prime and how to fire a flint-lock pistol. With a hunk of chalk, he'd drawn a manly figure on the wall of an outhouse, but only Jane and Fanny Bertram had been able to hit it at ten paces. Even so, a whiff of gunpowder, as we often hear, does the female constitution no harm.

And now, after two days of tension, the familiar, rowdy voices of Odysseus and Edward Trelawny were at the front door, together with the equally uncouth tones of strangers. What did it mean? Was it time to leave the consulate, grab their ready-packed bags, and face whatever horrors had erupted in the sinister streets of the town? And what then? Flight through cold, darkness and danger in search of some distant, scarcely accessible refuge?

The explosion of four burly and vociferous horsemen into the nest of five nervous chicks and their prudent husbands had an effect not unlike a petard exploding outside a prison gate, or the arrival of a watch of British tars in a sleepy whorehouse. Emma, as she led her little knot of guests from the drawing-room into the hall, quickly grasped Stanhope's mission to Athens. 'But why on earth didn't you say you were coming!' she exclaimed.

'We expected to stay with the Lord Governor,' Colonel Stanhope roared back: the newcomers had been engaged in a stentorian conversation outside, and it would be a while before they could moderate their voices. Stanhope pulled off his gauntlets and dropped them on the floor. He unbuckled the sword belt that engirdled his greatcoat and handed it to one of the servants. Spattered and wet from head to foot, he dripped onto Emma's floor a pool of Romelian mud, the accumulation of three days' hard riding.

'When I heard that they'd arrived in the Akropolis,' Captain Trelawny explained loudly, 'I said to Odysseus, *Let's take them down to the Knightleys. Mrs Knightley always knows what to do in an emergency.*'

'Well, not quite always,' Emma agreed. 'But we do have room. And if the gentlemen would like to stay…' She glanced demurely at her husband.

In response, Mr Knightley pulled a wry, consular face: surely the consulate was full enough already? It is, however, an established principle of English life that a husband who still enjoys the intimate companionship of his wife thinks twice before contradicting her in public. Accordingly, the Consul nodded and said nothing, a model of diplomacy, common sense and self-interest.

Odysseus offered to provide dinner for them all from the Eight Winds, a *taverna* which stood in the next street and which was, according to Uncle Trelawny, aptly named. The meagre supper of cold lamb, cold potatoes and pickles was quickly swept from Emma's dining table and back into the kitchen. Two extra wings of the table were unfolded, and places laid for the four new guests. Odysseus meanwhile ordered two of his waiting bodyguard to confiscate enough food from the Eight Winds to feed a dozen people, in fact to grab everything that was ready to serve.

It was half an hour before Colonel Stanhope and Lieutenant Humphreys had heaved their bundles and saddlebags up to their rooms and changed their clothes, before the weary horses had been stabled, and before George Knightley had raided the consular cellar for its second-best vintages. Supper took a little longer. The resources of the Eight Winds had proved inadequate, so Odysseus's soldiers had raided several other *tavernas*. One of the owners, a sturdy Russian with a row of medals on his chest, had accompanied the food from his own kitchen to the kitchen of the consulate. His raucous, bass voice rang through the house, demanding payment. Odysseus rose from his chair in cold anger and disappeared from the now lively circle in Emma's drawing-room.

'I assume Odysseus will pay what's owing,' Mr Darcy observed.

'And I assume exactly the opposite,' Captain Trelawny contradicted him. 'Usually Odysseus says something like this: *When I find out what you've done, and everyone in this sinful city has done something, I shall have you questioned, together with your wife and your daughters as accomplices. And if, by any chance…*'

'That's disgraceful, you know.' Fanny Bertram's voice, indignant and disruptive, broke in on the Captain.

There was a sudden silence. Everyone looked at her.

'My dear, my dear…,' her husband mumbled. 'Please…'

'I think perhaps what Mrs Bertram means…,' Mr Knightley began tactfully.

'I think Mrs Bertram means exactly what she says,' the Captain interposed. 'And what's more, I agree with her: it's disgraceful.'

'It certainly isn't the English way,' Mr Knightley agreed.

The Captain stood up. 'I'll go and pay the man myself,' he said. 'After all, it was my idea to bring the rude soldiery into your home, Mrs Knightley.' He made a neat bow in Emma's direction and left the room. He came back ten minutes later with Odysseus. The food was served, Mr Knightley's good wine washed it down, and the subject of payment was forgotten.

Elizabeth Darcy was far from delighted with the new guests: Jane would once again have military company thrust upon her. Elizabeth knew, from experience, the folly of mixing unattached army officers and impressionable young women. Emma thought differently. She asked the Colonel how long they planned to stay in Athens, clearly implying that a long stay would be preferable to a short one. Two men in uniform, a handsome old colonel and a young lieutenant, not exactly good-looking but well-knit, well-dressed and personable, were a robust addition to her circle.

'They come see *me*,' Odysseus answered in the Colonel's place. 'Importancy for discuss.'

'And you have no idea how long this business will take, Lord Governor?' Emma asked.

'*Lord Governor* is correct?' Lieutenant Humphreys broke in. 'Or would *Lord High Governor* be more in keeping? I ask only for information.'

Elizabeth flashed the Lieutenant a conspiratorial glance and suppressed a titter. As always Emma intercepted the glance: in her view it was a bad time to quiz Odysseus who seemed unusually nervous, but…the damage was done.

'*Lord Governor* is enough,' Odysseus replied ominously, sensing an insult but not sure where it might lie. For the rest of the meal he said nothing, listening like a death's head as Humphreys and his senior made light of the perils of the ride from Mesolongi to Athens with no guide beyond an infantryman's compass and a mediaeval map.

Just as coffee was served, the knocker on the front door sounded again: a message from Iannis Gouras. A guard from the Akropolis had gone missing: Odysseus should return to the citadel immediately. With Odysseus gone, Elizabeth steered the conversation down a well-worn track: safety. If the congress in Salona did not come off, she told the two military men, Odysseus's position in Athens might become difficult. If there was a struggle for power, if the city turned violent, how easy would it be, from a military point of view, to defend the consulate? The Colonel asked what weapons they had. Four pistols. How secure were the bolts on the doors and the locks on the shutters? After a tour of the consulate by lamplight, the Colonel offered Elizabeth a considered assessment: two determined men could take over the consulate in ten minutes. A mob would be inside in seconds. Captain Trelawny agreed. He'd been in some tight corners in his time, he said, and the consulate had one irremediable weakness: it contained five of the loveliest ladies in the Ottoman, or perhaps in any, Empire. While the men frowned at his frivolity, the women were more inclined to forgiveness.

It was not long before the Colonel's evaluation was tested in practice. The Russian restaurateur had not been paid. In fact, he had left the consulate before Trelawny had arrived in the kitchen. The cheated man now returned at the head of a small mob. Over the last months, Odysseus had driven his unwilling vassals ever harder. Too many confiscations, too many outrages, had fuelled the broad undercurrent of rebellion. And so, a dozen brave, or perhaps desperate, souls backed their burly Russian leader as he hammered on the door of the consulate.

Inside the now beleaguered building, Colonel Stanhope took over. The women were ordered into the drawing-room. The fighting men, each of them with a pistol raised, stood shoulder to shoulder a few feet inside the front door. Mr Bertram's task was to open the door on the command of the Colonel and then to stay out of sight behind it: like most military men, Colonel Stanhope had no time for fingerposts.

As the door swung open, the mob fell back a few inches, suddenly silent.

'Well?' the Colonel challenged the Russian impressively.

'Where is Odysseus Androutsos?' the Russian demanded in Greek.

'In the Akropolis,' George Knightley answered in the same language.

'You want money for the food?' Captain Trelawny asked in English.

'Yes,' the Russian replied, also in English. 'Money for food. Want.'

Mr Darcy offered the Russian a five-*piastre* piece. At the glint of silver, other hands were thrust forward. Mr Darcy put a silver piece into each.

'There was a misunderstanding,' George Knightley explained. 'Mr Androutsos thought you had already been paid. There was never any intention of taking food without payment.'

The Russian screwed up his face at the Consul, not understanding the words, though alert to the tone of apology. He raised the embroidered cap on his head and wished the Englishmen *Goo' night*. The pistols were lowered, and the door was closed.

'One thing is obvious,' Trelawny said, as the men exchanged rueful smiles. 'The ladies can't stay here.'

'But where else can they go?' Mr Knightley asked.

'I can speak to Odysseus,' Trelawny offered. 'Perhaps there's somewhere for them in the citadel.'

'I doubt it.'

'There's a mosque,'[71] Trelawny ventured. 'The Greeks kept horses in it. But it's empty now.'

'Empty mosque or not, we can't stay long in Athens,' Mr Darcy objected. 'We must head for Ionia. As soon as the road is open.'

The women, who had retired obediently to the drawing-room, now burst forth. They were quickly apprised of Captain Trelawny's plan for their safety.

'Live in the citadel with all those soldiers! Sleep in a mosque!' Mrs Darcy exclaimed.

Jane smiled at her. 'We'll be all right, Mamma,' she said. 'Papa says Captain Trelawny will look after us.'

'Exactly,' said the Captain. 'Exactly what I had in mind.'

Chapter 6

THE MOSQUE

When in 1822 the Christian Greeks reclaimed the Akropolis, they also took possession of a mosque their Ottoman overlords had built in the precinct. A mosque! The Greeks decided to pull it down. Weatherproof buildings were, however, scarce, so they simply pulled down the minaret and used the main building as a stable. One of Odysseus's favourite horses chancing to go lame, a Turkish soothsayer convinced him that stabling animals in the House of God was sacrilege, and for a month or two gunpowder was stored there instead. This was the mosque that Uncle Trelawny had in mind, and he started his campaign immediately. Unhesitatingly, he exposed the soothsayer's lie: a mosque is not a holy place nor is it the House of God: a mosque is simply a building dedicated to prayer. A quick investigation established that Trelawny was right. The soothsayer was apprehended and brought to the Venetian Tower for an 'enquiry' from which she never recovered. Even so, Odysseus was still unconvinced. Sacrilege was a delicate problem, and perhaps the housing of infidel women in a mosque was even more impious than the stabling of brute beasts. After all, he argued, the lame horse had never recovered. Faced, however, with a combined attack by two British officers, five English ladies and his sister's affianced husband, Odysseus caved in, Trelawny was given the key, and the privateer became the proprietor of a mosque, albeit a mosque without a minaret.

Next day the victorious British force reviewed the building it had so imperiously annexed. 'Change the lock, and you'll be safe enough,' Colonel Stanhope pronounced. 'You agree, Humphreys?'

Lieutenant Humphreys nodded. 'Absolutely, sir.'

'Mrs Darcy, Mrs Knightley,' the Colonel bowed slightly to each woman. 'You'll be perfectly safe here.'

'Unless they batter the walls down,' Elizabeth replied.

'Nobody,' Humphreys reassured her, 'nobody would dare do such a thing.'

'Hold your tongue,' the Colonel whispered in his ear.

The Colonel had already understood the strategic weakness of the mosque: the building was surrounded by *khlepts*. Currently these *khlepts* were loyal to Odysseus, but for how long? When, exactly, would Odysseus's grip begin to fail? The answer was obvious: the moment 10 million English pounds physically entered Athens, loyalties would evaporate, and Odysseus would be ousted. At that point, if the Christian *khlepts* battered down an unloved Moslem building, nothing could protect either the mosque or the women enjoying its shelter. Experienced as he was in military tactics, the Colonel saw immediately that the arrival of the gold was not only the problem, it was at the same time the solution: at all costs they should delay the gold, keep Odysseus safe: by this means they would greatly enhance the safety of the ladies. There were, of course, no guarantees. Luckily, despite rumours to the contrary, the Colonel believed that the money was still in England: a judiciously worded letter to London might block its shipment until July or maybe until the autumn. Until such time, a clear and unmistakable message must be delivered to Iannis Gouras and the other hell-hounds: Odysseus, and no one but Odysseus, would one day pave his yard with English gold.

'My dear,' Mr Darcy reassured his wife. 'If Colonel Stanhope thinks you'll be safe here, I'm sure he's right. Such a pity that Odysseus won't let *us* stay with you.'

'I asked him again,' Captain Trelawny confirmed, 'but he refused. *No man. Man bad. Englishman very bad. English soldier-man brother of Satanás.* You know how he goes on.'

'If he doesn't trust Englishmen,' Mrs Darcy questioned, 'how is it that Captain Trelawny stays in the citadel? He's English. Cornish, I believe.'

'Yes,' the Captain agreed, 'luckily, I do bed down here. If you're uneasy, we can give you a pistol. Fire it through the roof if you need help. I'm in the compound all night, so I'm certain to hear.'

Elizabeth flashed him a gracious smile. 'As Jane says, the Captain will look after us.'

Looking after English ladies? Why would Uncle Trelawny take the trouble? It is an interesting question, and my story cannot proceed until the Reader is clear as to the answer.

In the books he published later, Trelawny lambastes the gentlewomen of Europe as faithless, worthless creatures, an untreatable canker on the face of humanity. However often an Elizabeth Darcy or an Emma Knightley invited him to read at a poetry evening, smiled at him or otherwise pampered him, and however courteously he replied, nothing changed his underlying view: they were bloodsuckers. Why then, did he beg favours of Odysseus on behalf of these vampires? And why did the ever-suspicious Odysseus grant them?

Looked at from the Captain's point of view, the simplest answer is perhaps surprising: for the sake of Fanny Bertram. He had talked to her for perhaps an hour altogether: even so, she had caught his imagination. At first glance, she was less attractive than her social superiors: her dress was less costly, her hair less lustrous, her bosom less revealed and less compelling. But she was not spoilt, not faithless, and certainly not worthless. She interested him, and in the light of what happened later, a simple, romantic answer might suffice. On the other hand, Trelawny was never a man to regulate his actions by his desires: profit was his loadstone. And where lay his profit? As we have already said, in the equation Jane Darcy for Tersitza. Five women, including Jane, had been surrendered to his protection. He had been dealt, it seemed, five cards, three of them queens, as his first hand in a game from which untold profit might accrue.

And from profit must follow the two great gains he so deeply craved: social position and respect. When Uncle Trelawny arrived in Athens, his position in English society was, to put it politely, equivocal. During his sojourn in England just before he headed toward Greece, he had been unsparingly libelled by most of his acquaintance, most notably by Joseph Severn, a second-rate artist who had helped Trelawny design Shelley's tomb. A quick sketch[72] of Uncle Trelawny by Severn has survived: it is not flattering. Nor is a question in a letter sent by Severn to a friend in London: who was this *odd fish* washed up in Rome, he wanted to know, *this Lord Byron's jackal*. The nickname spread. People who had no personal knowledge of Trelawny began referring to him contemptuously as *Lord Byron's jackal*. What in heaven's name was that supposed to mean? Did he gnaw the bones of Byron's victims? Fiddlesticks! And so, with Uncle Trelawny ambiguously perched between jackal and defender of the faith, we can now proceed with the work on the mosque.

Improvement of the mosque had begun without delay, but, with the best will in the world, the place would never be comfortable. The smells of stored explosives and horse urine lingered in the air. In the daytime, the interior was dimly lit by four small windows, each about the size of a human face. There was one massive door, with a heavy lock but with, as yet, no bolts on the inside. Furniture, carpets, lamps and cushions could soften the cold stone, and a small pipe would evacuate the fumes from the charcoal stove, but in terms of comfort, the gatekeeper's hovel on an Irish estate was superior. At best, the mosque might offer a place of refuge, and with that lowly aim, Trelawny and his Suliots began their campaign.

Next morning, during his daily inspection of his domain, Odysseus reined in his horse to watch the preparations. He and Trelawny gruffly exchanged what passed for civilities in their world. 'But since you are here, Lord Governor,' Trelawny then asked, 'I have a request.'

Odysseus looked sour.

'This corpse?' Trelawny pointed at a female carcase suspended on a pole a few yards from the mosque. 'Can she be removed?'

On the night of Stanhope's arrival, as the Reader may remember, Odysseus was called away because one of the guard had gone missing. The soldier was not found, though a friend of his, a dancer in one of the *tavernas*, had remained in Athens. She was questioned. At first, she denied all knowledge of the deserter. Then, after a black eye, a bloody nose and two broken fingers, she admitted the acquaintance. Since neither silence, denial, nor confession protects a suspect from the wrath of a tyrant, she had been summarily impaled, and her corpse had been left hanging as a reminder to the soldiery of the fragile thread on which the life of a wife, a daughter, or a dancing girl depended.

Odysseus raised his chin and tutted refusal. Trelawny pointed out that the corpse had already been attacked by rats, carnivorous wasps and magpies and was no longer obviously female. Odysseus was unimpressed: terror, he said, works best when the actual image, in this case the body, is the stuff of nightmares, threatening the unimaginable, the unspeakable. In the end, a compromise was reached: the corpse on its stake was translated to a spot outside the men's barracks.

Despite his surly opposition to every new suggestion, Odysseus was not, in fact, unhappy. His spies had followed Trelawny, Jane and her father on their horseback rides round Athens. From Odysseus's standpoint, Trelawny's antics bore only one interpretation: he was preparing to separate Jane from the English crowd at the consulate. Then, just as the horse rides were going well, Jane's weakling of a father had fallen off his horse. Yet all was not lost: the ingenious

Captain had so contrived that Jane would be sequestered each night in the mosque, just a few yards from the Venetian Tower. Before long, the older women would certainly be whisked away so that Jane could be more readily transferred to the tower. Odysseus did not ask how the trick would be worked, but this he knew: Jane's time was nigh.

And so it came about that the mosque was cleansed of a malodorous and unsightly neighbour, the Suliots pressed on with their work, and the English ladies prepared to move in.

Trelawny's Suliots will play a significant, though a less than edifying, role in this story, and it may be useful here if I say a few more words about them. The Suliots were originally Albanian-speaking Greeks from Epirus. As a tribe, they had a reputation for ferocity and a history of rebellion. When Ionia became a British territory in 1815, riff-raff from the Adria, especially those who spoke a few words of English, gravitated to the capital, Korfu. Among them were more than a few Suliots. On his first arrival in Ionia, Trelawny had engaged a band of some twelve of these men. All spoke English, though after the Ionian fashion. In Athens, wishing to match the size of Odysseus's own Praetorian Guard, Trelawny had taken on another fifteen mercenaries, all claiming Suliot descent. Naturally, quarrels had erupted between the older recruits and the newer, as well as between the true-born Suliots and timeservers from other tribes. Trelawny's chamber in the Venetian Tower was distanced from the outer world by a vaulted anteroom where his guard was quartered. This room was in constant turmoil. Fistfights, knifings, one murder, one castration and a series of desertions quickly reduced Trelawny's troop to a kernel of ten. These ten, Trelawny believed, would follow him through the flames of Hell, with or without their *solde*. Two of them, he treated almost as comrades: Alexis was one and Bartolomeus, Tolo for short, was the other. How this brace of time-servers repaid Trelawny and how he finally settled his account with them will shortly emerge.

On the morning that the consular ladies moved from the consulate, a great deal of bustle, noise and confusion accompanied them. By afternoon the *zenana*[73], as they called their new refuge, had grown ever more tranquil until, as dusk fell, the ladies and their menfolk gathered for the last duty of the day: to thank the Captain for his efforts.

'As we so often say,' Elizabeth smiled broadly, 'Captain Trelawny will look after us.'

Jane plucked up her courage and smiled at the Captain too. If her father trusted the man, why should anyone doubt him? 'Captain Trelawny,' she said thoughtfully, broaching an idea of her own. 'There's another Englishwoman in the town.'

'Mrs Brandon?' he asked.

'Yes, Mrs Brandon. Marianne,' Jane replied. 'Do you think…?'

'Certainly not, child,' her mother broke in. 'Mrs Brandon has no connection with us. None at all. There's no imaginable reason for her to come here.' It was not so much that Elizabeth rejected Marianne Brandon. Far more, she disliked Jane's addressing such a proposal to the Captain rather than to her mother, or failing that, to her father.

'I agree absolutely,' Emma Knightley added, adding a dash of venom to Elizabeth's words. 'The woman is insufferably stupid. And in any case, she's content exactly where she is. In fact, I believe she would refuse an offer, however kindly meant. I, for one, don't want her here.'

'I take your point,' the Consul nodded. 'But…'

'Then perhaps you don't want me either.' The voice of Fanny Bertram was barely audible in the hubbub of agreement, but the fury in her eyes was unmistakable.

'My dear, my dear,' her husband admonished her. 'We should accept God's blessings without asking for more.'

'Stuff and nonsense,' his wife replied. An abrupt silence fell on the group. Fanny glanced at Jane, the only person who might support her, but then she looked away: it would be unfair to pit

Jane against her mother. Fanny would have to fight this battle on her own. 'Either we invite Mrs Brandon,' she threatened, 'or…or I shall leave this place myself at once. At once.'

'Don't be ridiculous,' Mrs Darcy warned her. 'I think you'll find *nobody* wants Marianne Brandon here.' In fact, she was less sure than she sounded, and she cast around the group for allies: 'Tilney!' she ordered. 'Tell Mrs Bertram what *you* think.'

'I have to say I feel myself obliged to agree with you, ma'am,' the governess muttered, dropping the slightest hint of a curtsey.

'And so I should hope,' Mrs Darcy growled, much as I hesitate to use the word. She had, correctly, detected insolence in Tilney's words. 'Gentlemen?' Mrs Darcy pressed.

The three husbands nodded awkwardly, Mr Darcy and Mr Knightley first, with Mr Bertram following when he saw which way the wind was blowing. During all this, the two soldiers studied the brickwork of the mosque as though looking for faults in the pointing.

'Far as I could 'ear, Miss Jane was asking *me* what *I* thought,' the Captain broke in with a sudden tone of authority. Silence fell again: if staying in the safety of the mosque was a blessing, it came, not from God, as the Chaplain had asserted, but from Odysseus via Captain Trelawny, and it was a blessing that could be withdrawn at any time.

'You know, in some ways Marianne Brandon sails to windward of 'ee all,' the Captain said, his west-country accent thickening as he confronted the gentry around him. 'She speaks a bit of Greek, she's got Greek friends, and she knows the town, better'n any of us. Prob'ly she's smart enough to take care on 'erself, which the rest of 'ee certainly ain't. But, 'aving said that, if she wants 'sylum 'ere, she's as much Christian right to it as anyone else.' In general, it is a bad sign when Uncle Trelawny slips into dialect or into preaching Christian virtue: either might mean a declaration of war. And now he was slipping into both.

'Then she'll sleep in the area we've curtained off for the

maids,' Mrs Darcy insisted, earning a long, hard stare from the Captain.

'That's as may be,' he said. 'But, if I may make so bold in the presence of your ladyship, it seems there's more Christian charity in your daughter's 'eart than what I see in yourn, twelve-year-old though she be.'

'I'll thank you, Captain Trelawny, to keep…,' the Consul began, leaping to the defence of his honoured guest, but then he thought better of it: for now, Trelawny had the whip hand.

The Captain strode off to his quarters and wrote a note to Marianne offering her refuge in the citadel. A messenger was sent to find Marianne and deliver the offer. How would Marianne reply? Until they knew, the women, apart from Fanny, busied themselves inside the *zenana*. On the terrace outside, the men kicked their heels. Outside too, a chair was found for Fanny. Sitting with her arms tight folded, she kept herself to herself, her quarantine broken only by an occasional word from the Captain. Marianne's reply, when it arrived, was short: she thanked the Captain, but she refused his offer. Her refusal was, of course, held against her. Mrs Darcy found it insolent, and Mrs Knightley found it insufferably stupid. But whether insolent and stupid or not, Marianne wasn't coming to the mosque. For the time being, that was the end of the matter, though it ignited a trail of gunpowder that soon led to a fiery conclusion.

That night, behind their excluding curtain, the maids quickly fell asleep on their comfortable, hay-filled paillasses. The hard kapok on which the ladies were lying was more expensive but less restful. Fanny Bertram simply couldn't close her eyes. She had quarrelled with her husband blatantly and openly. She had quarrelled just as openly with Mrs Darcy, and Mrs Knightley had joined the quarrel against her. Heaven knew where such disagreements might lead. Why? Why on earth had she taken the part of Marianne Brandon? And taken it so emphatically? She knew practically nothing about the woman, and the little she knew was unattractive. *Oh, my dear*

Herr Gropius! I'm old enough to be your mother! His mother: what twaddle! Marianne was at most ten years older than the Austrian consul. It was laughable, or it would have been if Marianne had not been so ill-mannered.

Fanny lay on her back staring at the unfamiliar dome above her, whitewashed and flickering in the uneasy light of the lamp. Marianne! Strange how young Jane had found something to like in the woman. Why else had the girl asked if Marianne should join them in the citadel? Common charity perhaps? And what had Jane got by it? Once the men had left the citadel, a rebuke from her mother, and a demand for an apology. Jane had not apologised, of course, but she'd cried for a long while, and only Catherine Tilney had been able to comfort her. And why had she cried? Out of hurt or anger? Knowing Jane better now, Fanny saw disappointment and vexation that her mother had taken sides against her and that neither her father nor Mr Knightley had defended her when she was so obviously in the right. Fanny herself was long familiar with such betrayal, though she no longer cried about it. In fact, the only Lohengrin[74] who had sprung to Jane's defence had been the bosom friend of the loathsome Odysseus.

Fanny listened to the breathing around her. It was disquieting. Most of her life, except in her father's house in Portsmouth and during the first few months of her marriage, she'd slept alone, in silence. With stirrings, sighs and sniffs all round her, how would she ever fall asleep?

Her thoughts wandered back to the Darcys and to another question. How would the mother and the daughter settle down together over the next few years, assuming they escaped from Greece in one piece? Perhaps Jane would be sent away: there were boarding schools for troublesome girls, expensive and soul-destroying, but with their doors always open to the likes of Jane Darcy. But perhaps Jane's mother was more understanding than she seemed. Women and their daughters? Of the five women in the consulate, none had a good word to say for her mother. And the men? They never spoke about their mothers at all.

And then the Lohengrin of the evening, Captain Trelawny? Not only had he defended Jane Darcy, but for the second time, he'd taken up the cudgels for Fanny herself. While, perhaps for the thousandth time, Edmund, her husband, had sided with the God-ordained *powers that be*. And she'd said *stuff and nonsense* to him. In public. He'd make her suffer for that. Really suffer. Toss and turn as she might, Fanny couldn't sleep. She got up from her mattress, pulled a blanket round her shoulders, and began to walk barefoot up and down the cold marble floor. The single oil lamp guttered, but it was bright enough for her to avoid tripping on mats and mattresses.

'Will you please stop making such an insufferable noise?' It was Mrs Knightley's voice, drenched in lethargy.

'Sorry,' Fanny whispered. 'I can't sleep.' She found her slippers at the end of her mattress and wriggled her toes into them. Her nightcap had worked loose: irritably she tugged it off.

'And nor can I with you prowling about like a jackal.' Mrs Darcy's voice.

'I'll go outside,' Fanny whispered. She unbolted the door. Like the lock, the bolts were new, fitted that afternoon under the supervision of Colonel Stanhope. The key stood in the lock, so new it smelled of lock oil. The key turned heavily through its wards. As Fanny opened the door, the *tutting* from the mattresses all but blasted her out of the mosque and into the silent, moonlit temple of Athene Parthenos. A figure rose from one of the fallen columns: it was a big man dressed in the red jacket and white *fustanella*[75] of the *khlepts*, Iannis Gouras, she guessed. Motionless and nervous, she waited in the shadow of the portico, three wide arches in front of the mosque, the door still a crack open behind her.

'Everything a'right?' a familiar west-country voice inquired. It was Captain Trelawny.

'Yes,' she replied with a little gasp of relief.

'Ah. That'd be Mrs Bertram, would it?'

'Mr Trelawny?' she whispered, trying to make her voice carry but at the same time to shield it from the women in the mosque.

'Maybe if 'ee come over 'ere,' the Captain said, 'I'd 'ear some clearer.'

It was improper, of course, to meet a man at the dead of night wearing only a night-gown, a blanket, and pair of pointed slippers. Even so, the hostility behind her in the mosque and the promise of understanding ahead of her in the moonlight propelled Fanny toward a heap of marble fragments in the south-west corner of the Parthenon. As she neared the stones, she caught the smell of tobacco: the Captain had been smoking a cheroot.

'Sorry 'bout my 'earing,' the Captain said. 'Been near the big guns too often. Never comes back 'ee know. Once 'tis gone, 'tis gone. Like a lot of other things in life.'

'Tobacco seems to make you philosophical, Captain Trelawny,' Fanny said, trying to sound at ease and stopping a few paces from him. She straightened her blanket to conceal her night-gown a shade more convincingly.

'Not essackly,' he replied. 'But what 'appened this afternoon, that were food for thought, or so I'd of said.'

The man was a friend of the great Lord Byron, a friend of Shelley. Was the yokel accent meant to insult her as it had insulted Mrs Darcy? Or had something shifted in the man? That was what she felt had happened to her: that afternoon, something had shifted, something had dislocated. It hadn't affected her speech, but it had certainly affected her judgement. What on earth was she doing gossiping with a man she hardly knew in the shadows and secrecy of a pagan shrine?

'Bit cold out here,' the Captain said.

'I don't mind.' And then, confidentially: 'I've been colder than this in my life.'

'If 'ee want, we could find somewhere a touch more sheltered.'

Might as well hang for a sheep as a lamb. 'Perhaps we could,' she risked.

'There's a spot in the old gateway, backs onto the fireplace in the tower. 'Tis always warm there.'

Fanny laughed quietly. 'If you know the place so well, you could set up as a guide. For the tourists,' she said. 'After the war.'

'Not much of a job for a sailor.'

'You can teach me then. I may need a job after the rumpus this afternoon.'

'They were wrong, all of 'em. Shameful, I call it.' He began to move, and, almost involuntarily, she followed him.

A distant wave of cheering and laughter spread from Odysseus's apartments high above them in the Venetian Tower. Then music, a *tamboura* and a clarinet, tentative and insinuating at first, but raucous and insistent as the musicians warmed to their work.

'You stood up to them. I was…,' Fanny hesitated, 'very grateful.'

'Stand up to that lot! Why shouldn't I? I got naught to lose.'

They were walking away from the Parthenon and toward what had once been the gateway of the sacred enclosure, the Propylaea. As they brushed past a mound of overgrown rubble, a thorn bush caught Fanny's blanket and dragged it off her shoulders. Reduced now to her night-gown, she stopped and tried to tug the blanket free.

'Need a 'and?' the Captain offered. He released the blanket from the thorns and handed it to her, turning his glance toward the cloudy, moon-dark sky above her. He waited, staring upward, giving her time to arrange the blanket round her shoulders.

They walked on, the Captain waiting for her to begin the conversation. 'Where's this warm place?' she asked at last, her self-possession all but exhausted. 'Not far, I hope.'

'Just round next corner,' he replied.

They found the place and sat for a moment with their backs to the warm wall, an inch or two of space between them. Odysseus's music was nearer now and louder.

'Like lovers,' the Captain ventured at last. At that moment, he had no intention of foisting himself on her, or indeed of betraying her into anything she might regret. On the other hand, she was an attractive woman. He'd thought so, when he'd seen her decked out in her simple finery at the New Year's party. And now, after his glimpse of her dishabille when she'd lost her blanket, he found this first impression not only confirmed but pricklingly enhanced. If she was eager, or, to enlarge the bull's-eye somewhat, if she raised no objection, it would not be the act of a man of the world to let her languish.

'Lovers?' she repeated. 'I don't know much about that sort of thing.'

'Come now! And 'ee a married woman.' The conversation was taking a favourable turn, the Captain thought.

'You're saying that if I married Mr Bertram, he must have come a-wooing? Like the frog in the poem? Is that it?'

'Handsome girl like you. Surely he come courting?'

'Not really. He's not cut out for that sort of thing.' She felt the disloyalty but waved it aside. 'At least, not when it came to his poor cousin Fanny.' The words were out before she could stop them. Ever since her husband had quacked *My dear, my dear* during the tussle with Elizabeth Darcy, her contempt for him had reached a new virulence. And the words *poor cousin* had been running through her mind ever since she'd said them to Jane in the scullery.

'So that was the way on it,' the Captain took her up. 'Let me guess. Your cousin, Edmund's his name, ain't it, flung himself at the feet of some haughty Belladonna, but she'd have naught to do with 'im. So cousin Edmund married plain little Fanny, who, all her life, 'ad been pining away for love of him, and who, unbeknownst to 'im, was the best-looking 'andful in the county.'

'Don't make fun of it,' Fanny said, admitting that he'd come close to the truth, painfully close, if you forgot the nonsense about *the best-looking handful in the county*. Though, to be fair, she *had* been good-looking. She'd come into her looks late, and she still hadn't lost them completely, or so she sometimes told herself. Back then, when she was eighteen, Henry Crawford, Mary's fastidious brother, had wanted to marry her, marry her for her pretty face and for what he'd called her *exquisite figure*. Exquisite? For sure she'd been quicker, lighter on her feet, and stronger than her cousins, than Mary Crawford, than any of the young ladies in the parish. And why? Running errands for her aunts, helping with the preparations whenever the family entertained, tossing hay even when they were short-handed: in a word, *work*. At the time, it had seemed an injustice. Now, looking back, it seemed more like a special providence.

'Damn dobeck,' the Captain's voice broke in on her reverie. 'Why is it men never see what's in front of their noses? Always 'ankering after what they can't 'ave.'

Should she let him get away with it, calling her husband a *damn dobeck*? Not that she knew what a *dobeck* might be. And *damn*? Was it some kind of insult? To her? Not really, she quickly decided. *Damn* was just a word men used to spice up their talk. A *damn* or a *goddamn* in front of a lady, it might be an insult, but it could also be meant as a compliment. In the Captain's case, it seemed to be a friendly *damn*: me and you, Fanny Bertram, we think alike, so I don't have to tidy up my language. It reminded her of her brother, William: he hadn't been too particular about what he'd said when they'd been alone. In a way she enjoyed it, the free and easy speech of sailors.

'Hankering? Do you think *all* men hanker?' Fanny said at last, trying to steer the conversation away from her personal history. 'I think Mr Knightley chose his bride with his eyes open, and Mr Darcy too for that matter.'

'And look what vipers they come up with. Couple of the cold-heartedest damn bitches as ever I clapped eyes on.'

For a moment Fanny had no reply. In a way he was right, though his language was uncommonly harsh. Perhaps she should rally him out of his bad temper, or at least try. 'Is that why you're always so polite to them?' she asked, with the naivety of the proverbial milkmaid.

'Can't a sailor be polite without a lady quizzin' 'im for it?' There was laughter in his voice: it was her reward, and it warmed her.

'Your *words* are above reproach perhaps, but the way you *look* at Mrs Darcy…'

'I look at what a lady chooses to show me,' he laughed. 'But what about it, my look?'

'Your look suggests that a cold-hearted b-i-t-c-h,' she spelled out the word, 'might suit you down to the ground.'

The Captain burst out in a roar of laughter that must have been audible in Piraeus, two miles away.

'You got a tongue in that 'ead of yourn,' he laughed letting his dialect soften. 'And could be you're right. But no,' he added, suddenly flat. 'Maybe last week, maybe yesterday, but not anymore. Not after this afternoon.'

'Was it so important? About Marianne Brandon?'

'I don't give two figs for Mrs Brandon, but…' He stood up and struck a defiant pose: '*Then she will sleep in the area we've curtained off for the maids.*' He raised his arms to the heavens: 'Who in the name of God does she think she is?'

'Sit down,' Fanny smiled. 'It makes me uncomfortable, all that arm-waving.'

He sat down, this time a shade closer, close enough for her to feel the pressure of his arm through her blanket. She didn't move away.

'So, your vicar never came a-courting?' the Captain asked. 'More fool 'im.'

'Do you think I'd have enjoyed it?'

She heard the coyness in her own voice, and it came as a shock. How could she be sitting in the moonlight with a man who was no better than a pirate and asking him such questions? That was exactly how Mary Crawford had trapped young Edmund, with her coy, deceitful innocence and her merrymaking. That was how Cousin Maria and Cousin Julia had led men on, poor Mr Rushworth and the rest of them. And, at the time, how young Fanny had despised them for it! And to be honest, how she despised them still. Of course, you could look at this gossip with the Captain in another way. Perhaps she was *worse* than her cousins: Maria and Julia were always nicely dressed when they did their damage: Fanny, on the other hand, had only a blanket between her and stark indecency.

'Never met a pretty wench who didn't enjoy the right kind a lovin' from the right man,' the Captain replied.

Fanny sighed and said nothing. It was years now since any man, the right man or not, had offered her any kind of lovin'. After her marriage with Edmund, she'd been the *vicar's wife,* and men had plied her with sanctimonious vapourings or paralysing banality. In all that time, had she been nothing but a wench in need of loving words? Could it be that the Captain had understood…? 'So, I'm the wench, and you're the right man?' she asked easily. 'Both of us here in the moonlight. What a coincidence!'

'But you did marry your Reverend, courting or no courting.'

Her Reverend? Come a-courting? Rather the opposite. She saw it all so clearly now: Edmund had treated her with little more than contempt, taken her grossly for granted! He'd whistled for his bitch, and she'd scampered after him, panting with pleasure at being recognised. For Fanny the game with the Captain collapsed. She pulled away from him, breaking the contact between them.

'Anything wrong?' he asked. 'I didn't mean to speak out of turn. If I did…'

'Maybe I married him. And maybe I didn't,' Fanny said very quietly. 'I must get back. The others will worry about me.'

'Worry? They prob'ly 'ope you fell off the parapet.'

'All except for Jane.'

'Except for Jane,' the Captain repeated. 'God bless her heart.'

In the moment that he blessed Jane's innocent heart, or so Uncle Trelawny recalls, he knew he could never betray her into the clutches of Odysseus Androutsos. Not for a million would he have done it, no, and not for 10 million either. Over the years, I have learned not to take my uncle's noble sentiments at their face value. Like many people, he has an alarming ability to believe two exactly contradictory notions at the same time. Betray her: not betray her. In the light of what happened later, it's hard to know which way he really inclined.

The moon disappeared behind a bank of clouds as Fanny and the Captain flitted among the broken columns to the door of the sheltering mosque. They found it locked.

'They shut me out,' Fanny whispered with quick indignation.

'Did they, by God?' the Captain replied. He tried the door handle himself. ''Tis locked all right,' he said. He felt the keyhole with the tip of his finger. 'But the key ain't in the lock. 'Ung up inside, prob'ly, like the locksmith said.'

'But I can't get in.'

'Yes, you can, 'less they shot the bolts,' he assured her, producing a key from his pocket. 'This afternoon when the smith put the lock in, I kepp one of the keys.' He gave the key to Fanny.

She took it and slid it into the lock. It turned stiffly, as before. She cracked the door open.

'Ain't bolted then,' the Captain whispered.

Fanny listened into the building. A peaceful snoring came from behind the maids' curtain. She removed the key and held it out to the Captain.

'Keep it yourself,' he said, still whispering. 'But don't tell anyone.'

'Thank you,' she said.

'You got a placket in that night-gown of yourn?' he asked.

'None of your business,' she answered, the indignation gone, the teazing back in place.

'Well, if you ain't, you'd better make one, so you'll 'ave somewhere to put the key tomorrow.'

'What tomorrow?' she objected.

'Tomorrow, when we 'ave our nex' little chat. No 'arm in chatting. Or is there?'

'And what if someone sees us?' she asked, incautiously raising her voice.

'If they cut up rough, just remind 'em who's in charge 'ere,' he replied.

'You are,' she whispered and slipped in through the door.

'Be a fine thing, wouldn't it?' the Captain said to himself as the door closed and Fanny locked him out.

Chapter 7

RELEASE

The mosque had no kitchen. In one corner, Captain Trelawny had set up a *sofra* with five cushions. At each mealtime, or so the Captain planned, the maids would leave the mosque, pick up food from the great kitchen in the Venetian Tower, and bring it to the *sofra*. On this, the first morning in the *zenana*, breakfast had been brought before sun-up, though it still sat untouched on the table an hour later.

Of the ladies, Fanny Bertram was the first to rouse herself, though she had been the last to retire. Gossiping with the Captain and a few hours of dreamless sleep had left her in a peaceable mood. They'd laughed together, she and Trelawny, or rather he'd laughed, and she'd shared his merriment with a smile. A smile wasn't much perhaps, but it had been a *real* smile, not a mask for submission and appeasement. When her brother, William, had been at Mansfield Park, she'd smiled like that, laughed her way through the hours they'd spent together. And later, after she'd married Edmund, there had been a happy time when Fanny had laughed in much the same way, not with her husband but with his father, Sir Thomas Bertram, unlikely as that might seem.

Sir Thomas had been the terror of Fanny's early years: Aunt

Norris's endless *I don't know what will happen if Sir Thomas finds out* had transformed the head of the family into an ogre. Then calamity had struck Mansfield Park. Young Thomas, the heir, had launched his career as an irreclaimable waster, Maria and Julia, the daughters of the house, had disgraced themselves, while Edmund had taken holy orders and become a carping bore. Sir Thomas might have caved in under his afflictions, had he not, after ten years of living with her, discovered Fanny, his niece and humble dependent. One rainy afternoon in the library at Mansfield Park, he'd asked her, despairingly, what she made of young Tom's latest extravagance. She'd told him, he'd pressed her, and in half an hour, he'd discovered how shrewd at least one member of his family could be, and how quick to catch his shades of meaning. After that, he'd begun gossiping with her about life at Mansfield Park in its many aspects. Soon, in the privacy of a tête-à-tête, he was sharing with her his loathing of his sister-in-law, Aunt Norris, his despair at the indolence of his wife, and his repugnance at the behaviour of his children. Sometimes he'd been sour, sometimes blistering, but Fanny had always detected in his words a vein of anarchic humour. Her uncle's humour met a streak of Portsmouth subversiveness in her, suppressed and inhibited, but never quite ironed out. Their intimacy grew, quite unsuspected by the rest of the family. When Edmund, lovelorn and desperate, had sought his father's permission to marry little Fanny Price, he had anticipated a proud rebuff. Had the rebuff been at all robust, Edmund would certainly have abandoned Fanny, but Sir Thomas took a different tack, grasping his son's hand and congratulating him on the first sensible action of his life. That evening at dinner, Sir Thomas had proposed a toast to the couple in which he warned Fanny that, in his view, she was throwing herself away on a plain country vicar. His words were received by the family as a kindly jest, though Fanny herself later remembered them as grimly prophetic After the wedding, Sir Thomas had showered the vicarage at Thornton Lacey with invitations to dine at the big house, invitations intended for Fanny but necessarily including her husband. Occasionally she had abandoned the vicarage for a month at a time and stayed at Mansfield Park. A long visit, it could be argued, was an economy, sparing Wilcox, the ageing coachman, and his now enfeebled horses a round-trip of some sixteen miles. The stays had become even longer, after Fanny's sister, Susan, had been invited to move from Portsmouth to Northampton in order to become Lady Bertram's companion and, as Sir Thomas put it, *the stationary niece*. Edmund had raised no objection to his wife's intimacy at Mansfield Park: Sir Thomas's unsuspected fondness for Fanny had allowed at least one ray of paternal sunshine to warm the vicar of Thornton Lacey. As young Tom's depredations increased and the financial prospects of Mansfield Park faded, Sir Thomas took a decision: by hook or by crook he'd allot some kind of portion to Fanny, his little favourite. When it was announced, Edmund welcomed the arrangement. After all, what belongs to the wife, belongs to the husband and that remains true in principle even if the couple separates. Was a separation likely? Evidently, Sir Thomas had sensed that all was not well in Fanny's marriage. Weighing the character of his fussy, sluggish preacher-son against that of his quick, agreeable daughter-in law, he slyly laid his plans.

This period, Fanny has told me, was the happiest of her life. It all ended abruptly, however, when she and Edmund left England. Since then, only one thing had offered her a similar pleasure: her cheerful afternoon walks with George Knightley, now discontinued.

But to return to the mosque and to Fanny, lying on her kapok mattress with eyes half-closed, remembering. Remembering how, last night, at the end of a quarrelsome day, something in her had rekindled, something that she had not expected to see again. Captain Trelawny had set it off, the Cornish rover with his Albanian fancy dress and his *damn-this* and *damn-that*. He'd teazed her. She'd repaid him with banter that had sprung out of nowhere. Trelawny had shouted with laughter when she'd spelled out the word b-i-t-c-h for him. Was that shout *her* triumph? Or was it *his*? His. Definitely his. He'd forced his way into her cave and established his right to shout there. Not that the cave was well guarded. No guard is necessary when there are no marauders. But now this unlikely Lohengrin… For as long as she could remember, Fanny had fought her own battles. Now it seemed she had a champion: not that she quite believed in him, not that she had any clear idea who he was, but somehow his words made her feel better: *They were wrong, all of them… The best-looking handful in the county.* What twaddle! Trelawny must have said the same thing, perhaps the identical words, to a dozen silly women. But still, there might, years ago, have been a shred of truth in it. At her wedding Sir Thomas had called her, more than once, *the prettiest bride Northamptonshire had seen in many a long year.*

Elizabeth Darcy sat up on her mattress. 'You're back,' she said to Fanny. 'We wondered if you'd flown the coop altogether.'

'In my night-gown?' Fanny replied cheerfully. 'I wouldn't get far in that, would I?'

'No, you wouldn't,' Elizabeth agreed. 'Not even as a nymph in this land of nymphs and shepherds.' There was an edge of playfulness in Elizabeth's voice. Perhaps she was regretting her unfairness the day before, or perhaps, as Trelawny had suggested, she was recognising who was *in charge round 'ere.*

'A land of shepherds anyway,' Fanny replied, sitting up. 'You see plenty of those around here. And sheepdogs.'

'More in Arcadia,' Emma pronounced, yawning herself awake. 'Or so they say.'

'Dogs yes,' Elizabeth agreed, standing up and pulling off her nightcap. 'But not so many shepherds. At least not when we were there.'

'On your way here from Medoni?' Emma questioned sleepily. Fanny wondered which of them had locked her out. And she wondered whether they would ask her how she'd got back in. 'Arcadia?' she said. 'That's where they had that dreadful massacre, wasn't it? Three years ago? In Tripolis.'

'Too many ugly swains probably, and not enough nymphs.' Elizabeth ran her fingers through her hair and nodded to the maid who stood nearby with her *robe de chambre*. 'Like a village dance in Lambton.'

Fanny relaxed: Mrs Darcy was back to normal, casual and caustic. With luck, hostilities were over.

Jane had been sleeping in the arms of her governess, as far away from her mother as the mosque conveniently allowed. She and Mrs Tilney woke at the sound of voices. 'Is everything all right now?' Jane whispered to her bedfellow, hearing the humour in her mother's voice.

'I think so,' the governess whispered back.

'How did Mrs Bertram get back in?' Jane asked, lowering her voice still further.

'I don't know.'

'I think it was hateful of Mamma to lock her out.'

'Well, it wasn't just your Mamma. Mrs Knightley had a hand in it too. Anyway, Fanny's back now, so perhaps we've heard the last of it.'

'Catherine?' Jane whispered.

'Yes, my dear?'

'You know what you said yesterday, about Mrs Brandon.'

'What did I say?'

'You said you agreed with Mamma: Mrs Brandon wasn't wanted here.'

'That's not quite what I said.'

'Oh?'

'What I actually said was I felt *obliged* to agree with your Mamma. That's a different thing altogether.'

'What are you two whispering about?' Mrs Darcy asked, gesturing the maid to help her with the *robe de chambre*.

'Whispering, ma'am? I heard no whispering?' Mrs Tilney replied, all innocence. 'Did you hear any whispering, Miss Darcy?'

'No,' Jane confirmed. 'Perhaps it was behind the maids' curtain.'

'There's no one behind the curtain,' Mrs Darcy rejoined. 'If you used your eyes, you'd see the maids are busy out here.'

For lack of a tart reply, Jane shrugged her shoulders.

'There's altogether too much whispering in this place,' Mrs Darcy insisted. 'Last night, for example. Under the portico.'

'I was out there,' Fanny risked. 'I didn't hear anything.'

'Are you all going deaf?' Mrs Darcy demanded, tying the silk belt of the *robe*.

'I'm not going deaf, and I heard nothing,' Emma volunteered with an enquiring glance in Fanny's direction.

Emma's hearing was, in fact, unusually acute. She'd picked up a *Mr Trelawny?* as Fanny left the *zenana* and a *What if someone sees us?* on her return. Weighing the two remarks, she could picture how Fanny had occupied the interval between them. Further, Emma realised, the words *What if someone sees us?* referred to the future, not to the past: evidently Fanny Bertram was plotting another meeting with the gallant Captain. Scandal was always welcome to Emma Knightley, but scandal involving the Chaplain's awkward, if ill-treated, wife was pure joy. And the two whispers she'd overheard weren't Emma's only clew. The day before, she had spotted the Captain paying the locksmith a *piastre* and receiving a key in exchange: the key would explain how Fanny Bertram had spirited herself through the locked door and back into the mosque. Emma delighted in secrets. Exactly what *use* she would make of Fanny Bertram's secrets, she wasn't sure. Perhaps she'd make no use of them at all, but, for now, she held Fanny in the palm of her hand.

Just before eleven o'clock, the three husbands arrived at the *zenana* on foot, wet and uncomfortable despite their waterproofs. Their visit would be a short one. Colonel Stanhope and young

Humphreys had agreed to keep watch in the consulate for an hour at most: at mid-day, the two officers had business in the Venetian Tower with Odysseus, London Committee business. That left the visitors a bare half hour with their wives, and even that had to be spent under the portico of the mosque, sheltering from the misty rain: the interior of the *zenana* was as much forbidden territory to them as it was to the *khlept* soldiery.

Mr Knightley brought disturbing news from the consulate, news which he broke as tactfully as he could. The evening before, a local gang, led by the Russian tavern-keeper, had approached the consulate for a second time. Now they demanded not money but information: Why were two English soldiers staying in the consulate? Had they brought the money from England that everyone was talking about? The Consul, backed by the other Englishmen and an array of small arms, had suggested that they apply for information to the Lord Governor, Odysseus Androutsos. The name had not been well received. To calm things down, the Consul had invented a diplomatic rule: he was forbidden by international convention, he had told them, to answer questions from local citizens about the local authorities. It wasn't true, but it had confused the mob.

'How clever!' Mrs Darcy said with a smile of appreciation: she was coming to rely on George Knightley's unostentatious cunning.

'So you see, you ladies should count your blessings, being out of harm's way in the citadel,' Mr Darcy added. He smiled encouragingly at Jane, who did not appear to have much inclination to count anything, least of all her blessings.

His wife pulled a wry face.

'Or am I wrong?' Mr Darcy pursued. 'Has anyone behaved insolently? I can easily have a word with…'

'Not at all,' Emma reassured him. 'Odysseus has told his *khlepts* to stay fifty yards from the mosque. Only the maidservants are allowed anywhere near us.'

'And do they keep their distance, the *khlepts*?'

'So far, yes,' Mrs Darcy conceded.

'They patrol along the battlements,' Mrs Tilney explained. 'Otherwise they stick to their quarters.'

'And where are their quarters?' Mr Darcy asked.

Jane pointed to a confusion of huts and lean-tos on the other side of the great temple. 'Over there, along the wall,' she said vaguely.

'Mrs Bertram? Any complaints?' the Consul prompted. Since the husbands had arrived at the *zenana*, she'd said not a word. He had learned to value her unpretentious shrewdness during their walks together: if Fanny had an opinion, then the Consul wanted to hear it.

'Complaints? None,' Fanny replied with a shrug. Unseen by the menfolk, Emma shot her a quick, conspiratorial smile, Elizabeth a dubious glance.

At this, the conversation faltered. After an uncomfortably curt greeting to his wife, the Chaplain said nothing, Fanny said nothing, and Jane clung in silence to her governess. No relief offered itself in the form of Odysseus or Captain Trelawny, though Iannis Gouras passed by twice, raising his cap and smirking.

'Who is that vile-looking man?' Emma whispered. She'd never seen Gouras before in the flesh. The others muttered agreement: he was vile-looking, absolutely vile-looking. Such features! Such an expression! Such whiskers! Altogether vile! What else was there to talk about? The rain began to fall more heavily.

The half hour was nearly up. 'Mrs Bertram,' the Consul concluded. 'Is there anything we might bring from the consulate that would make your stay more comfortable?'

Fanny shook her head. 'I'm sure we all have our inner resources,' she said. She heard the coldness in her own voice and regretted it: as always, Mr Knightley was trying to be kind. 'Though a few books might help,' she added with an attempt at a smile. 'Sir Walter Scott. You have eight of his novels in your cabinet. And I still haven't read *Kenilworth*.' It was the best she could do.

'Books, yes, a good idea,' Emma Knightley agreed. 'We can lay them out somewhere. Make the place look cheerful.'

'And you, Mrs Tilney?' Mr Darcy offered. 'Is there anything you and Jane might need?' *Mrs Tilney*. He hadn't called her *Catherine* since they'd arrived in Athens. In fact, he'd hardly spoken to her at all. And now, seeing how tightly Jane clung to her governess, he was sorry. Had he ignored the woman? Had she taken offence? He saw her drop a diminutive curtsey and shake her head. He tried a friendly smile, but she was already looking away.

'Not *too* many books,' Mrs Darcy said as she entered the fray. 'We may have to leave this place at a minute's notice. No point turning it into the Vatican Library.'

'No, indeed,' the Consul agreed.

'We have to be practical,' Mrs Darcy pressed. 'Bring the Scott novels and a decent mirror. That's all.'

Fanny said nothing. She had woken as blithe as a dunnock, and the sudden shift in her mood arrested her. Nothing had happened to make her so taciturn: nothing, that is, but the arrival of her husband. So far, he'd wished her good morning, but nothing more. Now he asked her, with some acerbity, when exactly she'd begun to read the works of Sir Walter Scott. The question meant mischief, and she made no reply, not even a grimace. The background of this contretemps may seem incredible to the modern Victorian reader, but Fanny has assured me it is true. Two years before, while they'd been packing to leave England, Edmund had forbidden her to pack too many books: novels in particular were outlawed. They'd quarrelled about it: after all, she'd reminded him, she'd read aloud half of Fuller's Circulating Library to Edmund's mother, and no harm had come of it. And why scorn novels? Some of them were religious in theme and as chaste as Paley's *Sermons*. Her defiance, though mild, had brought out the devil in Edmund. Imperiously, the injunction had been extended: not only was the packing of novels forbidden, she was prohibited from reading fictions of any kind, aloud or to herself. To avoid a battle royal, Fanny had asked if she might pack works of history, and Edmund had agreed in principle, though disallowing any actual title she incautiously put in front of him.

'I asked you a question,' her husband now insisted, not looking at her but, apparently, comparing the surviving columns of the Parthenon, or perhaps simply staring at the rain.

Still she made no answer. Indeed, how could she answer except by making public her husband's ludicrous tyranny and her wretched compliance? Mr Knightley rescued her by asking his wife about food: Were they getting enough? Did the quality meet her expectations?

Fanny was grateful to the Consul, and indignant with her husband. Indignant, yes. But she reflected, petty tyrant as Edmund undoubtedly was, were her own hands quite as clean as they should be? Last night she'd been flirting, yes, that was the right name for it, shamefully *flirting* with Captain Trelawny, and now she was shunning the man she'd married, rejecting him, and not for the first time. Of course, he was shunning her too, but that was how they were: isolated, remote, excommunicated. When had she last taken an interest in anything he had to say? An age. And why were they like that? Surely the blame lay with him and not with her. She was perfectly capable of maintaining reasonable discourse. During her now-abandoned walks with Mr Knightley, the Consul had freely questioned her, discussed with her, and listened to her. And she had asked his opinion on countless subjects. When, though, had she last shared *Edmund's* confidence or sought *his* judgement? On the other hand, what would have been the point? He had nothing to confide, and no opinions beyond the opinions of his church or his employer, and an unshakable belief that God had given him a wife to trample on exactly as he saw fit. Years ago in Mansfield Park, she now realised, he'd been no different, though, with the simple-mindedness of childhood, she'd ignored his shortcomings: perhaps she'd failed to see them. After all, until she married the man, she'd been in love with him. But, looking back, she remembered how he'd tolerated the vices and cruelties of his sisters, how he'd shamed himself by acting his part in *Lovers' Vows*, and above all how he'd humoured Mary Crawford and encouraged her pranking and preening. Had there ever been an issue, just one, on which he'd made a stand? In his whole life, had he uttered a single sentence to match Captain Trelawny's *If she wants asylum here, she's as much Christian right to it as anyone else*?

And the farce of her marriage! After her first bewilderment, she'd endured it, year in, year out, because there had been no escape. Marriage? She'd never encountered a happy marriage, not as she'd once imagined happiness. I find it strange that so many young women believe so fervently in something they have never seen with their own eyes and have heard tales of only in works of fiction. Silent, musing, ignoring the listless talk around her, Fanny abandoned the question of why her marriage had been so loveless in favour of a more immediate issue: should she keep company with Captain Trelawny that evening?

Deep in thought, she watched the three husbands take their leave and her four female companions retreat into the warmth of the *zenana*. She propped her back against the wall of the portico, and relapsed into a kind of truculent passivity. Captain Trelawny? The question was still unanswered. Abruptly, something in her recoiled. Never. Nothing on earth would persuade her to become the creature of a scoundrel and a womaniser such as Edward Trelawny. In most ways he was actually worse than her husband. The Captain was boorish. He was affected, untruthful, contemptuous, self-righteous, insincere, a cheap philanderer, and a familiar of the villainous Odysseus.

She saw a figure now making its way toward her. In the rain, it dodged among the columns of the temple, seeking shelter under what was left of the entablature. Iannis Gouras. It was the third time he'd passed the *zenana* in half an hour. The others had called him vile, and indeed it was true, but, at that moment, he seemed to Fanny furtive and unhappy.

In fact, Gouras was in trouble, or at least he was sailing dangerously close to the wind: the reason, indirectly, was the women in the mosque.

Just before Christmas, on all the roads out of Athens, Odysseus had set up barriers manned by his Ithakans. On the day after the women's move to the mosque, an old man on a donkey was stopped on the Korinth road about twenty miles west of Athens. What follows is based on a story told me by Uncle Trelawny, and it may be nothing more than an attempt to blacken the character of Odysseus. Naturally, the old man was ordered to dismount. He and his donkey were thoroughly searched. In the old man's pocket, the soldiers found a few *piastres* that instantly disappeared. And a letter.

The soldiers were illiterate as was the old man, so he and his letter were returned under escort to Athens, where both were examined, though without special effort or urgency. As soon as Odysseus awoke, however, the situation changed. He was handed the letter by his soldier-secretary: five Englishwomen, it reported, were being housed on the Akropolis in an old mosque. Against each woman's name stood her age, her family situation, and a brief description. That was all. Within minutes, the old man was removed to the Venetian Tower, to the *Chamber of Enquiries*, so that the Master Enquirer could educe where the letter was going, and who had sent it. The matter was urgent, and the Master Enquirer should use *all the means of enquiry at his disposal.*

In his own mind, Odysseus had already pinpointed the author of the letter: Iannis Gouras, his unloved deputy. Yet the Master had extracted not a scrap of information, even though the old man was already incoherent with pain. Impatiently, Odysseus told the Master to ask the question direct: *Did Iannis Gouras send the message?* The Master objected: a question direct never elicits more than a flood of eager and unreliable babble. It proves nothing. Even so, the question direct was put. The old man hazily grasped what was wanted and implicated Iannis Gouras. Who was to receive the message? The old man, at the end of his strength, could no longer grasp the words. He collapsed, struggling to understand. A bucket of cold water failed to revive him. Exhausted, broken and bleeding, his body was dumped in what might be called the *Post-Enquiry Chamber* to survive or die as chance dictated.

Later in the day Trelawny and Odysseus were walking round the battlements of the Akropolis, braced by a north-wester howling in from the hills.

'So, I can trust Gouras? Is possible?' Odysseus demanded of his friend. 'After what is happen?'

'But what *has* happened?' Trelawny asked. 'You torture an old man, and he agrees to the words you put in his mouth. It doesn't prove anything.'

'*Is* prove. Who in Athina send this letter not if Gouras?'

'Well,' Trelawny shrugged, 'I could have sent it. George Gropius, the Austrian fellow, could have sent it. The new soldier, Stanhope? He might easily have sent it.'

'But who to? And why?'

'You can ask the same questions about Gouras. Why would *he* send perfectly useless information to Korinth?'

'Gouras send because he is unlimited bastard, and because he hate me. I will rid him.'

'If you rid yourself of every *unlimited bastard* who hates you, my dear Odysseus, Athens will be a ghost town.' In fact, Trelawny had already plumbed Gouras's simple plot. In the race for the 10 million, Gouras might well come from behind and outstrip the less nimble Odysseus. The clew lay in the information in the old man's letter. It was useless, all of it. On the other hand, the facts were scrupulously *correct*. It was exactly the kind of letter Gouras would be sending to the Executive month in, month out, if he wanted them to trust him. First establish trust, then a plausible lie at the right moment, and Odysseus would be done for.

That was not a desirable outcome: if Gouras got his hands on the money, that would scotch Trelawny's own scheme. 'Keep a watch on Gouras,' Trelawny advised the Lord Governor. 'Don't let him see you suspect him. And when the time comes...' He made the gesture of slitting his own throat.

Some hours later, Fanny was brushing her hair, readying herself for bed. Despite her categorical and unqualified rejection of Captain Trelawny, she was taking a little more care than usual. In front of the foxed and unflattering mirror, the only one in the *zenana*, she arranged her hair in graceful curls. Tomorrow there would be a proper looking-glass, courtesy of Elizabeth Darcy. Reflected in a corner of the mirror, Fanny glimpsed Emma staring at her speculatively. The woman had made herself agreeable all day. Why? Had she guessed the secret of the night before? Would guessing a secret make a woman like Emma Knightley more friendly? Or more hostile? Friendly perhaps, at least until she could manoeuvre Fanny into some kind of trap. Fanny scrubbed her fingers through her hair, making the curls less graceful but, as she saw with a frown, more attractive. Then another change of heart: as long as a woman did nothing improper, she told herself disingenuously, a wife, even a chaplain's wife, could keep company with whom she pleased.

And so it was, with her wild curls drifting across her shoulders, that she ventured onto the portico as soon as the others were sound asleep. Fanny locked the door behind her and secured the key in the pocket she'd stitched into her night-gown that afternoon while re-hemming a skirt for Mrs Knightley. The rain had stopped, but the night was misty. Fanny had borrowed a big shawl from one of the maids, and now, in the style of an Ottoman peasant, she pulled it round her shoulders and over her head. In the whole of Athens, only one church still had a bell that sounded the hour though it ignored the quarters. It chimed once. She heard footsteps on the battlement: two guards walking together, invisible in the mist. She heard a challenge and a response, a demand for a password and a reply: Iannis Gouras, she guessed, going about his business.

She waited, shivering. Somewhere below the citadel, a frantic clucking erupted: a stoat in a hen-roost perhaps. Then silence once more, bone-cold silence. The guards passed again, disembodied footsteps on the parapet. Should she go to the wall, to the warm wall where she'd sheltered the night before with Trelawny? Probably not: for one thing she wasn't quite sure where it was. For another, if she met anyone… She'd wait till two. After all, she'd agreed no particular time with the Captain, so he could hardly be late. There was no frost, but the night was chilly: despite the shawl, she was trembling.

Finally, she detected movement, a shadow stirring among shadows. If it was Trelawny, good. If not, she'd go inside: it must be nearly two o'clock already.

'Well, I'll be damned,' the shadow whispered. 'Really 'tis 'ee then.'

She said nothing. Now that he'd arrived, she was angry with him for arriving so late, though at the same time she was ready to forgive him because, after all, he hadn't disappointed her. She compromised, hurrying toward the shadow but trying not to seem too eager. The shadow, no longer insubstantial, held out its arms. Only one man had ever held out his arms to her like that, her father-in-law, Sir Thomas Bertram. She had never distrusted the old man's offer of warmth and security: any distrust she felt for the Captain at that moment was quickly suppressed.

'I'm freezing,' she said. However banal, the words were true.

Arm in arm they traced the muddy path to the Propylaea. It was early March. Soon the rains would be over, and it would be spring. Fanny kept her night-gown held high, well off the ground. If next morning Emma Knightley discovered mud, there'd be an inquisition, silent perhaps, but an inquisition nonetheless. They found the warm wall. The Captain sat down and stretched out his legs in front of him. 'Sit on me,' he said, looking up at her. 'Keep your backside out the dirt.'

'So that's what I stayed up half the night to hear, is it?' She suppressed a sudden laugh. *'Keep your backside out the dirt.'*

'*My woman's heart grossly grew captive to his honey words*,'[76] the Captain quoted, dropping Cornish in favour of a theatrical London drawl.

It was funny. It was funny in a clever, allusive way which Fanny had rarely encountered, but which somehow lifted her spirits. She laughed outright.

'Are you laughing at me?' he protested. 'I'm doing my best, you know.'

'That's what frogs always say just before they turn into princes.' Her sudden merriment lit up the darkness like a kiss in a frog pond. She sat down as he'd invited, and he put his arms round her.

Her laughter collapsed. 'I wish I knew what I was doing here,' she said. The bell struck two.

'I looked for you,' he said. 'From eleven till almost one. You didn't come, so I went back to the tower. Then I thought, faint heart never won fair lady. And there you were.'

'There I was, like patience on a monument.'

'*She sat like patience on a monument, smiling at grief*,' he picked up immediately. 'Shall I go on?'

'Is there more?' she asked. She knew there was more: she'd read most of Shakespeare's plays aloud to her Aunt Bertram, taking all the parts and trying to read as Henry Crawford had taught her, adjusting her voice to the characters, and following the punctuation, not the lines. Usually her aunt had rewarded her efforts by falling asleep, to which Fanny had responded by breaking off immediately, often in mid-sentence. But even so, her stumbling attempts to read Shakespeare, and so many poets beside, had been an education of sorts.

'*Was not this love indeed?*' Trelawny struck up. '*We men may say more, swear more, but still we prove much in our vows, but little in our love.*' She felt his voice throbbing through his body, noble now, with no hint of Cornish mines or fisherfolk.

'Is it true?' she asked. '*Much in your vows but little in your love?*'

'Well, it's Viola who says that. In the play.'

'What play?' She knew perfectly well that the play was *Twelfth Night*, but she suspected that Trelawny might prefer his captives wide-eyed and ignorant. Feigning ignorance: that had been the game her flirtatious cousins had played with any man who came within range of their artillery.

'*Twelfth Night*.'

'Do you sit down and learn Shakespeare plays by heart?' she asked.

'*Twelfth Night*? We read it one night in Pisa, me and the Shelleys. Some other friends, too. Mary Shelley[77] was Viola. With a woman like her, you remember every word she says, even if she's just reading aloud.'

So, there were other games a woman could play: wide-eyed and ignorant wasn't the only choice. 'Mary Shelley? The woman who wrote *Frankenstein*?'

'Have you read it?'

'Only reviews.'

'Reviews?'

'The old consul left stacks of them behind, when he went home. *Monthly Review*, *Critical Review*, that sort of thing.'

'They weren't very good,' the Captain shook his head, 'the reviews. *A tissue of horrible and disgusting absurdity*. That's what John Croker called it. Something like that.'

Fanny nodded. 'Was she disappointed?'

'That was all a few years ago. I didn't know her then.'

'Did you *know* her? Or did you just *meet* her?'

'I knew her. I helped her leave Italy after her husband died.'

'Italy,' she echoed. 'Is that why you call yourself *Edgardo*? Because you spent so much time in Italy?'

'Italians can't say *Edward* properly. Nor can the Greeks.'

Fanny sighed. 'But *Edgardo* isn't your name.'

'Sailors are driven to all manner of artifices.'

'Humbug!' she broke in. 'My brother was a *real* sailor. A gentleman.'

'And I'm not?'

'Well, does a gentleman stay out half the night with...?' Her voice tailed off: she was making herself ridiculous. If her companion was no gentleman then she was no lady. '...with someone dressed in a second-hand shawl?' she concluded lamely.

'Not to mention what's underneath.'

'How would you know what's underneath, young fellow?'

'It's the kind of thing sailors talk about. I've heard it said that many women shed their shifts before a fellow can stammer out *You first, my dear.*'

No one had ever spoken to Fanny quite like that, though she was long familiar with Portsmouth banter. Perhaps a part of Fanny was scandalised, but the rest of her forgave the Captain, doubted indeed that he needed forgiveness. Even so, before her ungentlemanly sailor could turn his theory about discarded petticoats into practice, she should head him off. 'Didn't one of the reviews say that *Frankenstein* had good descriptions of scenery,' she remarked casually. 'Or was that *William Tell?*'

Her words were chaff, but chaff falling on safer ground. The Captain liked that: he'd taken things a shade too far, tried her mettle perhaps. Deftly, she'd kept their cheerful nonsense afloat, though on terms less compromising for her and less inviting to him. He should play along. Fanny had never seen Switzerland, and he began to tell her about the Alps and about mountains in India that were even grander. His travels brought him to his harrowing years in the King's navy, and to his bitter childhood. He asked her about Portsmouth, about the debts of young Tom, about the sale of Sir Thomas's estates in Antigua and the ruin of Mansfield Park, about the loss of her husband's living in the general wreckage. They made themselves more comfortable in a dozen different positions, but he still hadn't kissed her, hadn't tried to caress her impassive body. She teazed him with her words, but she didn't stroke his hair or try to excite him with her loins, pressed as they were against his body. With an inward smile, the Captain realised that she was ignorant, or innocent, of such devices. If her fortress were pregnable, it would fall through a *ruse de guerre* and not from her own desire or through force of arms. The solitary clock, unheeded, chimed away two more hours.

For all she was untravelled and apparently unread, Trelawny had never met anyone, man or woman, whose life so closely resembled his own, a life of callous usage and undeserved punishment, of striving and rejection, with, now and then, a sudden interval of elation or indulgence. Even so, he knew he hadn't understood her. 'Something you said puzzles me,' he told her. 'Will you explain it?'

'Perhaps you know enough about me already,' she replied evasively. It was a sore place he was about to touch, and they both knew it.

Trelawny hesitated. He'd already stopped calling her husband a *dobeck* even in jest. *Don't make fun of it,* Fanny had told him. *It? Him? Her? Her marriage?* She'd given him a warning, and he was taking it broadly. 'What you said was: *Maybe I married him. And maybe I didn't.* What did you mean?'

She didn't answer, admitting her words but at the same time regretting them. What should she do? Keep silent? Explain? Change the subject? He waited. Then, finally, she began to whisper a reply. 'The Bishop of Peterborough married us: Doctor Madan. In the cathedral. He was very old, over eighty. Then, when Sir Thomas had to sell the living, the new bishop found Edmund this job in Athens.'

'Does it pay?'

'£50 a year, less £30 for our board and lodging. Less than 8 shillings a week. Without my money we'd be lost.'

'Your money?'

'I have a portion, from my uncle and from my Aunt Bertram. It was my aunt's money.'

'So *you* keep *him*?'

'In a way.'

'*And maybe I didn't?*' the Captain prompted. 'What did you mean by that?'

She turned away, tossing her head. Was she baulking? He had no wish to compel her, none at all: he'd wait a second and let the question drop.

'I'm not quite sure,' she said at last, uneasy and tentative. 'There's what you might call a legal problem.'

This was painful territory for him too. It had taken him nearly four years to divorce his faithless wife, Caroline, years of discussions with lawyers, evasions, costs, hearings, filthy and degrading stories in the press, and yet more costs. He'd briefed the best lawyers in London, Sir James Scarlett[78] and Jonathan Pollock, Fred as everyone so oddly called him. Was there no way, he demanded of them, no way that he could rid himself of Caroline without publishing to the world the last sordid detail of his own cuckoldry? Sir James had been pedantic, crusty and unsympathetic, but clear. There was no way. Fred, who had been born in Charing Cross and started life as a saddler, was more down to earth. He was ready to call a spade a spade, and he had words enough, frank and robust, for the humiliations and infamies Caroline had heaped on her husband's head. In the end, however, he'd been no less clear than Sir James: there was no way. Five years ago, the divorce had been made final, but every last detail still rankled, and now, shaken as he still was, he had to turn his attention to Fanny's uncertainty. She had a *legal problem*? What legal problem? Bigamy? Unlikely among the gentry of Northamptonshire. Incompetence of the celebrant priest? Unlikely in the case of a bishop. Only one problem came to mind:

'Are you saying your marriage was never…?' He couldn't say the word: if his guess was wrong, the very idea was derogatory, insulting even.

'…consummated?' She finished his sentence for him. 'Isn't that the word they use?'

He was right then, and he nodded, accepting her courage.

'And was it?' he whispered. The sore place he'd touched was an old battle-scar that had never healed. His own pain helped him gain a sense of hers. And all he wanted at that moment was to help her, if only he could!

'To be honest,' she said stiffly, 'I'm not sure.'

Her body was taut now, tense in his arms. She was afraid. The clock struck five, but she didn't seem to hear it.

'Legally…,' she ventured. Then, confused and struggling, she fell silent.

Was she struggling to speak? Or not to speak? 'Legally?' he took up. 'As far as I know, if a marriage was never consummated, the law lets you annul it.'

'The law…,' she gasped. 'Are you…?' Then silence, a shivering, painful silence. How could he help her best? By holding his peace? Or by grasping the nettle?

'You say you're not sure,' he asked. 'Not sure of what?'

'Please, please,' she insisted.

Please talk? Please shut up? 'You want me to talk?' he asked gently.

'Yes,' she replied. She started to tremble, not to shiver, but to heave as though hostile and unhealthy waves were coursing through her limbs. He'd once seen George Byron overcome by epilepsy. Was Fanny…?

'Calmly, my pretty one,' he said. 'Calmly.' He touched her forehead with his fingertips, trying to soothe away the evil. He stroked her hair and held her close to him.

Abruptly the trembling stopped. With a sudden intake of breath, she'd brought her nerves under control. 'I'm sorry,' she whispered.

'And it will help you if I talk?' he whispered. 'Just let my words come to you?' In helping her, he felt the first relief from his own pain, the first relief in five wrenching years.

'Yes.' Her voice was lower than a whisper, but somehow it was firm. Clear and firm.

'Was it like this?' He tried to imagine the scene: a wedding night with an ignorant bridegroom unable to couple with his bride. Nothing similar had happened in his own life, not even when he'd been obstupescent[79] with drink. 'Perhaps...,' he began. 'Perhaps when he came near you, it seemed somehow wrong.'

'Wrong?'

'Well, you'd known him all your life. He was your cousin, but for years you'd lived in the same house. He was more like a brother. It was somehow forbidden. It felt wrong. Sinful?' It wasn't a word he often used, *sinful*. To him it meant nothing, but maybe to her...

'I don't think so,' she whispered again, though without conviction.

'Then perhaps you were frightened? You'd never kissed him, not really? You'd never cuddled up to him? Or to anyone else for that matter. You began to panic, like you did just now?'

'I wasn't... I wasn't afraid of him. Why should I be?'

'But you were afraid? What of? Afraid you wouldn't be good enough for him?'

He heard a sharp intake of breath: he was very near the sore place now.

'Were you afraid he wouldn't like you? That you weren't the wife he really wanted? You weren't...' He had no idea how to finish the sentence.

'I wasn't Mary Crawford,' she agreed with a gasp of relief: at last she could spit out the bolus that had been choking her.

'That must have been awful,' he said consolingly, though with no idea who Mary Crawford might be.

'Why *should* he want me?' she broke out with sudden vehemence. 'Mary was... Well, she was lovely. I hated her.' The idea of hatred wasn't new to her: she'd admitted it to herself for years and to Jane Darcy just a few weeks before. But the phantom of Mary Crawford stretched out on the nuptial bed in Thornton Lacey, ready for a wildly expectant Edmund, that *was* new. For a second, she saw her wedding night as her inexpert and fumbling husband must have seen it. Perhaps it had been, she realised with sudden clarity, even worse for him than it had been for her.

Trelawny now knew the answer to one of his questions: what had happened on Fanny's wedding night? His second question was just as delicate though in a different way: what had followed the disaster? What had been its repercussions? 'Did your husband ever…?' he began. 'Did he ever…?' How could he put his question in a way she'd understand? In a way that would help her?

She was beginning to tremble again. He had to be quick. Gross words, no others, ran through his mind: he'd have to risk it. 'You know what *fuck* means,' he said. It wasn't a question.

'Of course I know.'

'Did he ever…do that…to you?'

'Not really.'

'Not really?'

'Once.' She touched her mouth. 'Here.'

'And it disgusted you. I suppose…'

'No,' she said, suddenly articulate again. 'It disgusted *him*. He couldn't bear to see me looking like that. He hated what happened.'

'Dragging you down, you mean? Degrading you like a whore in an alehouse?'

'I don't know much about…alehouses,' she said, shying back into ignorance.

'He hated what happened. Did he hate you too?'

'No,' she replied uncertainly. 'I don't think so. Though I know he blamed me.'

'And after that once… Did he…?'

'No. After what happened, I don't think he could anymore. At least, not with me.'

At least not with me? What might that imply? There were men, so-called men, who couldn't make it, not with a woman however willing and attractive she might be. Some found a safer anchorage with other men: some sailed in that water but never tried to cast anchor, never understood how they really were. Was Edmund one of those? Better try other explanations first. 'You mean he chased after other women?' Trelawny ventured.

'Other women? You've seen him, *God, I thank thee that I am not as other men are, adulterers*. Such a Pharisee he can be sometimes!'

'That could be a game he plays.'

'You think so?' The hope in her words surprised him.

'You'd like that? If he secretly chased after women?'

'It would be better than it is now.'

'You think you failed him?'

'That's what he thinks: he thinks it was my fault.'

'He thinks that you failed him.'

'Yes, but he doesn't understand. He could have done anything he wanted. He could have forced me. Tied me to the bed. Flogged me. He could have. Anything.'

Trelawny heard in her words a clarity, a precision that startled him. A woman craving consummation tied to a bed and flogged? Was the image a fantasy? Or reality? Who was she? What had she lived through, this woman whom chance had flung so unceremoniously into his arms?

Fantasy or reality? A little of both, perhaps. The prisoners whom Fanny had visited in Northampton and Peterborough had, over the years, enlightened her as to a number of practices that seemed to her not only unforgivably malicious but also strictly incredible. Some, Fanny heard, were done in love, some in hate, and some simply in anger. She pressed no questions on the prisoners: her heart and mind rebelled at the vicious horror of what she was told. But the stories multiplied, and she began to believe at least the less lurid of them. After she and Edmund had arrived in Athens and he'd begun to tighten his authority over her, she had asked herself how far a man like Edmund might go. He had certainly shown a willingness to hurt her and had derived some inexplicable satisfaction from her suffering. He'd left scratch marks and bruises that took weeks to disappear. But the hellish persecutions she'd heard of from the prison women? In her imagination, that road had sometimes stretched out before her, but Edmund had never dragged her down it more than the first half-mile or so.

'You weren't fighting him then?' Trelawny prompted after a minute or two of nervous silence.

'Not at all. I wanted him to love me. That was all. But I didn't know what to do. In a way it was my fault, but if he'd loved me, he'd have found a way.'

'*Love will find a way.* That's what Byron says.'

'It was Mary Crawford he wanted.' The Captain could hear regret and blind anger taking over again. 'If *she*'d been in that bed, they'd have found a way. My God, it can't be so difficult.'

His first impulse was to say anything that might calm her: that her husband, in all probability, worshipped the ground she trod on. That every man fears the goddess he creates in the image of the woman he loves. But he said no such words. Partly, he despised Edmund too much to invent noble excuses for him, and, partly, he doubted that Edmund would have 'found a way' with any woman, Delilah, Jezebel and Salome included.

'Sometimes,' he said calmly, 'it isn't just difficult. It's impossible. Don't blame yourself. Truly, don't.'

'You're right. I've always blamed myself. Makes no sense, does it? It's just that I've never talked about it before. No one ever helped me to put it into words.' She hesitated. 'Not like you're doing now.'

'Good,' he said, giving her an affectionate hug.

'So, did I marry him?' she asked abruptly. 'Or didn't I?' Her voice was suddenly matter-of-fact, without fear.

'He spent on your face, once.' No need to mince his words now. The storm was over.

'Was it...?'

'...consummation?'

At this point, I pause to wonder how *I* might have answered Fanny's question. A doctor is used to temporising: *Well on the one hand... Though on the other...* Uncle Trelawny was, of course, a sailor, not a doctor, and he took a different tack. 'Fanny, listen to me. Absolutely, finally, without any argument, it was *not* consummation.' Trelawny had but slender sanction for what he said: despite his divorce, he had no more idea of the case law on consummation than he had of what the Code of Hammurabi[80] says about doctor's fees. Two things, however, were clear. First, nothing required Fanny to repeat his own path to social humiliation by demanding a public hearing. More important, perhaps, he had shined a first light on the depths of Fanny's undeserved misery. He saw her now as modern Andromeda chained to an imaginary legal rock. If the Captain seized his chance, he might kill her kraken and set her free. All he needed was the right words.

'You say it wasn't consummation?' Fanny repeated her question suspiciously. 'But how do you know? Tell me. Please.'

'Listen to me, Fanny. The way you were with Edmund, it's quite common. A lot of young girls are cut off from men and that sort of thing, and so they're frightened. On the wedding night, they tighten up like oysters. Some men just blast it away. But some can't. Edmund couldn't. I knew a fellow exactly like him, a messmate of mine in the *Fortunate*.'

'A friend?'

She was taking the bait. 'Yes,' he lied. 'Men tell each other things. Specially after they've been at sea a month or two.'

'And this man…?'

'Man and boy, a sailor, remember, not a vicar. Well he knew nothing about women, and he had no luck at all.' Trelawny hesitated. The story needed to sound good. 'Well…, to put it simply, in the end he managed to do to the girl what had been done to him all his life: he buggered her. Once. Just once. And she kicked him out. Out of her bed. Out of her house.'

Fanny said nothing, but she'd understood: it was another word she knew from her prison conversations.

'And when she went to the bishop's court for an annulment,' Trelawny explained, 'it all came out, about the buggery.'

'How awful.'

'For her especially,' Trelawny agreed.

'But it wasn't her fault, was it? What did the judge say?'

'Fault?' Trelawny cast around for an answer. 'The judge, the law, don't concern themselves with fault…but with fact. Consummation is a matter of *fact*, not a matter of *fault*.'

'And so she got her annulment?'

'It took nearly two years, but in the end, yes, she got it.'

'You know that for certain?'

'Yes,' Trelawny said with well-feigned conviction. 'For consummation, the woman must be…,' he hesitated, '…fucked. And in the right place.'

'So, what they call…'

'…buggery,' he said the word for her.

She nodded. 'So, it isn't consummation.'

'No, it isn't.'

You had to be f… She didn't say the word, even to herself. And…in front. That had never happened, never, never. 'But that isn't quite my case?' Fanny said. 'Is it?'

'No,' he agreed. 'But I had another messmate.'

Fanny said nothing, waiting for the explanation.

'Well, his woman… You know… With her mouth…?'

Fanny did know. It was a subject common enough with the women prisoners: it was their readiest way of earning favours from the prison guards. 'Yes,' she said. 'I know.'

'So again, seed was shed…,' Trelawny pressed on, 'but not in the right place.'

'And it happened *after* they were married? After the ceremony?'

'That's exactly the point. There was a ceremony, but they never *were* married because there was no consummation. That's what the judges said.'

'In England?'

'One judge was in York. The other was in Exeter, as far as I recall.'

'And did the women get married afterward? To other men?'

'That's why they wanted the annulment.'

Fanny paused. Apart from a word or two, used in the interest of perfect clarity, Trelawny had been tactful. She welcomed his tact, but welcomed even more his clarity: he'd left her with no shade of doubt as to her situation,[81] or at least her situation as he claimed to understand it. If only he was right! If only! She took one of his hands in both of hers and squeezed it in gratitude. She felt a slight pressure in return, but no more. No more. And yet he wanted her: she had already sensed something about him, a warmth perhaps, or a subtle fluidity in his limbs that she had never detected in Edmund or in Henry Crawford in his most amorous days. 'You certainly talk about some things,' she laughed. 'You and your messmates.'

'Messmates, yes,' he agreed. 'But I don't often discuss such subjects with ladies. They prefer *to leave a casement ope at night to let the warm love in*. Buggery between sanctified sheets, well, it's not a nice subject.'

'You never talked about it with Mary Shelley?' There was laughter in her voice again.

'Not really. Though we were both friends of George Byron...'

The name made Fanny thoughtful. 'For a long while I didn't understand things like that,' she said. 'It wasn't till I started visiting women, in prison, trying to help them...'

'In prison?' he repeated. 'Do you mean in one of His Majesty's gaols? Or is *prison* your way of saying *marriage*?'

She began to tell him about her prison visits, about the women she'd met, how she'd helped them, and what they'd talked about: like Trelawny and his messmates, they'd discussed some outlandish things. And she told him that she'd met Elizabeth Fry.

'You've met Elizabeth Fry!' he exclaimed. 'And you made a fuss of me because I knew Shelley and I've met Keats! You damn women, you've no sense of proportion.'

They talked on until a faint grey light cracked the eastern horizon. The clock struck six. The Captain left her again at the door of the mosque, taking with him her muddy slippers and promising to return them, clean, within the hour.

Fanny sneaked back into her cold bed. From a nearby blanket, she heard Emma wish her a sleepy good morning, but Fanny didn't care. She wasn't married to Edmund, she'd never been married to Edmund, and nobody could do a thing about it. And something else: the kiss she'd just shared with Captain Trelawny under the portico, it was *not* adultery. Just one kiss, unchaste perhaps and tending to her perdition as it might be, but thank God, yes, thank God, it breached not even one of the Commandments.

Note

Reading through my last two chapters, I understand that no publisher will ever print them. They would offend public taste, wound public sensibility, or even corrupt public morals. We must, at all cost, protect the morals of our womenfolk, and in particular of the young.

If female sensibilities are best protected by silence, if purity is best preserved by ignorance, and if ignorance is best induced by perpetual euphemism, then I consent to the expurgation of my last two chapters. *If?* Perhaps the word *since* would be preferable. Who am I, a simple doctor, to question the wisdom of society, of our rulers and their exalted ladies? Accordingly, if Mr Gregson so requires, I shall reduce the conversations between Fanny Bertram and my Uncle Edward, conversations that they both assure me took place more or less as described, to a single paragraph:

Fanny had married Edmund Bertram in Peterborough Cathedral, and she said as much to Captain Trelawny. She also knew that, on grounds unmentionable in a work of fiction in this sixth decade of the nineteenth century, a marriage might be annulled, and she had reason to believe that in her case an annulment might be possible.

Let Mrs Grundy rule.[82]

Illustrations: Characters and Scenes from
Jane and the Jackal

Edward Trelawney (at roughly the time *Jane and the Jackal* was written). See p. ix

Bourdzi Tower today showing (under water) the old sea wall, now destroyed. See p. 12

Medoni today showing the gate from the lower town into the upper town. See p. 15

Romantic image of Odysseus Androutsos, Governor of Romelia. See p. 43

Mary Bruce (née Nisbet), Countess of Elgin, based on a portrait by François Gérard 1804. See p. 49

The Funeral of Shelley, based on an imaginative reconstruction 1889 by Louis Fournier. See pp. 62-63

Sketch of the mosque in the Parthenon temple, c. 1830. See p. 141

Edward Trelawney by Seymour Kirkup, c. 1840. See p. 136 (National Portrait Gallery, London)

Road through Mountains near Delphi, sepia by Simone Pomardi, 1805. See p. 266

Acropolis of Amfissa, postcard c. 1920. See p. 267

Kervansaray, Smyrna, based on a sketch by William James Müller, 1843. See p. 268

Ford in the River Evinos, summer 2017. See p. 308

British graves in the English cemetery, Korfu, c. 1820. See p. 318

Tavistock Square today. See p. 318

Yarmouth Bridge catastrophe, based on a press sketch, 1845. See pp. 319-320

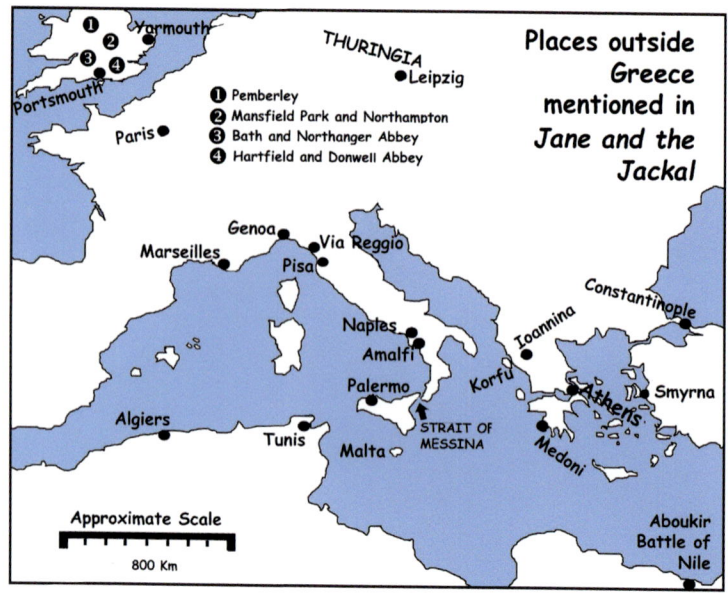

Map 1

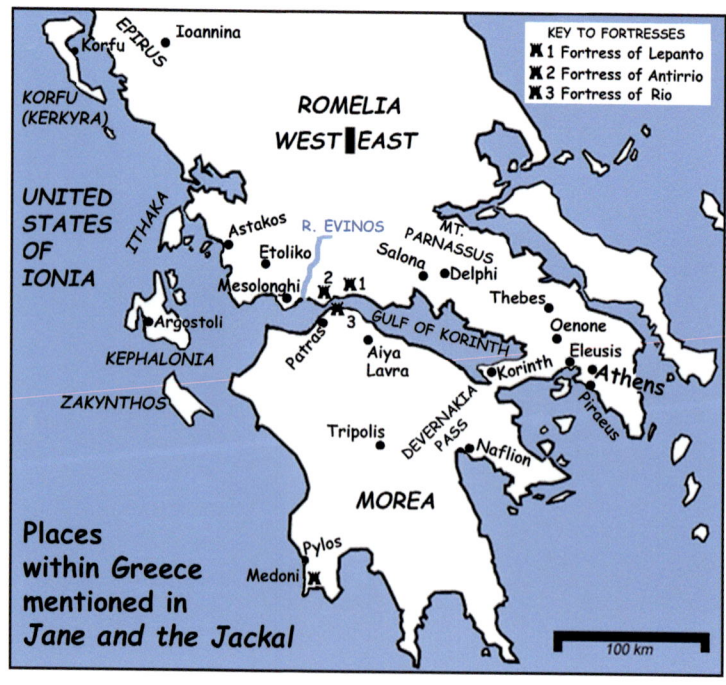

Map 2

Chapter 8

THE ASSAULT

The morning after Edward Trelawny slew Fanny's kraken was promisingly mild. The wind backed to the south, and the skies cleared. The smell of camellias and date palms was borne on the breeze, perhaps from the Morea or perhaps from far-away Egypt. It was Sunday, 7th March.

Apart from those who had guard duty, Odysseus's soldiers were allowed Sunday as a day of rest. A few went to the morning service in one of the town's still functioning churches. Most lay in bed till mid-day and then sauntered in twos or threes into the dull streets below the Akropolis. A handful sat in the spring sunshine repairing kit, polishing brass, or smoking a quiet pipe. As the Reader already knows, the men had been ordered to steer fifty yards clear of the mosque. As simple soldiers, they had obeyed without question: now, in the sunshine, they could see the reason behind the order.

After breakfast, the women had manoeuvred chairs and a sofa onto the warm terrace in front of the *zenana*. Jane sat with her governess refreshing French vocabulary, while Elizabeth and Emma hunted for common relatives among their extensive hordes. Fanny sat on her own, mending the lace trim on her night-gown. She was pondering her next encounter with Edmund. What should she say to him about their supposed marriage? And how might he reply? Would it be better to challenge him in front of Mr Knightley and the others? If that happened, Edmund would cringe and fawn and even perhaps lie. If she were alone with him, he'd act the bully, threaten her, hit her maybe. But at least he'd tell the truth: she'd find out what he really thought. And she wasn't afraid: not any more. Why had she put up with his threats and his blows and his beatings for so long? *Wives, submit yourselves unto your own husbands.* How those words had ground her down! But no longer! Whatever they actually meant, and despite what Ephesians went on to say about the behaviour of husbands, for her it was all dead and buried. She wasn't a wife, Edmund wasn't a husband: she could submit or not, just as she chose. And if he threatened her with his fists? Just let him try!

To Odysseus's soldiers, to men, that is, whose carnal experience of women was largely confined to dancing at weddings, dalliance in taverns, and an occasional fortuitous rape, the sunny domestic scene under the portico must have looked like paradise. The little band of angels, heavenly and vulnerable, was, of course, protected by a powerful barrier: Odysseus had given an order, and Iannis Gouras was poised to enforce it. Disobedience was suicidally improbable.

Lunch had been carried from the Venetian Tower at one o'clock, eaten, and cleaned up. Halfway through the afternoon, the three husbands and the two officers from the consulate arrived for a visit. In the balmy weather, tempers were lulled, laughter and gallantry could take over. Under their portico, the ladies now held court. When Captain Trelawny added himself to the group, the breeze seemed, at least to one member of the group, to blow more embracingly and the sunshine to cast a still more caressing light.

When the Captain asked Fanny, quite publicly, how she found life in her new dormitory, her wits reeled for an answer. Then mischief. As far as she knew, she replied, dormitories were for nuns, and the idea of sacred vows was, to her, unappealing. Such ambiguity was dangerous, but the danger roused her further. She saw her husband frown as he always did before *My dear, my dear, I think…* Perhaps it was time to desert the Captain for a moment and share a few thoughts with Edmund.

'Edmund,' she said. 'There are some curious inscriptions in the gateway.'

'In the Propylaea, I suppose you mean.'

'Exactly. Have you seen them?'

'I think not,' he replied with a shrug. 'I've seen everything I want to see in this God-forsaken town.'

Mr Knightley, ever-anxious for marital harmony, heard both question and answer. 'Why don't you go, Bertram?' he asked, with a complicit smile at Fanny. 'Might be something interesting.'

A broad hint from his employer was a command for Edmund Bertram. Fanny took his arm and steered him along the path she had trodden twice with Captain Trelawny.

'Edmund,' she said as soon as they were out of the hearing of the others. 'I've been wondering.'

'And not about gateways and inscriptions, if I understand correctly.'

'In a way, yes,' she contradicted. 'About gateways and inscriptions.'

'And I have been wondering too,' he said. 'Wondering why you ladies did not attend service this morning.'

'Mrs Darcy said we had more important matters to attend to,' Fanny rejoined quickly and, be it said, untruthfully: the subject of divine worship had been ignored completely.

'More important than the performance of your religious duties?'

'To be honest, Edmund, Mrs Darcy doesn't enjoy your sermons.' This at least had the merit of truth, but Fanny's saying it was something entirely new. In all their years together, she had never criticised, or passed on criticism of, his reading, his preaching, or, heaven forbid, his dog-like religion of facile compliance and unflinching inactivity.

'Mrs Darcy doesn't enjoy my sermons!' he bridled. He paused impressively. A reproach was imminent. What would be the subject this time? The throwing of ecclesiastical pearls before trampling swine?[83] Or the voice of the prophet that finds nothing but dishonour in his own house? No, he took a more personal line.

'Apparently that is a sentiment you share.'

'Why do you say that?'

He was silent for a moment, resentment swelling like an infected carbuncle. 'Because you never take the slightest interest in any of my sermons. Neither in my sermons, nor, it seems to me, in anything else I say.'

She made no reply. He was being ridiculous. He had eighteen sermons. Each was divided into three parts allowing, with exhaustive recombination, for some 5,832 deliveries: at a rate of one per Sunday, it allowed more than a hundred years of sermonising. She knew all eighteen sermons by heart, indeed she had known them for years, and in none of them could she find a trace of faith,[84] hope, love or charity.

'You don't deny it,' he said accusingly.

'If your own common sense doesn't deny it,' she said sadly, 'why should I?'

'Exactly,' he said. 'Exactly my point.'

She had no idea what he meant. There was nothing she could say. She waited for him to find fresh cause for lamentation.

'Have you any idea,' he began pathetically, 'how lonely I sometimes feel? With a wife who never thinks beyond her next meal, and, of course, her next letter from Brother William?'

Greed? Was he digging up greed again? A month before when she'd suggested buying fish once a week from Piraeus rather than lamb every day from the butcher, he had indeed accused her of greed: accused her in front of Emma Knightley. And an over-fondness for her brother? That charge she'd heard time and again, spurious as it was: after all, she hadn't seen William for five years.

'Oh dear, no!' he pursued. 'Poor Brother William! They never gave him another command, did they, not after the *Zebra* was broken up?'

Fanny made no reply. In William's last letter, months ago, he'd admitted that he was now first mate in the *Antelope*, a decaying troopship lying at Chatham. The Admiralty's plan was to convert the *Antelope* for the transportation of convicts to Bermuda. Once there, the ship would become a prison hulk. Edmund, as always, had seen the letter.

'First mate of a prison hulk! That's as far as William Price will ever go.' He sniffed with bitter relish.

Fanny refused the provocation: it was an exhausted argument, and she had no wish to renew it.

Edmund, however, wanted more. He rolled out another threadbare taunt: 'Do you remember when Brother William was a midshipman, how you wheedled your way round Henry Crawford to get him a promotion? You'd have done anything, anything, for William to be made lieutenant? I remember how disgusted Mary was. Disgusted. And my sisters too.' This was a blatant lie, a lie that drifted further from the truth every time Edmund repeated it.

'Pfff,' Fanny sighed. 'If I've told you once, I've told you twenty times, exactly what Mary said was this: *Henry was never happier than when he got your brother's commission.* Happy: he was happy, she was happy. Everyone was happy but you.' She did not add, *You miserable cur*, but her tone implied it.

Edmund fell silent. Fanny walked beside him now, despising his stupidity, his mendacity, his failure as a priest, as a husband, and as a man. Once there had been hope: now hope had vanished. Thank God, her need for hope had vanished too.

Before their marriage, Fanny had looked forward with some excitement to Edmund's new role as vicar of Thornton Lacey and to her new role as his wife. But there had been no roles, either for him or for her. He had hired a curate to conduct the necessary services, and the curate's wife had attended to the deserving poor, leaving nothing for Fanny to do.

Then had come the crisis in her life: her first visit to the prison in Northampton. Suddenly she'd been confronted with suffering a world away from Mansfield Park or Thornton Lacey, though she had certainly caught a whisper of it in Portsmouth. How should she react to what she'd seen in the women's gaol? As a Christian, as a woman neatly dressed in a world of filthy bodies and ragged clothes, how should she behave? She'd asked Edmund, begged him, to help her. What did the Word of God say about prisons and prisoners? The Bible, she was sure, was packed with compassionate instruction, if only she'd known where to find it. And what had been his reply? He'd quoted Saint Peter[85]: *Some things are hard to be understood, which they that are unlearned and unstable wrest unto their own destruction.* So, she was *unlearned* and *unstable*. And she should keep her nose out of the Bible or risk destruction. When she'd mentioned her biblical difficulty to her father-in-law, he'd taken her into his library and dug out an uncut edition of Cruden's *Concordance*. Sadly, her studies had produced little: biblically, prison visitation, as horseracing gentlemen say, was a nonstarter.[86]

They were nearing the Propylaea and the promised inscriptions. 'And above all...,' Edmund began again, working himself into a passion of self-pity. This was how he'd been at every crisis of his life: she remembered him begging her for pity because Mary Crawford wouldn't marry him! '...with a wife who takes no interest whatever in my profession?'

'In fact, Edmund,' she corrected him innocently, 'that's exactly what I *have* been wondering about.'

'About my profession?'

'No. About my being your wife.'

The blow was hard and direct, but it seemed to shock her more than it shocked him.

'I see,' was all he said, standing rigid as a gibbet.

'What do you see?'

His reply was glib and oddly self-assured. 'I see a wife who promised to love, cherish and obey her husband and who is now, apparently, questioning her vows.' The self-pity had vanished. His new tone was masterful, cruel even.

'I do obey you, Edmund. In all things. When have you found me disobedient?'

'There are things worse than disobedience. Far worse. You doubt that you are my wife! If that is true, then the abomination of desolation[87] stands in the holy place. The question is, shall we destroy it? Or will it destroy us?'

Really? Did he really believe that her questioning their miserable marriage was prefigured in the Bible? 'I don't see where the *abomination of desolation* comes in, Edmund, but I know I've never disobeyed you.'

'Very well, I'll give you an order. Whatever you are thinking, I forbid such thoughts. Do you hear?' He raised his hand as if to slap her, but lowered it instantly: they were in the open and someone might be watching. She welcomed his anger, especially if it loosened his tongue: perhaps now they could come to the point. It was time for her to fire her broadside.

'Edmund, you know as well as I do that our marriage was never...,' she screwed up her courage, '...never consummated.'

'What difference does that make?' He began to walk again, crushing her hand between his arm and his jacket, dragging her after him. 'The bishop himself said the words: *I pronounce that they be Man and Wife together*. It seems to me you are questioning the authority of the bishop.'

'Of course not.' She waved the bishop aside as an irrelevance. But, she realized, the bishop's words were ready on the tip of his tongue. What did it mean? Had he, like her, been puzzling over the conundrum of their marriage? Were they edging toward a real discussion? 'But if the marriage was never consummated...?' she pressed.

'And whose fault was that, may I ask?'

'Fault has nothing to do with it,' she replied. 'Consummated, or not consummated: it's a matter of *fact*. Isn't that what the law says?' She tried to pitch her voice diplomatically – to imitate Mr Knightley at his most consular. Edmund, she sensed, was struggling for an answer, and struggling too with his rising temper.

'And if I say it's a matter of *fault*,' he snapped, 'is my obedient wife going to contradict me?' Silly petulance was smothering their argument, and it pained her.

'It *is* a matter of fact, Edmund. Your opinion makes no difference.'

'And if I say the opposite?'

'Don't be so unreasonable.' How could he lower himself to such inanity? What kind of scatterbrain did he take her for?

'Me unreasonable! Have you been drinking *tsipouro*?'

'For heaven's sake, Edmund, talk to me sensibly.'

'*Man and Wife together!* That should be sensible enough for any woman.'

'And the fact that you never…?' There was a word that Trelawny had used, a word that the women in His Majesty's prisons used with monotonous frequency, but even under the present provocation, Fanny did not use it directly. Even so, the word hung in the air between them, perhaps provoking Edmund to lay out his best cards on the table.

'Listen, Mrs Bertram,' he said. 'You want the law, well here it is.' He cleared his priestly throat and began his homily: 'A marriage may be either void or voidable. For a marriage to be void, there must have been some insurmountable impediment preceding the marriage ceremony: consanguinity within the forbidden degrees, for example, or the previous and undissolved marriage of one of the parties…'

'You've been talking to a lawyer!' she exclaimed.

'Some years ago. Is that further cause for complaint?'

'Finding things out behind my back and not telling me.'

'There was no reason to tell you. You answer to the name of *Mrs Bertram*. To me that sounds like the behaviour of a married woman.'

'But why talk to a lawyer? Because you were in doubt? What other reason could there be?'

'My dear, my dear, surely you are familiar with the words of St Paul: *...he that doubteth is damned.*'

'Perhaps you are right, Edmund: remember, it is your doubt we are discussing, not mine. But I am certain, absolutely certain, of one thing: in the eyes of God, you and I cannot possibly be married.' There it was! The noose round her neck, and she'd put it there herself.

'And how would *you* know what God sees?'

You! The anger, the venom with which he loaded the word! She remembered the Edmund of her childhood, her only friend. He'd found a pony for her to ride when she'd been sorely in need of exercise, though, she had to admit, he'd taken it away again when Mary Crawford wanted riding lessons. And now, what a cheap bully he'd become!

They came to the place where she and Captain Trelawny had sat together, the wall with the warm bricks. She looked at the dust and the crushed shoots of early grass. She saw a button, embroidered with gold thread and gleaming, a button from the Captain's Albanian blouse. She grimaced and stood for a moment beside her cousin, motionless and silent. She was still holding his arm. To an onlooker, they might have seemed a respectable couple having, perhaps, an insignificant tiff.

'And what exactly is a *voidable* marriage?' Fanny began again. 'You mentioned it just now.'

'No reason for you to know. No reason for you to ask.'

'Is non-consummation a reason for a court to annul a marriage? What did your lawyer say?'

'Mind your own business.'

'If it isn't my business, I'd like to know whose it is.'

'All right then,' he said with an angry shrug. 'A court *can* annul such a marriage: any fool knows that. But a court requires *proof.* Proof, you understand. Proof.'

'Proof that the marriage was never…?' Her voice froze in her throat.

'Exactly,' he gloated, his snarl turning suddenly to a derisive smirk. 'Proof.'

'But you could never prove…?' she challenged him feebly.

'I don't have to prove anything. Nothing at all. As the matter was explained to me, *you* must prove *your* case: I don't have to disprove it.'

'And you'd force me to prove…?'

'There's nothing you *can* prove. I think we should forget this whole degrading conversation.'

He'd make her prove her virginity in public! She could see now how low he'd sunk. But, whether in public or in private, her case was lost. Irretrievably lost. The battle had been short, and Edmund had won. She simply stopped fighting.

But if Fanny was still a virgin, wasn't that proof enough? Why did she give up so easily? When she'd been sixteen, Fanny had been as tall as she was now, she'd been strong and lissom, but, as we have already said, the green sickness had prevented her from 'becoming a woman.' Mary Crawford, who had never seen Fanny as any kind of rival, had tactfully suggested to Fanny's aunts that a doctor in Northampton, a specialist in women's ailments, might be able to help: perhaps there was a way of curing Fanny's condition about which the village doctor knew nothing. Idle Aunt Bertram had agreed but had not pursued the matter. Skinflint Aunt Norris had found the expense of a city doctor intolerable for a disease that came close to a defect of character and afflicted neither Maria nor Julia, the daughters of the house. Generously, Mary had set up a consultation for Fanny, paid for it herself, and they'd gone into Northampton together. The doctor had mentioned the traditional emetics and purgatives with which the profession treated Fanny's condition and to which Fanny needed no introduction. How often over recent years, had she been forced to defecate and to vomit until she was too weak to stand, but without result? Then, the doctor had suggested, perhaps she might try beef tea: beef tea was coming into fashion in Ireland both as a drink and as a medication. And the doctor had another suggestion. He'd asked if he might examine her: possibly there was some kind of physical obstruction. Close to panic, Fanny had agreed. Never in her life had she been 'examined.' What would happen? What would she be expected to do? After the examination,[88] which in the event had been brief and discreet, the doctor had asked Fanny if she'd climbed trees as a young girl. No. Did she ride a lot? Whenever she could. Side-saddle? Always. Had she ever been thrown by her horse and landed awkwardly? Maybe with her legs apart? Once she had landed badly, she had admitted, but only once. Perhaps that was the cause then, the doctor had said. Perhaps that was how she'd ruptured her hymen, because in the purely physiological sense, she was no virgin. Her intactness or otherwise had nothing to do with her failure to bleed, of course. With luck the beef tea would take care of that.

At sixteen, Fanny had lacked any prospect of marriage, and the news of her missing virginity had caused her no sleepless nights. From Portsmouth gossip, she'd known, of course, that a girl had to bleed on her wedding night. Failing all else, a sharp fingernail and a quick scratch inside would procure the necessary bleeding. As her marriage to Edmund had approached, the subject had acquired if not urgency then, at least, immediacy. Fanny had thought over, and rejected, trickery of any sort. Two days before her wedding, she'd spoken openly to her husband-to-be, confessing the fall from her horse and its consequence. As she'd expected, her noble and forgiving husband had understood completely, and nothing more had been said about it from that day to this. But now? If a court demanded proof of her ongoing virginity, she had no way to provide it. Edmund knew that: it seemed that he had discussed the whole thing with his lawyer, and that now he was threatening to use her girlish honesty to destroy her.

Fanny pulled her hand free of her cousin's arm, bent down, and picked up Captain Trelawny's button. 'Look what someone's lost,' she said.

'You see how careless people are about losing things,' he replied. 'Things that later might be of the greatest value. Not that a button...' His words were almost light-hearted. He'd just won an argument that had brewed silently during his entire married life, a dispute that he'd dreaded as he dreaded shame itself.

'If I wanted an annulment?' Fanny asked gravely, wanting to clear the last uncertainty from her mind. 'What would you say?'

'I'd quote the Book of Proverbs: *Her feet go down to death; her steps take hold on hell.*'

'In other words, you'd tell me to go to the devil?'

'Your words, my dear, not mine.'

When they got back to the mosque, Fanny went straight inside. She seldom suffered from the headache, but as she squatted on her simple mattress, her forehead felt as though it would explode. Her temples thumped till she cried out in anguish.

Jane, under the portico outside, heard her. 'Mrs Bertram,' she whispered, coming to Fanny's bedside. 'Fanny, are you all right? What's happened?'

Fanny looked up. She held out her arms, longing for the compassionate touch of the girl's hand. Quickly Jane knelt beside her. Fanny pressed her face against Jane's shoulder and began to shed the accumulated tears of fourteen years. 'Don't call me Mrs Bertram,' she sobbed. 'Not ever again. Call me Fanny, call me Frances, but not Mrs anything.'

After sunset, the wind veered to the north-west and the temperature dropped. Men who had been sipping wine in the sunshine turned now to *tsipouro* for warmth and stimulation. One subject spurred their ever-rowdier conversations: the five women in the mosque. Rumour had it that they were English, exotic beyond imagination. Casual observation, coupled with concupiscence, added that all five were angelically beautiful, clean as saints, and as ready for love as the legendary blondes of Circassia. Only one thing kept the men from storming the *zenana* immediately: the threat of the cruelly sharpened spike. As long as this image held sway over that of exotic northern beauties naked and defenceless, the mosque was safe. But, notoriously, the more a man drinks, the more lust prevails over reason. By nine o'clock in the evening, the cauldron was seething. At ten, it boiled over. Fortunately, this calamity had been foreseen by both Captain Trelawny and Colonel Stanhope: the women in the *zenana* were not without resource.

Odysseus's men were accustomed both to hard liquor and to forcing doors bolted for the protection of comely women. What they were *not* accustomed to was working in silence. And silence was important if they were to obtain the women and avoid the spike. One of the men suggested battering down the door with the wooden wash-trough that sat in the yard, but battering was rejected as too noisy. Wrenching the door off its hinges with crowbars would be slower but quieter. And another thing: they'd need gags. Women kick up a dreadful fuss when they panic. Outraged cursing, a few bites and a couple of scratches were part of the fun, but women screaming the mosque down might arouse their Commander. They'd definitely need gags.

That evening, Jane Darcy moved her mattress next to Fanny's. The girl had never seen anyone so distraught, and she resolved to sit with Fanny through the night. And so it chanced that, when the *khlepts* inserted their crowbars between the door of the mosque and the doorframe, two of the inmates of the *zenana* were still awake, holding hands and listening into the darkness. Crowbars they heard, and men's voices whispering in Greek.

Instantly Jane was on her feet. Under her mother's pillow was a double-barrelled, cap-lock pistol,[89] the latest design from Thuringia, loaded, and deadly. It was a gift from Colonel Stanhope. Jane grabbed it, cocked one barrel, and fired a shot through the roof tiles, just as Captain Trelawny had suggested. Then she cocked the other barrel and stood facing the door: the first man to show his face would not live to tell the tale. But no one came. Crowbars rang and rattled on flagstones. Fleeing boots carried away what sounded like dozens of feet.

Trelawny was smoking a pipe at his open window when he heard the shot. The five guards on night shift, playing cards in the anteroom, heard the shot too and pushed into their Captain's room. Buckling on his sword belt, Trelawny gave instant orders. The wicket gate would not be barred till midnight, so one man should run to the consulate with word of an attack. The other four should follow Trelawny. A moment later he was at the door of the mosque shouting: 'Ladies! I'm here with my men. There's nothing to be afraid of.'

The commotion in the *zenana* can more easily be imagined than described. 'Are you in there, Fanny?' Again the Captain's shout.

'Yes,' she cried back.

'Tell them to calm down. There's no one out here but us. Open the door if you can.'

Fanny and Emma Knightley swung the door half open. A few seconds later, Odysseus arrived with Iannis Gouras and a bodyguard, all with scimitars drawn. Trelawny moved to the open doorway of the mosque, interposing his impressive figure between the Greek men and the English women. He began to explain to Odysseus the crowbars and the damage, stressing how ineffective the attack had been: if Odysseus suspected a complaint about his hospitality, he might throw the Englishwomen out of the citadel there and then.

Trelawny's messenger found the Consul drinking brandy round the fire with Mr Darcy and his two soldier-guests. The four men grabbed swords and pistols and hastened to the mosque. There they found Odysseus and his Ithakans crowded into the portico and Captain Trelawny barricading the half-open door with his body. Trelawny hailed the four new arrivals, and then ushered the Consul and Mr Darcy into the *zenana* despite Odysseus's rules on the seclusion of the women. The two officers needed no instruction: they took their places immediately and imposingly in the doorway on either side of the Captain.

Ignoring the new arrivals and the breach of the rules, Odysseus asked his friend, Edgardo, to finish explaining what exactly *is happen*. Odysseus listened in silence and then gave his orders: half-a-dozen men, the possible ring-leaders, were to be brought immediately from the barracks to the mosque. He explained the order to Trelawny in English, ignoring the others. When, a few moments later, the suspects arrived, Odysseus and Iannis Gouras questioned them for half an hour: of course, nobody had seen anything, nobody had heard anything, and nobody had (ever) questioned, let alone disobeyed, an order of the Lord Governor.

Deluged for half an hour with angry questions, outraged denials, accusations and threats in a language they did not understand, the English stood dumbfounded, asking nothing, contributing nothing. They saw Iannis Gouras repeatedly urge some course of action on his commander, and Odysseus baulk every time. When at last the Greeks fell silent, the Lord Governor explained his dilemma to Captain Trelawny. There were six suspects, he said: without evidence, it would hardly be fair to punish all six, or even one of them. Trelawny believed not a word: since when had fairness been of concern to Odysseus. Even so, he nodded agreement. For now, Odysseus pursued, it was better to let the matter lie. No outrage had been perpetrated, and no one should be punished. As far as he was concerned, the matter was closed. Of course, the accused froze with apprehension: unexpected leniency in a tyrant can be more alarming than straightforward cruelty. No one risked a word of dissent, concurrence or thanks. A few moments later, without as much as a *good night*, the little crowd dispersed, the Greeks to their beds, Trelawny's guards to their card game, and the English to the interior of the mosque. With the door firmly closed and no further restraint on speech, the *zenana* exploded with questions: What next? What shall we do? What*ever* shall we do now?

One husband was missing from the mosque, Chaplain Bertram. He'd been left to defend the consulate, together with Trelawny's messenger, though, as Colonel Stanhope observed, the value of such a *Schlappschwanz*[90] (the Colonel used a word he'd picked up while buying pistols in Thuringia) was far from obvious. The Consul asked Mrs Bertram if her husband should be fetched: they could hardly plan the next step without the Chaplain's agreement.

'Do as you think fit,' she replied. Edmund had told her that *her steps took hold on hell*. It was unusually plain speech coming from Edmund, but his words had, at least for her, two possible meanings: hell would swallow her if she sought an annulment, or her life would become a hell if she remained his wife. His wife! How could she be his wife? It wouldn't cost her a second's grief if she never saw him again till her dying day! It was a consummation devoutly to be wished.

'I feel he should be here,' Mr Knightley said. 'Trelawny. Can you send one of your men for him?' The wicket closed at midnight: the man would have to run.

'I think one thing is obvious to us all,' Mr Knightley began. 'If the women are not safe in the consulate, and if they are not safe in the citadel, then they must disappear from Athens, and the sooner the better. But how?' The discussion began. With the straits of Lepanto blockaded, the only route was by road across the mountains. No, Colonel Stanhope ventured, there was another route: they could sail southward from Piraeus, double the three capes that formed the fingers of the Morea, and then head northward for Ionia or westward for Italy. A ship from the Mediterranean fleet, the *Hind*,[91] Captain Churchill commanding, had been in Piraeus until a few days before: Churchill would certainly take the women on board even though he had no orders to that effect. Probably he would, the men agreed. At this point, Elizabeth Darcy stepped in. Did anyone know where the *Hind* was now? she asked coldly. Or when Captain Churchill would be back in Piraeus? Nobody knew anything, and the Colonel politely withdrew his idea.

With that alternative gone, the general direction of the retreat was now clear: Salona, Astakos, Korfu. Turning a sensible decision into a plan of action is always laborious, and so it proved in this case. Should the women walk? Should they ride? Should they travel in carts? With an armed guard? Or without? Which of the men should go with them? Should they seek refuge in the Turkish fortresses along the route? After all, they still had the *firman* from the Sultan offering imperial protection to Lord Darcy and his party. Or should they avoid the Turkish fortresses like the plague? And they'd need a guide through the mountains: should they wait for the next messenger from Korfu? Or hire a guide in Salona? So many possibilities, so many impossibilities, and, at first, nobody could tell one from the other.

Before long, however, two voices became prominent. The voice of George Knightley maintained order: one person should speak at a time, and everyone should have a say. Elizabeth Darcy seemed to find a new voice altogether. She examined theories in the light of such facts as were available: she was frank to the point of discourtesy and brutally clear-minded. Her new character surprised them all, perhaps Mrs Darcy herself more than anyone. Mr Knightley began to wonder how his life might have been with such a wife, and Mr Darcy to understand how different his life would have been without her.

After a while, with the outline of a plan emerging, Captain Trelawny started a new hare. 'And Mrs Brandon?' he asked. 'Is she to be one of the group?' Marianne's inclusion no longer aroused much passion. Emma Knightley shrugged: nobody spoke. At exactly that moment, the Chaplain reached the mosque. He was greeted by a sudden silence: everyone there, perhaps even Jane

Darcy, realised that he was a spent force, a man of no importance, a moral scarecrow.

'Mr Bertram!' the Captain asked provocatively. 'We are in need of your decision. The womenfolk are to proceed across the mountains to Astakos. Should Mrs Brandon, Marianne, be one of the party?'

'I hardly think it *my* role to make such a decision,' the Chaplain replied with resolute sanctimony. 'What does Mr Knightley think?'

'We know what he thinks. The question is, what do you think? If anything at all,' the Captain pursued.

'For one thing, I have certain scruples about deciding the fate of a fellow human being.' The Chaplain's words convinced nobody. His scruples were not at stake: he was simply afraid that a disagreement with the Consul at this critical moment might prove embarrassing.

'No, Edmund,' it was Fanny's voice. 'We are equally divided. We need your deciding vote.' She exchanged a quick glance with Captain Trelawny, a glance that Emma Knightley intercepted and understood correctly.

The Chaplain looked at Fanny with murder in his eyes. 'When I decline to make a decision, I would have thought that *my wife…*'

His wife had challenged him, fiercely and in public, something unheard of and dangerous. Worse perhaps, he himself had now publicly pointed his own finger at the sore place.

'Speak, Mr Bertram.' The Consul, one of the most even-handed men who ever lived, was evidently on the side of the wife: the Chaplain should drop his mealy-mouthed deviousness and say something to the point.

'We're waiting, Bertram,' the Captain broke in, not quite licking his lips.

The Chaplain looked anxiously at Mrs Knightley, then at Mrs Darcy. Both gestured in the direction of the Captain: Answer the question! In despair, the lonely man glanced at Fanny. Help me, his expression cried out. Help me.

'Since, my dear,' Fanny stepped in, 'you scruple at deciding the fate of another human being, I shall decide for you, if I have your permission.'

The Chaplain, appalled at the calm vindictiveness of her words and at the support she evidently enjoyed among the others, neither gave nor withheld his permission: he said nothing.

'Although,' Fanny resumed, 'I think that earlier today you *did* decide the fate of another human being, or at least you tried to.'

He looked at her viciously. 'And who was that?' he said.

'Me.' Fanny's voice was low but sharp as a bollock dagger.[92] 'You told me to go to the devil. Or have those words escaped your memory?'

'Mrs Bertram! In front of all these people!' he squirmed. 'How can you?'

'How can I what? How can I *decide*? Easily. Marianne speaks Greek. Marianne knows the country. Marianne comes with us. If that's what she wants.'

The Chaplain left the mosque in fury. Had Fanny gone mad? She was his wife! If she wasn't his chattel, she came damnably close. A nobody! A cousin rescued out of common charity from her depraved family in Portsmouth. Fanny, the scheming witch who'd driven a wedge between him and Mary Crawford. Fanny, the devious niece who'd wheedled a small fortune out of her uncle, Edmund's father: a *portion* as Lady Bertram had called it. £3,000! Infernal sight more money than had ever come his way! Though, he reminded himself, a wife had no property. What was hers was his.

The thought did nothing to dampen his fury, as, perhaps, he recalled the unusual terms of his father's settlement. In essence, the normal rules applied *unless the marriage were annulled*. He saw it all now! Fanny talked of annulment, but what she really wanted was to secure the money, to deprive him of it, to deprive him of everything but his miserable stipend. And why? What use had she for £3,000? To spend on her prisoners perhaps, on female felons sentenced for heinous crimes by courts of law. English courts! He really would see her in hell first. She'd fallen off her horse, and lost her virginity to a molehill. That simple fact put an end to her annulment game. And like a fool she'd told him about it, years ago, before they were even married. The shamelessness of the woman. He'd rub her nose in the dirt next time he caught her on her own. He'd unmask her: for all her claptrap about what was right and what was wrong *in the eyes of God*, she was no better than the Scarlet Bitch of Babylon.

Of course, nobody knows exactly what Edmund Bertram raved about on his way down to the consulate, but once, when I speculated on this subject with my Uncle Trelawny, the ramblings above, or something like them, were what we imagined.

During the remainder of the night, under the unremitting control of Elizabeth Darcy, *General Darcy* as Colonel Stanhope now baptised her, a careful plan emerged. Then, at dawn, an unexpected scuffle broke out in the enclosure of the Parthenon, twenty yards from the mosque. Stanhope went outside to investigate. He came back quickly and pulled the door tight closed behind him.

'Stay inside please,' he said. 'There's about to be some unpleasantness. It might be upsetting.'

'Is it Gouras?' the Captain asked.

The Colonel nodded.

'With one of the ring-leaders from last night?'

'With two.'

'And two wooden stakes?'

'I'm afraid so.'

'But Odysseus said no one was to be punished,' the Captain objected.

'Perhaps he's changed his mind,' the Colonel said. 'Or perhaps Gouras is taking the law into his own hands.' Stanhope had been only a few days in Athens, but already he understood how the place worked, at least in its disciplinary aspect. 'Either way,' he added, 'there's nothing you can do.'

A terrifying scream penetrated the mosque, a scream less than human, the death agony of some fiend. Another scream, another, another, each more soul-shattering than the last. A second of silence. Then cries and execrations: the squeals and yelps of a living corpse. Before it was over, came a fresh cry, a second victim like the first.

Mrs Tilney pressed her hands tight over Jane's ears. The savages! Lieutenant Humphreys blocked his own ears. Mrs Knightley did the same. The appalling screams quickly faded and then stopped altogether.

'Into the heart,' the Colonel said. 'Both of them. Thank God.'

The sobs of Jane Darcy and the consoling whispers of her governess were the only sounds in the mosque until the Colonel spoke again: 'You're safe here for a while. They won't be coming back.'

The two men had received exemplary punishment on the orders of Iannis Gouras. Odysseus was savage with fury when he heard about it. Edward Trelawny once confided to me the reason for Odysseus's unnerving clemency that night: Odysseus had believed that the attack on the *zenana* was a plot of the Captain's to carry off Jane Darcy, a plot that had miscarried because Jane had been given a pistol and had been ready to use it. The next attempt, Odysseus had imagined, would be more successful.

Chapter 9

AN ALLIANCE

Lizzy's Plan, as her husband called it, had been conceived in the early morning hours after the assault on the mosque. The Consul and the two army officers would stay in Athens. The women, Fitzwilliam Darcy, the Chaplain, and Captain Trelawny escorted by his Suliots would take the road to Salona and then on to Korfu. Hour by hour, the plan matured: questions were raised, objections explored and modifications debated.

Five women! Six if Marianne Brandon joined them! The Consul was alarmed. Even with an escort, wasn't that asking for trouble? Odysseus's soldiers had already attacked the women in the Akropolis itself. But on the open road...! Mrs Darcy took the point. Perhaps it would be easier if the women dressed as men. Jane and Fanny were no problem: they could ride on horseback, astride and with a kerchief round their mouths. A simple country cart with a tarpaulin cover would take the others, all dressed as men. Their disguise would be imperfect, of course: they could hardly compress a woman like Emma Knightley to manly proportions. Even so, their costumes should be good enough to pass casual inspection in a village or at a barrier. The practice and procedures of female disguise offered the women an inexhaustible fund of discussion, but, beyond a little harmless ribaldry, elicited scant contribution from the men.

And a place to lodge each night? Where could so many women, even disguised as men, stay in safety? If there were no lodgings, Mrs Darcy decided, they'd have to camp in the open. On the journey from Medoni, they'd camped out twice. No lice, no fleas, no black beetles. She described the heavy felt capes the *Sanjakbey* had given them: shepherds' capes, itchy and ugly, but warm and waterproof: if they had a cart, the capes would obviate the need for a tent. They still had four capes, and they could buy more in the town. If Marianne was coming, no doubt she could find what they needed.

How long would it take? Mrs Darcy referred the question to Colonel Stanhope. The first leg, Athens to Salona, he calculated, was something over a hundred miles. The road was good all the way. Judging by what the British army had achieved in the Peninsula, they should reckon with three days to Salona, maybe four. And over the mountains? That was anybody's guess. If they could find mules in Salona…

The great unknown, and unknowable, was Odysseus. Mr Darcy was in favour of frankness and candour: they should ask Odysseus to bless the whole enterprise, ask him perhaps to provide an escort. The others, led by Emma Knightley, took the opposite view: Odysseus should remain ignorant of their plans until the last minute. Captain Trelawny was firmly on Emma's side. Odysseus, he told them, had begun to see the English women as hostages, bargaining tokens in the power struggle that would usurp the Salona Congress. Odysseus might well understand their departure as an escape, which indeed it was. They should prepare the next moves with the utmost secrecy. That was easily said, Mr Darcy countered, but Odysseus's spies would report immediately any purchase by the consulate of capes, horses, ammunition and the hundred other things they would need. Nobody had an answer.

Tell Odysseus? Or keep it secret from Odysseus? The question was turned and twisted like a fox in the jaws of the hounds. Then they had a stroke of luck. A pair of messengers arrived almost simultaneously, one from Sir Frederick Adam in Korfu, the other from Lord Byron in Mesolongi.

Sir Frederick's courier brought startling news: Sir Thomas Maitland had dropped dead of apoplexy in Malta. Until instructions to the contrary were received from London, Sir Frederick would act as Lord High Commissioner of Ionia.

Byron's messenger brought the Consul three missives, all sealed in a single package. The Consul's own letter contained copies of the other two, one addressed to Odysseus and one to Captain Trelawny. Nothing was closer to his heart, Lord Byron told all his correspondents, than union among the Greeks. He fully intended to join the congress in Salona, preferably in April: in fact, nothing but death would keep him away. In his letter to Odysseus, the Consul saw, Byron asked him to arrange with the other Greek captains a date and an agenda for the congress. The instructions as to date and agenda were, however, missing from Trelawny's version of the letter. Apparently, Byron did not quite trust Trelawny with the details of his plans.

Elizabeth Darcy was serving tea at the daily conference on the terrace of the *zenana*. The Consul had just finished explaining the nub of Byron's letters: the great poet was coming to Salona. 'Wonderful,' Elizabeth commented. 'That's our passport out of Athens.'

The others looked puzzled. 'But how?' Fanny questioned, the only one honest enough to ask.

'Odysseus won't see Byron's letter to you, Captain Trelawny?' Elizabeth began.

'No,' he confirmed.

'Good. Then you can tell Odysseus that Lord Byron wants an *escort* from Mesolongi to Salona. And, of course, that he wants his old friend Captain Trelawny to provide it.'

'Be careful,' the Consul objected. 'Odysseus is no fool.'

'Fool or no fool,' the Captain agreed, 'I can see what Mrs Darcy is thinking.'

The Captain's word was enough for Fanny. 'Good idea!' she said. 'Lord Byron's Escort Party.'

'Yes, let's call it that,' Mrs Darcy pressed ahead. 'Ask Odysseus to allow it. You could even ask him for a safe conduct.'

'And if he refuses?' the Consul asked.

'What does Odysseus want most in the world? Byron's 10 million. So tell him how grateful Lord Byron will be, how extraordinarily grateful.' Mrs Darcy smiled, pausing for sounds of agreement.

'Clever!' Fanny exclaimed. 'I can see now why the Colonel calls you *General Darcy*.'

Mrs Darcy's smile broadened. The handsome compliment paid at exactly the right moment earned the Chaplain's sometimes fractious wife not only a smile of acknowledgement but also a change of status: at that instant, Fanny became a useful ally.

'I still don't see the point,' Emma said flatly. 'What's so clever about an escort party?'

'It means a dozen or more people will leave Athens at the same time,' Fanny explained to her quietly. 'If the women dress like men, as we planned, we can leave with them.'

Odysseus, when Trelawny asked him, accepted the escort-plan immediately: and he was happy to issue a safe conduct if it would help his so-good friend, Edgardo, and oblige the so-rich Lordship Byron. Of course, he wanted to know who exactly would ride with the *Escort Party*. Obviously his Suliots, Trelawny replied, though other details were still vague: perhaps it would be best if Odysseus signed a general safe conduct rather than using specific names. Odysseus agreed. And the route? First they would go to Salona, Trelawny told him, then south-west to Mesolongi where Lord Byron was waiting. Finally, with Lord Byron in tow, they'd double back to Salona for the congress. Again Odysseus agreed. Evidently, the sanctified odour of £10 million had numbed the nerves of his sensitive, rat-smelling nose.

Then, in an attempt to oblige Lord Byron even further, Odysseus offered to sell the Captain horses from his own stable: the escort of a so-famous Lordship should be well-mounted. Even though Odysseus's prices were double the market rate, his offer was snapped up: Mr Darcy enjoyed good standing with the bankers of Athens, cash was no problem, and Odysseus's nose was numbed still further.

In the meantime, at the Consul's request, Marianne visited the consulate. Did she wish to join the other women in their flight to Korfu? Yes, she would be delighted. The Consul expressed surprise: Marianne had spent so many years in Athens. Wouldn't leaving it cause her some distress? Not really, she reassured him: since the start of the war, nobody who came to the city was in need of a guide. The Darcys had been her last clients, and the last she expected. Luckily, Marianne had a sister in England who had offered her bed and board if ever she needed it. Mr Knightley was all understanding. So, would Marianne help Mrs Darcy and the others with the purchases necessary for the journey? Sensing a clutch of per centages ahead, Marianne replied that she would be *more* than delighted. Things were moving forward.

The two couriers were questioned in detail about the roads. Byron's courier reported throughout Romelia the worst flooding he had ever seen. Sir Frederick's man agreed: one span of a bridge between Astakos and Etoliko had been washed away completely, and he'd been forced to make a detour of fifty miles. Worse, late snow had blocked half the tracks in the high mountains. But when does a courier make light of his journey?

The couriers' reports drew Mrs Darcy's attention to a still-missing component in her plan: nobody in the escort party was familiar with the road. To them all, Thebes, Delphi, Salona, Mesolongi were just names on a map. Her husband agreed, they'd need a guide: perhaps he should talk again to Sir Frederick's courier. The man, Stavros, was cooling his heels somewhere in the consulate until a despatch was ready for Korfu. Mr Darcy tried the shed where the outdoor servants bunked, but Stavros wasn't there. The stable-boy suggested Madame Rifat's. This was a well-known establishment in the Street of the Winds. It was no longer run by Madame Rifat who, as a Turk, had been butchered by the *khlepts* during the siege of Athens. Nerissa, the statuesque Grecian nymph who took over the business, kept the name, however: *Madame Rifat's* was familiar to every mercenary, whore and bandit in Romelia.

Mr Darcy pushed open the door of Madame Rifat's and glanced round the tables. Stavros was sitting alone with a beaker in front of him. Two of Odysseus's henchmen were sitting at another table. Four young women were lounging behind a simple counter, gossiping. Seeing Mr Darcy in the doorway, the girls perked up. He waved them an easy refusal and joined Stavros at his table.

Stavros would have gossiped all night with anyone who was buying drinks, and so the two men fell into immediate conversation. After a while, Mr Darcy, as casually as possible, mentioned a plan to whisk six women from Athens to Korfu via Salona. By way of reply, Stavros tapped his forehead with two fingers and said: 'Can you carry one fart in one bucket over one mountain? No. But six farting women over twenty mountains! You think?'

'Not a good idea,' Mr Darcy translated. Nerissa's handmaidens were closing in. Mr Darcy gestured them to refill the two empty beakers on his table.

Stavros screwed up his face thoughtfully: perhaps he'd fired his shot without taking proper aim. 'But…'

Mr Darcy had successfully managed a large estate in troubled times, he had stayed solvent while many of his contemporaries had crashed, and he'd built a ship. He knew exactly what Stavros was thinking. 'But?' he repeated.

'If you need help, milord. Guard? Guide? Especially guide through mountains?'

'Yes,' Mr Darcy agreed. 'Now you're talking sense.'

The handmaidens brought to the table a jug of red wine and four extra beakers.

'Just the wine, not the beakers,' Mr Darcy told them. Stavros translated. During the indignant babble that followed, Stavros remained firm. 'I tell them we talk business,' he explained to Mr Darcy. 'But they say in back room talk business. In *taverna* talk friendship.'

'At the moment, tell them, I have all the friends I need.' Mr Darcy began to relax: after weeks of correctness in the consulate, the shrill indecency of the whores, not that he could understand it in detail, was as refreshing as a quick swim in the lake at Pemberley.

'Times are hard, milord,' the messenger sighed. 'No rich people in house like this, never. You are first since Napoleon.'

'Napoleon never came to Greece.'

'You are right. But you make them crazy just with your beautiful breeches. So beautiful breeches they never see. Never since Napoleon.' He laughed.

'Tell them we need five minutes,' Mr Darcy smiled.

'You have money?' Stavros asked.

'For you? Or for them?'

'For both. Most important for me.'

'Name your price,' Mr Darcy offered. 'One gentleman, six ladies, a navy captain and eight guards. From here to Korfu.'

'Mr Trelawny? He is navy Kapetan?'

Mr Darcy said nothing.

'And his guard is ten, not eight,' Stavros objected further.

'Two more disappeared this morning.'

Stavros nodded sagely. Desertion was not a shameful betrayal: it was a matter of business.

'How many days?' Mr Darcy asked, not understanding Stavros's nod.

'You are need ten days.'

'If you say so.'

'Fifty *piastre* one day.'

Something under twenty sovereigns for the whole journey. It was a fair price. 'Half tomorrow. Half when we arrive,' Mr Darcy offered. The two men shook hands across the table, emptied their glasses, and the handmaidens moved in again.

As a young man in his native Derbyshire, Fitzwilliam Darcy had kept his nose clean. In London, he'd been less particular, though without risking his health. Mr Darcy gave the maidens a friendly smile. In his experience, girls in taverns were harmless creatures if you treated them decently. Hungry and harmless. He stood up, took a five-*piastre* piece from his *so beautiful breeches,* and put it on the table. 'Spend it for me,' he said to Stavros. 'From tomorrow you're working for me, so you stay in the consulate.'

With a guide in place, it was now Trelawny's turn to negotiate. Perhaps unsurprisingly, the Greek mercenaries who constituted his bodyguard understood the art of negotiation better than the Cornish pirate who called himself their leader. That the Captain still had eight followers was less a tribute to their loyalty than to his readiness to increase their *solde* in line with their escalating sense of their market value.

The Suliots confessed immediately the one sentimental weakness of their negotiating position: several of them had wives on Korfu. This meant they would give their leader the best imaginable terms: a miserable 600 *piastres* a day. Per man. The Captain said he would try to raise the money. In the Levantine tradition, agreement is taken as a sign of weakness. The agreed 600, the men now insisted, was *in addition to* their normal pay. Captain Trelawny commanded no such sums, but he would see what he could do. All he could do, of course, was to speak to Mr Darcy.

'But I'm paying 500 for a guide,' Mr Darcy objected. 'For the whole trip! And they want 600 a day for each man. It's extortion!'

In the end, Mr Darcy, supported secretly by Marianne Brandon, took over the negotiation. He offered the Captain's men 300 *piastres* each for the whole trip, half now, half in Astakos. Without grumbling, and with a suspiciously cheerful promise to sharpen swords and clean pistols, the men accepted. Bartolomeus, who still inspired the trust of his Captain, did most of the talking.

Two days later Mr Darcy gave the Captain 1,200 *piastres* in silver fresh from two local banks, one in Athens and one in Piraeus. Tolo was to pay the money to the Suliots immediately. Predictably, it wasn't long before a goodly part of this sum had trickled back into the treasuries of the Athenian bankers through the hands of Nerissa and her sisters.

Between the dawn of Monday 8th March and the dawn three days later, without bustle and without alerting Odysseus's spies, *Lord Byron's Escort Party* was put together, supplies were purchased, and disguises were improvised. After catching a glimpse of herself in a mirror wearing fashionable tight trowsers and a frock coat, Elizabeth decided that she and Mrs Tilney would travel as countrywomen. With their walnut-tanned skin, their incipient wrinkles exaggerated with blacking, lumpy clothes, and ugly bucket hats masking their hair, two such fussocks, Mr Darcy assured them, would arouse neither the greed of the most indigent thief nor the lust of the most concupiscent satyr.

Odysseus may have wondered why the ladies spent so many of the daylight hours in the consulate or in the town, but equipping the convoy excused everything. The Captain's Suliots were kept busy providing an escort here and an escort there, but, as long as their services were recognised with an extra *piastre*, they raised no objection.

As the Reader already knows, it was part of *Lizzy's Plan* that Mr Bertram would travel to Ionia with his wife. And yet, in the event, he stayed in Athens. How was that small triumph achieved? To trace the whole story, we must first go back a little. On the same night that the mosque was attacked, Emma Knightley and Fanny Bertram entered a lifelong understanding that led, among other things, to my meeting them together in Cheltenham in 1845. After more than a year of coolness and misgiving in the consulate, the reconciliation surprised them both. Emma was, apparently, the first to hint at new possibilities.

'Thank God for Captain Trelawny,' she had whispered in

Fanny's ear after the Captain's anxious *Are you in there, Fanny?* had restored some measure of composure to the *zenana*. At the Captain's order, the two women, as we have already seen, together opened the door of the mosque. After that, they stood arm in arm watching events unfold. Emma would not have been Emma if she'd failed to remark Fanny's tussle with the Chaplain. Then she watched in awe as Fanny and the Captain baited the wretched man. It was better than a play.

Are you in there, Fanny? Emma had turned the words over in her mind many times: provided Fanny Bertram was unharmed, the rest of them be damned.

While Elizabeth Darcy and the others bickered about the suitability of *HMS Hind* as a vehicle of escape, Emma stayed close to Fanny. 'Trelawny's such a useful man,' Emma whispered to her.

'Yes,' Fanny agreed.

'You sly little thing,' Emma said, giving her waist a squeeze.

Fanny had no wish to confide her secrets to the Consul's wife. Even so, such was her loneliness, that, while the others abandoned the *Hind* and broached the issue of land transport, Emma wheedled the whole of Fanny's story out of her in a dozen earnest whispers.

'I think I can help you,' Emma offered.

'You already have.'

'You hear what they're planning?'

'Captain Trelawny is taking us to Korfu.'

'Exactly. And you're coming with us? Or don't you want to?'

'Of course, I want to. I thought Mrs Darcy…' For a moment, Fanny was close to panic: was there a scheme to exclude her?

'Yes, Mrs Darcy wants you with us.'

'I hope so. Really.'

'And your husband?'

'My husband?'

'My dear, if you're going to Korfu, wouldn't it be better if Mr Bertram stayed *here*? In Athens?'

'Here?' Fanny was overwhelmed. Leave Edmund behind?

Fanny's imagination, always ready to catch fire, kindled on the instant. Leave Edmund altogether? Go back to England alone. Start a new life. Without Edmund. She had her own money: she had her *portion*. If her Uncle Thomas had tied up the money as carefully as he had claimed, it was hers. For a moment Fanny was back in England, so far from Athens that she scarcely heard Emma whispering in her sweetest voice: 'Well, wouldn't it?'

No answer.

'Fanny?'

'Is there a way?' Fanny replied at last. 'Is there some way Edmund could stay here while I go to Korfu? On my own?'

Emma smiled to herself. You'll hardly be on your own if you're with Captain Trelawny, she thought, but what she said was: 'I'm sure there's something we can do. I know how unhappy you've been, this last year.' Sympathy may have been one reason for Emma's siding so boldly with the errant wife, if indeed Fanny was a wife. The more deep-seated reasons were, perhaps, Emma's love of romance, her delight in hoodwinking men, and her incurable habit of interfering in other people's lives.

'I have money in England,' Fanny whispered. 'Of my own. Enough to live on.'

'Then there's no reason you shouldn't go alone, if you're sure,' Emma prompted her.

Fanny made no reply beyond tightening her arm round Emma's comfortable waist.

'If I speak to George, he'll tell your husband to stay here,' Emma said.

Fanny wrinkled her forehead: she wasn't convinced.

'After all,' Emma improvised, 'a consulate without a chaplain is a poor sort of place.'

Emma, escorted by one of Captain Trelawny's Suliots, went down to the consulate early that afternoon. Even though she had picked just the right moment to approach her husband, she found him surprisingly firm: Bertram must decide. He could stay in

Athens if he wished, or he could go to Korfu. Obviously, nobody gave a tinker's cuss either way, but it must be *Bertram's* decision. Emma gave ground: yes, the Consul was absolutely right, as always, but it was a delicate matter, perhaps better handled by a woman? Should she ask the Chaplain herself? George conceded the point.

Emma was now in difficulties: she had boasted that the Consul's authority was in her pocket, but evidently she had deceived herself. What now? If she followed George's instructions and asked the Chaplain for his decision, she already knew which way the Chaplain would jump: he wanted to keep a hold on his wife, and, of course, on her money. Accordingly, when Fanny went to Korfu, her unloved husband would certainly come tagging after. Perhaps, then, it would be a mistake to follow George's instructions too slavishly. Emma should *interpret* them and avoid the question direct. And when she reported back to George, the truth might require some re-adjustment, but luckily Emma was a born *equivocatrix*, if I may be permitted to invent a word.

In the event, she sent for Mr Bertram and told him that the Consul required his presence in Athens for the next six months.

'How flattering,' the Chaplain replied cautiously.

'As you know, Mr Bertram, at the moment Athens is no place for ladies.'

'Indeed, it is not.'

'For that reason, we are planning to move to a safer place. To Korfu.'

'As I have heard.'

'And your wife...?'

At last a reaction: 'If I am to stay here, she will, of course, stay here also. Her place is at her husband's side.'

'She'll be exposed to danger if she stays in Athens.'

'She will not hesitate to stay here. With me.' How courageous he had suddenly become, Emma thought, courageous at least on Fanny's behalf. 'When God took a rib from Adam's breast and made Eve,' the Chaplain dogmatised, 'He taught us that a wife's place is at her husband's side. That is where she came from. That is where she belongs.'

'And my place?' Emma bridled. 'Is that also at my husband's side?' The impertinence of the man was making her head spin.

'You are going to Korfu. I believe that's what you told me.'

'Yes indeed.'

'Then in your case the matter is settled, and my opinion is of no importance.'

'Mr Bertram, I have spoken to your wife. While you are in Athens, she will wait for you in the safety of Korfu. That is her wish.'

'She has no business expressing such a wish. If a decision must be made, I make it on her behalf. As Saint Paul[93] clearly reminds us: *As the church is subject unto Christ, so let wives be subject to their own husbands in everything.* Everything, my dear Mrs Knightley. The text is perfectly clear.'

'Saint Paul no doubt offers excellent spiritual guidance,' Emma conceded. 'But it is Sir Frederick Adam who steers us on practical matters. And he has instructed that all Englishwomen are to be evacuated from Athens to Korfu.' Perhaps this was stretching the truth a shade too far. 'Or at least Mr Knightley has asked Sir Frederick if this arrangement is agreeable, and there is no reason to believe that it is not.'

With the Consul, the Consul's wife, and the acting Lord High Commissioner against him, the Chaplain knew that he had to tread carefully. 'Perhaps if I speak to Mr Knightley myself…,' he suggested.

'If you suggest to Mr Knightley that he is treating his wife improperly,' Emma's voice rose impressively, 'he will be most offended, of that I can assure you.'

'But I make no such suggestion.'

'Indeed you do, Mr Bertram! I am to go to Korfu and wait until I can re-join Mr Knightley in Athens. Or until he leaves Athens to re-join me. Is that in some way an improper course of action, in your opinion?'

'No, ma'am.'

'And yet you will forbid your wife to accompany me? Forbid her to wait with me in Korfu until the present emergency is passed? You will expose her to danger and yourself to calumny as a heartless man?' Emma paused before striking her final blow: 'As an *insufferable* man!'

With a sigh, the Chaplain surrendered, and Mrs Knightley waved him away, permitting him to return to his previous avocations. With a mischievous grin of triumph, she returned to her dressing room: it would soon be time to ready herself for her return to the mosque.

There was a familiar knock on the door of Emma's dressing room. 'Did you speak to Bertram?' Mr Knightley asked peeping round the half-open door. His wife was sitting in front of her mirror, hairbrush in hand.

'He wishes to stay.'

'Here in Athens?'

Emma nodded.

'He told you that?'

Emma needed to tread carefully. 'He and his wife do not see eye to eye. She wants to go: he insists that she stay here. In other words, he says it is *his* duty to stay here and she must stay with him. She must not *desert her post*, as he calls it. They almost came to blows about it.'

'Blows! Really?' the Consul said. 'If it comes to fisticuffs, I think I'd put my money on Fanny.'

Emma smiled. Thoroughly sensible, witty, *and* handy with her fists, she thought. Quite a paragon. 'But don't mention it to either of them,' she said. 'Bertram finds the whole thing embarrassing, and you can see why.' She gave her husband a look that made further discussion of the Bertrams improbable. 'I don't have to go back to the mosque quite yet,' she offered. 'If you've nothing urgent to attend to…' She smiled, and the matter was settled.

Chapter 10

FLIGHT

Before first light on 11th March, the women from the *zenana*, escorted by Captain Trelawny and his eight Suliots, descended to the gate of the citadel and asked the sentry to let them out. He refused. Without an order from the commander of the guard, Iannis Gouras, the gate would stay closed. It was a bad start. Two soldiers were sent to look for Gouras, but he was nowhere to be found. In fact, he was in the gate-tower, looking down at the little procession, biding his time, letting the thinly clad English women shiver a while.

Not until the Lord Governor's guests looked painfully cold, did he leave his vantage point, clatter down the wooden stairs, and summon the sentry. The two men exchanged a few crisp words. Gouras was pleased: the guard had done his duty.

Gouras then turned to Trelawny. 'Women? Where go?' he asked.

'To the consulate. Our convoy leaves for Mesolongi in an hour. The Lord Governor has already given his permission. The women wish to say goodbye to their husbands.'

'Husband?' Gouras pointed at Jane. 'She husband?'

'No.'

'She not go.' He scanned the others. 'And this,' he ordered, pointing at Mrs Tilney. 'No husband. She not go.'

'Miss Darcy wishes to say goodbye to her father. And Mrs Tilney is her personal servant,' the Captain said, in a tone of authority. 'The Lord Governor has given permission.' Odysseus's *permission* covered, if anything, the expedition to Mesolongi: it had nothing to do with the women visiting the consulate before dawn. Gouras, of course, suspected this, but he was unsure. The convoy to Mesolongi had one purpose, and one purpose only: to bring Lordship Byron and his money to Salona. If Gouras delayed the women, he might be delaying the money, and that was not at all in his interest.

'Remove cloak. What clothe under?' Gouras demanded, more to maintain his authority than because he wanted to know.

It was a danger Elizabeth Darcy had already foreseen. Under their cloaks the women wore light, indoor dresses and flimsy shoes. They were going nowhere. The clothes they would wear on the journey were waiting for them in the consulate.

Gouras nodded and gestured the sentry to open the wicket. The women glanced their appreciation at Elizabeth: she had insisted on light clothes in the face of rowdy opposition from the others.

Crowded into the yard behind the consulate, the saddle-horses were already fed and their girths had been tightened. Their hot breath steamed in the lamplight, their harness chattered, and their impatient hooves scraped the flagstones. The loaded mules snapped up the wisps of hay that littered the ground in front of them. The women's cart, a farmer's wain, was all but ready. The wain had unmatched horses but good wheels: after the breakdown on the road from Medoni, Elizabeth Darcy had insisted on sturdy wheels. As with a Romany cart, the contents of the wain were protected from the weather and from casual observation by a simple structure of wooden arches under a grey tarpaulin. Mr Darcy, it was agreed, would drive the wain until they were clear of Athens. Then Marianne would take over. She knew the cart already: in the past she'd used it to take tourist parties around the sites of Athens.

Marianne was already in the consulate, disguised as a man. A sheepskin jacket, baggy breeches, and a *bonnet rouge* (of indeterminate colour) enveloped her copious form. She had stippled her plump cheeks with a show of manly stubble. Whatever a casual viewer might have guessed about this ungainly figure, it bore no resemblance to an English lady. The women from the *zenana* changed quickly and took up their positions.

Jane and Fanny Bertram were now two sprightly young horsemen though hardly to be confused with heavy dragoons. The day before, Fanny had ridden astride for the first time. She already felt awkward and a little sore from the saddle. However, with Edmund watching, she hid, with some success, both her physical discomfort and her mental pleasure at leaving him behind. Like the authentic menfolk, Fanny and Jane had pistols in their belts.

The Suliots, with a hint of military discipline, followed Captain Trelawny's order to mount. They were cheerful this morning: their horses, the pick of Odysseus's stable be it remembered, were extra pay in the form of horseflesh, though as yet their commander had said nothing on this score. One of the riders trailed Mr Darcy's grey mare on a lead-rope.

When the cavalcade was ready, one of the Hampshire lads heaved open the big gate, and the Captain bellowed the order to move forward. The Consul and the two British officers stood in the stable-yard waving goodbye.

The Chaplain stood beside the Consul, but he did not wave. He was seething with futile anger: that morning he had tried to persuade the Consul that Fanny should stay in Athens, but the Consul had refused to listen. Athens was too dangerous, the Consul had informed him coldly. The Chaplain bridled: he was as close as he'd ever been to a quarrel with his bread and butter. 'You are coming between man and wife, sir,' he said viciously. 'I would advise you to have a care.' It was an empty threat from a weak man driven to the point of despair.

'*You*, Mr Bertram, would advise *me*?' The Consul snapped his fingers in the Chaplain's face, and walked away shaking his head in disbelief. Most of what happens to us in life is the result of how we go about things. If the Chaplain had put his argument differently, the Consul might well have agreed: *Excuse me, sir, I know it's the last minute, but would it still be possible for me to join the convoy?* The Consul would have said goodbye to his pestiferous Chaplain without a second thought. But no: the issue for Edmund Bertram was his wife's obedience, not their mutual escape from danger. He went about the wrong thing in the wrong way, and ere long he was forced to count the cost.

As soon as the gate was closed behind the convoy, the four men who stayed behind turned to their individual concerns: the officers to the planning of their next meeting with Odysseus, the Chaplain to a search, perhaps, for *religionis consolationes*, and the Consul to the despatch of a letter. This letter had already been dictated by Elizabeth Darcy and embellished by the Consul with diplomatic curlicues: it was to be sent to Odysseus that afternoon.

Most Respected Lord Governor

I think it right to inform your Lordship by these presents that, following instructions received from the Lord High Commissioner of the United States of the Ionian Islands appointed by His Majesty George IV, by the grace of God, King of the United Kingdom of Great Britain and Elector of Hanover, I have this morning despatched with the convoy known as Lord Byron's Escort and under the supervision of Captain Edward Trelawny and Fitzwilliam Darcy, Gentleman, six female subjects of the said King, <u>videlicet</u> Elizabeth Darcy, Emma Knightley (wife of the undersigned), Frances Bertram, Catherine Tilney, Marianne Brandon, and Jane Darcy, minor, daughter of the said Fitzwilliam Darcy, the destination of the female persons named being Korfu, also known as Kerkyra. Whilst in East Romelia, the convoy will follow the route already authorised by your Lordship for those members of the party proceeding to Mesolongi for the purpose of escorting Lord Byron from Mesolongi to Salona.

This letter is for your information only and requires no action on your part.

Your humble servant

George Knightley, Gentleman

British Consul at Athens

This artfully clumsy text was delivered to the Venetian Tower shortly before dusk, in other words, shortly before the failure of the ladies to return to the mosque might have sounded the alarm to Gouras or to Odysseus himself. Mrs Darcy had calculated that if, in the early morning hours, the convoy moved with sufficient noise and public display, Odysseus's spies would see no clandestine intention, nothing that required reporting to the Lord Governor. If indeed nothing were reported, then, by the time the Consul's letter reached Odysseus, the convoy would be well into the countryside, perhaps even ready to pitch its first camp. But would they be safe? Would Odysseus send troops to pursue and haul them back to Athens? Mrs Darcy argued in this way: preventing them from leaving Athens was one thing: arresting them and dragging them back as prisoners along the main highway, that was a horse of another colour. An English lord and his milady? The wife of the British Consul? How would Lord Byron see the matter? How would the British government see it? How might it influence the distribution of the 10 million? With Mr Knightley in Athens poised to ask such questions, Odysseus's hands were tied. No one was safe, no one would be safe until they all landed together in British territory, but with luck they would not be pursued.

By early afternoon, Stavros had led the little procession as far as Eleusis and the last barrier on their route. As usual, the soldiers scanned the safe conduct that Stavros presented, pretending to read it and to recognise Odysseus's signature. With greater facility, they recognised the silver coins with which Stavros greased their palms, and they waved the convoy ahead. A few hundred yards after the barrier, the road forked: to the left the road to Korinth, to the right the road to Oenoe, and then on to Thebes, city of the Sphinx. As soon as they were safely past the fork, Mr Darcy surrendered the reins of the cart to Marianne and mounted his mare. It was a fine spring afternoon, Athens was well behind them, everything was going to plan, but still their spirits did not rise.

Since morning, anxiety had kept them edgy and silent, and they remained so as they passed ancient Eleusis with its celebrated mysteries, countless ruins and handful of inhabitants. But now, as Phoebus's car sank toward the horizon, Captain Trelawny, riding stirrup to stirrup with Fanny, began to hint at the colourful legends of the ancient countryside. Naturally he embellished the narrative with anecdotal flourishes and neatly papered over the gaps in his knowledge. Fanny teased him about his more obvious paperings, and their mood lightened. Mr Darcy, riding with Jane, picked up the cheerful flow of conversation, and began to entertain his daughter with much the same legends, though I imagine that Fanny heard the more colourful version. Heard it, and enjoyed it. Never in her life, apart from her few excursions with her brother, William, had Fanny had such a man to herself, a man determined to amuse her, to meet her proclivities at every turn, and to put at her disposal the gifts of his mind. And Fanny could not deny it: Trelawny's gifts greatly outshone those of her long-absent brother. She enjoyed playing the *ingénue* to his master, though the game took many twists and turns as he cleverly exposed her extensive, though poorly organised, stock of information. Yet, despite Trelawny's company, the day was long, and the ride was making Fanny uncomfortable to the point where she could hardly disguise her bodily distress from the Captain.

Then trouble.

It began a few miles after Oenoe where the road begins its upward crawl into the foothills of Mount Parnassus. The road was dry, and the horses were good for another hour, though the Suliots were not. All day, the escort had been riding four in front and four behind, saying little, even among themselves. Now the front man, Alexis, raised his hand, and his three comrades immediately reined in. The column behind them bunched up and stopped.

Trelawny rode forward. 'What's the problem, Alexis?' he asked.

Rebelliously, Alexis growled three words in Greek.

'Speak English,' the Captain ordered roughly, sensing insubordination.

Alexis weighed the odds and took a decision. 'We camp here,' he said flatly.

'I decide where we camp,' Trelawny contradicted him.

Stavros, the guide, rode up. 'No good place camp,' he said, hearing Trelawny's last words. 'Field very open. No cover.'

'We camp here,' Alexis repeated. 'Open field, close field. Not important.'

'Is there a good place?' Trelawny asked Stavros. 'Within the next hour?'

'Half hour, yes, is good place,' Stavros replied. 'Forest. Ravine. Stream with clean water.'

'We camp *here*,' Alexis said for the third time.

'We move on,' Trelawny ordered. 'Half an hour more.'

Mr Darcy joined the group. 'Trouble?' he asked.

'We're discussing where to camp,' Trelawny told him. 'There's a good place half an hour ahead.'

'Then?'

Trelawny glanced back at the women. Fanny had jumped off her horse. She was walking painfully, cringing and flinching at each step. He watched Jane dismount too, putting her arm solicitously round Fanny, though Fanny seemed reluctant to accept her help.

He trotted back to the cart.

'You all right?' he asked Fanny.

'I'll be fine,' she said. 'Not used to the saddle, that's all.'

'You can ride in the cart,' Trelawny suggested. He remembered a hunting trip in Java and poor Zela after her first day of riding bareback.

'No. I'll ride my horse,' Fanny said with a hint of obstinacy. 'I'll be fine.'

'Luckily there's no more riding today,' Trelawny answered, changing his plans to suit the state of Fanny's backside. 'We're camping here tonight.'

'Thank God,' Fanny whispered and shot him a grateful glance.

Grudgingly Stavros sought out the best place in the vicinity. A hundred yards off the track he found a slight hollow, enough to hide the carts from the road, though it wouldn't hide the smoke of their campfire. There was a copse just outside the hollow where they could forage for firewood. Trelawny approved the place, and the convoy pulled off the road.

Leaving Stavros to set up camp, Trelawny grabbed Alexis and the real leader of the Suliots, Tolo, who was, or so Trelawny still believed, the most loyal of the bodyguard. 'Let's take a walk,' Trelawny suggested. 'We have something to discuss.'

The three men walked in silence until they were clear of the hollow and out of sight of the camp. Poor grazing land stretched to the horizon, broken by an occasional clump of trees. The first dandelions glowed among the new green thistles. The road onward to Thebes was hidden in a fold in the hills.

'What's your game?' Trelawny demanded at last. 'I pay you to obey orders, not to give them.'

'We say camp here, and you agree,' Alexis argued. Tolo nodded agreement. 'This is *your* order, Kapetan, not our order.'

'You know exactly what I mean.'

'We know nothing,' Alexis answered. 'We are soldier.'

'Call yourselves soldiers, do you? Soldiers who question orders?

My orders?' Trelawny's tone roughened. Eight armed bodyguards on one side against three men and six women on the other: unless he established control now, they'd never reach Thebes let alone Korfu.

'We *are* obey orders,' Alexis replied with the practised obtuseness of the trooper. 'Kapetan say camp here. We camp here.'

'Where we camp is not the question,' Trelawny said, his voice dropping dangerously low. 'I'm your officer. You do exactly what I say and exactly when I say it. No discussion, no argument, no talk.'

'Sometime talk is bess,' Tolo replied amiably, but with a glance back in the direction of the hidden camp. 'Is bess now.'

'Talk about what exactly?'

'Perhaps money,' Tolo said with elaborate vagueness.

'We have no money,' Trelawny told him. 'We don't need money till we get to Salona. Now we have paper. In Salona Lord Darcy will change the paper for silver: it's all arranged with a moneylender.' It wasn't quite true. They had silver with them though not enough, in all probability, to satisfy the Suliots.

'No silver, no soldier,' Tolo said, with a regretful shrug of his shoulders.

'So, is this a mutiny?' Trelawny growled.

'No unnerstann *mutiny*.'

'That's what they said at the Nore,[94] but they still hanged thirty-eight sailors afterward.'

'No unnerstann.'

'Hanging? It's like impalement, only it works at the other end.' He ringed his neck with both hands and made a sharp gesture of hanging.

The two Suliots laughed. 'And you, Kapetan? You unnerstann? Money?'

'There *is* no money, not before Salona. You know that, and you know why.'

'Then you go Salona. We go Athina,' Tolo said, without rancour. They were walking still across the rough grazing, slowly, easily. For a while nobody spoke.

Then: 'And perhap…,' Alexis began thoughtfully. 'We go Athina, perhap we take two lady.'

'Miss Jane and Miss Fanny,' Tolo agreed. 'Dress like man, but very pretty lady.'

Miss Fanny! It was a threat too far. The two pistols in Trelawny's belt were part of the consignment Colonel Stanhope had bought in Thuringia: cap-locks. Cock and fire. If he took the Suliots by surprise, he'd be rid of them both before they could turn round.

'I give you a choice,' Trelawny said calmly. 'I pay you more money in Salona: that's the first choice. Second choice: you ride back to Athens tonight, and I find new men in Thebes.'

'And lady?' Tolo asked. There was no need to elaborate: his argument was clear from his tone of voice. Surely the Kapetan could see how easily they could take the women. Naturally they had no wish to seize two English ladies who would be impossible to trade for a fair price. Much better to get money for leaving them behind. Miss Fanny was the Kapetan's woman. Miss Jane was Lordship Darcy's daughter. They must be worth *something*.

Trelawny shrugged. 'There isn't any money. Take the women,' he said.

Tolo was surprised: the Kapetan did not always bargain so cleverly. 'We talk?' he suggested.

The grazing land fell suddenly away in front of them: a ravine, though not deep. The three of them stopped, glancing round for a way ahead. Trelawny fell a pace behind his bodyguards, drew his pistols, cocked one barrel of each, and fired point blank into their treacherous backs.

Alexis fell dead on the grass, a bullet through his heart. Tolo fell too, twisting away and drawing his own weapon at the same time. He was too late. Trelawny cocked his second barrels. The first shot ripped into Tolo's chest, the second shattered his face.

Quickly Trelawny checked that the men were dead. He snatched up their pistols and checked them. Naturally there was no powder in the pans: he'd been in no immediate danger. He stuffed the four guns into his baggy satchel: old-fashioned they might be, but guns were guns. He began to run, circling the hollow. The four shots he'd fired must have alerted the camp. The Suliots would be scared: if he entered the camp from the other side, he'd be safer. He skimmed over the thistles and herbs and then burst into the camp, shouting: 'Ambush! Ambush!'

The English and the Suliots crowded round him: 'What's happening? What were the shots?'

'We were walking. Three men ambushed us. Locals I think.'

'Tolo? Alexis?' the Suliots wanted to know.

'I got away. I don't know what happened to them.'

'They hurt?'

'I don't know. I don't think so.'

'And now?' Mr Darcy asked.

'We stay here,' the Captain ordered. 'We mount guard. Round the edge of the hollow. Move on in the morning.'

'Without a guide?' Mr Darcy gestured toward Stavros already on his horse and poised for flight.

'The foe is *within* the gates, Darcy, not *without*. You take my meaning?'

Mr Darcy took the point. 'Within,' he repeated.

'Wait,' Trelawny told him and then bellowed, 'Stavros. Over here.'

Stavros slipped off his horse and led it nervously toward Trelawny.

'You men!' Trelawny ordered the Suliots. 'We're in a hollow. You four guard the circle.' He indicated four posts to them. 'You two search the trees. Move.'

The Suliots hesitated, glancing at each other: with Tolo and Alexis gone, they were leaderless.

'Move, I said,' the Captain repeated quietly. The men moved, though without much enthusiasm. 'You, Stavros, stay here with me.'

'It's some kind of mutiny,' Trelawny explained as soon as the

Suliots were scattered round the hollow. 'I shot two of them.'

'Mutiny?' Mrs Darcy asked. 'Your loyal and trusted bodyguard?'

'They'd *be* loyal if you Darcys weren't so rich,' the Captain retorted. 'They threatened me: more money, or they go back to Athens.'

'How much more?'

'Double now, double later, double again after that. Sort of a mercenary's martingale,[95] if you know what that is.'

Mr Darcy nodded: more than one friend of his youth had been impoverished by a martingale. 'So, what do we do now?' he asked.

'I think…,' Trelawny began, but Elizabeth Darcy interrupted him.

'Three choices,' she said. 'Stay here, go back to Athens, or go on. Obviously we can't stay here, so do we go on? Or back?'

'Go back?' Fanny baulked. She remembered her husband's baleful frown as the convoy had pulled away from the consulate. All day she'd held the pain of the saddle at bay with the knowledge that she'd never see that scowl again. And now…? 'Odysseus thinks we tricked him,' she improvised. 'Which we did. Go back and apologise? He'd never listen.'

Trelawny nodded. 'Fanny's right,' he said. In fact, Fanny was wrong. For her, going back to Athens was perhaps unthinkable, but for the others it might have been the best course. If they'd sent a message to Odysseus, if they'd asked him to take the women back under his protection, he might well have agreed. Until Byron's 10 million was in his hands…

'Apologise!' Marianne came down heavily on Fanny's side. 'You won't get the chance to apologise. If we head back to Athens, we'll vanish. That's how it's done here.'

'You think the wife of a British Consul can disappear,' Emma demanded, 'without questions?'

'Questions there may be, my dear Mrs Knightley,' Marianne replied. 'But no answers. Odysseus will say we left Athens without his permission: after that, he saw neither hide nor hair of us. He'll say he sent out search parties, did his best to find us, but there's a war going on. The Turks must have found us. And we all know what happens to women who fall into the hands of Turks.'

Jane began to cry. Catherine Tilney held out her arms, and Jane, as so often, clung to her for comfort.

'We go on then?' Mrs Darcy asked, turning her face away from Jane's tears. 'Tomorrow? Do we agree?'

'Yes. We go on,' the Captain said.

'With or without Trelawny's so-called bodyguards?' Mr Darcy wanted to know.

'Perhaps I can keep them on till Salona,' the Captain suggested. 'They won't fight, but they look impressive, even the half dozen we still have.'

'Salona easy find new men,' Stavros said ingratiatingly. He'd been on his horse ready to take flight: he'd have to work hard before Lordship Darcy and the Kapetan trusted him again.

'Perhaps we can find somewhere safe in Salona,' Mr Darcy suggested. 'Somewhere to stay. If we get a message to Korfu, Sir Frederick will send a rescue party, don't you think? A Consul's wife and a vice-consul complete with family, they'd be worth rescuing?' He shrugged, as though there were two sides to every argument. 'Or not?'

'Rest and rescue?' Trelawny added encouragingly. 'I think we all like the sound of that.'

The mood was suddenly more hopeful. They gathered firewood, started the cooking pot, hobbled the horses where the grass was better, and posted the Suliot guards in two watches.

Not long after midnight Trelawny was sitting with Fanny by the camp-fire. For a while they'd kept a thoughtful silence. Fanny broke it first. 'You think we'll get to Salona?'

'I think so.'

'What are your plans, if we do?'

'See you safe to Astakos, and then head south for Mesolongi.'

'To see Byron?'

'I have to see Byron. We started this trip together. We're friends. He's not a fighter, so he may need me.'

'And after that?' Fanny's voice faltered. A question direct trembled on the tip of her tongue, but she couldn't ask it. Instead she muttered: 'Will you go back to England? Ever?'

He put his arm round her shoulders, and they gazed into the embers together, a hundred unasked and unanswerable questions rising with the smoke into the night. 'I haven't thought that far ahead,' he said quietly, understanding what lay behind her question and unwilling to answer.

Fanny said nothing, but, with a nervous shrug, she shook his arm from her shoulder. There was no more to be said.

The Captain and Mr Darcy had split the night between them with the change of guard at two o'clock. Half an hour before the end of the Captain's watch, three figures loomed into the bright circle of the fire: the Suliots who were supposed to be sleeping. Two of them, Cosmo and Zander, had been with Trelawny since he'd recruited them in Ionia. The third was a newcomer. Trelawny stood up, put his hands on the butts of his pistols, and positioned himself between Fanny and the men. They stopped some yards from the Captain, respectful but agitated. They'd been out on the grazing land, Cosmo explained, where the shots had been fired. They'd found their dead comrades. Trelawny affected surprise. The Suliots made no accusations and demanded no explanations. It was simply time for them to return to Athens, Cosmo said, with the Kapetan's permission if possible, without it if necessary. The three Suliots who were mounting guard loomed into the bright circle round the fire, backing their colleagues. Trelawny offered them a hundred *piastres* extra if they stayed with him till Salona. They refused. Trelawny wanted to know how they planned to travel.

'We have horses.'

'They're Lord Darcy's horses, all of them,' Trelawny flared.

Fanny stood up. 'Captain Trelawny,' she said. 'Let them take the horses. And let them go in peace.'

Trelawny bridled.

'In *peace*,' Fanny repeated.

She was right, he realised. Six wakeful Suliots against him: Fanny and a sleeping camp on his side. 'Take the horses,' he said. 'And go. Now.'

The men still hesitated.

'You, Kapetan?' Zander asked tentatively. 'You go Athina? Now?'

'No,' the Captain replied, understanding the fear behind the question. 'I'll never go to Athens again. You're quite safe.'

'Never?' Zander repeated. If the Kapetan returned to Athina and spoke with his frenn the Lord Governor…

Fanny too perceived the danger: the Suliots would be well advised to dispose of the Captain here and now rather than risk his return to Athens in a few months' time. 'Never,' she repeated firmly. 'The Captain is coming back to England with me. I have money there, a big house and a farm. He has no reason to stay in Greece.'

'But you?' Zander said suspiciously. 'You have man in Athina. Priest man. Black crow man.'

'I'm not his wife,' Fanny said resolutely. 'I'm his…'

The men waited, curious to know her relationship with the raven of the consulate.

'…his cousin,' Fanny concluded. 'Now, you have your horses. Why don't you go?'

Chapter 11

A MISTAKE

The next morning broke as a spring morning should break in the foothills of Mount Parnassus.

'*Lovely Dawn[96] with her rosy fingers,*' Captain Trelawny quoted wearily, gazing at the eastern horizon. After the Suliots had pulled out, only Stavros had slept. Now it was time to eat, strike camp, and move on. They planned to move fast that day, pushing on to Thebes or even to Salona, if luck and the roads were favourable. Despite the urgency, however, vital, matutinal matters required attention. With these matters in mind, the women split into two shifts: The first shift, Jane, Catherine Tilney and Emma, would avail themselves of the privacy of the copse while the other three helped the menfolk strike camp.

A few minutes after they'd disappeared among the trees, Jane and Emma ran back into the camp screaming, Jane well ahead. She fell into her father's arms panting and trying to gasp out what had happened.

'Men,' she cried. 'Soldiers.'

'How many?'

'Four. Five.'

'What did they want?'

'Me.'

'You?'

'They said "We want woman call *Jane*".'

'Are you sure?'

'Mrs Tilney said, *I'm Jane*, and they took her.'

Emma caught up, floundering for breath. 'They took Tilney,' she panted. 'Soldiers. Looking for Jane.'

Galloping hooves stormed down the road a hundred yards away: the gang that had taken Tilney was heading back to Athens. Trelawny and Stavros sprinted to the edge of the hollow in time to see a thunderous cloud of dust, gilded by the first rays of the sun, disappear round the curve of the road. How many men? How many horses? How was Tilney secured? The dust obscured the details.

Trelawny sent Stavros back to the others and stood alone for a moment, transfixed. Had Odysseus sent men for Jane? It had to be Odysseus. Who else could it be? Had the Lord Governor gone insane? Then, with a sudden insight, Trelawny saw yesterday's exodus, and his own part in it, as Odysseus must have seen it: Trelawny, or so Odysseus must have thought, had spirited Jane out of Athens and taken her to a place where she was exposed and vulnerable, to a place where she might easily be snatched. And Odysseus had snatched her, brutally and expertly. Only one detail had gone adrift: his brainless Ithakans had taken Tilney by mistake.

When Tilney arrived in Athens, the Lord Governor's fury would be nightmarish. But Trelawny himself? His bargain with Odysseus: Jane for Tersitza? Where did that stand? Odysseus almost certainly believed that his prospective brother-in-law had kept his word. His dear Edgardo had readied Jane for collection: he'd camped in an undefended place, dismissed the escort, and allowed Jane to wander off with only her governess and the Consul's wife to watch over her. What more could he possibly have done? What more? Nothing. And that *nothing* resolved, more or less, the uncertainty that had troubled the Captain since his fateful words in the Venetian Tower: *Tell Tersitza tonight. She's to be my bride, before midsummer.*

He heaved a sigh of anticipation and relief: *terra firma* lay ahead. Although Jane Darcy was still free and likely to remain so, the fault lay not with Trelawny. Trelawny had played his part, and nothing now prevented him from claiming Tersitza and her share of the English treasure. And to crown his luck, Fanny Bertram had, the night before, brought their dalliance to a natural and convenient end. He set off back to the camp almost ready to whistle a hornpipe.

He caught up with Stavros, and they strode back together into the circle. General Darcy was announcing their next move: decamp immediately, and fly for Salona.

'I'm sorry to disagree, ma'am.' It was Marianne, suddenly tough as a farm cat and ready for a fight. 'We can't just forget about Catherine. Leastways *I* can't.'

'You think we should rescue her from a troop of horsemen?' Elizabeth's tone was icy.

'Of course, we *should*,' Marianne retorted. 'The problem is, we can't.'

'What then?'

'What Catherine did, ma'am,' Marianne's tone edged toward sarcasm, 'saved your daughter's life. I don't know exactly why Odysseus was after her, but I think we can all guess. Whatever lies behind it all, Jane is still with us. Thank God.'

Everyone looked at Jane as though to verify her existence. The girl clung now to Fanny Bertram who was holding her much as Catherine Tilney had done and whispering words of assurance.

'But Catherine,' Marianne pressed on. 'Catherine is gone.'

'I'm fully aware of the facts,' Elizabeth replied sourly. 'But there's nothing, absolutely nothing I can do. Nothing.'

'Not you, ma'am. Me.'

'You?'

'Yes, ma'am. You may have given her up, but I still see some hope for Catherine. Not much, but some.'

'Hope? Where?' Mr Darcy asked quickly. Catherine Tilney was his servant, and, just as he'd failed his servants on the *Pemberley*, he'd failed her. Shamefully. He was in dire need of hope.

'With the Consul, sir,' Marianne replied. 'With Mr Knightley. If word can be got to him, he can talk to Odysseus.'

'But yesterday,' Mr Darcy objected, 'you said if we went back to Athens, we'd disappear.'

'If we *all* went back together: we couldn't hide that. But if *one* of us sneaks back to Athens…? If I took the wain on my own, who would suspect me? And of what?'

'It would be an appalling risk,' Mr Darcy replied thoughtfully. Since their first meeting in the consulate, he had largely ignored the existence of Marianne Brandon. And now she was offering to *sneak back to Athens* and save the unfortunate Tilney. 'You think there's a chance?' he asked, his voice awakening with anticipation.

'Yes, but we must be quick,' Marianne replied. 'They were off at a gallop.'

'They won't keep that up for long,' Trelawny broke in. 'Last week we bought every decent horse in Athens, apart from Odysseus's roan. With luck, Marianne might even get to Knightley before Tilney's soldiers are back in Athens…'

'Never,' Mr Darcy agreed. 'The wain's too slow for that.'

'Hitch up our best horses?' Trelawny suggested.

'No.' It was Fanny's turn now. 'If you take that wain too fast over a bump, it will fall to pieces.'

'I think you're right,' Trelawny agreed with her.

'I have another idea,' Fanny said, stepping forward and addressing herself solely to Mr Darcy.

No one said anything. Mr Darcy nodded: he was listening, though his hope was fading.

'Catherine did something very brave,' Fanny began. 'She saved Jane's life as far as I can see. And now we must save hers. I hope you'd do the same for me if I was where Catherine is now – or where she's going to be in an hour or two.' She paused for agreement.

'Go on,' Mr Darcy said, not quite ready to see his salvation in the Chaplain's wife. 'Please.'

'Well, it's Marianne's idea really,' Fanny replied. 'A quick dash to Athens, a few words with Mr Knightley, and a dash back here. I can do it. Give me enough money to bribe the guards at the checkpoints. And let me ride the big grey. She wasn't worked hard yesterday.'

There may have been tears in Mr Darcy's eyes as he listened.

'So may I ride her?' Fanny asked. Again the question was to Mr Darcy: only he could take the decision.

'Damn plucky of you, Mrs Bertram,' he said. 'I can't tell you how grateful I am.'

'It's just a horse-ride,' Fanny replied modestly, a little startled, perhaps, at her own words. A helter-skelter run to Athens was far more than *just a horse-ride*. There would be danger at every bend in the road. Then she foresaw with the acuteness of a waking dream, that her half-hour in the consulate might easily be her last. Most harrowing of all, a final question assailed her: how much of her bravado was sparked by Trelawny's heartless rejection, *I haven't thought that far ahead?*

'What we'll do is this: Fanny will go,' Mr Darcy decided. 'The rest of us will stay here.'

'Me?' Stavros asked hopefully, still unsure of his welcome.

'You stay,' Mr Darcy told him. 'We need you here.'

Stavros nodded.

'Fanny will take the mare.' He hesitated: 'We can pad out the saddle with one of the capes.'

Fanny nodded gratefully.

'Now let's get her on the road.' Mr Darcy hurried off to find the mare where he'd hobbled her the night before.

'You'll be in Athens this afternoon,' Trelawny calculated,

reasserting his authority. 'And back here by mid-day tomorrow. We'll wait till the following morning, till Sunday.'

'Wait where? Not here?' Fanny questioned.

'No, it's too dangerous here. Specially for Jane. Half an hour up the road, there's a good place to hide. That's what you said yesterday, Stavros? Right?'

'Not right. Is left,' Stavros corrected him. 'Is ruin chapel. St Emilios. Just bell-tower. And track left. Narrow, very narrow. It go ravine.'

'To the left? You mean to the west?' Fanny confirmed.

'I disagree,' Elizabeth Darcy broke in, putting all her remaining authority into her words. 'We are not going to wait. We shall proceed to Salona. Mrs Bertram can catch us up there.'

'No.' Three simultaneous female voices countermanded Mrs Darcy's order.

'We'll wait in the ravine, Mamma,' Jane said quietly. 'For Fanny.'

'We'll keep a lookout for you, Fanny,' the Captain added. 'At the chapel. Don't get lost.'

In twenty minutes, the mare was watered and ready. The Captain gave Fanny the bandolier he wore under his shirt. Gold and silver: all the money he had with him, in fact more or less all he had in the world. She extracted from the belt two *piastres* for each barrier on the road back to Athens. She added a *piastre* or two more, dropped the handful of silver into her unfamiliar, masculine pocket, and buckled the bandolier under her shirt. Trelawny handed her the safe conduct signed by Odysseus, but he gave her no written message for the Consul: they all agreed it was too dangerous. Then he hugged her for a second. 'Come back safe,' he whispered. 'And in Athens…'

'What?'

'…stay clear of harm.'

Fanny broke away. She knew exactly what he meant. What gave him the right to say things like that? She'd asked him, *Will you go back to England? Ever?* It was the plainest offer a woman could make, and he'd turned her down. The Captain was toying with her. If she wanted to talk to Edmund…! Of course she didn't want to talk to Edmund. She would avoid Edmund like typhoid fever! But if she wanted to, she would: the Captain be damned.

The others hugged Fanny in turn, Elizabeth Darcy with especial warmth. 'Good luck,' she said. 'We'll wait for you. In the ravine. Then we'll ride to Salona together. All of us.' Elizabeth would have found an apology awkward, but her words were a plea for forgiveness, and they all knew it.

'All of us,' Fanny repeated, and she was gone. Stavros guided the others to the ravine. The remains of a chapel stood by the road, as he had said, and a shady track led up through a wood of twisted cork oak, scrubby pine and holly. A feeble stream beside the track oozed from one boggy pool to the next. The cartwheels left all-too-obvious ruts through the mud: with an effort, they manoeuvred the cart off the track and among the trees. They disguised the cart with branches, and the ruts with dead leaves. They'd camp half a mile further up the ravine. Stavros knew a good place.

Once their simple camp was set up, the four women and three men who remained of the initial convoy sat round a low fire watching the midday stew seethe in its pot. A promising, spring sun flickered through the branches above them.

'Why?' Mr Darcy asked. 'Why is Odysseus sending men to find Jane?' He glanced at Jane. She couldn't hear the question: she was combing out and plaiting the mane of Fanny's horse, making it fine for when she got back. Deliberately Mr Darcy studied the circle of faces round the fire. There was a long silence. No one wanted to reply, though the same thought was running through all their minds.

'Men…' Emma Knightley began at length, but stopped with a shrug.

'You think that's what it is?' Mr Darcy prompted.

'Once or twice I caught him glancing…' Emma tried again.

'Yes,' Mrs Darcy agreed. 'I think we all had our suspicions.'

'Well I certainly had none,' her husband rejoined. Women! The proverb was right: you had to get up early in the morning to stay ahead of a woman.

Emma exchanged a quick look with Elizabeth. *Husbands! Blind as bats and obstinate as mules.*

'Though we did all wonder about *you*, Trelawny,' Mr Darcy added. 'At least when you first showed up. The poetic privateer! Shelley, Byron! And God knows who else. But that seems to be over.'

'The wondering? The poetry? Or the privateering?' the Captain replied, hiding discomfort under half-hearted banter.

'All three, I hope,' Mr Darcy replied. 'But, you're a friend of Odysseus. Did he ever say anything? Let anything slip?'

'Certainly not, or I'd have mentioned it. Of course, I would. Anything else…' Too much denial? Methinks the pirate doth protest too much. Best keep his gun-port closed and his powder dry.

Emma grimaced but kept her thoughts to herself. She'd seen the flare-up between the Captain and Fanny just as Fanny was leaving. What was the man up to? Time would tell. But whatever twists and turns Time might finally unveil, Trelawny and Odysseus had been thick as thieves, and probably they still were.

Jane finished her plaiting and joined the now silent circle round the fire. As she sat cross-legged among the dead leaves, isolated and anxious, tears began to stream down her face. Elizabeth, who was sitting on the other side of the fire, glanced at her daughter and opened her mouth to say something. Then she saw the look on her husband's face. Tilney was gone, Fanny Bertram was gone, and Jane was without comfort. Darcy longed to console his daughter, that was miserably obvious. Somehow though, he couldn't stand up, walk the three paces that separated him from his child, and take her in his arms. Why was it so hard for men to show what was in their hearts?

Something in Elizabeth Darcy broke. All morning she'd reproached herself on Catherine Tilney's account. It was true what everyone thought: she'd abandoned Tilney immediately, given her up as lost, without regret and without a pang of conscience. How Marianne, loud, fat, impoverished Marianne, had put her to shame! And Fanny Bertram, a nobody with no past and no future, she'd jumped on a horse and ridden into the lion's den without a second's thought. Elizabeth gathered her courage. She walked round the fire to where Jane was sitting and knelt beside her. She took Jane's hand and gave it a little squeeze. If Jane rejected her… But no. She felt Jane's fingers tighten on hers for a second. With a quick gesture, Jane brushed her sleeve across her eyes, banishing her tears.

'There's no shame in crying,' Elizabeth whispered. 'I'm sorry… I…' She had so much to regret, that she was lost for a place to begin.

Jane looked hard into her mother's eyes, trying to fathom her mood. Then, 'I do try to be brave, Mamma,' she said. 'But what happened this morning… I know it's wrong, but I get so frightened.'

'So do I,' Elizabeth confessed. 'I think we're all scared out of our wits. Me especially.'

Jane grasped her mother's hand in both of hers. 'But you don't show it,' she said.

'Perhaps that's my mistake.'

'I want to be more like you, Mamma,' Jane whispered. 'Help me.'

On an impulse, Elizabeth raised Jane's hand to her lips and kissed it. 'The Captain says we have to post a lookout,' she said. 'Down by the chapel. For Fanny. When she comes back.'

'Yes.'

'Shall we go down together? This afternoon?'

'Yes,' Jane whispered. 'Just the two of us.' She glanced at her father. He was smiling at her, smiling at her and her mother. Despite their troubles, it was a warmer, more intimate smile than she'd seen on his face since the day they sailed out of Genoa.

Lunch was over. Perhaps it was already time for Elizabeth and Jane to go down to the chapel. They cornered the Captain. 'How long before Fanny gets back?' Elizabeth asked him. The Captain looked at them and smiled. They were an odd couple. Jane made a convincing boy, slender and strong-featured. Her mother, countrified and uncouth, had taken Jane's arm as though Jane were indeed a young man, a very young man, an inch or so shorter than his frumpish female companion.

'We're thirty miles from Athens,' he replied.

'It took us the whole of yesterday,' Elizabeth said.

'Fanny will be much quicker. That mare she's riding can canter fifteen miles in an hour.'

'But not for long.'

'No. At a trot she'll be half as fast. And she'll have to stop at the barriers.'

'So, the earliest she could be back is…this afternoon,' Elizabeth calculated.

'It's possible, but tomorrow is more likely. Who knows what she'll find in Athens?'

'It's Friday now,' Elizabeth said. 'We said we'd move on to Salona…'

'…on Sunday morning.'

'Will you take me and Jane down to the chapel? Now if you like. We'll keep the first watch for her.'

'Of course,' the Captain agreed. 'And Jane! Don't forget your pistols.'

'I should have had them with me this morning,' she said.

'No,' Trelawny said. 'That's the first rule: never get into a fight you can't win.'

'And the second rule?' Jane asked, suddenly cheeky, and glancing at her mother.

'The second rule is almost the same,' he improvised. 'Never win a fight when losing might be more profitable.'

'Sometimes it's best to lose?' Jane asked.

'Ask your mother. She must have lost some interesting battles in her time.'

Elizabeth said nothing. The Captain was right, of course, but even so the phrase *in her time* rankled. Just because she was dressed as an old woman…

'Shall we go now?' Jane asked.

'Take a canteen of water and some bread,' the Captain said. 'And make sure Mr Darcy knows where you're going.'

The Captain found them a good place to watch the road, a low cliff behind the dilapidated bell-tower, thick with dead thistles, foxgloves and cockleburs from the summer before. He smeared Jane's hands and face with mud so they wouldn't flash white in the sun. A farm cart drawn by a single ox creaked its way past them along the road. Crouching among the foliage, they were invisible.

'You'll hear Fanny coming before you see her,' the Captain said. 'When you're sure it's her, check that she's on her own. Then give a whistle so she knows you're here.'

'Whistle?' Elizabeth asked. 'How?'

For ten minutes, the Captain showed the two women how to whistle with their fingers in their mouths. Elizabeth gave up, but Jane soon acquired the knack: it was something her brothers had been able to do for years, though they'd always refused to teach her. Her brothers! She hadn't thought of them for weeks. If she practised enough, she'd be able to whistle ten times louder than them when she got back to Pemberley. Then, promising that they'd be relieved at dusk, the Captain left them.

The road was not busy. Occasionally a mule, a donkey, or a two-wheeled cart headed downhill toward Eleusis. If there was a load, it was firewood or chickens in bast panniers: the pillaged countryside had little else to offer. Once a troop of a dozen riders jingled past them uphill, making for Thebes.

It was a long while since Jane and her mother had gossiped together. When Jane was still small enough to fit comfortably on her mother's lap, they'd often chatted or read a story together, but those days were long past. In a way, Jane's Aunt Wickham, Elizabeth's sister Lydia, had come between them. Lydia had never been welcome at Pemberley, though she'd invited herself occasionally to stay with her rich sister. Wickham usually stayed away. During these visits, Lydia had still been, at least in the afternoons, the same cheerful romp as always. Most evenings, after dinner, she'd fuddled her head with drink, spending her mornings in bed nursing the headache. But in the afternoons, she'd been funny, cavorting Aunt Wickham, and little Jane had adored her. Seeing this, Elizabeth had warned Jane against too much frolicking with her aunt, a warning the child had not understood. Like any careful mother, Elizabeth had taken alarm. The devil that drove Lydia also threatened Jane: a devil like that would have to be exorcised. Where Lydia had been irremediably spoilt, Jane would be directed toward sobriety, gentility and virtue. Until she'd employed Tilney as Jane's governess, however, Elizabeth had done little to direct her daughter, beyond tut-tutting at some of her words and many of her actions. Such a drizzle of disapproval would alienate any child. Luckily, Pemberley was a large house, the park was enormous, and Jane had her pony, her father and her brothers to amuse her. If all else failed, there were books of all kinds in the library and countless hiding places in which to read them. In general Jane had no difficulty avoiding her mother. In fact, the two of them had seen more of each other in Italy and Greece than they'd seen in the previous two years. And now they sat together in the spring sunshine watching the road below for a sign of Fanny Bertram, the Chaplain's wife, as they still believed her to be.

'I think you like Fanny more than you did at first,' Jane ventured. 'But still...'

'I feel sorry for her,' Elizabeth replied.

'Why?'

'Well, her husband's in Athens for a start.'

'She wanted him to stay. I think she's perfectly happy about it.'

'Yes, she is. That's what I was thinking: how sad it is when a wife's happy about leaving her husband behind.'

'You're sorry for her because she's happy. That doesn't make sense.'

'You're right, it doesn't,' Elizabeth agreed. 'Very little does. Or hadn't you noticed?'

Jane giggled. 'What do you think it would be like? Marrying a priest, like Fanny did?'

'I had a priest propose to me once,' Elizabeth replied. 'Years ago.'

'Who was he?' It was a serious question. Jane was mildly shocked: her mother had had a life before she became Elizabeth Darcy!

'His name was Collins.'

'What was his first name?'

'I don't remember.'

'He proposed to you, and you don't remember his name?'

'It was probably Servilius, Sycophanticus or Obsequius. Something like that. He's Lady Catherine's chaplain at Rosings.'

'I know who you mean. Papa says he has a wax nose.'[97]

'What on earth does he mean by that?' It was a vulgar expression, but Elizabeth knew exactly what it meant.

'Probably he takes too much snuff,' Jane replied.

'Probably.'

'So, what was his name? Really?'

'William.'

'And why didn't you accept him?'

'I'd rather die an old maid than marry a man with a wax nose,' she replied with a smile.

'And you preferred Papa, of course.'

'Not at all. As far as I was concerned, they were as bad as each other.'

'But you *married* Papa.'

'I changed my mind about him.'

'When?'

It was a question Elizabeth had been asked more than once before. 'When I first saw Pemberley. When do you think, you little goose?' The answer was hardly romantic, but then Elizabeth was sure her daughter would not believe her.

'No it wasn't, Mamma. Tell it properly.'

By the time dusk had closed in and Stavros had relieved them of their watch, Jane knew her mother's simple, though not unexciting story, and she'd told Elizabeth everything she knew about the Bertrams.

Jane and her mother had been back in the camp for about an hour when the jingling of harness and the snort of a horse that smells rest alerted them. It was Stavros and Fanny. She was leading the grey mare, horse and rider both stumbling with exhaustion. Catherine Tilney was not with them.

Fanny told an incoherent tale in spasms and out of sequence: she'd ridden into Athens, bribing her way past the barriers. She hadn't needed the safe conduct. On the road, she'd seen nothing of Tilney or of Tilney's kidnappers. Nothing of Cosmo. Nothing of the Suliots. She'd reached the consulate and explained to Mr Knightley what had happened. He'd gone immediately to the Venetian Tower. She'd waited for him in case there was news of Catherine. The Consul had stayed away for several hours. When he'd returned to the consulate, he'd told Fanny what had happened. A few minutes after he'd reached the tower, he explained, Catherine and her captors had arrived at the citadel. For a while Odysseus had been too angry to speak. Then, slowly, everything had fallen into place: Catherine was to stay in the citadel till Mr Knightley could get her a passage on the *Hind*, or on any English warship. Fanny's job was done, and she'd ridden back to their camp as fast as the grey mare could carry her. That was all.

That was all she *told*, but there was a great deal more, much of which Fanny kept to herself for many years.

Chapter 12

THE SHOT

Chapter 12 is crossed through in the original manuscript. A note in Hawkins' hand reads: NOT TO BE PRINTED UNDER ANY CIRCUMSTANCES. The conversation between Fanny Bertram and Captain Trelawny in Chapter 13 is similarly excised. Making public the information contained in these pages would obviously have incriminated Fanny Bertram. On the other hand, without this information, the subsequent narrative makes little or no sense. This conflict may well be the reason that Jane and the Jackal *was not fully edited and published in Hawkins' lifetime. Eds.*

Before he rushed off to the citadel, Mr Knightley told his cook to put food on the table for Mrs Bertram: she'd eaten nothing since the day before, and there would be no meals in the consulate until breakfast next day: Colonel Stanhope and young Humphreys had ridden that morning to Piraeus to take stock of its defences, and Mr Knightley was invited to sup with the French consul. Ten minutes after the Consul had gone, the cook, grumbling under her breath, brought bread and wine and most of a cold leg of lamb on a platter: Fanny should help herself.

'I'm sorry, but there's no carving knife,' Fanny said, smiling and miming the carving of meat. The cook disappeared and returned a moment later with a carving knife and fork, heavy, bone-handled, and well worn.

As Fanny began to carve the lamb, the knife in one hand and the fork in the other, her husband entered the room. 'I know why you're here,' he said without greeting. The bitter anger that had gripped him the day before in the stable-yard was no less acerbic now. 'It's about Tilney.'

'Were you listening at the door?' Fanny put down the knife, leaving the sturdy, two-pronged fork stuck in the meat.

'When *my* employer talks to my *wife*, I have a right to listen. Or don't I?' His voice had sunk to a growl. There was a new, threatening note in it, yet somehow, buoyed by her new-found freedom, Fanny ignored the warning.

'Edmund. Let's try to understand each other once and for all: I'm not your wife.'

'Will you…! Will you stop saying that?' His words had a sudden shrillness in them, a nervousness that, in a woman, would be called hysteria. 'Understand each other! It's your duty to understand *me*! Me, do you hear? Me!'

'I do understand you, Edmund. You believe we're married, and I can understand why. But you ask for more than my understanding: you seem to demand my agreement.'

Ever since Fanny had known him, Edmund had sulked when things went badly. After they'd abandoned Thornton Lacey and set off for Greece, she'd watched with grief as his sulks degenerated into spleen and vindictiveness. Not that he behaved spitefully to *everyone* around him. He seldom appeared as the dyed-in-the-grain bully she knew him to be. A mistake by a porter, an imagined slight by a stranger, a rebuke by Mr Knightley: outwardly Edmund kept his composure and avoided scenes, but as soon as they were alone, he unleashed his rancour on his wife. He jeered at her and shoved her this way and that, though he seldom shouted, fearful that someone might hear him. Instead, he hissed out his words like a snake spitting venom. Once, not long after they'd arrived in Athens, he'd slapped her across the face, backward and forward till her head was dizzy. She'd warned him, if he did that again, it would be the end. And had he done it again? In fact he had. In response, Fanny had started to pack her trunk and threatened to explain to the Consul exactly why she was leaving Athens. That had frightened him, and she'd forced from him a promise not to exercise in future what he stoutly maintained were his rights. His rights! It was his perfect right to give her a good slapping, he insisted: in fact, it was his husbandly *duty* when she needed correction.[98]

He could do what he liked to her, short of killing her outright. And, as it turned out, his promise was no sooner given than it was broken, though perhaps with a shade less violence. This was, as she'd learned from many a long-suffering prisoner, the way of the world. But did it comply with the law of the land? She simply didn't know.

During her solitary ride back to the consulate, Fanny had mulled over the risk of meeting Edmund. With luck she might avoid him altogether. Failing that, he might be calm enough to talk reasonably. Might. But if the worst came to the worst? For this eventuality, she'd formed a plan, worked out a lie that would put an end to Edmund's claim on her once and for all. The lie was ready, if she needed it. In fact, if his *Me, do you hear?* was anything to go by, she would certainly need it, and heaven knew what beside. Edmund, it seemed, was on the verge of a nervous catastrophe. And yet, despite everything, her heart went out to him. After all, they had lived together since her childhood. He had never made her his wife, but she had promised before God *to obey him and serve him, love, honour and keep him in sickness and in health.* He was suffering and close to despair. He was menacing, but at the same time, and in greater measure, he was pathetic. Perhaps she should stay in Athens? For a while at least? Find a nurse for him? Help him?

'I do not *believe* we are married,' he picked up her words. 'We *are* married. Do I have to knock it into your stupid head? Because if I must, I will. And with a vengeance.'

Again, Edmund went about things the wrong way: if he'd found some words of conciliation, if he'd simply kept silent, then Fanny, who was trembling with indecision, might perhaps have stayed with him and tended his needs through whatever lay ahead.

'I've made you tremble,' he hissed. 'But not as much as you'll tremble when I'm done with you. I'm going to make you wish you'd never been born.'

His words, but even more his vicious tone, tipped the balance. It was time for her saving lie. 'A judge can annul a marriage like ours,' she said quietly. 'I shall apply to the court in Korfu as soon as I get there.' She'd planned and polished these words and tried to predict the replies he might make.

'You dare not,' he struck back. 'And we both know why.'

Defiance and blank rejection: of all the responses he could have made, this was the most probable. She knew what had to come next.

'Because I can't prove my virginity?' she asked calmly.

'Exactly.'

She was ready: 'But I can,' she said, almost without emphasis.

'You're insane,' he gasped. 'You belong in the madhouse.'

'Listen, Edmund. What I told you before we got married, I thought it was true.'

'It *was* true.'

'You don't know that. You thought it was true because *I* thought it was true. But I never saw a doctor, did I? Never.' By a stroke of good fortune, all he knew of Mary Crawford's doctor in Northampton was the prescription for beef tea: the lie was safe. So far, the conversation was running just as she'd anticipated.

'What are you saying?' His face was tight with malice, livid one second and purple the next.

Fanny waited, weighing her words. 'Listen Edmund. Listen

carefully. Before Catherine Tilney went out as a governess, she was trained as a midwife. I think you know that already.' Fanny tried to keep her voice low and calm, but her husband's rage began to confuse her.

'Midwife!' he cried, the howl of a beast caught in an iron trap.

'She examined me. Last night.' Her voice rose: she couldn't keep it down. 'Despite what I thought, I *am* a virgin. I can prove it. And if necessary, I will.' For Fanny, this was the weak point in her story: where, and how, in the wilds of Boeotia had Catherine examined her? Luckily Edmund was too enraged to see the weakness.

'Liar!' he yelped.

'You can scream all you like,' she jeered, suddenly vindictive in her turn. 'But you're wrong.'

'Wrong? How can I be wrong? What you told me? Was that a lie too? Like all your other lies?' He began to rage in words that made no sense, the words of a madman.

She heard the madness, but still she did not pull back: the urge to goad him was too strong to resist. 'That's why I came back to save Catherine! Because she saved me from a nightmare! She saved me from you!'

'Nightmare! I'll give you nightmares,' Edmund snarled. Stung beyond bearing he rushed at the table. He snatched up the carving knife, grabbed Fanny by her hair, and put the point of the knife to her throat. 'Stand up,' he ordered. He wasn't screeching now: his words were suddenly controlled and menacing. He had a plan.

She stood up.

'Take off those ridiculous breeches and whatever you're wearing underneath.' He spat at her, showering her face with spittle.

'You can't even spit properly,' she said recklessly, her voice cold but her mind collapsing into panic. 'Let me go, or I'll shout for the servants.'

He jerked the knife inexpertly against the skin of her neck. Blood spurted: she could feel it escaping, wet under her collar.

The trickle of blood spurred her fear: her defiance coarsened till it threatened her ruin. 'What are you going to do? Rape me? You, Edmund? You'd better get a *man* to help you!'

Outrageous as they were, her words seemed to calm him: his face became suddenly more concentrated, and he began to argue in his tedious, dogmatic way, as though this were a day like any other, and he had no knife at her bleeding throat. 'It's my perfect right,' he said, 'except it isn't called *rape*. You're my wife. Husbands can't rape their wives. Whatever a man does to his wife, it's allowed.'

'Not everything, Edmund.' She tried to match his tone, to divert his mad anger.

'Yes, Fanny. You told me about it. Remember? That woman in Northampton gaol. She made a fool of her husband, just like you make a fool of me, in front of Knightley, in front of everybody. And this man, he decided to teach his wife a lesson. A painful lesson. Exceedingly painful. And afterward she tried to pay him back, with a bowl of boiling water, or so you told me.'

'Yes, exactly,' she agreed. Edmund trying to argue was less immediately threatening than Edmund hacking at her throat with a carving knife. 'Boiling water.'

'And in the end *she* went to gaol,' Edmund concluded. 'Not him. That means I can teach you a lesson.[99] Anyhow I like. You know that as well as I do.'

'Maybe you're right!' she conceded. 'Maybe I deserve a lesson.' The knife was still at her throat. Even though he'd believed her lie, things had gone from bad to desperate. Anything, anything, anything to get the knife off her throat and his hands off her body.

'Yes, a lesson!' he agreed, his voice rising to a sudden snarl. 'The lesson you deserve. That thing there.' He nodded at the huge, double-pronged fork stuck into the leg of lamb. She strained to see what he was looking at. 'It would be a lesson, wouldn't it, if I…'

She glimpsed the fork and gasped with fear. 'Edmund. Calm down,' she said. 'We can talk. Edmund, talk to me. Tell me what I've done wrong. Help me understand.'

He jerked the knife again. This time Fanny felt more blood trickle and a sharp pain. 'Edmund,' she said. 'Edmund, please.'

'So now it's *Edmund please*, is it? Dear Edmund, kind Edmund, Edmund my husband.' She felt the knife slice again across the flesh of her throat, and blood spurt from the new cut.

'Now,' Edmund said, with the soft reasoning of insanity. 'As you know, my dear, God forbids women to wear trowsers.'[100]

'Of course, Edmund. Trowsers. Breeches. Take off the abominable breeches,' she repeated, a frantic awkwardness gripping her fingers as she fumbled with the buckle of her belt. 'Whatever you say. You're always right. You know everything. Do what you tell me. Yes. I must. And I will. Just give me more space.'

'So I know everything, do I?' he grinned wildly. 'I certainly know why you want more space. And the answer is *no*. I like this knife exactly where it is. For the first time in your life you're doing exactly what I tell you.'

For the first time in her life…! He was spouting insanity, beside himself with sick rage. Nothing she could possibly say would reach him now. 'I like this knife,' he repeated, twisting it a little in the new wound it had made. 'I like it.' And he *did* like it: she felt his liking in the filthy, gloating tone of his voice. This surely was the onset of the insane violence of which she had often heard but which she had never witnessed. With a last shudder of self-control, she choked back her scream of revulsion and denial. She had two cap-lock pistols lodged in her belt. Her right hand, invisible to him, found the butt of one of them. Grip it, she told herself. Calm down. Calm down and get it out of the holster. No mistakes now. Cock. And fire.

The explosion was shattering. It drove them apart. For Fanny, it was like a vicious punch in the belly. For Edmund Bertram, it was a consummation, the shears of Atropos.[101] Cutting him free. The bullet hacked through his entrails and shattered his backbone. He fell to the floor screaming, not beseeching heaven to forgive his sins, but calling down the wrath of God on the hell-hound he had married.

Fanny heard the curse. It cleared her mind for a few critical seconds. She ran to the tall veranda window, flung it open, and fired her second shot into the empty yard. The servants were now hammering on the dining-room door, alarmed by the shots, but too scared to enter the room.

Fanny's neck was trickling blood, but she ignored it. She skirted Edmund's crippled, still cursing body, hurried to the dining-room door and flung it open. 'Fetch a doctor,' she ordered. 'Quickly.'

Edmund died ten minutes later. After watching his last agony, Fanny stood above him saying nothing. Her right hand rested uncertainly on the butt of her second pistol: her left hand now pressed a table napkin to her wound, wet and bloody but somehow numb. The doctor arrived, a Greek from three streets away. Mother Yeter offered to translate. With the help of the old woman and the cook, the doctor laid out Edmund's broken body on the dining-room table. With that done, he turned his attention to Fanny: what should he do about the wounds in her neck? He gave her two choices: cauterisation with a red-hot iron or stitching with catgut. She chose the stitches.[102] When the wounds were closed, he doused them with brandy: alcohol sometimes prevented suppuration, he told her, though nobody knew why.

The Consul returned from the Akropolis in a good mood, entering the consulate by the veranda door, just as the doctor was preparing to dress Fanny's fearsome-looking wounds. The Consul glanced from Fanny to the bloody corpse on the table and back again. For a second shock and revulsion contorted his features. Then he blurted out a single word: 'What...?'

No one replied. With a respectful bow, the doctor began to attend to Fanny's neck. While the doctor was working, the Consul recovered enough of his equanimity to take in the situation: Edmund Bertram was dead and Fanny had been stabbed in the neck. The doctor had already been called and had started work, so Edmund had been shot perhaps half an hour ago. As consul, what should he do? First, he realised, he should help Fanny. He should stay calm and wait for her to explain. At the moment, with the doctor dressing her throat, she couldn't say a word. Perhaps she would never… Better not speculate. Better sit down and wait.

The wait was not long. As soon as the doctor was finished, Fanny turned to him, partly in expectation, partly in despair. Ever since the doctor's arrival, she had been rehearsing in her mind a story, a narrative of Edmund's death that would neither blacken his name irremediably nor brand her as a killer. 'Shall I tell you what happened?' she asked.

'If you feel strong enough,' the Consul replied gently. 'But don't strain your voice.' He nursed a painful memory from Donwell days: a fight between two scythe hands, a throat injury that left one of them dumb, and an arm injury that cost the other his left hand.

'I'll be fine,' she said, and began her story. Edmund had joined her in the dining room. They had been making plans for Edmund to go with her to Korfu after all. Then two men, not much more than boys, had pushed their way into the house through the veranda door. The door had been left open for fresh air, as so often in springtime. It was open now.

After each step in the story, Mother Yeter translated the information for the doctor, casting her eyes to heaven occasionally, perhaps in disbelief, perhaps in search of a word.

The boys had grabbed her, Fanny continued, put the carving knife to her throat, and demanded that Edmund give them all the money in the house. She had drawn a pistol to defend herself. One of the boys had grabbed it. Heroically, Edmund had flung himself on the boy and taken a bullet in his bowels. Seeing him fall, the boys had panicked, thrown the pistol down, and run off through the stable yard. Fanny had snatched up the pistol and fired after them, but the wicket in the big gate had been open, and the boys had escaped.

Mr Knightley nodded sagely and asked no questions. If this was to be Fanny's story, then so be it. Fanny was a brave woman.

The risk she had taken returning to Athens was extraordinary, and she had taken it solely to save the life of Catherine Tilney. He'd accept her story, incredible though it was. The housebreaking boys were obviously an invention: consulates were simply not invaded by thieves. Fanny and her husband, he surmised, had got into a fight. The damage to Fanny's neck was savage: it implied unforgivable violence on the Chaplain's part. And the Chaplain's injury…? Evidently it had been inflicted by Fanny's pistol fired an inch or two from her husband's body. Back home, George Knightley had been a magistrate, he had some idea of legal and criminal procedures, and he took his responsibilities as consul seriously, but after an initial hesitation he came down irreversibly on Fanny's side. Whatever he could do to protect her, he would do it.

What, then, he asked the doctor… What should they do next? What was the law? Within four days, Mother Yeter translated the answer, they must report the death to the citadel. The doctor would issue a death certificate: two if they wanted a certificate for the family in England. Another point: it would save the consulate and Mrs Bertram a great deal of trouble if the certificate stated that the death was accidental. The doctor cast his eyes speculatively to the ceiling. Which was clearly the case, he added, not quite winking, but almost. Of course, such a certificate would be more expensive. Even so, it was worth the money. The doctor would make it cheaper for poor Mrs Bertram if he could, his heart went out to her in her suffering, but the doctor's guild forbade discounts even in the most distressing circumstances.

Fanny did her best to look inconsolable, though at that moment she was still blazing with anger: anger that shaded into fury when she remembered his filthy threat…, his threat to ravage her with a carving fork. Would he have done it? He'd cut her twice in the throat with the knife: he'd been mad enough for anything. But… But there he was, lying on the table, with his backbone shot away, silenced for ever. She stood up and went to the table, looking down at him, not knowing if tears would flow now that every last issue was resolved between them. And the tears did come. Sobs of relief, remorse, and pity for her wasted years shook her shoulders and forced her to her knees. She began to pray, her lips moving though no sound came from her mouth:

Dear God, he had no time to make his peace with You. Be merciful to him. Be merciful to all of us. Especially to me, for I stand in great need of Your love.

While the doctor left the house and returned with two death certificates and his bill, Fanny knelt still at the table, contemplating the evil she'd done and the evil that had been done to her. She was not striking a balance: nothing could outweigh the sin she'd committed. Finally she stood up, and aimlessly crossed the room to the sideboard where the roast lamb now stood, the carving fork still plunged into the tender meat.

'There's something I feel I should tell you,' the Consul began quietly, seeing her rouse herself from her prayers.

What was coming now? What did the Consul *feel he should tell her*? He'd asked her not a single question. Not one. Because he didn't believe her? The doctor certainly hadn't believed a word of her tarradiddle: asking for extra pay to certify that Edmund's death was an accident! And so sure that he'd get it: *It would save Mrs Bertram a great deal of trouble.*

Fanny nodded to the Consul and made no reply.

'We had words, your husband and I, yesterday,' the Consul explained. 'He addressed some highly offensive words to me, and I felt obliged to dismiss him.'

Fanny trembled with relief: she had expected much worse.

'He didn't seem in his right mind,' the Consul continued. 'He was to work here until Midsummer Day, and then leave.'

'I see,' Fanny said turning her mind quickly to Edmund's dismissal: it certainly explained some part of his vehement despair.

'But, in view of what has happened, I can withdraw the dismissal,' the Consul offered. 'No point in it now. The government will pay his stipend till the year's end. Only £25, but it may help. I know you're not wealthy.'

Whether he believed her or not, Mr Knightley was going to help her. She fell to her knees again and covered her face with her hands. 'But I'm not…,' she sobbed.

I'm not his wife, she was going to say, but she bit back the words along with the sobs that threatened to overwhelm her, letting her mind clear again. As far as the Consul was concerned, she was Edmund's *widow*: nothing could be simpler. *Widow?* In truth, she had never been Edmund's wife, but from now on she would be his *widow*. The picture broadened. For Sir Thomas too? Edmund's father in England? For him too she'd be *Edmund's widow*.

'You're not…?' the Consul prompted, giving her time to recover.

'I'm not penniless,' she ended her sentence, looking up at him.

'You'll need to be thrifty though.'

'You're very kind,' Fanny muttered, with wrenching sincerity. He was a fair-minded man, Mr Knightley: she wished she could tell him the truth.

'Will you stay tonight?' Mr Knightley asked. 'Longer if you wish.'

'Being in Athens frightens me,' she replied, rising to her feet. He extended his hand to help her. 'Does Odysseus know I was the one who rode back?' she asked. 'With the message?'

'No. He didn't ask.'

'Good. Then nobody knows I'm here. Except you.'

'And the doctor. I paid him off by the way. And I sealed one of the certificates with the government seal, while you were…' He gestured at the table.

'Thank you,' she said, leaving her hand resting in his.

'The certificates…?' she muttered.

'One is for you. The other is for his family.'

'In Mansfield Park.'

'Yes.'

'Could you...' She hesitated. 'Could you send it to Sir Thomas? I just don't know what to say to him. Not properly. Not for a while. And he should know straight away. I'm sorry, I'm sorry...'

'I'll write. Willingly. But can you write too, just a few words. I'll put it in with my letter. Otherwise he might think...'

'A few lines. Yes. I'll do it now. Thank you, so much...'

'I'll have your things boxed up and sent to England.'

'Care of Sir Thomas Bertram, Mansfield Park.'

'Northamptonshire. No problem.'

Fanny's heartfelt thanks took shape as a warm but wordless smile.

'He didn't leave a will. I asked him about it yesterday after you all left. The lawyers will have to sort it out. In England.'

'He didn't have anything to leave.'

'Anything else...?'

Yes, there was something else: a small sandalwood box containing some 200 sovereigns in gold. Edmund kept it in his desk. It was her money, but he'd refused to surrender a penny of it to her when she'd left the day before. Mr Knightley helped Fanny break open the desk and retrieve the coins.

'Can I write the note...?' There was ink, pen and paper on Edmund's desk, but Fanny was too squeamish to touch them.

'...in my office,' the Consul offered, seeing her difficulty.

She nodded. He went with her to his desk, sharpened a pen for her, and left her to her work. It was almost an hour before she presented him with a single sheet of paper, open, for him to read.

'And tonight?' Mr Knightley asked folding the letter in two. 'You're welcome to stay here. Or would you prefer to go back? To the others?'

'They're waiting for me. There's nothing more I can do for Catherine, is there? I'll go. Now if I may.'

'You're sure you're strong enough? It's a long ride.'

'I'm stronger than I look,' she replied bravely. 'Don't worry about me.' But she had one last question: 'Was Odysseus terribly angry? When you told him? About Tilney?'

'About Tilney, and about Jane. Yes, he was furious at first, but he got his temper under control: he had no choice really. Then Tilney arrived with the gang who'd seized her.'

'Did you talk to Odysseus? About Jane?'

'No. The subject of Jane is utterly shameful. We just talked about what will happen to Tilney.'

'And what will happen?'

'She'll be fine. She'll be on the first English ship that puts into Piraeus, though that might be months off. A couple of Odysseus's soldiers might not make it through the night, but he won't do anything to Tilney.'

'So, you threatened him with Byron's millions?' Fanny said, struggling to make her voice sound brisk and conspiratorial rather than lost and plaintive.

'Exactly.'

'You saved her life, then.'

'No, Fanny, *you* saved her life.' He paused, heavy with uncertainty. 'You don't think…?' He indicated the dining-room where the body of his unloved, unmourned Chaplain was lying on the table. 'You don't think he should be sent back to England?'

Fanny realised that, as his grief-stricken widow, what happened to her husband's body should have been one of her first concerns. 'I think he should be buried here,' she said with no show of emotion. 'With the Gulf of Korinth closed, it might be difficult…'

'I'll put it in the report.'

'Should I leave you money for the funeral expenses?'

'The Foreign Office can afford to bury its own,' he replied. 'After all, Chaplain Bertram died in the performance of his duties.' A myth was being born: no investigation of the truth would be necessary, now or ever.

'And Odysseus?' Fanny asked, turning toward the door that led to the stable-yard. 'Did he really send those men after Jane?'

'It's an important question.'

'Yes,' Fanny nodded again. 'And if he sent them, why?'

'I suppose we could ask Trelawny,' the Consul mused. 'Odysseus is his friend, in so far as either of them has a friend. But... Even to ask a question like that is to insult a man. And you'd get the same answer whether Trelawny knew anything or not.'

'I think I trust the Captain,' Fanny said, 'for all his being a pirate. I won't ask him any awkward questions.'

'Better that way,' the Consul agreed. 'Though it's a sad fact: in a country like this, with a war going on, a girl anywhere between Jane's age and yours is always vulnerable. So many vile men about.'

'Yes, so many,' Fanny agreed with an involuntary glance at the dining-room door. 'One day, God will be their judge.'

'Perhaps,' the Consul replied. 'Though why God allows what He allows, I've no idea. I can't see much sense in any of it.'

Chapter 13

CONVERGENCE

Despite Fanny's brave words to the Consul, her body was exhausted and her mind was, for a while, painfully confused.

'Can you start for Salona tomorrow?' Mrs Darcy asked, putting a blanket round Fanny's shoulders and then an arm. 'You can ride in the wain if you'd prefer.'

'Wain,' Fanny repeated uncertainly. 'What wain?'

In some of the novels I've been reading, *Wuthering Heights*, for example, the words *What wain?* would be the cue for brain fever[103] and for all manner of non-existent medical exigencies. In Fanny's case, I would simply agree with Marianne Brandon: 'She's tired out, poor love. A good night's sleep, a restful day tomorrow, and we'll see.'

The day's rest meant that it was Sunday 14th March before Mr Darcy and his little troupe set off again for Salona. Naturally, Fanny Bertram was affectionately nursed and pampered by her companions. In fact, their cossetting contributed greatly to her quick recovery: she wasn't used to it, she didn't like it, and she was eager to bring it to an end.

Not until they were well on the road, did Fanny break her silence about Edmund's death. Though nothing loomed larger in her mind, she had not found, at first, the right moment to broach the subject. Then, as her first day of saying nothing blurred into the next, she had no explanation for her silence.

It was Emma Knightley who finally burst the bubble. 'Did you see Edmund by any chance?' she asked bluntly, after a dozen skilful hints and probing questions had produced nothing. At that moment Fanny was riding in the wain with Emma and Elizabeth. Marianne was driving.

'Edmund?' Fanny repeated. 'Yes. I saw him.'

'How is he?'

'How? I don't know how. What can I...? I should have told you before. Edmund... He's dead.'

'Dead? What do you mean dead?' Emma's tone of disbelief was anything but polite but the word itself, and more particularly the way Fanny said it, had, for once, taken the wind out of her sails. Elizabeth was equally startled.

'He's dead,' Fanny repeated in the same wooden voice. Surely the words were plain enough. She floundered for the words a grief-stricken widow might say, but she came up with nothing. She *was* a widow, in a way she *did* grieve for him, but somehow she could not *heave her heart into her mouth*. 'I have his death certificate, if you want to see it,' she said. It was the best she could do, but it sounded inhumanly callous.

'I don't understand. What did he die of?'

'It was an accident. It's on the certificate.' Fanny paused. The image of Edmund's broken body lying on the consular dining table fixed itself in her imagination. An accident? What on earth could she say?

'My dear...' Emma was also floundering: neither the information itself nor Fanny's attitude toward it made sense. And why had Fanny said nothing the evening before when she'd arrived back from Athens?

'If it's too painful, you don't have to talk about it,' Elizabeth said with quiet consideration. 'We understand.'

'I should have told you before. Perhaps I should have put on an armband or something, but...'

'We understand. We understand,' Elizabeth repeated, much to the annoyance of Emma, who understood nothing.

Fanny gathered her strength. She had already given Mr Knightley her improvised account of Edmund's death. She dared not deviate from that now, though she might embroider the story a little: her new audience, Emma and Elizabeth, would want far more detail than Mr Knightley or the Greek doctor had wanted. And so Fanny began to retell the story in a version she was to repeat so often in the future. At appropriate moments, she tried to strike a tragic note, but she failed. Emma saw the failure and understood it as a kind of guilt: Edmund was dead, Fanny was not sorry, and her lack of sorrow made her feel somehow awkward. Elizabeth saw things differently: she believed that Fanny was as deeply moved as she herself would have been if her Fitzwilliam had been murdered by thieves. She saw Fanny's coolness and confusion as a sign of affection. Marianne, through her *bonnet rouge*, heard little more than the word *dead* without realising that it applied to the Chaplain.

Cool and lacking in detail though it was, the story was impressive. Emma, in whose dining-room the extraordinary event had taken place, bombarded Fanny with trivial questions which Fanny answered with an irritating lack of precision. Jane and the menfolk heard the tale when they stopped for lunch, but not from Fanny herself: Emma took over as storyteller-in-chief. Trelawny listened thoughtfully to Emma's version of the tale, glancing at Fanny now and again for confirmation. He offered no comment, not even a polite attempt at condolence.

The little convoy skirted Thebes and took the long straight road across the plain to the west. They found a place to pitch camp just beyond an outcrop of rock with a blackened cave beneath it and an ancient watchtower above. After they'd eaten a supper of bread and beans, Trelawny asked Fanny if she'd like to walk back to the cave: it had a curious look to it. His silence during Emma's narrative had alarmed her, and she agreed to the walk without pretending an interest in the cave. Had it still been on view, the Sphinx itself would not have roused much curiosity in her weary mind.

'So, your problems are over,' he began familiarly as soon as they were out of earshot of the others. He steered her away from the road and into the bare, open fields.

'Some are over, some are just beginning,' she replied cautiously.

'I'd congratulate you, though I don't suppose congratulations are in order.'

'No, they are not.'

'Nor condolences neither, if I understand c'rrectly.'

The Captain's shaky grammar, the rustic edge to his voice alerted her: they were heading for an argument. 'As you see,' she replied coldly, 'I'm not prostrated[104] with grief, but neither am I ready to dance a jig.' It would have been closer to the truth if Fanny had said she was *both* prostrated with grief *and* ready to dance a jig. Her feelings were extraordinarily confused.

'Tidy though, weren'it? Convenient, as you might say?' The rustic voice thickened in a spirit of contradiction.

'What do you mean?' Fanny knew exactly what he meant. How much better her story would have been, she thought, if they could have sat down and concocted it together.

'Never in all my travels did I hear of a consulate being burgled,' he said. 'Ransacked, pillaged and burnt to the ground maybe, but burgled never. In Athens, Odysseus takes care of that. And…'

'And?'

'The timing. It's too good to be true. You go back to Athens. You're on your own in Mrs Knightley's dining-room. Edmund enters, friendly and ready to discuss travelling to Korfu. Edmund? Friendly? Makes a pleasant change, don't it?' He paused, waiting for her to comment, but she said nothing. They walked on for a moment, silent.

'Well,' the Captain resumed at last. 'Two thieves turn up at that very moment. They put a carving knife which happens to be on the table to your throat, and demand money. A carving knife. They're housebreakers, working in the daytime, but they got no knives of their own, no swords, no pistols, nothing.'

Fanny put her hand to her bandaged throat as though her wounds proved her story, but still she said nothing.

'So, you draw your pistol. One of the thieves snatches it away. Not so easy, with your finger through the trigger guard? Or was it?' Another pause, another silence. 'Edmund sees the pistol and flings himself into the fray. Remember, this is Edmund we're talking about, not some fire-eating buccaneer. And the thief who has your pistol, doesn't hold it like this...' Trelawny held an imaginary pistol at shoulder height, aiming it. 'But roughly on a level with Edmund's...groin. There's a scuffle, and Edmund gets shot: here.' Trelawny put his hand on what a medical man would call his *os pubis*.

'Exactly,' Fanny said simply. The Captain saw her story through the eyes of a brawler and a fighting-man. To him, it was as full of holes as an old stocking.

'Then the thieves runs away, and no one sees 'em again,' the Captain concluded.

'You don't believe me.'

'Of course, I believe you. Everyone else believes you: why shouldn't I?' There was no overt sarcasm in the Captain's tone, but Fanny knew him well enough now to grasp his meaning exactly.

'You tell so many fairy stories yourself,' she retorted, 'you've forgotten what the truth looks like.' It wasn't much of a defence, but she was sure he would take her meaning as she had taken his: Doubt me if you wish, but keep your doubts to yourself.

'The issue is not what I doubt or what I believe, Fanny,' he said. 'It's whether you're goin' to tell me what actually happened.' It was time for plain speaking, and the yokel accent had more or less vanished.

The fields around them were poor. The soil was sandy and drained too quickly. Most of the coarse plants that grew there were torn up by goats as soon as they showed green. Nothing in that bleak landscape could have been further from the neat, sheep-nibbled pastures of Northamptonshire. Fanny felt a sudden longing to be away, away from Greece and the city of the incestuous Oedipus, away from Odysseus and his filthy plots, but most of all away from Edward Trelawny and his cold-hearted questions.

'I shall register Edmund's death in Korfu,' Fanny said quietly. 'It was an accident. The doctor issued a death certificate. And George Knightley confirmed it.'

'So, you're not going to tell me.'

'I don't know what right you have to ask.'

'You wanted freedom. You are free. Free to tell me. Or not, as you please.'

'There's nothing more to tell,' Fanny said. Her story had fallen apart in the Captain's hands. She had to defend herself, to shut his mouth before he mentioned his doubts to the others. But how?

'Captain Trelawny,' she said. 'I have a question for *you*.'

'For me? I'm honoured.'

'Why did Odysseus send men after Jane? I've never heard *your* side of the story.'

'*My* side? I don't have a side.' He remembered Mr Darcy's earnest question: *You're a friend of Odysseus. Did he ever say anything? Let anything slip?* It was an insulting question, a question for which, under different circumstances, one man might call another out. Fanny, of course, hadn't heard Mr Darcy's question: she'd been on the road back to Athens when he'd asked it, but, clearly, she was thinking along the same lines. 'I know nothing whatever about the matter,' the Captain said resentfully.

'I wonder what Mr Knightley meant then.' It wasn't until the sentence had slipped out that Fanny realised how alarming the Captain would find it.

'Knightley!' the Captain exclaimed. 'What did *he* say?' The

Consul spelled danger: he was in touch with Odysseus, with Gouras. Perhaps he already knew about Tersitza's engagement to be married.

'Nothing much. I can't remember really.' Fanny had heard the alarm in his voice and decided to try a little sarcasm of her own. 'I was so busy murdering Edmund, I didn't have time to listen properly.'

'Fanny?'

'Edward?' What had Mr Knightley said, in fact? *Even to ask a question like that is to insult a man. And you'll get the same answer whether Trelawny knows anything or not.* Something like that. The Consul had made no accusations, though his words were hardly a testimonial to the Captain's integrity. Well, she'd asked the question, and now she had to pick the bones out of Trelawny's reply: he knew nothing whatever about the matter.

'Let's not bother with the cave,' the Captain said. 'We should go back to the others.'

'As you wish,' she replied. 'The sooner we get to Salona the better.'

Four days later as the Darcys and their caravan neared Salona, it no longer seemed a stage on their long march: it had become a destination. At first the road from Thebes had been easy, but as they neared Delphi,[105] invisible in the swirling mists above them, the road wound its way from one gorge to the next, from one short, exhausting climb to another, fearsome and fraught with delay. One of the wain-horses went lame, as is the wont of unmatched animals. A fast melt of snow had washed away one of the innumerable decaying bridges on the road and cost them a day's detour. What might lie ahead in the mountains *beyond* Salona, they were too weary to contemplate.

A long, final descent brought them again within a mile of the Gulf, and then the Salona road swung inland across a fertile plain: two hours of weary plodding lay ahead of them, two last hours in the oppressive heat and damp that follow the Ides of

March. Finally, beneath the ancient arch of the Delphi Gate, the city of Salona, noisy, putrid and bustling, offered them its graceless welcome.

At the outbreak of the War of Independence, Salona had been a Turkish stronghold. It was the first city in central Greece to declare for the rebels, the first to be reclaimed by the Greeks, and the first to witness the massacre of a surrendering garrison. In addition to setting these precedents, Salona was the only sanctuary for Greeks between Athens in the east and the islands of Ionia in the west. Wealthy Greeks from the region had moved there in shoals: bankers, doctors, landowners, beneficed priests, tax farmers, every kind of moneyed riff-raff. Prices were high, and markets flourished.

But where in this sprawling chaos, could four English ladies and three gentlemen find shelter, and find it quickly? There were, of course, inns in Salona, one of which grandly called itself a hotel, but, as Mr Darcy, with the aid of Stavros, soon discovered, they were all unnegotiably full and likely to remain so. The last of the innkeepers suggested that they try the famous Fortress of Oria[106]: there were always rooms in and around the castle, he told them. He took Mr Darcy into the street and showed him the fort, towering above the town on a huge cliff.

Stavros wasn't sure. He knew the fort: everyone who travelled in that part of Romelia knew it. In fact, it was here that Odysseus planned to hold his congress with Lord Byron. But the place was swarming with soldiers, most of them irregulars, undisciplined and dangerous, and the area round the fort was no better. The womenfolk might feel uncomfortable. Mr Darcy replied that he would see for himself.

The cart-way up to the castle was steep, and the paving dilapidated. The fort itself appeared proudly invincible, though it had, in fact, changed hands many times. Half a mile before the massive gateway, houses and shops gave way to taverns and hostelries, gardens and terraces. In some of them, tavern-girls were gossiping in lazy groups, waiting perhaps for their first customers. Mr Darcy asked the Captain to ride ahead and see if the fortress offered a better chance of rest and safety. After a brief survey of the place, the Captain returned shaking his head: 'We have to find somewhere else.'

Stavros had one card left to play. Below the castle was an ancient and rambling *kervansaray*[107] built by the Ottomans to house, for a night or two, the camel trains which until recently had plied across Greece, and which still served most of the Turkish Empire. The keeper of the *kervansaray* offered them a cavernous room with an oak door, heavy bolts and a usable antechamber. Mr Darcy saw no sense in argument: his poor Lizzy was exhausted, Mrs Knightley was exhausted, and the animals were exhausted after the climb up to the fortress and the steep descent. Fortunately, after Mr Darcy's nod of acceptance, things moved quickly. A moneylender named Jethro Solomonides appeared as though invoked by the rubbing of a magic lamp, and cheerfully converted Athenian paper into Salonian silver. Supervised by Marianne and Stavros, both of whom understood the calculation of per centages, the silver began to flow out of the *kervansaray* and comfort began to flow in.

The *kervansaray* of Salona, though small in comparison with the great establishments in Syria and Egypt, had safe stabling, grooms, cleaners, kitchens complete with cooks, and messengers ready to depart at a moment's notice. There was also a supply of fresh water piped in from a nearby fountain. With guards in the anteroom, curtains to divide their much corbelled, yawning chamber, new mattresses and a score of other conveniences, rest and safety were soon assured.

That evening a plan was agreed: they would stay in Salona until a letter had been sent to Sir Frederick in Korfu and an answer had reached them with instructions for their rescue.

The letter was quickly written, but who could be trusted to deliver it? Stavros undertook to find a government courier before morning and began his search immediately. As it happened, two couriers presented themselves within the hour. The first had no credentials of any kind, and he was told to come back the next day. The second showed Mr Darcy the outer wrapping of a letter bearing the handsome seal of the Sublime Porte and addressed to Sir Thomas Maitland, Lord High Commissioner in Kerkyra. Sir Thomas, as we know, had died on 17th January, but the Sublime Porte had evidently not been informed. The courier himself was a foul-looking, foul-smelling Armenian crookback, though otherwise unobjectionable. Instructed by Marianne, Mr Darcy paid him three *piastres* and gave him a note to Sir Frederick requesting the payment of a further ten in Korfu. With the letter now written and despatched, they had, at last, time to catch their breath and settle down to a good night's sleep.

After Captain Trelawny's discussion with Fanny on the road between Thebes and Delphi, he had become restive. Sometimes he spoke of riding ahead to Mesolongi, of linking up with Lord Byron and setting up the *escort party*, though the plan to escort Lord Byron had always been a pure fabrication. Next morning, in Salona, his restiveness became pronounced. He had to be on his way, he insisted: events were unfolding in Athens, in Mesolongi, everywhere but in Salona. Secretly, he sent a messenger to Lord Byron, asking for orders: When should he join Byron in Mesolongi? Were any messages to be sent to Odysseus in Athens? The messenger was sworn to return with Milord's answer as soon as may be. While he was waiting for Byron's reply, Trelawny began to distance himself from the others. He had no time, he declared, for a sewer like Salona, rotten with a thousand fevers, and he had no interest in rendering habitable a filthy vault in a prehistoric *kervansaray*. He found the idea of waiting for Sir Frederick to send a rescue party timid and pusillanimous and saw no reason not to say so.

His behaviour was unexpected in another way too. Although everyone, led by Emma Knightley, saw him as Fanny's particular companion, he no longer sought her out, and she reciprocated by steering clear of him. Had they quarrelled? Was the shock of Fanny's widowhood making her unapproachable? The reasons for their mutual coolness were, of course, well-known to Fanny herself and to the Captain: Trelawny had all but accused Fanny of murdering her lord and master, and she had all but accused him of backing Odysseus's plot to kidnap Jane Darcy. Safety lay in silence and in mutual avoidance, that was clear.

Three days after Mr Darcy sent his letter to Sir Frederick, Captain Trelawny announced that the noise and disorder in the *kervansaray* were intolerable: he pined for the mountains: *Oh! There is sweetness in the mountain air*, he quoted, as though a verse from *Childe Harold*[108] explained everything. Tomorrow he would seek out a room in a cottage somewhere in the hills above the fortress, quiet and clean. There he could plan his next actions. In fact, his next step was already clear to him: as soon as he received Byron's invitation to head for Mesolongi, he would set off instantly, avoiding all farewells and all feminine reproaches, express or implied.

Trelawny's threat to leave the *kervansaray* alarmed the Darcys: how would they cope without the Captain? Elizabeth suggested that Fanny might still have some influence with Trelawny. If *she* asked him to stay… Mr Darcy was unsure. Even so, he extracted a reluctant promise from Fanny: she'd have a quiet word with Trelawny.

That evening Fanny hatched her plan. Fanny and Jane would rise early, and don, as usual, their boys' clothing. When next morning the Captain set off for Mount Parnassus, they would accompany him. Two lads eager to explore the fortress and the mountains: the Captain could hardly refuse. With luck during their climb, Fanny would find the right moment for her *quiet word*. Elizabeth approved, though she wasn't sure about Jane's disguise. Did she really look like a lad? No, Marianne agreed: Jane's locks, and Fanny's, had been lightly shorn in Athens, but something more radical was needed. She produced her sewing scissors and cropped the two sets of curls into the short, unruly style that the young blades of the Regency had generally affected, at least until the onset of baldness.

Next morning, when Captain Trelawny strode off in search of new accommodation, two young men strode beside him. The track up to the fortress was steep, and the Captain attacked it as though he were attempting to soar like a buzzard. Breathlessly, the boys stayed with him. Fanny's neck began to hurt. She had hidden the scars and the stitches under a bandage and then covered the bandage with a fashionable cravat: it was altogether too tight and very uncomfortable. Then a strange encounter.

They reached the level ground to the west of the castle and the chaos of *tavernas* that they remembered from their first hour in Salona. About a hundred yards before the gate of the fortress, two Suliots in their characteristic dress were sitting on a low wall, deep in conversation. During their brisk ascent from the town, Trelawny and his companions had already passed countless peddlers, peasants and loungers, and the Suliots were in no way unusual. Then, ten yards behind them, they heard, 'Kapetan Trelawny! Is you?'

They stopped and turned round. Fanny now recognised the two men, deserters from the first night of their journey, Cosmo and Zander.

'You boys go on,' Trelawny said out of the corner of his mouth. 'Best they don't recognise you.'

Without thinking, the two boys hurried on their way. 'What is he talking about?' Fanny exclaimed suddenly. 'They've seen us in these clothes before. Of course they recognised us!'

'Is it a problem?' Jane asked.

'Not necessarily,' Fanny reassured her. But in Fanny's mind, awkward questions had already surfaced: Why were the two men looking for their captain? Had the meeting on the hill been planned? Was this meeting the reason for Trelawny's sudden need for mountain air, and for his race up the hill?

At the gate of the fortress, the boys stopped and scanned the road behind them: there was no sign of Trelawny or of the Suliots. Probably they'd disappeared into one of the *tavernas*.

'Jane, I don't want to worry you,' Fanny said. 'But you recognised those two?'

'Yes. Cosmo and Zander.'

'They went back to Athens.'

'Yes,' Jane agreed.

'So, there's a possibility that in Athens they talked to Odysseus.' It was more than a *possibility*, far more, but Fanny wanted to warn Jane, not frighten her out of her wits.

'Talked to Odysseus? You mean…?'

'In plain words, it's not out of the question that Odysseus sent them.'

'Sent them…?' Jane went white. 'Like the men before, only this time…'

Only this time, men who would be sure to recognise their prey: that was the chilling thought. 'Where have they disappeared to?' Fanny asked urgently.

They scanned the road again. Nothing.

'Forget them,' Fanny said. 'We'll get around the fortress as fast as we can. There are plenty of tracks down the mountain. I saw them from the road when we came in.' They set off at a run. The great walls and the keep of the castle towered above them. Ahead were pine trees and a pell-mell slope downward. They paused at the brink, finding no track. Then with one accord they plunged down the forest slope, half-running, half-sliding on the loose stones, pine needles and ungathered cones that littered their way. At last they reached a path, trodden white, and leading down to the town. They stopped.

'Do you really think…?' Jane began, rubbing her shin where she had barked it on the trunk of a fallen tree.

'No,' Fanny panted. 'But we can't be too careful.' She slackened the cravat and the bandage at her neck. Then they walked briskly down to the town and the *kervansaray*. In their anteroom, out of hearing of the others, Fanny explained to Mr Darcy what had happened and why they were still out of breath. 'You and I shall have a word with the Captain when he gets back,' Mr Darcy said grimly.

'Yes,' Fanny agreed. If the Captain really was actively taking part in the kidnap of young Jane, then things had taken a turn for the worse, threatening or perhaps even fatal.

'I'll talk to him,' Mr Darcy said. 'You stand behind him with one of your pistols cocked, but hidden behind your back.'

'You want me to wing him? Or kill him?'

'It depends what he says.'

'You'll give me the signal? How?'

'No, young man, I won't have time. You decide for yourself.'

'But Mr Darcy…'

The sound of running footsteps echoed along the corridor outside. The door of the anteroom was flung open. It was the Captain. Seeing Fanny, he stopped dead. 'Thank God!' he said. 'Thank God! I panicked when you disappeared like that. And Jane…?'

'Jane is with her mother,' Mr Darcy said calmly, moving to confront the Captain.

'Those two scoundrels!' the Captain exclaimed.

'Fanny says they were two of your bodyguard, not Tolo or the other one, because you've already shot them, but two men whose names…' Mr Darcy became prolix, giving Fanny time to move behind the Captain without attracting his attention.

'Exactly,' the Captain agreed dismissively.

'And what did they want?'

'They'd thought better of it,' the Captain explained. 'Said they were fighters, not deserters. They knew I was going to Salona, so they came here, hoping to bump into me. Hoping I'd take them on again.'

'And what did you say to that?'

'I told them to go to the devil. Absolute impertinence. I said if they're still here at sundown, I'll take them to the commandant, and they'll finish up in the clink.'

'And then you came back here?'

'No. I spent a while looking for Miss Darcy and Mrs Bertram. I thought they might have gone into the fortress. But apparently they're here.'

'Yes,' Fanny broke in. 'We're here.' She slipped her pistol back into her belt. The Captain's story added up: she had no reason to shoot him in the back.

'Yes, you are. Thank God.'

'You've said Thank God three times this morning,' Fanny tried to smile. 'Are you becoming a believer?'

'Have I ever been anything else?' he asked equivocally.

'So,' she shrugged. 'No luck today with the *sweet mountain air* and a simple hut?' She tried to recover the teazing note in her voice, but she couldn't. Had she really been ready to shoot the Captain? In the back? In cold blood? She'd shot Edmund, but he'd had a knife to her throat and she'd panicked. She'd been over those horrible moments in her mind time and again, sometimes trembling with guilt, sometimes euphoric with the joy of escape. But to butcher the Captain on suspicion that he was plotting with Odysseus Androutsos! No! Mr Darcy had no right to ask it of her, and she should have refused. But she had *not* refused. The fact did not fit the character of the Fanny Bertram, or of the Fanny Price, she thought she knew so well: *she had not refused*.

'You're right,' Trelawny nodded uncertainly. 'No hut. And I never quite reached the sweet mountain air.' He caught Fanny's eye: her doubts were all but tangible. And he was far, very far, from trusting her. Somehow they had to reach an understanding, soon and in detail.

'If you want to try again…,' Fanny offered. 'I'll come with you.'

'Now?' He heard the readiness in his own voice.

'Unless you're too tired?' Fanny herself was tired: the race up the mountain and the long detour back to the *kervansaray* had cost much of her strength and her neck was throbbing, but she'd have to put her weariness behind her. Hiding what she felt: it was something she'd been practising for years.

They set off again. It was mid-day. In the huge courtyard, they headed for the fountain and the main gate.

'You don't drink cold water, do you?' the Captain asked indicating the fountain. It was the first straightforward question he'd asked her for days.

'I prefer tea,' she replied. 'Why?'

'Something a Chinese cook in Shang-Hai told me: boil water, make tea. Or toddy. Stops you getting a bad stomach.'

'Does it?'

'Always worked for me.'

'Let's find some tea then,' she offered.

'Or wine? Plenty of taverns in this town,' he said. '*Tsipouro* if you prefer. Which?'

'Wine then,' she said, lowering her guard. 'But not too much.'

They set off through the busy town, two men without a care in the world apparently, and one of them, if you looked at him closely, a very pretty fellow.

'So?' the Captain said. They were sitting at a rickety table in a *taverna* halfway up to the fortress. A jug of wine and two beakers stood on the table between them. 'What's this all about?'

'I wanted to ask you a question,' she said, pouring wine for them both. 'And I was hoping for an honest answer.'

'Ask. But then I shall claim the same privilege.'

She nodded, accepting the exchange. She sipped her wine and said, into her earthen beaker, 'An hour ago, we met Cosmo and Zander, two of your bodyguard.'

'Yes. But that isn't a question.'

'When they deserted us, did they get as far as Athens?'

'I don't know. Is it important?'

'Did they talk to Odysseus?'

He looked at her shrewdly. 'You mean, has Odysseus sent them after Jane like he sent those other men? And do I know all about it?'

'You see why I might ask such a question?' She took a deep draught of wine to avoid the confrontation in his eyes and then refilled the beaker.

'Yes,' he said. 'I see why. But will you believe my answer, Mistress Fanny?'

She reflected for a moment. 'When we were planning to leave Athens, I thought...'

'I know what you thought. And I remember exactly what you asked me that first night in camp: *Will you ever go back to England?*'

'And your answer: *You hadn't thought that far ahead.*'

'It was a stupid thing to say, and it upset you. I regretted it as soon as I'd said it.'

'However much you regretted it, is it true?'

He nodded reluctantly. 'Fanny, I'm what people call an adventurer. I don't need to be rich as a rajah, but I won't go back to England till I'm rich enough to hold up my head as a gentleman.[109] Can you understand that?'

'You gave me a belt full of silver and gold. And you paraded round Athens with all those guards. They must have cost you a fortune. I thought you *were* rich.'

'The money in that belt was, more or less, all I have in the world.'

'And you gave it to me without knowing if I'd ever come back!'

'Listen, Fanny. If you'd needed that money to escape from Athens, it would have been yours: yours a hundred times over, if I'd had it.' There was a warmth in his words, a strength that she'd never heard before in a man's voice, except perhaps when Edmund had told her how much he loved Mary Crawford.

'Well,' she said, more impressed than she cared to admit. 'You've got the belt back now...'

He touched his shirt in confirmation.

'And it contains all your worldly wealth,' she said easily.

'Oh, I shall be rich one day, never you fear.'

She smiled. Edward Trelawny would never make his fortune, of that she was certain. 'And what about my question?' she asked. 'You haven't answered it.' His words and the wine had already calmed her, lulled her natural caution. It was pleasant to be back on her old footing with the Captain, or almost.

'Your question.' He became suddenly serious. 'The answer is *no*. I know absolutely nothing about any plan to kidnap Jane Darcy, not now, not in the past, not ever.'

She accepted his word: what could she do but believe him? 'So tell me. Why are Cosmo and Zander in Salona?' she asked. 'To get work from you? Or to track down Jane?'

'I honestly don't know. We must be doubly careful of Jane, that's obvious.'

The word *we* was her clew: it was time to risk Mr Darcy's question. 'Can you stay with us? In the *kervansaray*?' she asked. 'It's important. For everyone.'

'If you wish,' he agreed simply. He drank down the wine in his beaker.

'The noise won't be too much for you?'

He laughed. 'The noise was an excuse. I wanted to disappear because you weren't talking to me anymore.' It wasn't true, Fanny realised, but it was the sort of thing a gentleman might be permitted to say: Fanny forgave him.

'But I *do* talk to you,' she objected in the same frivolous vein. 'I'm talking to you now, wouldn't you say?'

'Fanny, can you be serious for a minute?' His voice betrayed a rare hint of vulnerability.

Fanny nodded: what on earth did he have in mind?

The Captain cleared his throat. 'When I first met Mary Shelley,' he began diffidently.

'In Pisa, you said.' Fanny tried to sound interested, but the blank irrelevance of the subject took her by surprise.

'Yes, in Pisa. She was…' He hesitated. 'She was finishing a book.'

'Reading it? Or writing it?'

'Writing. She called it *Valperga*.'[110] His voice trailed off, uncertain.

'What was it about?'

'Cruelty.'

Fanny nodded: she had a slight premonition now of where he was heading.

'What most worried her, at least in the book, was men and their cruelty toward women, especially toward their…' He shied away from the next word like a nervous horse.

'Wives?' Fanny asked.

He nodded. 'I've thought over what she says. Specially since our talk…'

'…in Athens?'

He nodded again.

'So, what *does* she say?'

'In the story, a man thinks his wife has insulted him, so he takes revenge by treating her badly, villainously in fact.'

It was Fanny's turn to nod: it was a subject she probably knew more about than Mary Shelley, but she held back the least reply until she'd heard what the author of *Frankenstein* had to say.

'Mary says this: it amazes her that a man should dare *so to idolise himself as to sacrifice human victims at the shrine of his pride, jealousy and revenge.*'

'Yes!' Fanny agreed, taken aback.

'*Idolise himself*: that's what she calls it.'

'And that's really what it is: self-idolatry! Thank you for telling me. If you see it that way, it explains…'

For a long while, they sat on either side of the simple table without moving. It was a moment of equilibrium, a moment of unexplored, and perhaps unexplorable, possibility.

'Of course,' the Captain said at length, 'we can sit here all day philosophising, but there is a *much* better idea.'

'Shall I guess? Or will you tell me?'

'I'll tell you.' The lines of his rugged face softened. Humour played at the corners of his mouth, his brow lost its hard wrinkles, and… What could she see in his eyes? An expression that was entirely new to her. 'Why don't we two enjoy the sweet mountain air?' he asked. 'Together?'

'The two of us? Alone?'

'That expresses my idea exactly.'

'I think not, Captain Trelawny!' She tried to put some energy, some indignation into her reply, but without success.

'*And thus the heart will break, yet brokenly live on,*' he quoted tragically.

'More Byron?' she asked. Byron, Shakespeare, Pontius Pilate: she had no interest in the authorship. *Why don't we two enjoy the sweet mountain air together?* His own simple words, and the passionate invitation in his eyes, that was all she could think of.

He nodded. 'More *Childe Harold* in fact.'

'And me a widow of barely a week,' she objected. 'How could a man be so heartless?'

'I may appear heartless to you, Fanny Price, but it seems to me you are truly pitiless, the original *belle dame*[111] *sans merci*.'

Fanny Price? No one had called her that for years. It made her shiver.

'Yes,' he repeated, 'if you are not the *belle dame sans merci*, who is?'

'Never heard of her.' Fanny shrugged. 'Who was she? One of Byron's ladyloves?'

'No. She comes in a poem by John Keats. There's a knight.'

'The knight is you, no doubt.'

'Listen to the poem and decide for yourself.'

She nodded: he knew so much poetry, and he could recite it with such romantic fervour. Wherever this strange courtship might lead them, the poetry he taught her would always be one strand of her life. She watched him close his eyes and begin:

*'I met a lady in the meads,
Full beautiful, a fairy's child;
Her hair was long, her foot was light,
And her eyes were wild.'*

'So, she's definitely not me. But what happens to the poor knight? I can see – trouble ahead.'

'In the end she drugs him, and he falls into a trance:

*'I saw pale kings and princes too,
Pale warriors, death-pale were they all;
They cried – "La Belle Dame sans Merci
Hath thee in thrall!"'*

'No, the knight isn't you. Nobody *hath thee in thrall*, Captain Trelawny, and I don't expect anyone ever will.' Fanny began to laugh outright, a woman's laugh, clear, provocative and enchanting.

'Your disguise is slipping, young man,' the Captain said, enjoying her laughter but not quite understanding it. In Pisa, he'd learned the poem to impress Claire Clairmont,[112] Mary Shelley's half-sister. Claire had listened in rapture. And now this half-educated parson's wife couldn't stop laughing: *Nobody hath thee in thrall, Captain Trelawny.*

He watched Fanny knock back her wine in one gulp as men did, and fill her beaker again from the wine jug. 'So, you're a *widow* now,' he said, their intimacy restored and somehow deeper. 'That's strange, because last time we spoke on the subject, you'd never been married. Or did I miss a step somewhere?'

'I think widowhood is something a young man should decide for herself,' Fanny replied. And then, trying to be serious: 'It's a matter of inheritance.'

'You expect one?'

'It's a possibility. But only distant. No reason for pirates to get their hopes up.'

'If you mean me, I was never a pirate. A privateer, perhaps, but never a pirate.'

'What's the difference?'

'Not much. If I tell you to walk the plank, you still have to walk it.'

'And how many people walked the plank for you?'

'Thousands,' he said. 'Half the population of Bombay. Men, women and children. And a dozen lap-dogs.' He watched her intently as a man watches a woman whom he desires and has reason to believe he will soon possess. 'And now *my* question,' he pursued. 'If you allow.'

'I allow,' she said.

'Did you kill Edmund? I don't care if you killed him in cold blood, by accident, or with mandragora[113] and honey. Simply, did you kill him?'

She'd known the question was coming, but the starkness of the word *kill* three times repeated, and the sudden seriousness in his voice shocked her. They'd been drinking together, laughing together, and she was not entirely sober. He'd just made a thoroughly indecent proposal, and by way of reply, she'd quaffed her wine and quizzed him. Edmund? Of course, she'd killed him, but somehow it seemed long ago, in another lifetime. If she confessed to Trelawny now, what difference would it make? He already knew the truth: he just wanted to hear it from her own lips. Why shouldn't she tell him? In preparation, she moistened her lips with another sip of the wine.

'No,' she said. 'Edmund died, but I didn't kill him.'

Chapter 14

FEVER

Fanny had only a vague idea how men behaved when they were out of sight of women. On the wharves of Portsmouth, she'd watched her brother, William, clowning with fellow midshipmen, in the kitchens of Mansfield Park she'd seen Tom Bertram in his cups with half-a-dozen local oafs, and from the top window of the vicarage she'd watched her husband explaining to farmhands how to lay flagstones over her flowerbeds. Now, however, she was the drinking companion of a hard-bitten and unrepentant buccaneer, and she was at sea without chart or compass. The Captain saw the problem and amused himself instructing her. On the next two mornings, they wandered through the town partly to keep a lookout for Cosmo and Zander, and partly to improve Fanny's performance as a rowdy. The Captain taught her how to walk so that the two of them took up half the street, how to make a handsome lady blush by suggestive doffing of the hat, and how, as he put it, *to take the wall of any man or maid of Montague's.* The afternoons were more sedentary. He taught her how to sit with her legs sprawled apart, how to plant her elbows squarely on a table, how to tip back her head in contempt, how to laugh without giggling, how to wipe her lips with the back of her hand after a mouthful of wine, and then, when she'd drunk a shade more than was good for her, how to stagger home.

'A widow has to make a fresh start in life,' he told her on their second afternoon together, stopping outside a shop which sold daggers, scimitars, rapiers and antiquated firearms.

'You think a widow needs a sword?' she asked, not perfectly sober.

'If she can walk without tripping over it.'

'Perhaps she doesn't want to be a gladiator. Perhaps she prefers to be a woman, a *belle dame sans merci*.'

'Perhaps there's no such animal,' the Captain rejoined. 'Perhaps you laughed her out of existence.'

Despite Fanny's objections, they went into the shop. Fanny was a boy, on the small side and slight of build: she would need a rapier short enough to clear the ground when it was in its scabbard, and light enough for her slender wrist when it was in use. He made her try a dozen weapons, and still he wasn't satisfied.

'Captain,' she teazed him, 'I once went to Northampton with Mary Crawford. She was looking for a new muslin. You seem twice as hard to please as she was.'

'Never choose a weapon lightly,' he replied. 'Your life may depend on it. Mary Crawford obviously took such rules seriously. I think I'd have enjoyed her company.' He was taking a risk, joking about Mary Crawford, but Fanny simply shoved him into a rack of muskets, a dozen of which clattered to the floor, and rolled her eyes to the ceiling.

With the help of the armourer, who seemed uncommonly eager for them to leave his shop, Trelawny made his final choice and buckled the sword-belt round Fanny's waist, taking particular care that it sat comfortably on her hip. When he was satisfied and the weapon was paid for, he gestured her ahead. She swaggered, or tried to swagger, out of the shop with the sword banging against her leg. It was strangely arousing, one more excitement to add to the many she'd felt since she'd deserted her husband's company for the sisterhood of the mosque.

'I'll teach you the basic moves,' the Captain promised. 'The lunge, the parry, the feint. And another thing, young Price, we need a new name for you. I never met a boy called Fanny.'

'A new name?' she asked naively. 'What, for example?'

'Perhaps Frank?' he suggested. 'I believe Mrs Knightley once had a beau of that name.'

'And Catherine knew a scamp called John Thorpe,' she replied. 'No. Not Frank. Not John. I won't be named after a scoundrel.'

'You choose then,' he offered.

'What about Fitzwilliam? Or do you think Mrs Darcy would object?'

He laughed and slapped her on the back, as he would any other drinking companion. 'Some women might enjoy exchanging one kind of Fitz for another,' he said. 'But not Mrs Darcy. I don't think so.' It seemed that Fanny's *abominable breeches* and the weapons decorating her waist, changed not only her appearance, but, at a deeper level, changed the way the Captain saw her, changed what he *expected* of her. Coyness and decorum were banished. And why not? Good riddance to them. And perhaps the breeches, now that she wore them with conviction, changed her expectations of herself too. It was a curious thought.

Back in the *kervansaray* after that cheerful morning, the time for curious thoughts ended abruptly. Fanny's first intimation that something was amiss was the door to the inner chamber: it was closed and, as she discovered, locked from the inside. A guard, a man she'd seen lounging in the yard waiting for work, accosted her and the Captain.

'*Oki*,' the man said, holding out his hand to restrain them. *No.*

'My friends are inside,' Fanny told him. 'Please open the door.'

The man mimed turning a key, shrugged, and said something unintelligible in Greek.

'He has no key,' Trelawny guessed.

The lock clattered, and the door was opened from the inside. It was Mr Darcy. 'I heard voices. I hoped it was you. You've been gone for a while.'

'What's wrong?' Fanny asked, suddenly serious.

'Everything,' Mr Darcy said, ushering them into the chamber. 'Elizabeth is ill, Jane can't stop crying, and Mrs Knightley wants to go back to Athens.'

Fanny darted across the chamber to the curtain that marked off the women's sleeping place. The ridiculous sword rattled against her leg: what must Mr Darcy think of her?

Behind the curtain, Elizabeth was lying on a low divan. Marianne was sitting beside her, dabbing the sick woman's forehead with a wet cloth. Jane was kneeling at the end of the divan, her face buried in the white sheet. She wasn't crying, but she was breathing stiffly, like someone who has just come out of a fit of sobbing.

'What happened?' Fanny asked.

'Headache. Giddiness. Pains,' Marianne replied, touching her own stomach high up to show where the pains were.

'The wet cloth? Is it fever?'

'Some, I think. Not much. Not yet.' Marianne rinsed her cloth in a bowl of cold water, wrung it out, and began again to cool Elizabeth's face.

'You don't think it's...?' Fanny mouthed the words *enteric fever*. Jane was upset enough already.

'Stavros is out looking for a doctor,' Marianne said flatly. 'Mrs Knightley went with him.'

'Then we'll soon know.' Fanny went to the end of the divan and knelt on the flagstone floor. The hilt of her sword jabbed into her stomach, and she pushed it angrily to one side. As gently as she could, she rested one hand on Jane's shoulder, but Jane flinched away.

'I haven't deserted you,' Fanny said quietly. 'I've been trying to sort out something with the Captain.'

Jane raised her head, her face streaked with tears and smitten with doubt. 'About those men?'

'Of course, about those men.'

'You've been looking for them?'

'Among other things.'

'You didn't…?'

'No, we didn't find them. The Captain says we must be doubly careful of you.'

'Papa says I should stay in here. He's locked the door.'

'I think he's right. There's a guard outside too. That's a good idea. Till we find out what's going on.'

'Find out? You'll find out?'

'Me and the Captain. Don't worry.' She looked around for the Captain, but Marianne had already shooed him out of the sick-room. 'The Captain won't let anything happen to you,' Fanny said soothingly. 'And nor shall I.'

Marianne hushed them both: they were disturbing her patient. Fanny nodded and stood up, stretching out her hand to help Jane. Jane was still wearing her boy's clothing, but the disguise had lost its effect: she looked like a washed-out little girl in fancy dress. Fanny searched the luggage for their skirts and dresses. She found Jane's simple day-dress and helped her change into it.

Trelawny soon gravitated to the open yard by the fountain and sat on a stone bench. There his messenger, newly arrived from Mesolongi, found him, gave him a note sealed with Lord Byron's seal, took his promised reward, and disappeared. The note was not at all what the Captain had expected. Byron had discussed the matter with Mavrokordatos, who, as the Reader may recall, was a sworn enemy of Odysseus. Since the Captain and Odysseus had formed an alliance, it might be better, Byron suggested, if the Captain return immediately to Athens. That was what Mavrokordatos also recommended. Naturally, of course, the Captain could do as he wished, but the difficult journey to Mesolongi was, at this juncture, of no immediate use to anyone.

Trelawny was indignant. So Mavrokordatos was Firemaster now! The Captain's outrage warmed quickly toward fury, and then froze to disgust. Byron had always seemed to Trelawny, or so he now remembered, a puny, sickly sort of fellow, arrogant as Napoleon, wicked as Caligula, and disloyal as Judas Iscariot. He had the poetaster's knack of versification, but none of the deep emotions required of a real poet. He was fickle, selfish and perfidious. Just look at the way he treated women! A self-idolater to the last hair of his miserable pelt. Percy Shelley had been ten times the man.

But now, sitting on a bench beside the cool fountain, with the road to Mesolongi barricaded, what was the Captain's next move? Go to Mesolongi despite Byron's coldness? Return to Athens and patch up any remaining problems with Odysseus? Or stay in Salona for a while and see how far he could stretch his liaison with Fanny Price?

Trelawny looked up from his letter. Stavros had just entered the great yard with a professional man, evidently a doctor. Stavros gave Trelawny a friendly wave, and hurried off with the doctor in the direction of the sick-room.

The doctor was an Italian who spoke English. As he explained at some length to Mr Darcy, he had been Medical Officer with the Levant Company in Famagusta until 1821 when the company had been dissolved. Cyprus offered no prospects for a doctor. But Greece since the start of the war! The harvest there was bountiful beyond all precedent! Salona, as perhaps Milord had observed, was swimming in money. And the patient? As soon as he'd glimpsed Elizabeth Darcy on the other side of the chamber, the doctor had concerned himself largely with avoiding her and the miasmal air[114] at her bedside. He listened now to Marianne's explanation and asked half-a-dozen questions. He felt Fanny's hand, decided that her temperature was normal, and asked her to feel Mrs Darcy's forehead.

'No fever,' Fanny said a few minutes later. 'As far as I can tell.'

'You know what we're all thinking, Doctor,' Mr Darcy said. 'Could it be…? Typhoid?'

'Yes,' the doctor replied. 'Very possible.'

'In that case, what should we do?' Mr Darcy asked.

'You have money for nurse?'

'Yes.'

'I send excellent nurse. One week, twenty *piastre*.'

'I'll pay her when she arrives.'

'Not pay her. You pay me. One week now.'

Mr Darcy nodded. 'What shall we do till the nurse arrives?' he asked curtly, repelled by the doctor's haggling.

'Wash lady. Keep lady cool. Lady health is delicate. I will come every day. Ten *piastre*?'

Mr Darcy nodded again. 'Food?' he asked.

'Chicken. Vegetable. Not wine. Not beef.'

'Drink?'

'Only lemon juice mix with vinegar made from apple.'

'Where do we get the vinegar?'

'From apothecary.'

'Medicine?'

'*Basilico*. In English *basil*. In Greek *vasilikos*. Boil twenty leaf in cup of water, and *zenzero*. In English *ginger*. In Greek *tzintzer*.' Evidently the doctor intended to earn his ten *piastres*, if not as a physician, then as a walking lexicon. 'Boil until half water is boil away.' With the fingers of both hands, he imitated water evaporating into the air. 'Add some *miele*. You know *honey*? Lady take one small spoon two hour, two hour, two hour.'

'Understand that?' Mr Darcy asked Marianne.

'Yes, sir,' she said.

'Nurse can make medicine,' the doctor assured them. 'I return tomorrow.' He held out his hand. 'Twenty for nurse. Ten for me.'

After the doctor had been paid, Fanny brought up an entirely different problem: could the doctor look at the wounds on her neck. If everything was healing properly, could he perhaps remove the stitches? Mr Darcy nodded approval. 'Outside though,' he said. 'I don't want to disturb Mrs Darcy.'

In the antechamber the doctor admired the work of his Athenian colleague: the stitches were beautifully done. He cleaned the wounds and neatly removed the catgut. Fanny must have wonderful blood, he said: healing was well under weigh. If she left the wounds open to the air, by Easter the only trace of the cuts would be three scars, and even scars fade with time.

'I'll keep them covered a while longer,' Fanny replied. 'Please refresh the dressings.'

As the next days passed, it became ever clearer that Mrs Darcy was indeed suffering from enteric fever. Marianne, who had endured the disease herself long ago in Athens and who had afterward tended two of Lord Elgin's artists, took over the patient, sharing the duties with the local nurse, an Italian woman of perhaps thirty-five who kept house for the doctor and tended his richer patients.

Mr Darcy would now need more ready money than he had foreseen. Jethro Solomonides was summoned. He brought with him gold coins and silver, the necessary papers for Mr Darcy to sign, and, free of charge, the latest rumours about the Greek Loan. According to the moneylender, the Greek Committee in London had kept its word: already barrels of gold were sailing toward Mesolongi.

With cash in his strong-box, Mr Darcy still had two problems: keeping his wife in something like isolation, and keeping his daughter out of harm's way. The problem of Mrs Knightley's wish to return to Athens, he politely ignored. To keep Elizabeth isolated, he improvised a fever ward in a small chamber on the opposite side of the corridor. He asked Stavros to write a Greek sign with the words *Beware Fever*, but Stavros declined: fever victims were quarantined, usually under horrible conditions. Surely the master did not wish… He was right: the master did not wish, and the sign was not written. To keep Jane a little safer, her father doubled the guard outside their chamber. At night, he and the Captain took turns sleeping in front of the locked door. Mr Darcy had never enquired exactly how Fanny had persuaded the Captain to return to the *kervansaray*, but his gratitude was sincere. He even offered her his gold-inlaid pistols to enrich her display of weapons, but, for reasons she did not disclose, she preferred her trusty cap-locks. All they could do now was pray and wait: it would be three weeks, maybe four, before Mrs Darcy could travel.

Turning with relief, which I'm sure the Reader will share, from the sick and endangered to the healthy and free, I can report that the Captain kept at least one of his promises. Each morning, after exercising the horses, he gave his young *protégé* (or *protégée* if the Reader so prefer) a lesson in the noble art of fencing. A second lesson followed each afternoon. Fanny's rapier was too short and her wrist too weak for her to make rapid progress, but her eye was keen, and she was quick as a hungry ferret when she saw an opening. Although Trelawny himself was more at home with a cutlass or a dagger, his practice with Fanny in the yard was professional enough to attract attention: expert counsel in many languages was lavished on him and his novice. Naturally, Emma Knightley was also interested in Fanny's progress both as a swordsman and as an established, or perhaps as a prospective, *inamorata*: she missed none of Fanny's lessons, and few of the Venusian signs. But the signs puzzled her. Fanny obviously revelled in her new freedom. She acted more like a man with every day that passed: her stride lengthened, and she landed an ever-harder punch on the Captain's shoulder when he teazed her. When the three of them took a stroll together, Fanny's arm was offered as confidently as the Captain's. More surprising, perhaps, it was just as comfortable to lean on. Against all the proprieties, Fanny still wore no sign of mourning for her dead husband and never mentioned his name in conversation. Such behaviour was, perhaps, no real surprise: as Emma well knew, widowhood had brought Fanny a release from bondage, the first taste of liberty in her bottled-up and demanding life. Yet all was not sweetness and light. Often in the consulate, Fanny had been offhand and hostile, and that had not changed. Her moods alternated, like sunshine and showers in an English April. The Captain, of course, was equally puzzling. If he was not in love with Fanny, he was devoting time and trouble to an inspired imitation. Was it love or a well-played game? Emma favoured the idea of love. But even so, teaching Fanny to lunge and parry, and gallivanting round town with his ladylove dressed as a desperado, hardly made for a conventional courtship. On the other hand again, neither the Captain nor Mrs Bertram was cut from common cloth. With so many *other hands*, Emma was in an ecstasy of surmise and speculation. Her wish to return to Athens evaporated completely.

Late each afternoon, food was brought in from a *taverna,* and Marianne left the sick-room to join the others for the big meal of the day. These suppers weren't solemn, but neither were they cheerful. The symptoms and cure of typhoid fever do not make for lively conversation. The subject of the kidnappers from Athens was addressed briefly at the supper table but not discussed: no one had seen Cosmo and Zander, and no one had any idea where they might be found.

Each evening, some half an hour before dusk, Mr Darcy set off for a stroll, taking Stavros for company. Where they went, whether to one of the countless *tavernas* in the town or to the open fields, nobody asked. A few minutes after their departure, the Captain also disappeared, taking Fanny Bertram, as she was still known, for company. At first, the Captain and Fanny stayed away for an hour. Soon this hour extended to two and then, as time passed, to the whole evening and part of the night. Fanny, of course, owed nobody an explanation of her behaviour, and she offered none. To herself she explained it, with some measure of sophistry, in this way: she was fulfilling Mr Darcy's request, keeping the Captain with them, and ensuring, as far as possible, the safety of them all. What compromises she made with propriety, what concessions she made to the Captain's ardour, what novel pleasures she enjoyed in the Captain's company, these were matters for her own conscience and of interest to nobody.

Nobody? As I have already indicated, all this uncertainty inflamed Emma's imagination almost to the point of spontaneous combustion.[115] One evening Emma could restrain her curiosity no longer: she excused herself toward the end of supper and retreated behind a curtain. Here she resumed her disguise as a portly countrywoman and prepared to follow her quarry. Of course, they were too quick for her: they sped up the hill in the direction of the castle like wolfhounds. Not wishing to lose the scent quite so easily, Emma continued her slow trudge up the hill, pausing now and then to rest her weary knees. Maybe she'd find her hounds somewhere in the hills or meet them again on their way down.

In fact, much to her relief, she spotted the Captain in the garden of a *taverna* just short of the castle. The place was crowded: soldiers drinking together, soldiers drinking with the usual miscellany of women, and women drinking together as they waited, or perhaps prowled, for escorts. It did not rival *stations de plaisir* that Emma had investigated in Marseilles, but even so it was engagingly improper. The Captain was busy manoeuvring a chair, elegantly and attentively, so that a woman in a white gown trimmed with blue lace, a young woman apparently, could sit down. An Indian shawl was spread on the chair, perhaps for the lady's comfort, perhaps to protect the white fabric of her gown from the grime deposited by previous sitters. The woman's head was concealed in a fashionable poke bonnet, and a white chiffon scarf protected her neck. She was enjoying the fuss which generally attends the be-seating of an elegant lady, enjoying it mercilessly. Emma, sweating, hot and dowdy in her disguise, recalled such manoeuvres with a flutter of envy. But where was Fanny?

When the princess was finally seated, the Captain signalled to the waiter. Trelawny's dress was somehow different, less exotic than it had been in Athens. Each day he had toned it down a little, as Emma now recalled. Only the *fustanella* remained, and even that, she observed, was gathered at the knees to resemble breeches.

As she looked round for Fanny, the truth dawned: the young

lady *was* Fanny. Emma could be vindictive when she felt provoked, but there was no provocation in the couple at the table: they evidently wished to be alone for a while, and who could blame them? But even so it wouldn't do: it wouldn't do at all! Secret excursions to places of ill repute: it was shameless, very possibly it was immoral, and, worst of all, it was inexcusably public. Emma steamed into the garden like one of Brunel's expresses puffing into Paddington Station.[116]

The Captain saw her approach, and immediately stood up with a well-feigned smile of welcome. 'My dear Mrs Knightley!' he exclaimed. 'You should have said that you wanted to accompany us. We would have been delighted.'

'Yes,' Fanny agreed, pointedly standing as one does for an older woman, though Emma was, in fact, slightly her junior. 'Delighted.'

The Captain seated the new guest, making, if possible, more fuss of the hobgoblin who joined him now than of the *houri*[117] who had joined him earlier.

The waiter came and drinks were ordered: *tsipouro* and water for the Captain, wine for the ladies. When conversation began, it went straight to the point.

'You're very sly, you two,' Mrs Knightley remarked, surveying the garden, with perhaps a hint of disappointment at its decorum, though one might wonder what exactly she expected. Half an hour before sundown, even in a place of assignation, lowered voices and polished manners should hardly have surprised her.

'Sly? Anything but!' the Captain replied. 'An open garden on the main road halfway up a mountain! How could that be sly?'

Emma eyed Fanny's pretty dress. It was much lower cut than the dresses she'd worn in the consulate and more skilfully supported: it made Fanny look girlish and, Emma had to admit, surprisingly close to buxom, the little witch.

The conscientious Reader will have observed that, so far in this book, this is the first scene in which all three of my informants participate with no one else present. Each of them has described the scene to me in detail, and the descriptions are worth comparing, if, for no other reason, then as an illustration of the difficulties facing a writer in search of historical truth. To begin with the Captain's view: he said that the only thing he clearly remembered of that meeting was how extraordinarily attractive he found Fanny. She was a woman, not a girl, and a few minutes before, she'd been a boy. Now she was everything a man could desire. It was as though her spirit had escaped from some prison cell, as though her throttled voice had burst forever free. At that moment, if she had, *sans merci,* offered him a chalice containing some unknown elixir, he would have drained it in one draught and followed her to any of the ends of the earth. Allowing for Uncle Trelawny's usual hyperbole, it seems that she had made some small impression on his fickle heart. The Captain did recall that Emma Knightley had joined them, but he remembered nothing of what she was wearing, what she said, or how she behaved. He saw Fanny, *And nothing else saw all day long.*[118] Much in my narrative reflects badly on Uncle Trelawny. That he could shut out the world of calculation and advantage, of spite and strategy, and naively sigh for this simple woman (simple, if you ignore the fact that she had just murdered her husband) speaks well of him, I think. Most men, myself included, do not have this streak of lyricism, of romance, in their nature.

Emma recounts the scene as a victory and a vindication. Down in the *kervansaray* she'd known something was 'going on.' The glances of two people in love could not escape her long-cultivated power of observation. Perhaps the rest of the world allowed itself to be hoodwinked, but not Emma Knightley: since the poetry-reading in the consulate, her vision had been sharp as that of an unhooded hawk. In the garden of the *taverna* in Salona, she confronted the guilty pair, boldly and without hesitation. What were they up to? They must have rented a room somewhere in the neighbourhood, probably in the very *taverna* where they were sitting. The idea of the room was suggested by Fanny's dress. A dress like that, while it was waiting to be flaunted, must be stored and hidden, together with the bonnet, the scarf, and whatever Fanny might be wearing underneath, though that seemed to be fashionably little. A room? In a tavern? What use might a freebooter and his idol find for such a room? No great mystery there. On the other hand, Emma had not the least intention of betraying the secret she had so assiduously uncovered. Later, of course, Emma had to admit that the *actual* secret was only half the secret she had anticipated. But even that half was rich enough in detail and copious enough in interest to sustain a lifelong friendship between the female detective and the sylph in the Neapolitan bonnet.

Fanny, which comes as no surprise, remembers the scene altogether differently. Yes, the Captain had hired a room in that very *taverna*. Yes, she'd bought the white dress in the bazaar in Salona, and a dressmaker had taken in the waist for her and subtly (or so she believed) adjusted the neckline. And yes, the dress did spend its mornings and afternoons in the room with a servant appointed to freshen it up with needle and flat-iron. But what she most clearly remembered was that, when she had been discovered philandering with the Captain, she had, as yet, made no commitment, she was still *free*. On the two evenings previous, the Captain had rapturously rehearsed his role as lover, proclaiming a passion irrevocable, undying and unsurpassable in its intensity. She had no reason to believe him, but it was agreeable to hear the words, and it was exciting, perched on a cliff-edge halfway up a snow-capped mountain, to hint that she might reciprocate his feelings. The evening before, in what had been an entirely new experience for her, she'd allowed him to press his warm lips to her fingers, to her shoulder, and once to her mouth, and all that in the cheerful publicity of the garden. On the other hand, Emma's intrusion had not been entirely unwelcome: although it postponed Fanny's next skirmish with the Captain, such postponement gave Fanny time to breathe, a full evening to recover her equanimity.

Ever since they'd heard the rumour that Byron's millions were approaching Mesolongi, Fanny had looked for some diminution in the Captain's ardour, but, so far, he had firmly maintained his stance, unbent, unbending and ready for action.

A moment of youthful romance? A moment of shrewdness rewarded? A moment of reflection and insecurity? Or all three? How, O Clio, Muse of History,[119] should the faithful historian explain what happened that evening in the demesnes of Mount Parnassus, the sacred dwelling-place that Thou hast shared with Thy Sister-Muses since time immemorial?

Dusk descended quickly. The night was cool. The ladies drank wine enough to bring merriment, but not enough to unstring their tongues completely. When Fanny began to shiver, the Captain gallantly tucked her shawl round her shoulders. It was a handsome shawl, Emma observed, though not new. The dress, too, Emma noted, had been turned once, or possibly twice. The three of them talked about clothes, about weapons, about the thousand and one things sacrificed by desperate travellers to the merchants of Salona and now on sale at bargain prices. Fearlessly Trelawny shepherded them through the names and the roles of the Nine Muses, but Fanny refused to be impressed. She accused the Captain of inventing the whole thing for the amusement of two ignorant women who wouldn't know a muse from a myrmidon if they met one in the marketplace. In fact, of course, she was perfectly familiar with the Muses, and even helped the Captain with the name of the Muse of Comedy when he pretended to forget it.

Despite the lively talk, Emma too began to shiver. A peddler of shawls kept his stand by the garden gate, but no one suggested patronising him: the evening had plainly come to an end. Fanny went to her secret room and became a boy again. Then the three of them walked back to the *kervansaray* with Emma enjoying the protection of her gentleman friends and wishing, sadly, that she was dressed for the occasion.

The next evening began similarly with Mr Darcy and Stavros taking their walk. This time, however, before the Captain set off for the castle with *his* companion, he asked Emma if she would care to join them. She declined: she would stay in the *kervansaray* and give up her evening to a game of *piquet* with Jane. With a flattering show of reluctance, the Captain, *Fanny's buccaneer* as Emma now called him, accepted her decision.

Freed of Emma's intrusive company, Fanny and her buccaneer were free to make their own entertainment. The Captain suggested that instead of scampering up the hill so that Fanny could transform herself into the most charming, winsome, etc. etc., they attend first to a little unfinished business: that afternoon while fencing, Fanny had caught her foot on an uneven cobblestone and had almost fallen. Now he wanted to see if the rough place might be made plain, especially since Fanny's movements were becoming more agile. For their practice, he had chosen a shady corner of the great yard, well away from the stables, the water fountain and the main gate. They quickly found the problem: a fig tree had established itself against the wall, and its roots were unsettling the cobbles. As they examined the offending stones, a scuffle near the fountain caught their attention. Two men and a woman. They saw one of the men throw a cloth over the woman's head, a big cloth, heavy and smothering. Then the men grabbed her and dragged her toward the fountain where a donkey cart stood waiting. The woman wasn't fighting: either she was too weak or the men gripped her too closely.

'Jane?' the Captain asked with sudden urgency.

'No,' Fanny said. 'Jane wouldn't leave the room.'

'Let's make sure,' the Captain insisted.

The kidnappers, if indeed they were kidnappers, bundled the woman into the cart. One of them slammed up the tail-board, while the other grabbed the donkey's bridle, tugging hard. The cart gathered speed toward the great portal, as always wide open until dusk.

'Quickly,' the Captain urged. They started to run, but the cart was through the gate and into the street before they could head it off.

They reached the fountain. A woman's headscarf lay trampled on the wet cobbles: red chiffon. Jane had a scarf just like it, a gift from Cora Shrubb as it happened.

Despite the crowd in the street outside the *kervansaray*, Fanny quickly spotted the cart, heading toward the Delphi road. One man was dragging the unwilling donkey forward, the other, not much more than a boy, was guarding the tail-board. They were armed with daggers but not, it seemed, with pistols. The cart was making slow progress through the traffic. The Captain stopped, grabbing Fanny's arm to slow her down.

'Careful,' he said. 'We don't know that it's Jane.'

'We can find out,' Fanny replied sturdily, her hand, like the hand of a man, finding the hilt of her sword.

'It's too crowded. Let's follow them a while,' the Captain said. 'Me ahead. You behind.'

Fanny nodded. 'How far behind?'

'Ten yards. Keep an eye on me. When I stop them, you come up from behind and nail the boy. Tip of your sword, you remember where?'

Fanny touched her chin just below the root of her tongue. Through her neckcloth, she could feel the scars which itched but no longer hurt her.

'Scarface,' the Captain said with a grin. 'We'll make a pirate of you yet.'

Fanny watched him as he pushed ahead through the crowd. Who was he after all? Was he really *Fanny's buccaneer*, as Emma Knightley now called him to his face? And Fanny herself? What was Emma's *nom de guerre* for her? *The buccaneer's moll* perhaps? In any case, something to fit a silly woman transformed from a clergyman's wife into a brawling quean on the road from Athens to Salona, like a character in a novel by Lesage?

A *quean*? A *moll*? They were words she'd heard but never used. *Moll*... The sound was soft, comfortable somehow. Surely a buccaneer would love his *moll*? Wasn't that a rule of piratical romance? And did Captain Trelawny love his Scarface? No more than she loved him, probably. And how much was that?

The cart ahead jolted over a gap in the paving. The cart! She should watch the cart and forget about love. Alert now, she saw the Captain scan the kidnappers as he strode past them.

Jane? Was it Jane in the cart? She pictured again the scene at the fountain: a female figure, small, the same build as Jane. But the image was obscure: Fanny had only glimpsed the woman before the heavy cloth had swallowed her up.

Fanny stayed, unobtrusively, ten yards behind the cart, stopping when it stopped, moving when it moved, alert for a signal from the Captain. Whether he loved her or not, he trusted her. At that moment, he was trusting her with something difficult and dangerous, something on which his own life might depend. She felt the pommel of her sword, then the grip: if she drew it... She went through the movement in her mind. Draw. Clasping the drawn sword, her hand would be above her face. Drop her hand. Flick the foible of the sword upward. Lunge so that the point was at the boy's throat, and all before he had time to think, let alone draw his knife. And then she panicked: it was impossible. The Captain was asking too much. There were twenty tricks to disarm a swordsman: the onlookers in the yard had discussed them endlessly and acted some of them out. And for every move there was a counter-move. All this Fanny knew from watching and listening, but almost none of it from practice. She should give up now, overtake the Captain, and tell him to think again.

But she didn't: she followed the cart, sweating and suddenly timorous.

After the cart had passed through the Delphi Gate, the road broadened and the traffic eased. Fanny saw the Captain stop and pretend to fasten his shoe. That must be the signal for her to move closer. She strode forward. She saw the donkey draw level with the Captain, she saw him stand up, and she heard him shout something at the donkey-driver.

Her hand went to the hilt of her sword. She drew it half from its scabbard. Then a shock. The boy, fourteen she now saw or perhaps younger, spun on his heel and charged blindly toward her. Awkward, her sword half drawn, she stepped aside, letting him rush past. He didn't stop, but disappeared back though the Delphi Gate and down the first side street, perhaps to escape, perhaps to summon help. The other man, with the Captain's sword at his throat, stood with the bridle in his hand, making no show of resistance.

'Check the cart,' the Captain shouted.

Fanny sheathed her sword. In three steps she was at the tail-board. The woman was struggling now, her shouts and screams muffled by the cloth. Two ropes secured the cloth, one round her elbows, one round her knees. Her feet were naked. The soles were rough as the bark of a mountain ash, grey and purple. Her toenails were bruised and blackened. Clearly not Jane.

'It's not her,' Fanny cried, her voice shrill with excitement. 'Shall I let her go?'

'No,' the Captain shouted back, lowering his sword. 'Nothing to do with us.'

The little scene had already attracted a knot of spectators: Fanny and the Captain should escape before the crowd grew threatening.

Fanny unlatched the tail-board. Quickly she untied the rope round the woman's ankles. Then she leaned into the cart and released the second rope. Maybe the woman had been kidnapped, maybe not: the local people would sort it out. 'Let's go,' she bawled.

The Captain followed her, sheathing his sword. 'Some pirate you are!' he laughed. 'Master Scarface!' Yes, she had her new name, and it wasn't Frank or John. But, she had to admit it, *Fanny* really didn't match the way she dressed or the way she swaggered about the town: the way she was *obliged* to dress and to swagger, as she'd almost come to believe, relying on her promise to Mr Darcy to keep an eye on the Captain.

Trelawny took her by the arm, hurrying away, but not running. They went through the Delphi Gate and turned into the first side street. Behind a drainpipe at the corner, cowered the boy from the tail-board. The Captain grabbed him by the scruff of his neck and shook him as a gundog shakes an injured duck.

'Don't be unfair,' Fanny said quietly. 'He never hurt us.'

The boy crashed to the ground and then sat up feeling his neck and shaking his head: he was in some pain. Fanny put her hand in her pocket.

'If you give him a *piastre*...,' the Captain began.

'Shall I?'

'If you do, I'll never talk to you again.'

Fanny took a *piastre* from her pocket, bent down and pressed it into the boy's hand.

The Captain said nothing more as he and Fanny made their way through the town and up the hill toward the fortress. On previous evenings, he'd waited for her outside the *taverna*, in the garden: now he followed her closely through the open door and into the *taverna* itself. The tavern-keeper, sitting behind his bar, held out a simple, iron key to the pretty young man who took it and smiled his thanks. The tavern-keeper smiled back. Often enough he'd seen the gentleman disappear into his room, emerge as an eye-watering doll, and then reverse the change a few hours later. To his experienced eye, she was plainly a girl, though clever at disguises. And not to his eye only. Several regular customers had asked about her already: if she stayed in Salona, he'd find her plenty of work when her Albanian tired of her. Or at least that was how Captain Trelawny read the man's expression.

Fanny stopped abruptly a few steps from her door, with the Captain still behind her. What did she want? What did she expect? There was still time to tell the Captain to wait in the garden. Or should they take the next few steps together? And if that happened…? If she allowed it, what would Captain Trelawny be to her when she saw him next morning? And what would she be to him?

Chapter 15

THE RING

Mrs Darcy mended slowly. The doctor called each day, though the benefit his patient derived from his visits was blatantly overpriced at ten *piastres*. His appointed nurse, however, worked well with Marianne Brandon: the two of them played cards at Mrs Darcy's bedside and drank what Fanny calls half a bottle of *tsipouro* a day, and what Emma describes as two.

At this time, a fresh anxiety struck Mr Darcy. Fanny's new intimacy with Trelawny had prevented his desertion. Yet now this same intimacy itself posed a threat: why should not the two of them, Fanny and Trelawny, desert together? The world was their oyster. Why should they wait, trapped in Salona, while Elizabeth recovered from her fever and the diplomatic mill in Korfu ground out a rescue plan?

One morning, exercising the horses in the fields, Mr Darcy put the question to Fanny directly: 'Wouldn't you be safer riding ahead with the Captain?' he asked. 'Leaving us all behind?'

'Have you been talking to the Captain?' she replied. 'He asks the same thing five times a day.'

'And would it impose too far on a lady's privacy to ask what you reply?'

'I tell him he's making a mistake. The same mistake you're making, apparently.'

'And what mistake is that?'

'You both seem to think I'd turn my back on young Jane, forsake my friend Emma, and abandon Elizabeth and Marianne in the midst of this terrible fever. Is that really your opinion of me?' *After my ride to Athens*: she didn't say the words, but her voice was pregnant with them.

They rode on, Fanny slightly ahead. For a moment, Fanny's rebuke stung Darcy into silence. Then, 'I must apologise,' he said. 'Your loyalty goes beyond my previous…'

Fanny turned to smile at him. She shook her head. 'At least *you* believe my answer,' she said, hinting that the Captain did not.

They began a conversation, kindly on his side, friendly on hers. Perhaps Mr Darcy found it easier to like her as a young swashbuckler than as a chaplain's wife, but neither in Salona nor in their later relations, did he discover the lively, feminine side of her nature as George Knightley had done, the side which the Captain was now busily exploring.

And so things remained until, toward the end of her third week of sickness, Mrs Darcy had had enough. She dismissed the Italians, both nurse and doctor, and declared herself sufficiently recovered to walk about the chamber. If she could lean on Marianne, that would be support enough.

Under normal circumstances, or even under the abnormal circumstances prevailing in the consulate, the mosque and the *kervansaray*, Elizabeth Darcy would have chosen Marianne neither as her nurse nor as her friend. But three weeks of Marianne's gentle and patient concern had built a bridge between the well-respected lady and the squalid exile. In the sick-room, Marianne had emerged as a tender-hearted, devoted woman, ready to risk her own health, ready to lavish care on a sick acquaintance: care and *affection* one might almost say. Elizabeth, in a desperate hour, had responded to Marianne's generosity with the (sometimes hidden) warmth of her own nature. And so it was that Elizabeth began to lean on Marianne as she had never leant on any woman, apart perhaps from her older sister, Jane.

And then, as she recovered her strength, Mrs Darcy began to lean on Marianne in a new way. Marianne's knowledge of painting and antiquities was impressive, at least to Mrs Darcy who knew little of either. If, or more optimistically *when*, they all returned to England, Marianne could, perhaps, advise on the redecoration of Pemberley: find the right sculptures, choose the right pictures, combine the right colours, and so on. If that were a success, she might go on to oversee the work on the Darcys' new townhouse in London. At this stage, Mrs Darcy had not discussed with her husband the employment of Marianne or the redecoration of his family seat, let alone the purchase of a townhouse in London, but she foresaw no difficulties.

Three times a day, Fitzwilliam visited her bedside, looking the picture of Gloom. During one visit, to cheer himself up, he told her a secret: each evening (this was the secret) he and Stavros prayed for her recovery. Salona offered few places of prayer: two mosques and half-a-dozen Greek churches in all. Mr Darcy chose a different church each evening. He could have prayed in the fields, of course, but God, he believed, would hear his prayers more readily if he said them in a place sanctified for the purpose. Elizabeth saw no reason to disagree. Turning, however, to *serious matters*... By this means, of course, she intended to introduce the subject of her future London residence, but she failed: her lord insisted that *serious matters* must await her full recovery. Unsurprisingly perhaps, Elizabeth was not discouraged: knowing her husband's gallant nature, she also knew that the best time for winning his approval lay, at the latest, some days *before* her return to perfect health.

On the day that Mrs Darcy rose from her sickbed with no intention of returning to it, the long-awaited letter from Korfu arrived.

My dear Vice-Consul,

I understand both from your good self and from your principal, Mr Knightley, that you are currently escorting a number of ladies, including your wife and daughter, from Athens toward Korfu. I further understand from your letter that you are at present trapped in Salona with no evident path open to you across the mountains to the N. You ask for my assistance.

First, I would strongly discourage you from attempting to cross the mountains. Heavy, late snow has fallen, and it will be some weeks before the tracks are open to any but the most intrepid. It seems improbable that your ladies fall into this category.

I would counsel taking the SW route from Salona, passing, but not entering, Mesolongi, and then heading N to Astakos.

A recently recommissioned vessel of His Majesty's Navy, the <u>Laconia</u>, Captain Wentworth commanding, has recently joined the Ionian squadron in Korfu, and I have ordered Captain Wentworth to stand by in Astakos from 24th April to take you on board and to convey you to Korfu. Mrs Wentworth[120] accompanies her husband aboard the <u>Laconia</u>, and her presence will certainly ease the transport of six (or is it five?) ladies on board what is, after all, a warship. Once in Astakos, give word to the harbourmaster that he should flag the <u>Laconia</u> of your arrival. A word of warning, the <u>Laconia</u> must leave Astakos by 28th April.

By means of the messenger who brings you these presents, please inform me that you accept, and will comply, with this arrangement.

Please convey my particular respects to Mrs Knightley of whose visit to Korfu, during the late Sir

Thomas Maitland's Commissionership, I retain the most pleasant memories. Please inform her that the Governor's Residence is now almost complete and that she is welcome to stay there for as long as she chooses.

Yours respectfully,

Emma preserved this letter, perhaps on account of Sir Frederick's *most pleasant memories*, and allowed me to make a copy of it.

The journey could now begin. It took a day to repack the wain, to refurbish their food supply and to prepare the horses. Other purchases were necessary too. After Emma had described the receptions and the banquets which constituted her own *most pleasant memories* of Korfu, she agreed with Mrs Darcy that the clothes they had brought from Athens simply would not *do*. And Jane must be considered. At present Jane was hidden, disguised, sequestered. She would resume her male costume for the journey, but it was imperative that Jane enter the capital of Ionia in the character of a young lady. Mrs Bertram was a problem too: despite her extraordinary attitude to widowhood, she would require full wifely mourning. All in all, at least another day must be devoted to shopping. In view of her new closeness to Mrs Darcy, Marianne helped her and the others scour the markets, not only as chief negotiator but also as a tastefully reluctant beneficiary. In a flurry of activity, clothes were bought and altered, and a week's supply of medicaments was prepared for Mrs Darcy.

It was Good Friday, 16th April, before everything was ready and they could leave Salona behind them. At first light, the cart, five horsemen and three pack mules rattled toward the Delphi Gate. Early as it was, the churches were already full, alabaster windows glowed golden-brown, while mournful singing and the tang of frankincense spilled into the empty streets.

The Reader is already familiar with the mode of travel adopted by Mr Darcy and his party and with the condition of the roads in Romelia, so I need not repeat the details.

Sir Frederick Adam's letter had reported the mountain weather correctly. The heavy snow he had mentioned, however, was now melting. It was running off the hillsides in rock-rolling torrents. On the first morning at a swollen ford, the little troupe lost a mule: its leg was crushed by a boulder that came loose from the bank and smashed into the kicking, panicking animal. The mule's body, still lashing out and violent, was washed onto a shingle bank half a mile below the ford. Fanny and Stavros with one of the spare horses trotted downstream to recover the load. Stavros wanted to leave the now useless mule to drown. Fanny, however, overruled him. Despite the expenditure of a cap, a ball and a quantity of black powder, all of which might be needed later, she blew out the animal's brain.

On Tuesday, at about mid-day, the grumbling of the River Evinos[121] made itself heard ahead. The stony riverbed growled beneath the torrent like the hounds of hell roused, fretted, and ready to kill. Trelawny, Fanny and Jane led the way, as they had done for many miles. Jane could, of course, have ridden with her father and Stavros, but Fanny's words in the *kervansaray* had acquired for Jane something like the authority of the Sultan's *firman*: *The Captain won't let anything happen to you. And nor shall I.* And so, for a while, young Jane Darcy became the inseparable companion of an unrepentant mariticide and a ruthless privateer. When they had left England, the Darcys, husband and wife, had promised themselves that a European tour would enhance the education of their only daughter. Did her dealings with Cora Shrubb, did the impalement of Odysseus's victims, did the treacheries of Lord Byron's jackal advance Jane's education? Or set it back? As she grew up, Jane's character took an unusually serious turn. It would interest me as a medical man to enquire how much of that seriousness came from her ancestry, and how much of it came from these harsh days in Greece. Perhaps, one day, science will give us the key to unlocking such secrets.

The three riders reached the gravel-bank that ran beside the turbulent water. Ten yards from the water's edge they reined in. Only five miles separated them now from Mesolongi and barely forty from Astakos, but it might as well have been five hundred. The river was a mighty obstacle: an intrepid horseman might cross the flood, but a cart must inevitably be swept away and destroyed. Trelawny and his two companions waited for a moment in silence, giving the others time to catch up.

Mr Darcy and Stavros were the first to arrive. 'There's a ford?' Mr Darcy asked, more by way of stating a fact than of asking a question. 'Where is it?'

'Sometimes here, sometimes there,' Stavros replied with a shrug. 'In winter Evinos is big river. Dangerous river.'

'You have not travelled this road before?' Mr Darcy asked.

'Not with cart. Never with cart,' Stavros confirmed.

'So you have no idea where the ford might be.'

'Idea, yes. But certain, no,' Stavros equivocated.

The cart pulled up, and Elizabeth Darcy climbed out, once again a rough and ready countrywoman. She took in the situation at a glance. 'If this is the only road between the hills and the sea,' she said, 'it must be busy. If we wait, someone will know how to get across.'

'My dear!' Mr Darcy exclaimed, raising his hat. 'We would be lost without you.'

'And not long to wait,' Trelawny added. 'Look!' He pointed across the river. 'People already.'

At that moment, on the far bank, a troop of three riders trotted into sight.

'Mrs Darcy, get back in the cart. The women stay out of sight.' Trelawny was taking charge. 'The rest of us, pistols ready. Stavros, go down to the edge. You do the talking.'

Fanny checked the caps in her pistols. All correct. She was watching the river intently, her stirrup a few inches from Trelawny's. Jane had taken refuge on Fanny's other side, but not so close. Emma, peeping out of the cart, saw Trelawny's foot reach out to Fanny's, and the two feet exchange a second of silent pressure. Emma was annoyed. She knew that Fanny had come to an understanding with the Captain, but, try as she might, she could not fathom the details. Most of the day, the Captain and his lady, if indeed she were such, rode together, well away from the cart. Jane was always with them, laughing and joking. With each day that passed, Jane had grown more sanguine, released now from the oppressive gloom of the *kervansaray*. The nights, Jane spent in the cart, safe between her mother and Marianne Brandon. That left the other four to keep guard, Mr Darcy with Stavros, and the Captain with Fanny. During the Captain's spell, Emma, had forced herself into wakefulness. She had detected a stream of minor improprieties, but none of them allowed a firm conclusion. Emma, with curiosity worthy of a Michael Faraday, wanted to know the inalienable truth. You, dear Reader, may share Emma's curiosity, but, on this subject, as on the final events in the Salona garden of assignation, I am forbidden to satisfy it: my lips are sealed. Naturally, of course, if I have told my tale as it deserved to be told, the discriminating Reader will draw the appropriate conclusions with no further prompting.

Fanny watched the three distant riders hesitate at the water's edge, then urge their horses into the wide, rippling surge. Shallows apparently: the riverbed on that side was stony and solid. The fast-flowing water covered the fetlocks of the horses, but seldom rose above their knees. Then, in midstream and still in shallow water, the three riders stopped. The mid-day sun flickering on the water dazzled Fanny's view: even so there was something familiar about two of the men. She shaded her eyes. Was she looking at Cosmo and Zander? She turned to the Captain who had the eagle-eye of a sailor. 'Is it who I think it is?' she asked. He ignored her question, slapping his reins on the neck of his horse, and urging it forward.

The Captain trotted across the shingle, passed Stavros, and splashed into the water, holding his horse on a painfully tight rein.

The water was deeper on this side of the river. With a whinny of panic, the horse slipped, its foreleg trapped in a cleft of some sort. The water surged as high as its stifle. The animal twisted and strained against the rein and against the riverbed. It plunged forward for a minute, fighting the current, and then found shallow water again. The Captain joined the three horsemen, still stationary in midstream. Fanny saw one of them open a leather budget and give the Captain a letter, which he took without unsealing it. For a while the four men talked, letting their horses drop their heads and sniff the water. Then the conversation grew suddenly earnest, and the horses huddled closer together. Finally, Fanny saw the Captain turn toward her and cup one hand to his mouth. 'Fanny!' he shouted.

'What?' she shouted back.

She saw him beckon. She glanced up at Mr Darcy, who had been watching the episode from the top of the shingle-bank. He waved her forward: she should join the Captain.

Fanny negotiated the river easily, slackening the rein and relying on her horse to keep its footing. She liked horses and trusted them, unlike the Captain who despised all animals with one exception: an elephant which, or so he later claimed, had saved Zela's life during a tiger-hunt.

As Fanny neared the group, she saw that two of the men were indeed Cosmo and Zander. What was going on? What was the Captain's game?

'It's Byron,' the Captain said as soon as she was near enough to hear him.

Fanny stared at the unknown, third horseman. 'He's Byron?' The man looked no more like an English poet than his gelding looked like Marie Antoinette.

'No, no. He's just one of these damn Suliots.'

'And Byron?'

'Byron is dead. He died yesterday. That's what's in the letter.' He held out the letter toward her, the seal still unbroken.

Fanny shook her head. 'In Mesolongi?' she asked. For weeks she'd been dreaming, and now the dream was ending. In a few minutes, it would be played out completely. There was no point in arguing, no point in fighting: it was all but over.

'This changes everything, you understand?' the Captain said. 'I have to go.'

'You have to go to your dear, dead friend?' Or to the millions stacked in his house, she added silently.

'Of course. To my friend. How could I do otherwise? How could anyone do otherwise?'

'Will you burn his body on the beach?'

'Probably not.' The Captain winced at her sarcasm.

She looked around, absorbing the exotic scene: five horsemen standing in a torrent with snow-capped hills looming behind them. The scenery was the stuff of adventure, but the moment was not: it was a separation, a severance, as final and as brutal in its way as her last seconds with Edmund in the consulate.

'Shall I come with you?' she asked. 'Or shall I go to Astakos with the others?' She already knew Trelawny's answer, and she knew he was callous enough to make it.

'Go,' he said, trying to hide the quaver in his voice.

'Is that all? Just *go*?' Her voice was stronger than his, stronger by far.

'There's something I want to give you,' the Captain continued awkwardly, aware of the fierce, prescient light in Fanny's eyes. On his little finger he always wore a silver ring, a gift from Zela, as he had once whispered to her, of no great value, but, to him, a priceless relic. He pulled the ring from his finger and gave it to her. 'If ever you need me,' he said, 'send a messenger with this ring, and I'll be there. Wherever it is.'

Fanny took the ring. It stirred some distant memory of Lancelot and Guinevere. Was that how the Captain saw himself? As a knight of the Round Table? Inside the ring, an Arabic word was deeply engraved. *Zela,* she guessed. She gripped the ring in her hand, and looked Trelawny hard in the eye. Then, with all her strength, she hurled the treacherous piece of silver far away into the turbulent stream.

In fury, Trelawny's hand flashed to the grip of his sword. For a second he struggled, subduing some inner fiend. Then a look of brute resolution crossed his face. 'I'll be on my way then,' he said flatly. He jerked up his horse's head and set off for the far bank of the river as fast as his hard-pressed animal could bear him. The three Suliots made no move.

'Zander, you stay,' Fanny ordered. 'You two others go back to Mesolongi. With Mr Trelawny. Now.'

The two men turned tail and rode away. Regret arises from hope betrayed. Grief arises from undeserved cruelty suffered or inflicted. Almost without grief or regret, Fanny watched them go. 'Is there a proper ford? Further up the river?' she asked Zander. 'We have a cart.'

'I show you,' Zander replied, trying to sound helpful.

'First tell me,' Fanny said. 'This letter you gave Mr Trelawny?'

'From Mr Fletcher. You know Fletcher? He is Lord Byron man. He send us find Kapetan Trelawny.'

'Lord Byron is dead. You're quite sure.'

'Yes, milady.'

'Zander?' Fanny asked. There was a great deal that Zander might be able to tell her if she were cautious with her questions. 'That night? The night you deserted?'

'You told us *go in peace*. You gave us horses. You, not Kapetan.'

'Yes, I gave you horses. And you went to Athens? To Odysseus?'

'We are stop at city gate. We not go Odysseus: we are *take*.'

'Did Odysseus give you orders? Tell you what to do?'

'He ask: do we know Lord Darcy daughter, Jane?'

'And you told him *yes*.'

'Yes.'

'What else? Did he offer you money to find her? To bring her back to Athens?'

Zander made no reply: why admit the obvious?

'And you *did* find her. In Salona. With Mr Trelawny.'

Still Zander said nothing, waiting, evidently, to see what this strange Englishwoman wanted of him.

'Did you and Mr Trelawny talk about Jane?'

'Yes.'

'You told him you were looking for her?'

'Yes.'

'You told him Odysseus promised you money?'

'Money for Jane Darcy. Yes.'

'And what did the Captain say?'

'He say, not good idea. He say Odysseus is *not* pay us. He say perhaps we take Jane, Odysseus...' Zander briefly mimed throat-cutting. 'Kapetan say, forget Jane.'

'And did you? Forget Jane?'

'The Kapetan give us letter take Lord Byron.' He shrugged. 'Forget Jane, Kapetan say. Go Mesolongi.' Zander shrugged. 'For us is safer. You unnerstann?'

It was exactly as she'd feared: the Captain knew about the abduction of Jane Darcy, had known about it all along. He'd told no one. On the other hand, she thought, maybe that was for the best. He'd kept an eye on things, stayed close to Jane and her family so that he could protect them. Looked at in that light, he'd saved Jane rather than betrayed her. Perhaps she shouldn't condemn him till she'd spoken to him again. But when would that be? Never. *I'll be on my way then.* Those would be the last words she'd hear from him. Ever.

She tugged at her rein, turning her horse back toward the riverbank where Jane was waiting with her father. Jane saw the movement and waved. Fanny waved back.

'Zander,' she said. 'You come now. With me.'

Some thirty yards from the bank, a question crossed her mind: 'Zander,' she asked. 'What will Mr Trelawny do now? What's going to happen?'

For a moment, Zander seemed to anticipate a false step by his horse. He *brr-brred* a warning and tugged at the rein.

'Well?' Fanny urged him.

'Perhaps is something you not know, milady.'

'Something I don't know? About Mr Trelawny?'

'Kapetan...,' he hesitated. 'You know Tersitza Androutsos?'

'I've heard of her. Odysseus's sister?'

'Yes. The Kapetan, he marry with her.'

'Marry? When?'

'When Odysseus have 10 million gold, they marry.'

'The 10 million that is now in Mesolongi, with Lord Byron?'

'You know another 10 million?'

Fanny let go of the reins and her horse stopped. Zander stopped beside her. Fanny said nothing for a long while, lost in thought. 'I see,' she muttered finally. She listened to the rippling of the water and the sucking of the eddies, she felt her horse shake its head as the waterflies began to crawl toward its eyes, and she smelt the harsh wind blowing from the mountains.

'Zander,' she asked at length. 'Was there a deal? Did Odysseus demand a price for Tersitza? And the price was Jane?'

'I am soldier. I not can know. But after Christmas this everyone in Athina say: Jane is price for Tersitza. Kapetan give Jane Darcy to Odysseus, then Kapetan marry with Tersitza.'

'But Jane is still free. She's with us,' Fanny objected.

'Perhaps 10 million more important as Jane? The Kapetan bring Lord Governor 10 million, then he marry with Tersitza? I not can know what Kapetan is think. What Lord Governor is think.'

'Then he almost certainly will marry Odysseus's sister, and I can thank God,' Fanny said quietly.

'Thank God for Kapetan marry?' Zander was puzzled. 'You not want he marry with you?'

It was as though a serpent had been coiling and twisting after her, ready to sink its fangs into her heel.[122] 'No,' she said. 'Some women never marry. And... And I count myself among them.' At these words, the snake gave a final *hiss* and disappeared. She had bruised its head, smashed its skull, and she was free.

'Zander? Do you know the way to Astakos?'

'Yes, milady. First Etoliko. Then forest of oak tree. Very old road.' He hesitated. 'But guide for you is Stavros.'

'But you could come with us?' she asked. 'We'll pay you, of course.'

'Thank you, milady.' He laughed, showing his decayed brown teeth, and suddenly she laughed with him.

POSTSCRIPT

I seem to have come to the end of my material more abruptly than I had intended. My only remaining task is to satisfy the curiosity of my Reader as to who lived happily ever after and who did not, though I have already let several cats out of several bags.

The *Laconia* was waiting in Astakos exactly as planned. When Mr Darcy and the others boarded the ship, they were astonished to find Mrs Tilney already on board and waiting for them. In late March, the *Laconia* had taken on water in Piraeus, and Mr Knightley had arranged with Captain Wentworth a passage for Jane's exhausted governess. Under the kindly eye of Captain Wentworth and the soothing hand of his wife, Catherine had sailed without event to Astakos where, as planned, the ship had picked up the Darcys and their friends. Some weeks later, when the *Laconia* was ordered home with despatches, most of the refugees from Athens were once more aboard.

As to the fates of my various heroines, let us begin with Emma. George left the consular service some six months after Emma arrived in Korfu, and the couple returned safely to the fields and barns of Donwell Abbey. The mining project had collapsed. For a pittance, the Knightleys bought back their largely ruined estates from the mining company which had acquired them in 1817. Not long after the repurchase, when Emma was already thirty-five, she gave birth to a daughter, her first and only child. From the medical perspective, a first conception at thirty-five is unremarkable, but Emma heralded it as a miracle re-enacted from the Book of Genesis. When I last spoke to Emma, her daughter, named Frances in honour of Fanny Bertram, was about to marry a young man by the name of Weston, the youngest son of Emma's old governess.

Of Catherine Tilney, I know only what Fanny has told me. When the *Laconia* sailed for England, she (Mrs Tilney, not the *Laconia*) found work in Korfu as the governess of three simple girls, the daughters of an English wine merchant whose wife had died of enteric fever. Mrs Tilney had no wish to return to England: the balmy air of the Adriatic was gentle with her rheumatism, and she was not ready to exchange sunny skies and cheerful company for the cold, the damp, the tears and tiresomeness of an English country house. In fact, Mrs Tilney had no need to 'go governessing' again. For two brave words, *I'm Jane*, spoken one morning in a wood north of Eleusis, she received from the Darcys a handsome annuity. As far as I know she died in Korfu, and was buried in the English Cemetery there.[123]

The Darcys returned to Derbyshire in the summer of 1824. Fitzwilliam set off immediately for North Africa to track down the servants who had been snatched from the *Pemberley* by the corsairs. He traced only one, Brinkley. She had never reached the slave market, but had drowned herself in the harbour of Tunis. In a gesture of kindness unusual outside the fantasy world of Selim Pasha,[124] Brinkley's body had not been left for the crabs and the water rats but had been buried in an unmarked grave in the infidels' cemetery. By the time Fitzwilliam arrived back in Pemberley, the house had been radically, but tastefully, redecorated under the supervision of Marianne Brandon in what is now called the *late Empire style*. Marianne herself had moved on to London, where she was fitting out the Darcys' handsome new townhouse in Tavistock Square.[125] From her connection with the Darcys, Marianne built up a circle of clients. The fee for her services was modest. Her profit, and it was princely, was derived not from her honorarium, but from the per centages she negotiated with every supplier great and small. She retired to a handsome house in the County of Devon, not far, incidentally, from the house where Sir Thomas Bertram and Lady Maria, his indolent wife, had secluded themselves after the sale of Mansfield Park.

Despite her mother's precautions, Jane Darcy was 'spoilt,' if, by that term, one characterises a charming young woman, fearless in her social address, full of her own opinions, and pretty enough to bring tears to the eyes of the *Venus de Milo*.[126] In other words, she was all that her mother had been a quarter of a century earlier. Jane kept in touch with Fanny Bertram after their return to England, and from Fanny she acquired an interest in social issues, especially in prison reform and the administration of the New Poor Law Act.[127] The prison reform movement, as the Reader already knows, was led by Elizabeth Fry, a notable Quaker. In this circle, Jane met and married a Quaker by the name of Zekiel Smith, a banker, and she herself became a Quaker. At first, her family was horrified, but luckily the family horror was short-lived: Jane and her mother, after their rapprochement at the bell-tower of Saint Emilios, had become inseparable. Jane Smith bore her husband five children.

Elizabeth Darcy, sad to say, came to an untimely and tragic end. The Yarmouth Catastrophe[128] was the occasion. In case, dear Reader, you do not remember the circumstances, I will, briefly, recount the story here.

In 1845, Elizabeth Darcy took two of her grandchildren, Fitzwilliam Smith, a boy of eight, and Lizzy Smith, a girl of nine, on a holiday tour of East Anglia. Both children were weak in the chest, and the bracing climate of Norfolk in May was recommended by their physician. They stayed for several nights in a town called Caister. In Caister high street, they saw a poster: a circus was coming to Yarmouth, a mile or two down the coast. To anticipate the delights of the circus itself, as the poster expressed it, one of the clowns, Nelson, was to sail down the River Bure in a barrel drawn by four geese. The two little Quakers were wild to see the spectacle, which was to take place on the following day, and their grandmother agreed to take them. The carriage conveyed them to Yarmouth, but it could not approach the riverbank. The passengers dismounted and joined the crowds lining the banks on both sides of the River Bure. A footbridge, suspended on two cables, spanned the river. The approach of the barrel was heralded by cheers and shouts, and the barrel itself soon hove in sight. It was propelled not so much by the geese as by the current of the Bure which, with a spring tide ebbing, was rapid. Nelson, clowning as he went, steered his simple craft, followed by a flotilla of rowing boats. Grandmother Darcy had taken up her station just before the bridge. The children's maid, who was as eager as the children to see the barrel, stood beside her. Then occurred the catastrophe. As Nelson neared the bridge, hundreds of eager spectators rushed onto it, Mrs Darcy and her grandchildren among them. Four hundred persons, *The Times* reported, lined the bridge to watch the barrel disappear beneath it. The crowd, in the manner of crowds, stampeded to the other side of the bridge to see the barrel emerge. Then the bridge, in the manner of suspension bridges, and in full accordance with the laws of mechanics, collapsed. Seventy-nine people, most of them children, drowned in the River Bure. Grandmother Elizabeth and young Fitzwilliam were among them. The maid, who could swim though not strongly, carried little Lizzy to safety. Mrs Darcy was the most prominent of the Yarmouth victims, and her death was widely reported. I recall one newspaper headline the day after the catastrophe: *Grandmother's Nightmare* it read. After his wife's death, Mr Darcy sold the London house and retired to Derbyshire.

Fanny Bertram fulfilled the prophecy she had made about herself halfway across the River Evinos: she never married.

Note: *The following paragraph is struck through in the original manuscript. It has been included here as it offers a clue to much else in* Jane and the Jackal.

However, if I look up from my writing table, I can see Fanny now, a woman well over sixty, but still strong and straight as an arrow, still alert enough to act as keeper of records to a busy London doctor who spends more time than he should writing unpublishable fiction. As I watch, she stands up to put another log on the fire. A bell and a servant stand ready for such tasks, but Miss Price prefers to wait on herself. It is some years since I offered her a room in my house and a position of responsibility: at the time she was financially hard-pressed enough to accept. Neither of us has regretted her decision from that day to this.

Finally, since much of this book concerns the Greek war against Turkey, what happened to Odysseus Androutsos, Iannis Gouras, and the English millions? First let it be said that, despite the wild rumours of 1824, there were no millions. Two much smaller loans were made considerably later: they totalled, after commissions and discounts had been deducted, £900,000. Most of the money was squandered on decommissioned warships and other prestigious toys.

As for Odysseus, he did retreat for a while to his bolt-hole on Mount Parnassus, heavy, as mentioned earlier, with the fruits of a lifetime of theft, extortion and plunder. In the mountain cave, Odysseus, whose belief in the English millions was unshakeable, united Captain Trelawny and his sister in marriage. Odysseus then made the mistake of returning to Athens. There he was inveigled into the hands of Iannis Gouras, he was incarcerated, and fell to his death 'while trying to escape.' By inheritance, the cave and its treasure passed to Tersitza and Trelawny. When Trelawny returned to England he was accompanied by some part of this treasure, though not by his young wife. In fact, the marriage was not a happy one. By the end of 1825, at the age of thirteen, Tersitza gave birth to a daughter. The child was named Zella (with two *l*'s). A second daughter was born a year later, though by this time Tersitza had abandoned Trelawny and sought refuge in a convent. Tersitza sent the second child to Trelawny to be looked after, but the baby died in the care of a wet-nurse. Trelawny sent the body back to his wife in a plain wooden box, unembalmed and already stinking. Not long after this, in court in Korfu, Tersitza divorced Trelawny. The court awarded her alimony[129] of twenty-five *piastres* a month.

Iannis Gouras then, the survivor, what of him? Today Gouras is a General in the Greek army: he earned some international opprobrium for his brutal suppression of the revolt against King Otto in 1843, but otherwise he lives on, honoured and esteemed by all (except, I imagine, by the families of his victims). He has already, sad to say, outlived many a worthier man, and will probably outlive many more.

Greece was given its formal independence in 1832, some twenty years ago. Under its Bavarian King, Otto,[130] it has now achieved nationhood, though it is still foul-tempered, still disunited, and still desperate for foreign money.

Note: *The following paragraph is also struck through in the original manuscript.*

Fanny has just intimated to me that the hour is late and that I should stop writing. I see no reason to disagree with her.

THE END

Editing Jane and the Jackal: A Note

The editors of *Jane and the Jackal* discovered the manuscript by chance in the archive of the Tauchnitz Publishing House in Leipzig. It is a mix of history, surmise and invention, written by a Victorian doctor who struggles with historical fact, narrative tangles, and the demands of Victorian propriety. The text had never been edited for publication. The challenge was somehow irresistible.

The manuscript is written in various hands. Hawkins' own handwriting is what one expects of a Victorian doctor: a rapid scrawl with many abbreviations. Luckily, parts of the manuscript have been transcribed by a neat, careful hand, possibly female. Hawkins began writing his story in 1854. Countless changes to the ongoing manuscript were made in various hands and at various dates. It is not clear when, or why, he abandoned it. In selecting a 'final' version, the editors have tried to keep the narrative self-consistent and fast-moving. We have adjusted Hawkins' punctuation, though preserving his unVictorian aversion to dashes and semi-colons. We have regularised his spelling while keeping some 'historical colour,' for example, the archaic *clew* for *clue* or *trowsers* for *trousers*. We have made no attempt to expurgate the text. Rather the opposite: we have rescued obscure references with explanatory notes, provided a sketch-map showing the places Hawkins mentions, and added a handful of historic illustrations.

Jane and the Jackal? Hawkins never gave his story a definitive title, though *All Her Turkeys* is written on the bundle of papers in the Tauchnitz archive. *Jane and the Jackal* was the editors' working title, and we liked it well enough to preserve it.

Among the well-documented historical figures mentioned in the story are Hawkins' uncle Edward Trelawny, Sir Thomas Maitland, Odysseus Androutsos the villainous Governor of Athens, and Iannis Gouras the Governor's nemesis. Hawkins took some trouble to get his facts right; for readers interested in modern documentation, we have added a short appendix.

Although Hawkins sought publication, he seems to have written largely for his own amusement. The editors hope that the reader will share some of that amusement in this, his only novel.

Jim Pinnells   Isabel Otto
Easter 2024

RESOURCES

If the reader wishes to look further into the historical events that form the background of Hawkins' narrative, the handful of sources listed below offers a starting point.

Wikipedia has proved helpful on some characters and events, but the Greek War of Independence is not one of *Wikipedia*'s strongest areas.

Edward Trelawny's memoir, often derided as fiction, was published *as* fiction in the *Oxford English Novels* series:

> Trelawny, Edward John. *Adventures of a Younger Son*, ed. William St Clair. London: Oxford University Press, 1974.

A scholarly biography of Edward Trelawny by the editor of the *Adventures* (including a detailed bibliography) is:

> St Clair, William. *Trelawny: The Incurable Romancer.* London: John Murray, 1977.

A more up-to-date, though hostile, biography of Edward Trelawny is:

> Crane, David. *Lord Byron's Jackal: A Life of Edward Trelawny.* London: HarperCollins, 1998.

The Greek War of Independence is well accounted for in:

Brewer, David. *The Greek War of Independence: The Struggle for Freedom from Ottoman Oppression and the Birth of the Modern Greek Nation.* New York: Overlook, 2001.

Were the Bertrams married? Two authoritative (and surprisingly readable) books depict the tangled state of English marriage at the beginning of the nineteenth century:

Stone, Lawrence. *Road to Divorce: England 1530-1987.* Oxford: Oxford University Press, 1990.
Stone, Lawrence. *Broken Lives: Separation and Divorce in England 1660-1857.* Oxford: Oxford University Press, 1993.

If an interested reader were to search for Doctor Hawkins' manuscript in the great archive in Leipzig, it would not be found. The manuscript is what is sometimes called *an enabling fiction.*

The editors wish to express their heartfelt thanks to two early readers who helped greatly with the final structure and detail of Jane and the Jackal: *Elaine White and Kirstin Winterfeldt. Thanks also to Susan Pinnells for her help with the Illustrations.*

EXPLANATORY NOTES

1 *Greek uprising*. In the original manuscript, a brief history of the Greek War of Independence was included in the Author's Introduction but subsequently struck through. Since the information may be useful to a modern reader unfamiliar with post-Napoleonic history, the main points of the deleted text are given here as a footnote.

> *After the battle of Waterloo in 1815, Europe slipped into an uneasy peace... To the east of Europe lay two Empires: the Russian and the Ottoman, two mysterious and hostile worlds about which we in England knew (and know) next to nothing. The Ottoman territories were Mussulman with one major exception: what we now call Greece... The mighty Ottoman Empire had begun to crumble after its westward advance was halted at the gates of Vienna in 1683... In 1821 in the monastery of Ayia Lavra, a group of Greek nationalists raised a newly invented Greek flag. This marked the start of the Greek War of Independence. All over Europe, high-minded individuals, the Philhellenes or 'Greek-lovers,' supported the Christian Greeks against the Moslem Turks, among their number the poet, Lord George Byron... Unlike the Philhellenes, European governments disapproved of the emergent Greece. The British government, for example, had valuable diplomatic and commercial ties with the Sublime Porte in Constantinople. Until the Greeks had won their war, they enjoyed little support from any European emperor, king or elected government... The Sublime Porte resisted Greek independence with the fury of a dying lion.*

2 *Long life*. When Hawkins was writing this book, Trelawny was sixty. In the story itself Trelawny is 33. A sketch of Trelawny at about this age is included in the Illustrations. He died in 1881, aged 88

3   *Buttered bun*. According to the *1811 Dictionary of the Vulgar Tongue*, 'One lying with a woman that has just lain with another man, is said to have a buttered bun.'

4   *Tauchnitz*. Charles Hawkins' manuscript kicked its heels in the Archive of the Tauchnitz Publishing House in Leipzig for over 150 years. Tauchnitz was an unusual publisher. In 1842 it began publishing cheap, paper-bound books (the original 'paperbacks') in English for sale *outside* the British Empire and, in the case of American authors, *outside* the United States. Tauchnitz had celebrities such as Dickens, Thackeray and Hardy on its list. Our author, Charles Hawkins, evidently hoped to be among this number, but his book was never published. In 1955 Tauchnitz published its last English-language title.

5   *Book*. Mr Gregson evidently found Hawkins' numerous drafts unmarketable. A number of notes in the Archive advise Hawkins to study the style and story-telling techniques of the best-selling writers of the day and to copy them. Scrawled on these notes are Hawkins' bitter comments. An example: *I had always thought that medicine was a mercenary occupation. How often, for a stiff fee, do I take a cab and hurry to the sickbed of a wealthy patient (or more often to the sickbed of a wealthy hypochondriac) and, on the way, rattle through street after street where the poor, the feeble-minded, the maimed and the diseased parade in their hundreds? Even after years in the profession, my own avarice sometimes gives me pause. But now, under the tutelage of Mr Gregson, I find that the career of the artist, at least of the literary artist, is no less predatory than that of the pill-monger.*

6   *Charles Hawkins*. The editors have been unable to discover if (1) Charles Hawkins, the second son of John and Hester Hawkins (née Sibthorpe) and nephew of the sailor Edward Trelawny, (2) the Charles Hawkins mentioned in the *British Medical Directory for England, Scotland and Wales, 1853* as living at 22 Savile Row, London, and (3) the Charles Hawkins who in 1857 became head of the Anatomy Inspectorate (the inspectorate that provided corpses for dissection in training hospitals), are one and the same person.

7   *Chapter*. Hawkins named only a few chapters. The editors have added the 'missing' titles.

8   *Mamma*. Hawkins spells the word *Mamma* in four different ways: *Mamma, Mama, mamma,* and *mama*. Many writers of the era are similarly inconsistent. The editors have decided, somewhat arbitrarily, to follow R.S. Surtees whose book, *Ask Mamma*, was published in 1858.

9   *Elizabeth Darcy*. The following paragraph is struck through in the original

text. It is not without interest. *The* Elizabeth Darcy *mentioned here is indeed the beautiful and tragic heroine about whom so much has been written. Her unhappy fate after her return to England is well-known. The Greek episode in her life when she was but two-and-thirty is largely unreported.*

10 *Mild breeze.* Differing accounts of the design of the *Don Juan* and of the reasons for its failure are found in the various sources. The interested reader is referred to Donald Prell's *Edward John Trelawny, Fact or Fiction* (2011) for a discussion of this, and other Trelawny riddles. The *Hercules*, a limping 'two-gun collier,' in which George Byron and Edward Trelawny sailed to Greece in 1823, was pointedly *not* a Trelawny design.

11 *Sanjakbey.* Each province of the Ottoman Empire was a separate *sanjak*. The provincial governor was the *Sanjakbey*.

12 *Australia.* Felons were transported to Australia between 1787 and 1868.

13 *Bourdzi.* A recent picture of the Bourdzi Tower and the seawall is included among the Illustrations.

14 *Janissaries.* Janissaries were originally young Greek (and other Christian) boys enlisted into the Ottoman army and trained with considerable ferocity. They were neither particularly loyal nor particularly efficient soldiers, but they did much of the dirty work of Empire. The Corps of Janissaries became excessively powerful in Constantinople, and it was abolished by the Sultan in 1826.

15 *Curtain wall.* Included in the Illustrations is a picture of the curtain wall as it is today.

16 *Buntling.* According to the *1811 Dictionary of the Vulgar Tongue*, 'A petticoat.' (Or the female wearing, or perhaps not wearing, it.)

17 *Mopsqueezer.* According to the *1811 Dictionary of the Vulgar Tongue*, 'A maid servant, particularly a housemaid.'

18 *Swell.* A pompous, puffed-up person. The term was derogatory at this time.

19 *Morea.* The southern part of Greece, known today as the Peloponnese, was called the *Morea* at this time.

20 *Tripolis.* Literally *Three Cities*. Tripolis in central Greece is not to be confused with Tripolis, the capital of Libya, or with other cities of the same name.

21 *Muff.* According to the *1811 Dictionary of the Vulgar Tongue*, 'The private parts of a woman.'

22 *Going rate.* Hawkins is often vague about currencies and exchange rates. The difficulties lie (a) in the ongoing debasement of the Ottoman coinage and (b) in the revaluations of currencies that took place during and after the Napoleonic

wars. As a rough guide, the editors have established that in 1820, a British sovereign was worth in the Levant roughly 28 Ottoman silver *piastres* (in Turkish called *kurush*). This exchange rate can be applied throughout *Jane and the Jackal*.

23 *Notch.* According to the *1811 Dictionary of the Vulgar Tongue*, 'The private parts of a woman.'

24 *Vathek. Vathek* (William Beckford, 1786), *Udolpho* (Ann Radcliffe, 1794), *The Monk* (Matthew Lewis, 1796) are sensational Gothic novels. *The Monk* was decried as indecent and its second edition was heavily expurgated. Mrs Darcy would (probably) have preferred the more domestic (though scarcely less sensational) novels of Maria Edgeworth or Fanny Burney. The so-called 'sensational' school of fiction first emerged in the 1860s.

25 *Sour throat.* Sour throat is probably the disease usually known after 1826 as *diphtheritis* and after 1855 as *diphtheria*. *Putrid throat, putrid sore throat* and *sour throat* appear to be used interchangeably by physicians and by lay writers until Victorian medicine provided more secure diagnoses.

26 *Sofra.* Turkish word for the low table around which the company gathers to eat.

27 *Firman.* A decree, ordinance or permission issued by an Islamic sovereign.

28 *Khlept.* A *khlept* is not quite a bandit or an outlaw, but a 'free spirit' notoriously quarrelsome, unscrupulous and untrustworthy. As key figures in the Greek War of Independence, the *khlept* captains have enjoyed good as well as bad press. Odysseus Androutsos, who features later in this narrative, is the archetype.

29 *Dandy prat.* According to the *1811 Dictionary of the Vulgar Tongue*, 'An insignificant or trifling fellow.'

30 *Faith.* For faith, hope and charity, see *I Corinthians 13:13*.

31 *Cassandra.* Cassandra, in Greek mythology, agreed to grant certain favours to Apollo in exchange for the gift of prophecy. He gave her the gift, but she failed to deliver the favours, so Apollo added a curse – her prophecies, though true, would never be believed.

Cassandra was the daughter of King Priam of Troy. She prophesied the destruction of Troy; she knew that the Trojan Horse was full of Greek soldiers; as a Greek prisoner, she predicted the murder of King Agamemnon. No one believed her, ever. Hawkins' comparison of Fanny Bertram with Cassandra is startling but shrewd. The choice of John Collier's *Cassandra* as a cover picture for this book reflects Hawkins' comment.

32 *Silenus, Peitho or the Nepenthes.* Wine, women, or drugs.

33 *Dutch.* The nationalities of the four consuls are confirmed by David Brewer in his *The Greek War of Independence.*

34 *Fuller's earth.* A highly absorbent clay with many uses including the preparation of wool.

35 *Lovina.* Today a whole district of Colombo, Sri Lanka, is named *Mount Lavinia* in honour of Lovina.

36 *Castlereagh.* From 1812-1822, Robert Stewart, Viscount Castlereagh, was Secretary of State for Foreign Affairs. He cut his own throat in August 1822 in an attack of paranoia brought on, it is believed, by syphilitic meningitis. He was 53.

37 *Lord Strangford.* Percy Clinton Sydney Smythe, 6th Viscount Strangford, was British ambassador to the Sublime Porte from 1821 until 1824. Like Lord Elgin, his famous predecessor, he combined diplomacy with the collection of antiques. Two of his pieces, the Strangford Apollo and the Strangford Shield, are now in the British Museum.

38 *Nonsense.* 'No bigodd nonsense about her' is a phrase coined, by Charles Dickens in *Little Dorrit*, a book published (in serial form) in 1856, two years after Hawkins began writing *Jane and the Jackal.*

39 *Culloden.* The Battle of Culloden in 1746 brought to a bloody end the attempt by Bonnie Prince Charlie to overthrow the House of Hanover. The reign of terror imposed on Scotland by 'Butcher Cumberland' during the following years displays all the elements of 'terror from above' as seen in countless 'clean-up' campaigns before and since.

40 *Ali Pasha.* Among the despots of the last 200 years, Ali Pasha, the Lion of Ioannina, must be allowed some pre-eminence. He was an Albanian Muslim of great personal courage and administrative skill, but his pleasure in bloody atrocities, and the extraordinary number of them perpetrated by his followers, outweigh by far his organisational achievements. He was murdered in 1822, and his head was sent by the Ottoman field commander, Hursid Pasha, to Sultan Mahmud II in Constantinople. For more information, a recent book by Drs Quentin and Eugenia Russell, *Ali Pasha, the Lion of Ioannina* (2018) does, if anything, more than justice to this notable villain. Byron describes a visit to Ali Pasha in *Childe Harold*, Canto II, Stanzas 54-66.

41 *Hanging.* The last exemplary public hanging in England took place in 1868.

42 *Recent.* David Crane's biography of Trelawny states that from 'November 1823 until April 1824 almost no records [of Trelawny's activities] survive' (p. 110). Certainly, Trelawny's collected letters published in 1910 as *Letters*

of Edward John Trelawny contain nothing written in this period. This, as the Reader will note, is exactly the period of Trelawny's life covered by *Jane and the Jackal*.

43 *Dress*. A romantic image of Odysseus Androutsos in Albanian court dress is included in the Illustrations.

44 *Daniel O'Connell*. Known as 'the Liberator,' O'Connell (1775-1847) led Irish opposition to the Act of Union imposed on the Irish in 1800 by the government in London.

45 *Suliot*. For more on the Suliots, see Chapter 6.

46 *Heart*. At this point in the margin of the manuscript, in an otherwise unknown hand, is a quotation from Act IV Scene 1 of *As You Like It*: 'Men have died from time to time, and worms have eaten them, but not for love.'

47 *Piss-proud*. According to the *1811 Dictionary of the Vulgar Tongue*, 'Proud that he is still able to piss, though other functions of his p---- have largely deserted him.'

48 *Nisbet, Mary*. A sketch of what may well be this portrait is included in the Illustrations.

49 *Ozymandias*. The reference is to Shelley's sonnet (1818). All that survives of the empire of King Ozymandias is the buried face of a broken statue now reduced to a frown, a wrinkled lip and a sneer of cold command, together with the masterfully ironic inscription: 'Look on my works, ye mighty, and despair.'

50 *Backgammon*. The *1811 Dictionary of the Vulgar Tongue* defines a *back gammon (sic) player* as 'A sodomite.'

51 *Son of Laertes*. 'Son of Laertes, seed of Zeus, resourceful Odysseus' is the epic formula used by Homer to name Odysseus in the *Iliad* and the *Odyssey*.

52 *Funeral pyre*. An imaginative reconstruction of this scene was painted by Louis Fournier in 1889. A sketch of this painting is included in the Illustrations.

53 *Dr James's (Fever) Powders*. A powerful emetic based on antimony.

54 *Wilberforce*. According to William Wilberforce, Captain Norris claimed that the lot of his slaves was enviable: if shackles were fitted, it was only to protect the poor, brainless lambs in this wicked world. The slave decks of Norris's ships were perfumed with frankincense and lime-juice, and his slaves were fed on costly dainties procured in their native countries. (*Hansard*, 1789.) Fanny's Aunt Norris appears to be just such a slave-driving hypocrite.

55   *Elizabeth Fry.* Information on the great prison reformer, Elizabeth Fry, is widely available. It is probable that on a tour she made of northern prisons in 1818, she included Northampton and/or Peterborough. In addition to her revolutionary and ground-breaking prison work, Elizabeth Fry bore ten children.

56   *Salona.* In ancient times, this city was called Amfissa. In the late Middle Ages, it was captured by various European tribes, among them the Catalans. Its name was changed to La Sole and then to Salona. Salona recovered its ancient name, Amfissa, in 1833 after the War of Independence. Hawkins calls the city *Salona*, which was correct in 1824.

57   *Corsair. The Corsair, The Giaour,* and *Mazeppa* are narrative poems by Byron with archetypal Byronic heroes.

58   *Objection.* Hawkins gives Tersitza's objection in Greek. His intention was perhaps to confuse the reader just as Tersitza herself is confused. The words mean roughly: 'He doesn't speak Greek. How can I marry him?'

59   *Cave.* Odysseus' hideout is still there today, minus the treasure. With some resourcefulness and a head for heights, it can be visited.

60   *Mavrokordatos.* Alexander Mavrokordatos was a Greek aristocrat and one of the original Society of Friends who spearheaded the Greeks in their War of Independence. After Prince Otto of Bavaria was made King of Greece in 1832, Mavrokordatos was twice prime minister and served in many key embassies. He died in 1865 at the age of 74.

61   *Algiers.* Katie Hickman's *Daughters of Britannia: The Lives and Times of Diplomatic Wives* (1999) describes the daily life of the British consul in Algiers, Henry Blankley, a little before this era. The full name of his wife is not known, but even nameless, Mrs Blankley's role in tending ransomed captives makes interesting reading.

62   *Class warfare.* This is the normal translation of *Klassenkampf* as used by Marx and Engels in their *Manifest der Kommunistischen Partei*, 1848. *Class struggle* is more accurate.

63   *Mercer, Alexander.* Mercer's exploits at Waterloo are well documented. The Royal Horse Artillery still has a troop named after him: G Parachute Battery (Mercer's Troop).

64   *Fingerpost.* According to the *1811 Dictionary of the Vulgar Tongue*, 'A parson: so-called, because… like the fingerpost, he points out a way he has never been, and probably will never go, i.e. the way to heaven.'

65   *Tsipouro.* A strong liquor, the forerunner of ouzo.

66   *Unsuitable.* During his lifetime, Byron had a reputation for romantic defiance of conventional morality. In that sense he was 'mad, bad and

dangerous to know' as Lady Caroline Lamb famously remarked after meeting him in 1812. (Though Lady Caroline was *a fine one to talk*.) Later reworkings of the Byron legend levelled three accusations against him: (a) incest with his half-sister, Augusta, (b) anal rape of his wife, Anne Milbanke, and (c) a predatory and indiscriminate homosexuality. Such scandals are irrelevant to *Jane and the Jackal*, since they had little circulation during Byron's lifetime and during the following fifty years. (Incidentally, Harriet Beecher Stowe, author of *Uncle Tom's Cabin*, was one of Byron's more vituperative accusers.)

67   *Isle de Roi*. The name of the island of Mauritius from 1715 until 1810.

68   *Enslave*. Hawkins digresses at this point into a brief history of slavery. Since the history of slavery in the United Kingdom is again under discussion, these paragraphs have been relegated to a footnote rather than deleted altogether.

> *Uncle Trelawny's scheme was to enslave young Jane Darcy.* Enslave *is a strong word, and, in this year of grace 1854, it may help if I clarify what exactly the word meant in 1824, thirty years ago. Slave trading was abolished by an Act of Parliament in 1807. Under the Act,* owning *slaves remained legal outside Britain itself:* trading *became illegal on penalty of a heavy poll tax. The Royal Navy was ordered to patrol the high seas for slavers of any nationality. Accordingly, the captain of a slave ship, when approached by a British warship, might throw his captives into the sea, leg-irons and all, to avoid the threatened tax. Only in 1833 was slavery itself abolished in the English colonies, though the territories administered by the East India Company were still exempted. Slavery on Company land was ended only a few years ago, in 1843. It is also worth remarking that in 1833 owners who lost property rights in their slaves were compensated out of a £20 million government fund.*
>
> *What am I trying to suggest about Uncle Trelawny's plot? Since ancient times, slavery has been with us. In many parts of the world, it remains a curse to this day. As a subscribing member of the British and Foreign Anti-Slavery Society, I deplore any kind of slavery. To be honest, however, I see Uncle Trelawny's plot as no worse (though no better) than a million acts of enslavement performed by, or on behalf of, respectable English ladies and gentlemen, shareholders perhaps in the East India Company, who slept until 1843, and who sleep peacefully today, in their comfortable beds surrounded by inalienable riches on their well-guarded island.*

69 *Tric-trac.* The board game of backgammon.

70 *Letter.* Both letters are correctly quoted. Byron's correspondence on the subject of Greek resourcefulness in extorting money is extensive.

71 *Mosque.* The mosque built within the precinct of the Parthenon was pulled down in 1834. A sketch of the building not long before this date is included in the Illustrations.

72 *Sketch.* Severn's mediocre sketch is often reproduced. The editors have included a less celebrated sketch by Seymour Kirkup as revealing more of Trelawny's character.

73 *Zenana.* Hawkins uses a word more appropriate to India. He may have picked it up from Trelawny's *Adventures of a Younger Son* where it is used frequently. A *zenana* is a part of a house or compound reserved for higher caste women.

74 *Lohengrin.* Hawkins puts the word 'Lohengrin' into Fanny's mouth, though she could not have picked up the name from her reading of Arthurian legends. Lohengrin was not the name of this exemplary hero until Wagner's opera which was written in 1848. This is one of the few anachronisms in the manuscript of *Jane and the Jackal.*

75 *Fustanella.* The skirt-like garment worn by men in the Balkans since ancient times.

76 *Honey words.* The quotation is from Act IV of Shakespeare's *Richard III.* The words are spoken by Queen Anne, recalling how Richard Crookback seduced her.

77 *Mary Shelley.* Wife of Percy Bysshe Shelley, née Mary Godwin. Her father was the philosopher, William Godwin; her mother, the celebrated proto-feminist, Mary Wollstonecraft. Mary Shelley wrote the ever-popular *Frankenstein* while on holiday with Lord Byron (and others) in Geneva in 1816. It was published in 1818. She and Edward Trelawny corresponded extensively over the years, though they seldom agreed about anything. She helped Trelawny with the first edition of his *Memoirs of a Younger Son* published in 1831.

78 *Sir James Scarlett and (Sir) Jonathan (Frederick) Pollock.* Both lawyers represented Trelawny, and both later rose to become attorneys-general.

79 *Obstupescent.* Victorian medical term meaning a 'state when the patient remains still, with open eyes, as if astonished, and neither moves or speaks.' Or as the Captain might have said, 'Drunk as a wheel-barrow.'

80 The Codex Hammurabi (c. 2000 B.C.E.) laid down (among other things) fees for specific services, it established procedures for keeping medical records and explained patient's rights.

81   *Her situation.* Trelawny's understanding of Fanny's situation is, broadly speaking, in line with the jurisprudence of the time. For full detail see Lawrence Stone's *Road to Divorce: England 1530-1987* and *Broken Lives: Separation and Divorce in England 1660-1857.*

82   *Mrs Grundy.* A (non-appearing) character in a play by Thomas Morton, *Speed the Plough* (1798). Mrs Grundy soon passed into the language as the personification of self-righteous censoriousness and the ill-natured repression of all matters sexual.

83   *Swine.* The references here are to the Gospels. *Give not that which is holy unto the dogs, neither cast ye your pearls before swine, lest they trample them under their feet, and turn again and rend you* (Matthew 7:6), and *A prophet is not without honour, but in his own country, and among his own kin, and in his own house* (Mark 6:4).

84   *Faith.* See note 30.

85   *Saint Peter.* 2 Peter 3:16.

86   *Nonstarter.* If Fanny consulted the edition of Cruden's *Concordance* published in 1800, she would have found over 50 references to *prison* and over 30 to *prisoners* but only 1 to *prison visitation.*

87   *Abomination of desolation.* There is no agreement as to the interpretation of these words in *Daniel Chap. 11* and in *Matthew Chap. 24.* The general sense is that this particular abomination will destroy everything sacred to God's people.

88   *Examination.* As a doctor, Hawkins appears sensitive to Fanny's fears and objections, but he does not go into detail. The reader may recall the devastating impact that an examination by a male doctor has on young Kitty in Tolstoy's *Anna Karenina (Part 2, Chapter 1).* But why a male doctor? Were there no women doctors in Fanny's time? A largely unsung heroine of Victorian England was Elizabeth Garrett. In 1865, she obtained the first licence to practise medicine given (albeit unwillingly) to a woman in England and who immediately opened St Mary's Dispensary for Women and Children in London. The clinic attracted 3,000 patients during its first year of operation.

89   *Cap-lock.* Until the invention of the cap-lock mechanism, patented in 1807, a pistol depended on a flint striking a steel to generate a spark. This spark ignited gunpowder in the flash-pan. This, in turn, caused the charge of gunpowder in the gun-barrel to explode and to fire the ball out of the barrel. The cap-lock mechanism replaced the flint, the steel and the flash-pan. As a weapon, a cap-lock pistol was massively superior to the old flint-lock, as Fanny was to discover during the next few days. The cap-

lock was an intermediate step in the direction of modern ammunition in which the ignition, the charge and the bullet are contained in a single casing.

90   *Schlappschwanz*. A German term of opprobrium signifying roughly a *limp dick*.

91   *Hind*. HMS *Hind* was in Piraeus on 1st March 1824. Apparently, a group of notables including Odysseus Androutsos, Iannis Gouras, Edward Trelawny and Frank Hastings were invited to a party on board. At the height of the party, the *Hind* got under weigh. Fearing abduction, Odysseus took over the ship and regained the shore. The affair ended without bloodshed. The facts are hazy, and the ship's log for this date has been lost.

92   *Bollock dagger*. The name is derived from the dagger's shape rather than its function. A bollock dagger (sometimes called a *kidney dagger*) has two spheroids protecting the hilt.

93   *Saint Paul*. Edmund slightly misquotes the King James Version of *Ephesians* 5:22-24.

94   *Nore*. Two mutinies shook the British navy in 1797, Spithead and the Nore. After the Spithead mutiny, a general pardon was issued. After the Nore, 29 mutineers were hanged, not 38 as Hawkins suggests.

95   *Martingale*. A gambling tactic based on doubling one's stake after each loss. In *Pendennis* (1848-1850), Thackeray expatiates on the risks of the 'infallible' martingale system.

96   *Lovely Dawn*. Homer frequently refers to *Lovely Dawn with her rosy fingers*.

97   *Wax nose*. According to Partridge's *A Dictionary of Historical Slang*, 'any person, very pliable, exceedingly obliging or complaisant.' A modern equivalent might be *brown nose*.

98   *Correction*. Several ostensibly Christian websites today, particularly in the US, advise husbands to help their wives overcome sinful inclinations by means of corporal punishment. There is some biblical authority for this view. For the avoidance of doubt, the editors wish to distance themselves emphatically from this barbarous practice.

99   *Lesson*. Edmund is overstating his case. The legal position until 1840 and for some time thereafter was summed up by Judge Coleridge: '… the husband hath by law power and dominion over his wife and may keep her by force within the bounds of duty, and may beat her, but not in a violent or cruel manner.' In a famous case in 1891, R *v* Jackson, the Appeal Court Judge, Lord Halsbury, stated, obiter, that 'If a husband ever had the legal right to beat his wife, that entitlement is now obsolete.'

100 T*rowsers*. The reference is to Deuteronomy 22.5: 'The woman shall not

wear that which pertaineth unto a man…for all that do so are abomination unto the Lord thy God.'

101 *Atropos*. The mythological Fates – Clotho, Lachesis and Atropos – together prepare the fabric of each human life: Clotho spins, Lachesis weaves, and Atropos cuts the cloth.

102 *Stitches*. It was not until 1860 (six years after Hawkins began *Jane and the Jackal*) that Joseph Lister first soaked sutures (made of sheep gut) in carbolic acid to prevent infection. The Athenian doctor's use of brandy in 1824, if historically correct, is surprising.

103 *Brain fever*. The reference is to Chapter 12 of *Wuthering Heights*. To be fair, Brontë, says that Catherine Linton's illness was *called* brain fever, not that it *was* brain fever.

104 *Prostrated*. A marginal comment in Hawkins' manuscript is worth at least a footnote here. *Interesting conversation in the club with Thomas Wakley. In Paris he heard a lecture by Jules Baillarger at the Academy of Medicine on a newly discovered illness called folie à double forme: the patient alternates uncontrollably between fits of exuberance and fits of depression. Perhaps relevant to Fanny Bertram's situation?*

Baillarger gave his lecture in 1854. The condition he describes was later called manic depression (*and more recently* bipolar disorder). *Thomas Wakley founded The Lancet in 1823 and remained editor-in-chief until 1862, the year of his death.*

105 *Delphi*. Unlike the modern road from Thebes to Delphi, the old road snaked its way through the valleys below the peak of Mount Parnassus. A sketch of the road as it was in 1805 is included in the Illustrations.

106 *Oria*. At this time, the fortress in Salona/Amfissa was in ruins. Today it is handsomely dilapidated and romantically overgrown with pine trees. A postcard of Amfissa in the early 1900s is included in the Illustrations.

107 *Kervansaray*. Literally, a *caravan palace*. A sketch of the *kervansaray* in Smyrna (Izmir) at about this time is included in the Illustrations.

108 *Childe Harold*. A long narrative poem by Byron.

109 *Gentleman*. In a letter to his prospective bride, Claire Clairmont, dated 15 May 1823, Trelawny writes: *As to my fortune—my income is reduced to about £500 a year… so you see… how thoughtless and vain was my idea of our living together: as Keats says 'Love in a hut with water and a crust, is… cinders, ashes, dust.'* At the other end of the scale, according to a reliable source, the annual income of Fitzwilliam Darcy at the time of his marriage was £10,000 a year.

110 *Valperga*. Mary Shelley completed *Valperga* in Pisa (the novel is set in mediaeval Italy) and published it in 1823.

111 *Belle dame.* Keats' poem, *La Belle Dame Sans Merci,* was written in 1819 and published in 1820.

112 *Claire Clairmont.* Half-sister of Mary Shelley. During his time in Italy with the Shelleys, Edward Trelawny courted Claire with a view to marriage, but was rejected. The two remained (irregular) correspondents, however, until Claire's death in 1879 at the age of 80. Claire had a daughter by Lord Byron, Allegra. The child died in 1822 at the age of 5.

113 *Mandragora.* Perhaps a reference to the 'root' in *La Belle Dame Sans Merci.* Mandragora (mandrake) is a narcotic and hallucinogen; at one time it was also used as an anaesthetic.

114 *Miasmal air.* It is difficult for the modern reader to realise that, until the seminal work of Louis Pasteur, Robert Koch and Joseph Lister in the 1860s, the role of microorganisms in the transmission of diseases was not understood, and hygiene played little part in medical practice. The ancient miasmal theory held that disease was spread by bad air. One of the first breakthroughs was an observation in 1847 by Ignatz Semmelweis in the General Hospital in Vienna: in the delivery ward, childbed fever was more common in women who were attended by a doctor. A midwife was far safer, as indeed was home delivery. Why? Because, Semmelweis discovered, doctors following hospital routine had mostly conducted autopsies and similar tasks before delivering a baby. Knowing nothing about germs, they had not washed their hands. In 1849, John Snow, a London doctor, was the first to recommend boiling drinking water to kill germs. Incidentally, the prescriptions of the Italian doctor, which Hawkins spells out in such detail, are in line with modern 'alternative' medicine.

115 *Spontaneous combustion.* The reader may recall that in *Bleak House,* a novel published in 1852-3, the rubbish merchant Krook dies of 'spontaneous combustion.' In the Preface to *Bleak House,* Dickens manfully asserts that spontaneous human combustion is a commonly observed phenomenon.

116 *Paddington.* Several of the main stations in London were completed in the years immediately before Hawkins wrote his novel: Waterloo 1848, King's Cross 1852, and Paddington 1854, to name only three.

117 *Houri.* It is impossible to say what Hawkins imagined a *houri* to be. This is one description from a ninth-century Moslem text: *A houri is a surpassingly beautiful young woman. Her body is transparent. You can see the marrow of her bones like the deep flaws in a pearl or a ruby. She is like red wine in a white glass. She is white, and she has none of the mortal flaws of normal women: she does not menstruate, she experiences no menopause, she does not urinate neither does she defecate. She bears no children and is free of the pollution*

that comes with child-bearing. A houri is a very young girl with large pointed breasts which do not sag. Houris live in palaces of great splendour. Tirmidhī (824-892).

118 *And nothing else saw all day long.* A further line from Keats' *La Belle Dame Sans Merci.*

119 *Muse.* Accounts of the Muses vary greatly. The most popular nineteenth-century variation derives from Hesiod: each of the nine classic arts (dancing, epic poetry, history, etc.) has its own muse. The Muse of Comedy, mentioned by Hawkins a few lines later, is Thalia. The nine sister-Muses live on Mount Parnassus.

120 *Mrs Wentworth.* Like the wives of many naval officers in this era, Anne Wentworth evidently accompanied her husband on his voyages. For more information on the subject of women on warships, see Roy Adkins, *Trafalgar: The Biography of a Battle*, p. 76 et seq.

121 *River Evinos.* Today the Evinos at this level has been confined between two dykes. The area is a nature preserve, though, shamefully, both dykes are used as informal tips for stinking rubbish. A (rubbish-free) photograph of the river is included in the Illustrations.

122 *Heel.* Hawkins alludes to *Genesis*, Chap. 3, where God says to the Serpent, 'And I will put enmity between thee and the woman, and between thy seed and her seed; it shall bruise thy head, and thou shalt bruise his heel.'

123 *Cemetery.* The English Cemetery in Korfu contains many well-preserved graves, headstones and memorials dating back to the period of *Jane and the Jackal*. Most of the dead are either young British soldiers or very small children born of garrison wives. A photograph of a group of these graves is included in the Illustrations.

124 *Selim Pasha.* The noble and generous Moslem overlord in Mozart's *Die Entführung aus dem Serail*. In the original score of the opera, he is called Bassa Selim.

125 *Tavistock Square.* A photograph of Tavistock Square as it is today, is included in the Illustrations.

126 *Venus de Milo.* This famous statue was found in 1820 on the Greek island of Milos. It was purchased by the French Ambassador to the Sublime Porte and shipped to France in 1821.

127 *New Poor Law Act.* This act was passed in 1834. It sought to regularise and regulate the parish workhouses in England and Wales. Readers familiar with *Oliver Twist* will recall the workhouse scenes. The workhouse system survived until 1930.

128 *Yarmouth Catastrophe.* A memorial commemorating this accident was

unveiled in Yarmouth in 2013. A depiction of the catastrophe is included in the Illustrations.

129 *Alimony.* The facts stated in this paragraph are broadly historical. The story about the baby in the box has been questioned. It derives from Tersitza's divorce application and appears to have been accepted as a fact by the court in Korfu.

130 *Otto.* Otto, the second son of King Ludwig I of Bavaria, was made King of Greece by the London Convention of 1832. He was deposed and exiled in 1862. In 1863, he was replaced by Prince William of Denmark who became King George (the First) of the Hellenes and, incidentally, great-grandfather of King Charles III of the United Kingdom.

This book is printed on paper from sustainable sources managed under the Forest Stewardship Council (FSC) scheme.

It has been printed in the UK to reduce transportation miles and their impact upon the environment.

For every new title that Troubador publishes, we plant a tree to offset CO_2, partnering with the More Trees scheme.

For more about how Troubador offsets its environmental impact, see www.troubador.co.uk/sustainability-and-community